# APRIL

# RAIN

## JENNY MAC

JENNY MAC

Copyright © 2018 Jenny Mac

All rights reserved.

ISBN 978 0 6483536 1 4 (Paperback)

No part of this publication may be reproduced or transmitted in any form or by any means, without permission in writing from The Author.

*****

# APRIL RAIN

The Author JENNY MAC was born in the Country of Central Australia, but now lives near the ocean on the South Coast of NSW in Australia, where she completed her first Novel 'APRIL RAIN.'

For the latest information on
Jenny Mac, and April Rain
Visit her Website at: www.jennymac.com.au

Website developed by Website Software Solutions.
www.website-software-solutions.com

April Rain is a Fiction Novel.
Towns, Places, and areas are fictional.
All products devised within the Author's imagination.
Characters are fictional, and bear no reference to anyone.

\*\*\*\*\*

# JENNY MAC

APRIL RAIN

## *Acknowledgements*

A special thank you to Todd, Renee, and Brad for your continued belief in me, and providing a modern way of presenting my Novel to my viewers.

Todd for his patience in designing my own website. Renee for being my best critic, and advisor. Brad for his continuous interest, input, and advice. 'Thank you all.'

*****

'I would like to dedicate this Novel to My Family.'
Without all your support, it would have been impossible.
Having you all by my side, has been a blessing.
'Thank you.'

*****

# JENNY MAC

## *'Introduction to Shallow Siding'*

Shallow Siding, a small Country Town renowned for being the last point of call for The Country Railways Australia, is an important vital link into The Outback. Surrounded by native gums and fauna the township sits in a beautiful valley, seeking the back drop of gradual hills. Enormous pine trees scaling the slopes, take on another shade of green to compliment the landscape, but in the paddocks, still wet from recent rain, the abundant grasses sway to the breath of the gentle breeze.
Train tracks snake a pathway to skirt the town, and the escarpment where the fog hangs low in the early dawn.

Steeped in history of its bygone years, Shallow Siding reaches a new millennium, and has been rejuvenated to an historic landmark. A tourist trade evolves as visitors seek The Outback for a Country welcome, and a holiday adventure. New businesses have paved the way for a transformation of the Town Center which sold the main necessities and everything from a sack of flour, to a pick, and shovel.

The little town boasts a close-knit community combining locals, and farmers. A population of 1450 people, and their hub, and pride is the quaint, Historic Railway Station. 'The Siding.' Entertainment is provided locally from the Hotel, and The Community Town Hall, which catered for social events, and dances, and a small café.
Two hundred miles away, the nearest town links the outside world. Travel is by rail, or road-train, but roads tough in the wet, so the Country Train is heavily relied upon. Usually the town is a safe, sleepy little place, not much happened out of the ordinary.
*... Until Today ...*

# APRIL RAIN

## *Prologue*
*The Year ... 1996 ...*

Jacqueline Coby was born, and raised in the Outback Country but now she had returned to her birthplace of Shallow Siding, a small but picturesque Country town in Outback Australia. After thirty-one long years away, her life had turned a full circle, and though in trepidation, at last she was back armed with a fierce determination to face the demons of her past, and move on.

Hope soared in her heart with a real purpose, and the aspirations of a new outlook on life.

*... Or so it seemed ...*

Be swept away on a reverie of her past life. Share in her jubilations, and her harrowing misfortunes. A deep love bared for her family who raised her on a Cattle Station, and the people who touched her heart, and life during her journey into young womanhood, and beyond.

Jacqueline's story is of her life, and of true love. Of heart wrenching drama, and devastation, which left her life in tatters as she groped blindly to make ultimate sacrifices which then haunted her very soul, and being, as she was propelled headlong, alienated, and so lost. As the world she knew, and loved, was turned upside down.

*... April Rain ... Is from the Heart ...*

# JENNY MAC

APRIL RAIN

## Chapter 1

I gazed longingly over the escarpment but shivered as the first threat of mist drifted down to cloak the town at first light. 'My birthplace.' I thought, as mixed feelings surfaced, then surged within me whilst I reveled in the magnificent countryside which seemingly had beckoned me to this hillside, a special place of my childhood.

Shallow Siding was spread out before me nestled in a beautiful valley. 'It used to be a quaint Country Town.' I thought. 'But not anymore, it is much larger now, many changes have occurred.' Just to see chimneys billowing with smoke now triggered my thoughts, and stirred up long forgotten memories of a past life within the recesses of my mind. 'Of my past life.' As it had been back in my childhood. Then as the early risers moved around going about their chores, my heart seemed to miss a beat with the sight of it, and tears sprang into my eyes.

Sadness overcome me, as I realized how much I had missed. I felt such deep regret for my life that could have been. 'My young life when I was growing up was just so perfect.' I remembered, and I shuddered with dread in recollection of the time it had been so cruelly altered, and taken from me by disastrous events that alienated me, and changed my life forever. Fate had taken me on a journey into the unknown to live out a life of loneliness, deep sorrow, and of pain that had taken me to hell, and back. I had now returned to Shallow Siding to face all those demons of my past after thirty-one long years, but once again I was armed with a fierce determination.

Yesterday was definitely a huge shock to endure as we drove into this Country Town of the Outback that I loved. I used to always daydream of how it would make me feel to return to my home, but I had struggled to associate myself with something familiar, or even just one thing from my past to relate to, because now the old town I had known, loved, and grew up in, was lost in its renovation, and the revelation of a new era.

Now my first impressions of my homecoming stayed fresh in my mind. Especially thoughts of my unexpected arrival by a semi-trailer, which I felt was quite a bizarre return, not how I imagined it to be at all.

When the truck driver braked his rig, and then parked outside the Hotel at the end of the main street in town, I offered him some money. "Thank you for the lift, Ed." I said. "That is not a problem Jackie! Thank you, but the pleasure was all mine." he said, and he jumped down to retrieve my luggage. "Will you be ok Jackie?" he asked.

"Yes, I will be fine Ed, I used to know my way around here!" I said, as I climbed down.

## APRIL RAIN

I headed towards the Hotel, but realized that it was not the same place that I knew at all. 'It was a Hotel-Motel now, and all renovated in a Heritage Style that was quite appealing to the eye.' I stepped up onto the boardwalk that led me to the front reception area where a colourful artistic painting displayed a welcome sign.

Once inside the entrance double doors, I rang the bell on the desk, and was at once greeted by a short, plump lady, with bright red hair who bounced through a door wearing a big smile on her face. "Morning! How might you be? Julie's my name. You're new in town aren't you, and how can I help, did you want a room?" she bubbled.

"Good morning Julie. My name is Jacqueline Coby. Yes! I have just arrived in town, and yes, I would like a room please. I will probably stay a week at least, I will confirm that later with you." I replied.

"That's fine Jacqueline, just let me know what you decide. Your room is number five, a lovely room with a nice private verandah, the laundry is around the corner. If you want anything at all, just call me on the phone in your room. You can also order meals from the restaurant to your room if you like. Otherwise, all meals are in the dining room. Breakfast 6am, Lunch 12pm, Dinner 6pm." Julie said, as she handed me the room key. "Thank you Julie." I said. "Just head down the boardwalk, up onto the back verandah, take a right, room's on your right. Swimming pool is out back, and a covered bar-be-que area. Enjoy your stay Jacqueline." Julie said.

"I appreciate your help Julie, thank you." I replied. I stepped through the door, and was at once presented with a huge array of colour that emanated from various bush plants as I made my way along the boardwalk up to the wide verandah where the wild flowers tumbled profusely from hanging baskets above the timber railing.

As I turned the corner to my room, I was immediately amazed by the colourful, leafy, and private setting that graced the entrance of the room overlooking a pool area. 'This will do nicely.' I thought as I unlocked the double doors to room number five, and went inside.

A magnificent showcase of solid blackwood was on display in the making of the furniture that adorned the room in a most amazing colour scheme. Immediate memories of my Father's wattle trees flooded into my mind, and the sadness crept in again. 'What would their property be like today, and who lives out there now?' I wondered. 'Such a long time ago now, it is almost like I had dreamt it all.' I thought.

A kitchenette, set in a corner of the room had a small fridge, a table with two chairs, and a comfortable lounge setting sat opposite a television set. The amenities were very adequate in an ensuite providing convenience, and everything that I would require for my stay. 'At least I will be fine here.' I thought, as the long trip began to take its toll. Tiredness immediately consumed me, my eyelids felt heavy from want of a good sleep. I lay on the soft bed, and drifted off into a deep sleep. I woke much later to a sudden burst of sunshine streaming through my curtains.

I showered, dressed, and while I unpacked, I became eager to seek out the town.

## APRIL RAIN

It was a beautiful day outside I noticed as I walked out on to the verandah, and into the brilliant sunshine. 'Different in contrast to the last few days when it hadn't stopped raining, but this is the Country.' I thought, as I stepped onto the boardwalk which led out to the main street where I was immediately startled in noticing the tarred road on each side. Huge Jacaranda trees governed the center, and splashed the colour purple up along the thoroughfare, with bench seats scattered in their shade.

How different it all looked now. A flashback of a one road, dusty street came to mind with rough cobblestones in the side-streets. I recalled driving to town for supplies in the horse drawn wagon, which I hitched up outside. 'That was so long ago.' I thought. Many shops lined the street now, the Heritage Style evidently a theme set here as colours amassed, adding to all the splendor. I looked down as I walked along a footpath. This was strange to me also. 'There were no paths before either.' I thought.

Suddenly I paused, but came to a halt as I stared at a building set off the main street where 'The Hall' once stood. The print in the stonework read. 'Shallow Siding Community Town Hall.' Tears slid down my face as I faced this building. 'So much joy in my life had revolved around this site, but now it's gone, all gone!' I thought.

Wiped off the map as if it never existed, demolished, and replaced. 'Out with the old, and in with the new.' Visions came back quite vivid now, it had been a special place so long ago in my upbringing. 'Nothing is forever.' I thought, as sadness consumed me. I tore myself away from the new building, and walked towards the Town Center, and The General Store. I noted they still sold mostly the same things, only more of everything, but the building had undergone massive renovation in its time, so now its appearance was alien to me. I selected some items I would need, then proceeded to the check out.

This was different also. I remembered the old layout where a long counter went across the back wall, and I could still picture the owner sitting behind it with his old till sitting up on top, while produce overfilled small shelves to spill onto the floor. Now all stock seemed to have a place on high shelving units in the shop. A young girl proceeded to file my items through. 'It is just not the same.' I thought. 'We used to have a special bond with the store owner, chatting endlessly with him every time we came into town to catch up with news, and gossip that filtered in from the Outback.' "Is that all ma'am?" asked the young girl. "Yes thank you." I said, as I paid.

I left the store to walk down the street where a small Café with colourful umbrellas attracted my attention. Seating was arranged amidst surrounding partitions, an inviting hand painted sign read. 'The Sidekick Café.' 'I could do with a coffee.' I thought, and noticed all the new building additions in passing as I strolled along. An image came to mind of a little milk bar which once stood in the same place as the Café. 'Another part of my youth gone.' I thought, as I walked inside. "Morning, Nice day! How can I help?" asked the young girl at the counter. "Good morning, yes it is a nice day, I might sit outside if that is ok?" I asked. Just a small coffee please." I said, as I paid. "Sure! I will bring it out to you." said the girl.

Once outside, I desperately tried to suppress all my feelings of anxiety. 'This was not how I imagined it to be.' I thought. 'There are just too many changes now to comprehend.' Absently I thanked the girl who brought my coffee out to me, and set it down, but then I sat in bewilderment as the doubts clouded my mind about the following day, until finally I came to a decision. A plan for in the morning, something I was looking forward to doing. So with determination I returned to the Hotel.

Now in the early morning as the thick fog drifted in around me, I sat upon the hillside overlooking this town that I had loved, but now felt a stranger to. I felt unsettled, and apprehension gripped me as my old fears returned, until thoughts of more importance entered my head to clear my mind as the main reasons for returning to Shallow Siding to face my past resurfaced. It was my sole purpose, and of course. 'Meeting the train.'

That would be so difficult for me, my feelings were in a turmoil about this meeting after thirty-one long years, especially with the person I was to marry so long ago. I had shunned him, and broke our engagement, and wedding plans, because of events beyond my control.

'Would we still have feelings for one another?' Was the question on my mind? I had no idea what to expect from this reunion, but with a definite purpose I rose, and climbed down from the hillside, and started striding out determinedly for 'The Historic Railway Station.'

# JENNY MAC

# APRIL RAIN

## *Chapter 2*

The air was heavy in Shallow Siding, and fog hung low like a curtain of massed cloud blanketing the town in the early morning dawn. It was early in April, during the wet season, but still a very busy time at the Historic Railway Station, and as always, the Country Train was running late. Most locals thought this was not unusual, as they mingled on the platform of the Station.

Jake Hardy applied himself to the enormous task of preparing his outgoing parcels in wait of its arrival. He was a stocky man in build for his average height, but a fit man for fifty-two years. His pate was bald but a huge fringe of his ginger hair, greying at the sides now, was poking out from under his cap, and around his ears. His friendly brown eyes reflected a special warmth.

His pride was the uniform he wore, as he had served as Station Master at 'The Siding' the past twenty-four years, including when the new 'Station' was built. He was eighteen when he first arrived in Shallow Siding looking for work, and a place where he might like to stay, to settle down. He loved the unique Country Town, and was fortunate to get a job at 'The Siding.' It was his start, his chance. Jake fit in with no effort, mixing well with the locals, and station people. He made some good friends, never looking back as he worked his way to the top position at age twenty-eight. He was a local now, or so the locals, and the station people told him.

Jake observed the mix of people from his side office

window. Passengers already checked in, sat waiting. He knew that they would mingle until they boarded the outbound train. Others were there to collect people off the train, but some locals always came out just to be a part of the excitement of the train's arrival. It was a big event for them, a chance to catch up with people, and all the news around the district.

Shallow Siding however, was to be host for a huge reunion which was to take place the following week, so the majority of the locals had offered billets to visitors who were attending, and a lot of people were expected, so everyone was pitching in to help.

'That's what I love about this town.' thought Jake, as he gazed outside. 'Nothing is a problem to anyone here. In their Country way, they all stick together, and I guess I am the same now.' he thought.

Jake realized that the host of station hands, gathering together at the end of the platform had travelled long distances from Outback Properties, and were waiting to pick up supplies for their various stations, and to offload goods to be dispatched today. They all milled together chatting, then something one of them said caused a big uproar, and they were horsing around with the joke. 'Good to see them enjoying the break from all their hard work.' he thought.

As their laughter drifted inside to him, for some odd reason Jake felt the opposite, as he tried to shake off the sense of doom that had just overcome him. For some unknown reason, he felt uneasy. 'Or is it just me?' he asked himself. He knew for sure he was in for a busy day today. When the Station Owners finished loading their livestock, and all goods for dispatch were onto the wagons, they would rush the café for lunch as they usually did. It was their usual way of keeping in contact with what was happening in the town, by meeting up with some local friends, and to find out what might be coming up. 'But it wasn't that.' he thought. 'It's just this feeling I have, a premonition even!' He knew that his gut feelings were usually spot on. 'But what?' Everything is fine here, and I am up to my ears in work, so I'd better move! 'Get a grip Jake!' he thought, as he tried earnestly to push the feelings aside.

While he was working, Jake's thoughts turned to the people of Shallow Siding, and their work. There was always work in Shallow Siding, it was a thriving little township. Some newcomers though, can't handle the hard work, or country life, and tend to come, and go a lot. So there are always positions available on large acreages, like cattle properties, sheep properties, even market gardens with tourist attractions, and bush style accommodation, and even recreation farms. So hiring for those jobs was usually a selection from those known to work hard, they were the ones who had the monopoly.

Alternately, further into The Outback. 'Stations,' as they were so often called, mainly consisted of huge cattle ranches that ranged for many, many miles across the beautiful, wild, Outback Plains, so come muster time in the dry season, extra hands were needed.

Jake knew, that the early settlers of Shallow Siding had set the benchmark for huge success in this little town, and had been an inspiration to the town folk here.

He was honoured to have been a part of it all, he had lived, and experienced through an era of his thirty-four years all the hard times, the good times, and a coming of rejuvenation to a great Outback Country Town, to the splendor of their Heritage that the Country people had always been proud of.

Jake Hardy reflected on his life in the thirty-four years that he resided in Shallow Siding. He had everything a man could wish for, and he was contented with his lot.

He loved the Country, and life in The Outback, and it amazed him to think how easy it was to settle here. His job was the key to his success. He had worked very hard to obtain his goals, and had achieved most of them.

Though his most memorable achievement he mused. 'Was meeting a local girl Anne Giles, who worked in her parent's bakery shop.' He was always finding excuses to visit the bakery, just to chat to her, and then had finally summed up enough courage to ask her out to a dance.
'This first dance date was a special one.' he recalled, with the fondest of memories as they had starting dating after that.

They both enjoyed dancing so they made sure their agenda incorporated the 50/50 dances held every two months in 'The Hall.' A special place to all. A band selected by 'The Entertainment Committee,' played old time music, and rock'n'roll, which was all the rage back then, but now a new Heritage venue 'The Community Town Hall' stood in place of the well-loved 'Hall' the original modest weatherboard building, and the local community were disappointed to see it go.

Jake remembered fondly of Anne's huge passion for shooting. Her involvement competing in competitions at the rifle club was part of her life for years, but these days they played tennis once a week. Anne's parent's shop was sold after her parents had passed on, but Anne still worked at the bakery two days a week, and two days a week at 'The Siding.'

'It was twenty-seven years ago they married in the little town chapel.' Jake thought. Then they had bought their pride, and joy, a small house on the outskirts of town. 'It looks a million dollars' Jake noted. Their only regret was not having any children but Jake regarded two young employees who he thought very highly of, as part of his family, taking them firmly under his wing.

His thoughts were cut short when he heard Anne calling to him as she came through the rear doors, and walked into his office. "Good Morning Jake. I was just talking to some people outside. They are all getting concerned because the train is so late, have you heard anything yet?" she asked.

"Hello pumpkin! No not yet, I'll give them a bit more time to call in first, there is no need to worry just yet I don't think!" Jake replied.

# JENNY MAC

Anne Hardy was an attractive woman for her later years, her short wispy brown hair fell around her face, and her big brown eyes seemed to light up when she smiled.

"There are a lot of people in town today Jake, most I've seen for a while in 'The Siding,' and the weather is a bit ordinary at the moment, fog everywhere, but I guess it will lift." Anne said. "Yes the fog is bad, and there are more people out, but a big week next week!" said Jake.

"Yes, I must talk to Mitch when he arrives about that, and sort some details!" Anne said. "I'd better start now Jake, there's bound to be a rush on." replied Anne. "Ok pumpkin." said Jake.

Jake was expecting Mitchell Stringer any moment. He usually arrived early before the train was due to come in to deliver all his supplies of fresh produce for the Café Diner, and also for the Outback Stations. Mitchell had restructured his Market Gardens Property to become co-owner with his son Pete in a new joint venture of an Outback Bush Camp for Tourists. Jake looked up from his desk when he heard him call.

"You there Jake?" Mitchell called as he came through the back door all loaded up with boxes. "In here Mitch!" called Jake. "I'll be back in a second Jake, I have more in the truck." he said, as he set the boxes down to go back outside. "Ok Mitch!" Jake called.

"How's things Jake? Good to see you. Damn fog is so thick out there this morning that I could hardly see as I drove in today, but then I couldn't see the train either!"

Mitchell said laughing, as he walked inside Jake's office.

"Very funny Mitch. Good to see you too. Though I am tired of explaining about the train, because I don't know anything yet!" Jake answered.

"Oh I see! I guess that you would be, but everyone is in a big rush anyway getting their trucks unloaded out the front. I guess the train will be here soon enough though." Mitchell said to Jake. "It hasn't missed yet!" he joked in his Country style.

Mitchell Stringer stood over six feet tall, all muscle, and very fit for his fifty years, a handsome man.

His full head of sandy hair showing a distinguished hint of white now around his temples, was creeping to his collar, and his deep blue eyes seemed to twinkle in his tanned face. He had lived his life in Shallow Siding, a typical country man, but an important figure in town. His wife was killed in a car accident fifteen years ago to leave him with an only son. Mitchell, and Pete shared a huge bond, and were best mates. He never remarried, so involved himself in work, his son, various fund raisers, and was a member of The Entertainment Committee.

Just Mitch's mannerism, and his broad country accent never ceased to fascinate Jake Hardy. 'He always was a true Cowboy!' he thought to himself as he looked up at him. Their friendship was as solid as a rock, starting a long, long, way back, to when Jake first came to Shallow Siding. "How is the new business going now Mitch?" Jake asked. "Pete's got that all sorted, you've got to hand it to that boy Jake, he knows his stuff alright! From the two parties of tourists who arrived just last week, one pair extended their stay already, so it's all happening. We are all busy! Your order is here for the kitchen, but the orders to go with the mail truck, where do you want those put Jake?" Mitchell asked.

"Thanks Mitch! Just put the station orders out in the back room, inside there!" he pointed. "I will get young Sam to load all those up onto Pete's truck when he gets here! Pete should be here soon, he doesn't like being held up!" replied Jake. "Tell me about it!" said Mitch laughing. Jake joined in with his hearty laugh, and added. "Might come out to see the Outback Bush Camp when I can Mitch the whole town is talking about The Outback Gardens! New name for the property too, and a new venture. You must be set now?"

"Yes! Full steam ahead now Jake, lots of changes, but we have put a lot of hard work towards it! You both can come out anytime, second thoughts, might be best in the afternoon. I will have more time to show you around then, and you can join us for dinner! I'd better move now Jake!" said Mitch. "Ok Mitch!" said Jake.

Mitchell was stacking orders on the kitchen bench when Anne walked in from cleaning restrooms, and was heading to the Café Diner area. "Hi Mitch! So good to see you again. It looks like some good produce there!" she said, as she poked her nose into the boxes. I hope the rain hasn't ruined your gardens Mitch?" "Hi Anne! No the rain has been kind this time, not too much luckily, everything is flourishing, so I have top stuff! he replied. "How have you been Anne?" he asked.

Anne's eyes lit up as usual as he spoke to her. She just loved Mitch's country demeanor, he was like a brother to her. "I am great thanks Mitch, how are you, and Pete? Sounds like you have a community out there now, with all your employees, and tourists, things must be going ok?" she asked.

"Yeah, all good Anne. I have just organized with Jake for you both to come out to The Property one afternoon for a look around, and stay for dinner, just let me know when!" he said. "Sounds good to me Mitch, we've been meaning to go out for some time now." said Anne. "Oh! Also Anne, I almost forgot to mention …

Regarding the reunion next week. We might get the Committee together on Sunday, and go over some details. I've had so many replies it is ridiculous, I hope we can cater for them all. Most of them will arrive today on the train, but others will be driving from all different areas so pray for good weather." "Does that suit you at all Anne?" asked Mitch.

"Yes, all good Mitch, you leave it up to me! I will call everyone, and we will meet at the 'Hall' on Sunday, say 11am. Is that alright?" Anne asked.

"That is just perfect Anne, thank you!" said Mitch.

"Should be an interesting group of people when they get together I think, and I am really looking forward to meeting old friends myself!" he added.

# JENNY MAC

Mitchell had put a huge effort into organizing this reunion. Being a member of The Entertainment Committee, he wanted to see if it interested others. He researched well, and finally sent letters to whoever he could find, people he remembered. Trying to target the generation from around 1950's-1970, to get the people back that had grown up here years ago, but had left, people that had made Shallow Siding what it was way back then, and what it is today.

The new residents in the town were excited about this, as were the locals, and station owners, and were looking forward for their chance to mingle with the legends of The Outback. All responses were positive, so it looked to be a winner. "Ok Anne, better keep on. Have to deliver some orders in town, and get back home."

"Time is money, see you Sunday!" Mitch said. "Will do!" said Anne.

He made his way into Jake's office. "Ok Jake, I will take all this through now." he said. As he passed the office window he noticed Susan Hind making her way through the people, talking as she passed.

"Susan has arrived for work, she's outside." he said.

Mitchell liked Susan, and he felt that his son Pete did too, though Pete kept his personal feelings to himself, but Mitchell could tell there was something there.

Susan had become an important part of their business, so reliable, and very good with the tourists.

"Always on time is our Susan!" said Jake. "I will have to go now Jake, I've got deliveries to do in town. Tell

# APRIL RAIN

Susan I said hello. I will see her out at the property." said Mitch. "Will do! See you later Mitch, I'll ring you." said Jake. "Ok good, bye Jake!" he said.

Susan Hind, who operated the Café Diner through breakfast and lunch twice a week, was smiling as she walked through the doors of Jake's office, arriving for work. "Morning Jake, you can expect a big day today, I fear. There is a lot of action going on at the cattle yards, caused me a wait getting over the crossing, and visibility is not too good either, a lot of fog this morning. Sam said that he won't be much longer, he is helping someone outside unloading a Ute. But I see the train is not in yet anyway!" she said.

"Good morning Susan! No I don't know what's going on with the train yet, it is very late now, and I am getting a bit concerned actually." replied Jake. "Oh! By the way Susan. Mitch just left, he said to say hello, and he would see you out at the property." said Jake. "Oh thank you Jake. He is such a nice person." replied Susan.

Susan was a real country girl, quite slim, and medium height, with a suntanned skin from being outdoors.

Her auburn hair fell in a cascade of curls over her shoulders, and thick eyelashes shadowed her soft brown eyes. Susan, like her brother Sam, worked two days at The Railway Station, and for the rest of her week, she worked for Mitchell, and Pete Stringer at The Outback Gardens. Susan was very fond of Pete Stringer, always had been, but was very shy around him. She sensed that to have a relationship with Pete, then the first step must come from him, she would not push him. Being twenty-nine, she had waited a long time for his attention, a little longer wouldn't hurt. She would be just devastated if she lost his friendship. He was a great boss too, and she loved working out at The Outback Bush Camp where he hired her as assistant cook to Joe Banks, and organizer for the tents, where she catered for his guests. It was so different to working at the Historic Railway Station.

Sam Hind worked as Jake's casual assistant, and was Susan's kid brother. He noticed both Jake, and Susan chatting together in the office, as he walked through the front doors.

"Morning Jake! Hi Susan!" he said, as he walked into the office. "Good morning Sam!" replied Jake, and Susan in unison. "Just as well the train is late, no-one would be ready today Jake. I had to give them a hand out front to unload!" said Sam. "That was good of you Sam!" replied Jake. "I guess so." replied Sam, with a laugh. Sam was a jovial sort of guy, a real likable person. Nineteen years of age, and full of fun. He was medium build, light brown hair, and brown laughing eyes.

"Looks like we are in for a big day. I suppose we have heaps to do?" Sam asked. "So where is the train Jake?"

Jake's brow knotted to frown when his eyes met the huge clock that suggested the train was already forty minutes late. So much later than usual. "Not too sure Sam, might be some trouble!" he said. "Just get ready anyway. My list can wait, firstly go back out to assist the other hands offloading. We need all the outgoing parcels ready, and stacked in the holding room for now, then come back." "Oh! Mitch put the station orders in the back room, you can load them onto Pete's truck when he arrives, thanks Sam." said Jake.

"Sure thing Jake! No problems at all. I'll go outside now, then get back to help Pete. He won't be too much longer, he's always on time!" said Sam, as he left the office, and walked out through the front doors, onto the crowded platform of the Railway Station.

There were people everywhere today, he noted. 'Busy day for us.' he mused, as he strained his eyes to see through the fog as it hung low around The Historic Railway Station, making it hard to visualize the train tracks which disappeared into its depths.

Being a local boy, Sam knew all the people there. He had grown up in Shallow Siding, and he had been schooled at the little schoolhouse. He had some great mates who he grew up with, and now they all worked here. Sam thought himself fortunate getting a casual job at 'The Siding' twice a week when the train came in. He had lots to do, people to talk to, and Jake Hardy was a great boss.

Sam's main job though, was at The Outback Gardens working for Pete Stringer, and his Father, Mitchell. Mostly, he was out there every other day. He loved the outdoors, and met some interesting people amongst the tourists, who had lots of tales to tell. He loved working with, and being around the animals, that was his main role out there, tending to all the animals, and having them ready when Pete had guests. Pete was tops, a great guy, a real legend, and a good boss too. Sam was feeling satisfied with life, he had a sense of achievement now, was independent, and self-supportive. He lived with his parents, but could afford his own place now.

Sam walked along speaking to people as he passed. "Morning all, lovely day coming up today at Shallow Siding, once this fog lifts, it will be a beauty. Jake hasn't had any word on the train yet, but we will let you all know soon as someone calls in." "Morning Sam! Hi Sam! Thank you Sam!" People were talking back to him as he made his way through as Sam was well known identity throughout the town. He stopped suddenly to talk to a local couple that he knew well, and he knew they were waiting patiently for the train to come in because their daughter was on board.

"Good morning Mister, and Missus Worthington! I guess you're both getting anxious to greet your daughter Rebecca? She has been away for a while, quite a long trip by train from the city." he said.

"I will be pleased to see her again also!" Rebecca had attended school with Sam, but had moved to the city when she enrolled in a college there to train, and study to be a vet, and she was in her last year at the University.

The Worthington's owned a hardware store in town, where they had both worked for many years until just recently when they had hired permanent staff to help, so they only worked a couple of days each a week, which gave them both a break.

"Hello Sam!" said Eli Worthington. "Yes, we are very excited! Rebecca is coming home for four long weeks, so much catching up to do. She is really doing very well at college, and no doubt she will fill us in with all her plans when she gets home. You must come over to dinner one night Sam, I'm sure Rebecca would love to see you." "Hi Sam, good to see you. You had better come round for dinner, Eli has spoken!" said George Worthington with a chuckle. "It will be good to have a chat, and a few ales.

Hear tell you have two jobs. Very versatile I think! We've heard accolades of your work efforts. Good on you Sam, you can tell us more when you visit."

Eli, and George Worthington were like a second family to Sam, they had watched him grow up, and had known him all his life. Sam, and Rebecca were great friends from a long way back. "Yes work is going good Mister Worthington, I'm loving it, and I'd love to come over to your place for dinner, thank you both for the invitation." said Sam.

"Just let me know when, and I will be there with bells on! It has been good to see you both again, and I'm sure I will get to see Rebecca later when the train is in, we will all talk more then. I will have to go now, got a lot of work to do for Jake today, but I will be helping the station hands outside with some unloading first though, and that will take some time. Bye for now!" he said.

George Worthington looked up at Sam, and replied. "Don't let us keep you Sam, no doubt we will catch you later." "Yes we will Sam!" said Eli Worthington.

Sam made his way on down the platform, and was confronted at once by two of his very best mates. Charlie Boyle, and Boyd Summers had stepped out into his path to meet with him, and have a chat.

"Hi Sam. You will have your work cut out for you today!" said Charlie. "How's things Sam?" asked Boyd.

"What are you guys doing here?" asked Sam. "Every time I look around, you guys are there!" "That's what friends are for." replied Boyd. "Just here to look, you never know I could meet my future wife!" said Charlie, as he laughed.

They all laughed. Charlie had a unique way of setting the mood, as he was always cracking jokes.

"No, seriously." said Boyd. "We've got plenty of time, we don't have to start as early as you in the mornings, so we came to say hi, before we went to work."

"Well thank you both! How is the job going Boyd?" Sam asked. "Just love it Sam, and the outdoors." he said.

Boyd worked for the Jones family, who owned the property across the river, and he was their maintenance person for the grounds, tennis courts, and the pool.

"Have my own pad now Sam, the owners have given me the hut to live in, subsidized rent too, so no more riding the bike." he said, and laughed. Sam cracked a smile. "Good for you Boyd!" he said.

Boyd was tall, and lanky but quite good looking, with

black hair that curled in a mass on his head, and dark blue eyes. He had always been Sam's friend, they had gone to school together, and were the same age. "Yeah, I'm independent now, and saving for a car, second hand of course, but yeah, no more pushbike then. Will visit Mum, and Dad in style then!" he said, laughing.

Charlie Boyle laughed. "Maybe I won't have to be the chauffeur then, but I bet your plans won't happen overnight. If I know you Boyd, you aren't too good at saving!" said Charlie. Sam laughed, and said. "I think for once you may be right Charlie." "You guys have little faith!" replied Boyd. Charlie worked at the local Hotel, he was a cellar man there. He had saved up, and bought a second hand car from one of the property owners, so he had wheels now, but he knew how hard it was to get them. He was the chief chauffer for the boys, driving to the river for a swim, or just getting around town. He was twenty now the typical country boy, and quite a larrikin. His spiked ginger hair enhanced the hazel eyes, and his trimmed beard. He often got chided for being the shortest, but made it up with his wit. He too grew up with Sam Hind, and were best mates.

Sam looked hard at them both. "Guess who I was just talking to?" he asked. "Who then?" asked Charlie. "The Worthington's. Rebecca is coming home on the train today!" said Sam. "Oh really! You will be waiting too, I guess?" asked Charlie, with a slight grin on his face.

"What about Sarah at the bakery, she was getting

pretty close to you at the last dance, for what I could see!" said Charlie. "Only going to dinner, is all!" replied Sam. "Her Mother, and Father just invited me, it will be good to see Rebecca again! Besides, Sarah is a friend too, you know." he added. "Really, I bet she is, and I bet it will be good to see Rebecca too! Don't hold back on our account old chum." he said.

"Only dinner." he says! "Can you believe him Boyd?" asked Charlie, as he looked towards Boyd for some support. "That will be good for you Sam! You were always fond of Rebecca, and you will both have some catching up to do." said Boyd, as he grinned at Sam, and made a face at Charlie. "Can't have them all Sam, you have to share you know. Don't you realize, if you get all the girls, what chance do we have?" asked Charlie. "Get away with you two!" uttered Sam. "Always ribbing me about girls. You both have plenty of girls chasing you."

"At some other time, we can go into that in depth, but right now I have work to do, so I will see you two later!" he said, as he gave Charlie a shove, and Boyd a jab. They all laughed, and they both said. "Ok Sam, see ya!" said Boyd. "Don't work too hard!" said Charlie.

Sam left them with all their taunts, and headed down towards the end of the building where he couldn't help but notice the lady sitting alone.

'A real looker.' he thought. He knew she was new to town, as he hadn't seen her before, but she looked a little uptight, and sad, so he stopped to speak to her.

# APRIL RAIN

"Good morning!" he said. "The train's a bit late, but it will get here soon I guess, and don't worry this fog will lift soon, it's sure to be a great day!"

My name is Sam, I work here. I haven't seen you here before, have you come in from the Outback Properties, or are you from the city?" 'Must be one or the other for the way she is dressed!' he thought.

"Thank you for all the information Sam, and no, I'm not from the city, though I came from that way, and no, I am not from The Outback Properties, though I used to a long time ago, and yes, I am new in town I suppose you could say. I arrived yesterday! My name is Jacqueline Coby!" she said, putting out her hand.

He took her hand in a handshake. "Pleased to meet you Jacqueline, and welcome to Shallow Siding, I hope you enjoy your visit!" Sam replied. "So do I Sam!" said Jacqueline. "I am sorry to rush off now Jacqueline, but it is busy today, and I have work to do out the front. I will catch up with you later." said Sam.

"Of course Sam, you go ahead. It has been very nice meeting you though, and thank you so much for your hospitality, I had almost forgotten what that means to me until now. I hope you have a good day too Sam. No doubt we will meet again!" replied Jacqueline.

"It has been my pleasure meeting you too Jacqueline, and yes, I will be around here somewhere, we will meet again no doubt!" replied Sam, then he walked quickly towards the end of the platform.

# JENNY MAC

## CHAPTER 3

Jake stepped out onto the platform, but could see no sign of the train when he peered down the tracks through the fog. People were milling around in groups so he called out. "Morning all, can I have your attention please. There is no call in about the train so I will try to contact Old Riley again, I will keep you up to date!"

"Thanks Jake!" they called. Jake looked up, and saw Sam coming back. 'Oh good, Sam is finished outside already!' he thought. 'Good timing.'

Just as he turned to walk away, Jake's eyes seemed to rest on the solitary figure of a lady who sat down the end on a bench seat. 'She is a stranger in town, I haven't seen her before.' he thought. He couldn't help but notice how attractive she was. Her beautiful face, and tanned skin had an inner glow, and her slim petite body was shaped to perfection, enhancing the presentation of her dress. 'She must be about forty-five or so' he guessed.

Her short cropped blonde hair tossed around in the early morning breeze as she sat waiting patiently, but anxiously upon the bench seat. Oblivious of everything around, her eyes seemed focused only on scanning the mist for the train tracks rounding the outskirts of town, searching for the first glimpse of the train's arrival.

'Who would she be meeting?' he mused, as he turned to walk inside. Sam entered the office interrupting Jake's puzzlement. "All finished out there Jake!" he called.

"Sure Sam, that's good!" Jake replied absently.

# JENNY MAC

There was an uneasiness in Jake's chest, his mind blank. There was something so disturbing about the woman. Something familiar, which tugged the depths of his memory, and he desperately searched for some type of inkling but his recollection was in vain as he racked his brain, only to be distracted once again as he saw the local legend Pete Stringer, a professional bushman, come property owner who always delivered all the mail, and parcels twice a week to nearby stations, was making his way through the throng towards him.

Pete Stringer was a big man for his age. He was just twenty-nine, but his tall lean body was bulked with muscle. His sun-bleached hair reached his shirt collar, but falling forward onto his tanned forehead, though his deep blue eyes darkened with annoyance as he spoke.

"Hey Jake!" he called, as he made his way into the office. "What is the hold-up today? Don't you know I have a schedule to keep? This train is always late, but today I am not going to finish my run till dark, and if it rains again I might have to stay out bush, or to try and make it home with the chains on. You know what the roads are like in the wet! So what's up Jake?" he asked.

"Hi Pete. Sorry mate!" said Jake. "I haven't heard anything yet, I can only guess all is ok! Someone will contact me soon to let me know the arrival time!"

"Ok then. I might have to go back to the property for a while. I've got some people out there, and I need to organize a few things before I head off. Have to keep the tourists happy!" he said to Jake.

## APRIL RAIN

He turned to acknowledge Susan Hind, and Sam Hind, who had stood back due to his outburst. They both knew that he could be impatient at times, and that he had a short fuse. His outbursts, and impatience were well noted by all who knew him, but he was the most caring person, and would do anything for anyone.

Pete was of a mind that everything had to be done yesterday. He had a massive workload, but relished the challenges his life entailed. He was an extremely busy man, however now he was thinking. Things are getting a bit hectic lately, might just be about time to pass on some things to others who are worthy.

"Hi Susan! Hi Sam! How is everything?" he asked.

"Morning Pete." said Sam. Susan blushed, as she said. "Good morning Pete." then looked down at the floor.

She was relieved when Pete resumed the conversation with Sam. "Sam, if you finish here early enough, I might get you to work the mail run today, and then if you are interested in doing it permanently, it might tie in with your other jobs. I will talk to you more tomorrow when you come out, come and see me!" he said.

Sam had been out on the mail run with Pete before, and he had learnt the ropes. He knew all the station owners, and directions to the properties, he was excited about being given the opportunity. "Sure thing Pete." replied Sam. "I've got sorting to do, and Jake has a list for me, so I will wait for the train. When I'm all done here, I can start on the unloading of the mail, and parcels off the train.

I just have to get my jobs done here for Jake, and I'll be ready to go. "Ok good, here are the keys for my 4WD truck, thanks Sam!" said Pete. "I'll get a lift home with one of the boys who are unloaded."

Pete was a little embarrassed when he faced Susan, he sensed her shyness, and he too seemed at a loss for words some times when he was around her, but lately though, he had a feeling of closeness with her that he rather liked, and a real friendship had blossomed.

However he still didn't have the nerve to ask her on a real date. He had just quit a long relationship which hadn't worked out, and he wasn't quite sure how to approach a new one yet.

"Susan, I've got a lot of organizing for the weekend, could you come to work early tomorrow?" he asked. "Sure Pete! That's fine, I will be out there very early in the morning!" she replied, managing a smile. Pete had to smile back, and said. "Thank you Susan, that's great!

"Oh Jake, be sure to call me when the train is in!" he said. "Will do!" said Jake.

Pete was not only worried about the mail service, he had to greet potential, and existing customers off the train, find out their requirements to set up bookings for the following week.

Pete and his father Mitchell were a good combination, very good partners, but best mates who worked together running the property out of town which backed onto The Siding River, that they called The Outback Gardens.

## APRIL RAIN

The Outback Bush Camp had become a huge tourist attraction, and a successful addition, not only for the town of Shallow Siding, but also for The Outback.

Mitchell Stringer liked the new concept, and was very keen to join Pete in his new venture.

He became aware that word of Pete's bushman skills and expertise, had preceded him, when stories filtered through the Outback, and Pete had become a legend in his own right. He was very proud of his son, and of his new found fame.

Mitchell knew Pete loved the bush, his animals, and he reveled in all challenges even at an early age. Pete had a gift of natural talent, and he had acquired a lot of knowledge along the way. Mitchell had introduced Pete to the ways of country life very early in his life, and he had given him hands on experience in bush lore, bush tracking, survival, and all about firearms.

When he gave Pete his first rifle he found Pete an avid learner who became an expert at shooting at a young age by continuously practicing at targets.

He taught him personally the art in handling horses, and the other animals, something he had learnt himself at a very young age.

Pete learnt the business side of running the property, and was hands on with the organization of the cattle, The Market Gardens, and now The Outback Bush Camp, where he kept a close eye on his trade, and the interests of tourists, who came from all different areas he noted, so he could tell that word was getting around now as he had been flooded with enquiries, and he made bookings three months ahead. So he guessed he must be doing something right.

Business was going great, the last four years they had put a huge effort into getting everything just right, and Pete was very particular in the care, and upkeep of his Bush Camp, and care of the animals.

He had raised six camels from a young age, and had trained them himself, so the last two years things were operating smoothly, and a constant flow of tourists were coming to Shallow Siding, and to their Property, and they were reaping the benefits.

Initially, they had built a huge shelter for the camels in the first paddock, which was the holding yard. Pete had even installed an electric fence around it, and in the adjacent paddock which was a grazing paddock for the camels, huge water troughs had been installed, and salt licks for the camels, and a new hay shed was erected.

Water was pumped up from the river to the camp, and then out to the Gardens for irrigation. Pete's unique camel trail rides were an important asset to his side of the business at The Outback Bush Camp.

Pete's camp set up was very Outback Style, but very professional, and no expense was spared.

After meeting his guests at the train station, his initial warm welcome to the property was a ritual of serving

Billy Tea, and Damper made on the open campfires, and to add to their adventures. Camel rides were the norm through the hills on his property, and along the river.

He had all the very best of everything on offer for his guests. From the large recreation tents erected for their comfort, to separate tents for sleeping quarters. A large dining tent, set up like a restaurant with table cloths, and the finest of cutlery. All beverages were supplied, and a cook always on hand to cater for them.

Bush style amenities kept in with the theme, the river was utilized with canoes available, and fishing for fun.

Being renowned for his various skills, Pete was not only a great bushman with expertise of the Outback as a professional tracker, but also as a great hunter. His experience being forged from hands on training since his youth had now proved his status.

Pete Stringer was in great demand, and many tourists came to the Outback Country, and to Shallow Siding just to seek him out, and then experience the raw wildness of the Country, and the thrills of adventure with him. His name was wide spread, so now his Outback Bush Camp was a huge attraction.

He offered his guests an opportunity to go on hunting parties, or roo shooting trips, all depending on his guest's requests, or their requirements which ultimately became a part of their agenda during their stay.

Whatever their needs, he could cater for them.

# JENNY MAC

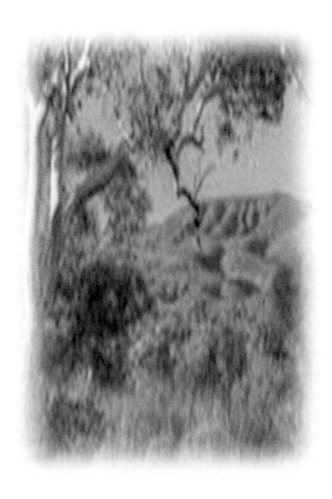

## Chapter 4

Pete Stringer recalled his meeting with the last two groups of people he had welcomed at the Historic Railway Station just last week, and all the events that followed. They had arrived on the last train into Shallow Siding for the week from the city, and were having a great time at The Outback Gardens.

Royce, and Riana were the first of the group to alight on the platform of The Siding. They saw a big man with a friendly face, and a huge smile standing there holding a sign which bared their names, and the other couples names, Col, and Fiona, who were going to The Outback Gardens also. Royce at once stepped up, and said. "Hi, my name is Royce Chalmers, this is my wife Riana."

Royce was the typical city guy, very well dressed in his jeans and check shirt, and very polite. His age would be round about thirty, Pete guessed. He wore a dark pair of shades, and a baseball cap covering his thick black hair which curled around to the collar of his shirt. 'He looked quite fit.' Pete thought.

"G'day mate, nice to meet you Royce, and welcome to Shallow Siding. My name is Pete Stringer, and I am your host from our property, The Outback Gardens!" said Pete, as he extended his hand to Royce, and they both shook hands.

"Good morning Riana, welcome to you too. I hope you enjoy your stay with us." he said.

"Good morning Pete," said Riana, as she looked into Pete's face with a twinkle in her hazel eyes, and she was thinking how handsome he was, but in a very rugged, country, sort of way. "And thank you Pete! I am sure we will enjoy our stay."

"Royce, and I have been looking forward to this for a long time." Riana said, as she smiled at him. Riana was quite short, and only reaching to Royce's shoulder, but she looked like she was very fit also, Pete noted.

She had very black short hair which seemed to stick out in all directions, and she had a lovely smile.

"Nothing beats a holiday in the Country." said Pete, as he returned her smile.

Col, and Fiona stepped forward. Pete greeted them both. "You must be Col, and Fiona Selmy! Hello, and welcome to the Country, and Shallow Siding." he said.

"Thank you Pete!" said Fiona. "I am very pleased to meet you, it has been a long trip, and it is good to be here finally." "Hello Pete, I am pleased to meet you also. This Country stay is a first for us!" Col said, as he shook Pete's hand.

"Well, we will have to make sure that you come back for your second stay, you both will love the Country I'm sure. We'll look after you!" said Pete. "Just to let you know Pete, we can both ride horses." said Col. "Yes that is good to know Col. I need to have a different program for learners, thank you for that." said Pete.

Col, and Fiona were both avid horse lovers, but they had never been on a camel ride, so that would be a first for them. They were staying over the weekend, and had planned their return on the first train out the next week back to the city, about four day stay in all.

However, the other pair, Royce and Riana Chalmers, were staying a full week, and they possibly would extend their stay if Pete could arrange a shooting trip for them. Royce was a keen shooter, and a member of a gun club at home, and always wanted to go on a shoot with a professional bushman.

Both of them were also very keen horsemen however, competing in showjumping back home, but had never ridden camels before. They wanted to relish the whole Outback Experience while they were here. "You might need to know we both can ride too Pete!" Royce said.

"Thank you that's great, and after a hand shake all round, he said. "First things first, luggage!"

"I have my vehicle outside, we have a four mile trip to drive to The Outback Gardens, so I would suggest we load up, and then let's get this show on the road!" said Pete. 'Pete is so very likeable.' Riana was thinking. 'And so friendly too.' She really felt at ease with him.

Already they were all feeling quite at home here, and were excited with their laughter, and chatter when they collected their luggage, then they all made their way to the carpark, and to Pete's huge land rover.

"Keep in mind everyone, if you want a tour of the town, or a shopping trip ladies, I can arrange it, or bring you in, and pick you up. Just name the day. Shallow

Siding has lots to offer and History goes way back in this little Country Town." offered Pete.

Fiona Selmy was just twenty-eight, but very tall in stature, with bright blue eyes. Her light, brown hair, hanging down her back in a cascade of curls bounced as she walked. She was most interested in The Historic Town, as well as the concept of living bush style on an Outback Property, and she had a lot of questions to ask.

"Pete, I would be very interested in a tour of the town! That is certainly an option for me if that can be arranged! Could you also tell me if you have horses at the property? I do love riding horses. And Pete, will there be mosquitos in the tents?" she asked.

"That's a yes, a yes, and a yes!" said Pete. "Better save all your questions for when we get out to the property, I think. Looks like I'll have to have a special question time just for you Fiona, then all will be revealed!" he said, as he laughed. 'It looks like I'm not the only impatient person here.' he thought.

She laughed back, and said. "Sorry Pete, I tend to get carried away at times, and my impatience is my worst fault you will find. I will try to be contain myself till then I guess!" she replied earnestly. Col Selmy laughed too. "Don't mind Fiona, Pete." he added. "She tends to want to know everything at once!" "That's ok!" said Pete. "I'm a bit like that myself!" Col was used to all her questions.

They had been married for only two years now, and they had decided to venture on this holiday before they started to have any children. Fiona was very meticulous in almost everything, and very decided in her opinions, and she was also very inquisitive. He guessed that he loved the strength that she had.

Col was the same age as Fiona, and even though they were of a similar height. He was very solid in build, and was quite strong looking. His brown hair fell shoulder-length, and pulled back with a leather strap at the back of his head, and he had unusual eyes of brown, flecked with gold. He worked for a machinery company back home, and was the mechanic who fixed all the heavy machinery from farm equipment to bulldozers. He was quite used to heavy work, and being in the outdoors at work had tanned his skin.

They all helped Pete loading the vehicle with their belongings, then taking their seats, they were set for the trip, and were full of anticipation by then. Each had their own thoughts as they left the little Historic Town.

The drive was amazing, the countryside left nothing to the imagination, the wild life in abundance. They saw kangaroos hopping in all directions, and herds of cattle grazing in the paddocks. It looked like a big cattle area, probably with some big stations here. As they climbed the escarpment, they were all amazed at the view that panned out before them from the gradual heights.

Looking back, they could see the town nestled in the valley. The early fog had lifted now, and the sun that was presenting itself in all its glory above the hills, now streamed through the trees.

## JENNY MAC

Splashes of deep green graced the paddocks that were still wet from constant rains, and the colour scheme was relentless. The Siding River, swelling now from the recent rains, rounded the hills effortlessly on its way to Shallow Siding.

Pete chatted endlessly as he drove the vehicle. "You are all going to be in for a treat today." he said. "Best weather that we've had for a while, not a rain cloud in sight. So we had better take advantage while we can! We do get a lot of rain here in April, but it is nearing the end of the wet season now, so we get a good day or two, and today is going to be magic. Won't be long now, and we will be at my property, so I'll give you a rough idea of your itinerary, what to expect, and not necessarily in this order, but close! Hold on to your hats!" he said, as he threw his head back, and laughed.

"Allocate your sleeping tents, freshen up. A welcome from the cook, and meet my Father, and staff. A short tour of The Outback Gardens Property. Then breakfast, at which point we will have a bit of a chat to get to know each other, and discuss all your needs for your stay, and any special requests that you might have, and we can organize it all for you. Keep in mind, the weather!"

"How does that sound for starters?" Pete asked, as he put on a big grin.

Everyone laughed at Pete's citation. They were all in the same frame of mind, and obviously could not wait to get there now. 'This was going to be a special holiday to remember.' Riana thought to herself.

## APRIL RAIN

Fiona's thoughts though. 'Were of riding horses.' That was her passion, and she just couldn't wait.

So finally they had arrived at The Outback Gardens. The Bushman, and the Tourists.

As Pete maneuvered the vehicle around the dirt track, they veered down through the hills to pass along a forest of tall pines until the property then spread out before them in the morning sunlight, as far as the eye could see.

A forest of majestic gum trees lined the winding road that arrived at the front paddock and double gated entrance. A hand painted sign which towered over the entrance, picked out colours of the earth, and splashed them across the timberwork in an artwork depicting animals, gardens, orchards, bush flowers, and landscape scenery, all surrounding a Homestead.

It was breathtaking. They all sat in awe, and speech was stilled for a heartbeat. "So beautiful!" said Riana. Fiona smiled, and said. "This Outback Country has got so much to offer! How lucky we were to choose this place. It's amazing."

"I'll get the gate." said Col, as the vehicle come to a halt, and he jumped out to undo the double gates. He swung one aside, and proceeded through to open the other gate so the vehicle could move on through.

"Thanks Col!" called Pete. Col closed the gates, and jumped back inside. "We have got about a mile to go!" said Pete. "Enjoy the scenery!"

The road followed the river on their left, which was almost at its peak now, and was flowing quite strongly.

# JENNY MAC

On their right, the paddocks seem to go on, and on, towards a small group of hills in the near distance, that were still basked in shadows of the early morning.

There was bird life, and animals galore. They noticed emus, and the kangaroos scattered, and bounded away. As they passed on, horses grazed on lush grasses in the adjoining paddocks. "Oh look! Horses." said Fiona. "Are they yours Pete?" she asked. "Sure are." replied Pete. "I have six horses, six camels, ten milking cows, two dogs, fifty head of cattle, all on the property.

As they passed they could see the dairy cattle grazing in the next paddock, and little calves hovering around. They were all distinctly marked in colour. Continuing on, they crossed a grid, and their eyes captured a timber hand painted sign, which read.

*WELCOME TO THE OUTBACK GARDENS*

They drove on until eventually they emerged from around a huge bend, and captured the first glimpse of the large Homestead through the towering Jacarandas enclosing it, and it was complimented by the backdrop of gradual hills, and the river ambling along as it wound around the back of the property, and out of their view.

Secluded, and protected by nature within the house paddock sat a large Historic, double story weatherboard Homestead majestically positioned above the ground on solid pilings, and painted in the colours of a heritage theme, which gave the homestead a grand Historic look.

Bush flowers, and ferns, abundant in their blooms, provided a colourful display along the driveway, and were mixed amongst the other plants, which flowered throughout the gardens in close to the house. A split staircase angled upwards to the wide verandas, which provided the most outstanding views of the property, and surrounds, and timber railings graced the verandas, where double doors spilled out from all sides. "This is it, we are here" said Pete.

"That is the Outback Gardens Homestead, my Father and I live there. We won't be going in there just yet though, but no doubt you will get an invite to a tour of the House, and the Gardens, and probably a dinner one night, at some point, when Father arranges it with the homestead cook. Her name is May Jeffries, she has two daughters, Marie, and Sandy who are housemaids for both places, and their son Tim, is our grounds person." he said. Joe Jeffries, her husband, is our Bush Cook. His assistant is Susan Hind. You will meet them all in due course." said Pete.

Pete went on introducing them to the surroundings as he was driving past the Homestead. "The house paddock is quite large, but it accommodates the Main Homestead, and three bungalows for our employees."

"The Jeffries live in the larger one. Dale, and Hannah Best in one, and the other, is for the outback hands that work here. Take notice as we go along, that, the orchards go all the way down to the river. The gardens closer to the house, just outside the house paddock, and a nursery behind the house. They are all irrigated from the Siding River." Pete was saying. "Rain water tanks are installed here to service all the houses, and are also at the Bush Camp. The Outback Camp Site is in a separate paddock, we have two water tanks to service there, which are for drinking, cooking, and bathing water."

"All other water is pumped up from the river. I have extended electricity to the camping area, but for those of you who prefer the bush feeling, we have plenty of gas lights, and candles as well!" he said.

Riana was the first to speak as they passed by the Homestead, and drove on. "Is that a tennis court that I see there, Pete?" she asked. "Yes! Two clay courts, Riana. All the equipment is at the big house, and you all will be shown where we keep everything, so you can play whenever you like." Pete replied. Riana noticed all the Bungalows also, as they made their way down the winding track. They were set out quite individually, and well apart from each other at the back end of the house paddock just like a small township amidst the enormous gum trees which grew everywhere on the property.

"Your workers are well looked after here, Pete. I bet they love their life here!" said Riana. "Yeah they sure do. They are all great people, we couldn't manage without them!" replied Pete, as he then went on with information he had to get off his chest.

"We also have canoes on the river." he said, then he pointed. "Look over there, you can just make out the river bending around the back of the Homestead, and passing the next paddock in which is The Outback Camping Area, and your home for a while." he said.

## APRIL RAIN

"It is just a short stroll to the river from there. It is safe to swim in the river or do some fishing also, we have fishing equipment in The Outback Camp.

Keep in mind though, if I am not with you, safety is in numbers, so always go in a group if you want to go to the river, it is outside the paddock so there will be wildlife around. Joe has put his hand up, and will be your guide if needed, so if you want his assistance, just ask him." Pete said. "What wildlife would we expect to encounter?" asked Royce. "Ok!" said Pete. "For starters, there are wild boars in the bush, they don't normally come in too close to the camp, but don't take anything for granted out here, always be on the alert. Never walk close to the boars if you see them, come back inside the paddock, or if in real threat, just climb a tree! Also, wild dogs roam the outback. I haven't seen any here on our property but have heard of attacks elsewhere, so just be aware. There are lots of kangaroos too, don't think you can pet one like in a zoo, they can, and will attack you. They are the main dangers, not too bad really, except for snakes, lizards' etcetera." Pete said, as he laughed.

"Oh look!" called Fiona. I can see tents just ahead, I guess we're here now." Everyone strained to look ahead when they passed through the final grid. It was like an amphitheater. Several tents were dwarfed by one huge central marquee taking pride of place in its dominance. The atmosphere was electric, and they all gaped in awe at the massive set up. Pete braked the vehicle as he said.

*"Final Destination!"*

# JENNY MAC

## Chapter 5

Jacqueline Coby sat very tensely against the platform bench at 'The Siding' station. Persistent fog only added to her dilemma, making her feelings more foreboding as she was barely able to see the train tracks. 'This is a new Station with a new name too!' she thought, as she looked around in disbelief. Many people were arriving now, she noticed, though she knew not one soul. 'How terrible to be an outsider here!' she thought, as she hunched up on the bench seat.

'Waiting is just the worst part!' she thought to herself. Though it seemed she had been doing that all her life. 'Why is the train so late, especially today, this important day in my life!' she stressed. With a fierce determination she finally had submitted, and returned to the Country seeking redemption so long overdue. Though she waited with huge trepidation, her heart heavy, her mind was on a specific purpose.

This was her old home town, her birthplace, and since she had fully committed by making her final decision to return, so many distant miles had been covered getting here, but the last few days had been rough, by far the worst she had spent travelling. She had chanced to meet a truck driver in the city, and accepted his offer of a lift on the final stretch to The Outback, but now every bone in her body ached from the cramped cabin in the truck. It was a slow trip, road conditions causing extra time to the already, long trip.

Now after thirty-one long, lost years, Jacqueline felt

estranged as she waited at The Historic Shallow Siding Railway Station. 'It is so different to how it was all those years ago. A lifetime ago really!' she thought. 'When the town took its name from the modest station called. 'The Siding.' where now a new building stands, and bears a new name. 'What changes have been made' she thought.

*It was her home, but, she knew it not.*

She was a stranger now. Gone were the days of her special childhood, and upbringing by her family that she loved deeply. She had known love here. Though her roots were here, and her existence, there was no family members, or loved ones anymore.

Deep memories surfaced here. She was a local, born, and bred, now she felt like an alien, an outsider, and she didn't belong here. It made her feel so unbelievably sad, and impossibly lost as a massive feeling of apprehension came over her like a veil. 'Why are you really doing this to yourself Jackie? Are you prepared to face the shame?' she asked herself.

'Why come back and relive all the sadness again?'
She could already feel the heartache eating away inside.

It crept into her very soul. Twisting, like a knife had been thrust into her, except there was no blood, only the pain, unbelievable grief, and sorrow. She thought she had already been through the worst that life could offer her, and felt she was climbing the hill towards a normal life. Only now she was not so sure, life had a cruel way of tricking her, as bad feelings persisted now.

Her memories were just too raw.

## APRIL RAIN

'Whatever had she been thinking?'

She was fighting her body to stay in control. 'Maybe it was a huge mistake coming back.' she thought.

'I should have let things lie, but no not you Jackie, you just had to challenge fate didn't you, and you had to face up to the demons of your past!' "Your determination can sometimes work against you Jackie, so be very careful of that, or you can become your own worst enemy!"

*'I can almost still hear Mother saying that to me!'*

'I wish that she was here, so I could tell her that my determination was all I had to get me through. I would have been lost without it.'

Jacqueline's depressing thoughts were beginning to hound her. Just thinking about her Mother caused her so much grief, something that would stay with her, and haunt her all the days of her life. Tears flowed down her beautiful face in despair, but her mind wandered as the memories returned, and she could picture her Father's face very clearly now, as thoughts of him surfaced to fill her being. 'Such a great Father he was, and a great man to all who knew him!' she thought.

'I can only hope that in some way he understood, and forgave me for what I done!' 'Please god, let that be?' she prayed. I loved him so, and Mother also. I still do!'

Jacqueline's mindset was not in a good place. She felt distraught right now as her whole life flashed before her. Feelings she had tried so hard all her life to suppress, were now resurfacing. 'There were so many good times!'

she thought. However, it was the bad that consumed her, and it was imprinted inside her mind so severely that it seemed to cloud everything.

She had known in her heart the only way she could go forward, was to come home to Shallow Siding to face her past, and to bear her soul! To try, and make things right, especially to all the people she loved, if they were here. Maybe then, and only then, her conscience could be restored. That would be her salvation.

'Oh dear!' she thought. 'Why am I doing this, I think it may be too late. I had my opportunities back then, and rejected them. But I did have many good reasons at the time!' she recalled.

Sorrow plagued her, but she knew not be sorry now, for if she could have it all over again, there would be no other outcome, no way out. Her fate had been sealed. She could not have predicted, or prevented the incidents that ruined her life, forcing her to become an outcast. She felt so tired, and exhausted that her mind wandered, and drifted in recollection of her memories.

*Into a Reverie reminiscing her past life…*
*Her young life… Gone by…*

## Chapter 6
*The Year was 1960: 36 Years ago*
*Jacqueline Coby was 14yrs old*

I remember it well. The day of the beginning, or was it the end. My first journey into the unknown, and my coming of age. I travelled the unfamiliar one way road, into young womanhood, and barely struggled to come to terms with the enormity of it.

There was no prior warning, and no insight into my future, though I sensed that this was the time that my life, my childhood as it had been, would change forever, and never ever being the same again.

This momentous day started like any other ordinary, carefree, day of my life. A child's life, where everything was an adventure, and every new day was blessed with a new challenge. I was bursting with energy, and a sense of gaiety, and a deep love in my heart for my family, my home, my life, and friends. I can still hear my Mother's voice, as she called out to me that morning. She was a very special person in my life, in all our lives, and I loved her dearly. I was the last daughter she had given birth to, and the baby of the family, and I guess I was a tomboy as well. I say that because I was always with my Father out on the property, and not really into things a young girl, would, or should do.

My Mother would always say, that I was the son that my Father never had. I just reveled in learning all the interesting, and difficult things that he achieved every day, and what effort it took to run a big property. He was also my Idol, and I followed him around asking questions all the time, and nothing could ever sate my appetite for more information. I was like a sponge, just soaking it all up.

Father was my confidence booster as well, and made me feel as if I was the most important person, someone who was clever, and talented, and had a will to compete, and succeed in life.

Clayton Coby was my Father. He was not only an ideal parent, but a hugely important man to our town, and district. He was one of the first settlers to set the benchmark for prosperity, and success, that other country farmers could emulate, on how to run a cattle station, and his introduction of a new source of farming. 'Wattle growing.'

He was an inspiration to all who knew him, and his success was widely known throughout the Outback. He run cattle on his property Shallow Downs, about 200-250 head at times, sometimes a lot more, depending on sales, but always improving, and buying more stock, or a good bull when he needed to. He was a noted figure at the Annual Show in Shallow Siding, and he always had a prize awarded for best Bull, or Heifer from his breeding stock. He was quite proud of his breeding stock. The property was undulating land, initially 180 hectares, well grassed with ample water supply, even though paddocks could get quite dry in the summer.

Rainfall was plenty in the wet season, winter was very

cold, but summer very hot in contrast, and at certain times drastic measures were taken to care for stock.

Over the years my Father extended the homestead, also building more cattle yards, stables, work-sheds, machinery, and hay storage-sheds, and meat houses, as well as several outbuildings. Bungalows for permanent staff, workers huts for the hired hands, and he had purchased tents for temporary wattle crew to camp in.

Because in earlier years he had expanded his property as well, by purchasing some land next door. He had, had, a brainchild, all about wattle. So he had looked into the requirements for growing wattle trees on his land, and came to the conclusion that he would like to gamble on the prospects of growing wattle, as the possibilities were endless.

There didn't seem to be any waste in the trees. Once they were at maturity the hardwood trees would be cut down, providing the best Blackwood timber for making fine furniture, and the bark would be stripped to be used for tanning for the oil it contained, and also processed into different oils or medicinal oils.

His immediate need was to find a reliable timber mill, and a refinement center to send his trees, and bark to, preferably by rail. Then to hire workers, and of course, to purchase the wattle tree plants. So he had done his research well, then refinanced with the bank to buy more land to pay for expenses, as well as a shed to be erected for the purpose of drying bark. So the wheels turned in motion, everything was going according to his plans, and

# JENNY MAC

a new theme was born.

Now that was all past history, as they had felled one good crop of wattle four years ago, and his paddocks were filled now with a mixture of mature trees, and younger ones of different ages.

Progress had been slow to start until the cycle had started to eventuate, but his plants had thrived, and at the cutting of the first crop he had hired up to eighty casual workers who lived temporarily on the property. After the initial organization and hard work of planting, nurturing, and irrigation of the wattle had been done, everything got a lot easier as time went by, and now it was all paying off.

My Father is very proud man, and his determination almost fierce, to a point where he believes he can move mountains, and nothing is ever too hard.

'There is always a way!' he says.

He is so stubborn, and set in his ways, once he makes up his mind. I guess that my Father also instilled in me a determination beyond no other, something that would stay with me forever.

*And I loved him so.*

Jackie! Jackie! "Where are you? Your Father wants you to meet him this morning. He has gone up to the hill-side of the top paddock!"

It was my Mother calling. Breakfast was cooked, and ready to serve when I walked in, and Mother was busy with her arms up to the elbows in flour, making bread, and big beef pies for lunch.

## APRIL RAIN

Morning Mother! "I am here now. I will just have breakfast, then I will go. I will ride Sailor, he will get me there faster! How did Father get up there today?" I asked. "Oh there you are Jackie! Good Morning!"

"Father took the jeep! He had to take some fencing wire, and tools, looks like you might have to do some repairs to the fences. The damn kangaroos have been digging under the wire again, and jumping fences, and the cattle have got through, so you will have to round up the cattle too. Ok then, ride Sailor but take care! I have packed you both some food for your morning tea!" Mother said.

"Make sure you take a coat Jackie, its cold out, and try not to be too late home today, you have lessons this afternoon. Jim told me he would be here at 3pm!" she said. Jim Hale was my tutor, a retired teacher, who lived alone on our property in a bungalow, down near the creek. I was doing correspondence for schooling at home with him now, since I finished my school years in town. I did not choose to leave home, and go to college. My future was here at Shallow Downs, and that was where I wanted to stay.

Jacqueline finished breakfast, and looked up into her Mother's smoky blue eyes. Her Mother had suddenly stopped talking to her, and was now just staring into space. Jacqueline immediately recognized that faraway look that her Mother sometimes got in her eyes, as she had seen it many times before on her Mothers face.

She had a closeness with her Mother, always had, she knew her well. Jacqueline smiled in a meaningful way.

# JENNY MAC

Mel Coby had been preoccupied inside the kitchen of their homestead at Shallow Downs when Jackie walked in, and she looked up. 'What a beautiful child, my baby! Such a wonderful young woman she will become!' Mel thought, as she looked to Jackie's deep green eyes, with pride, and smiled.

Mel was in her fifties now, and her body was quite petite in build, but held with a sense of pride, which was elevated up to her deep smoky-blue coloured eyes. Her features were striking, her tanned olive skin, shone with health, and her golden blond hair which was shoulder length, seemed to fall all about her attractive face in wisps, making her a very attractive woman for her age.

She proceeded in giving last minute instructions to Jackie on where to go. "Now please be careful Jackie!" she said. "I will be Mother, don't worry!" I replied, and getting up to leave, I kissed my Mother on the cheek.

"I'll be off now Mother, I hope you have a good day!" I said as I threw my pack over my shoulder, grabbed my rifle off the rack, and walked towards the door. "Take water, Jackie, and bullets for your gun!" Mel said. "Got all that, Mother, will probably be home for lunch!" I said, as I walked out through the door.

'She's growing up so quickly.' Mel Coby thought, as she watched Jackie walk outside. Previously, she was standing watching Jacqueline having her breakfast, and her mind had wandered a little.

'She had a lot to be thankful for!' she had thought.'

'She had given birth to her four daughters in this house, and their Father, Clayton Coby, was a very proud man, a good provider, a hard worker, and great Father to their children!' 'She felt so proud of the way they had raised them, they were all such lovely girls. She was a very protective Mother with her girls, and had liked to keep a tight rein on them all, when they were growing up.

She was very proud within herself for that fact!' Jacqueline was the youngest daughter born to Mel, and Clayton Coby. She was delivered at the property, by a midwife, on the 10th April 1946.

Their property was a huge enterprise, comprising a large cattle property with many cattle paddocks, a huge house paddock with other areas for lodgings, and, behind the Homestead grew a wattle plantation.

Their undulating land scattered with native gum trees was elevated with a backdrop of the nearby hills, and the wattle trees swayed, and climbed the gradual slopes.

The property had been in the Coby family for over two generations, but Clayton's hard work had seen the property built up to where it is today. Major extensions were done to the house, and Clayton had refused to give up on his new ideas about growing wattle. Mel smiled to herself as she thought of his fierce determination in making this venture succeed, so they had gone into debt, to make his dreams become a reality.

Now they were benefiting from his incite, and were in a very comfortable position. Clayton, and Mel Coby had become very rich people. Their Homestead existed of a rambling split level weatherboard house bearing three chimneys on the roof for fireplaces, and several double doors opening out onto wide verandas, which captured the cool breezes in warmer weather, and displayed the most magnificent views of the Property, the lawns, and colourful gardens. Large water tanks were set up behind the house.

It was an elite property for the day, and age. A sign on their mailbox at the front gate of the Property read. 'The Coby's Shallow Downs' aptly named for the area where they lived, and Shallow Creek which rolled along through their Property, blessed them with consistent water.

Axel Hall arrived at the back entrance to the kitchen of the big house. He walked up the steps, loaded up with an armful of wood, and knocked on the kitchen door. "Are ya there Missus?" he called out. Axel was the caretaker, as well as grounds person at Shallow Downs.

He had worked for the Coby's for ten years. He was part aboriginal with a wiry body, long black hair, soft dark eyes, and a flashy smile. His wife was an aboriginal woman, she died giving birth to their son Deakan nine years ago.

Deak lived with his Dad in a property bungalow. His job as a stable boy was to muck out the stables, and feed, and water the horses. "I'm in the kitchen, Axel!" Mel called out. "Come on in!"

## APRIL RAIN

Axel walked into the kitchen, and smiled. "Mornin Missus! Do ya want all the fires lit now?" he asked.

"Good morning Axel! Yes please, it is a bit cold this morning, just go on through Axel!" said Mel.

Mel was busy occupying herself in the kitchen after Jacqueline had left. She was quite enjoying herself this morning as her cooking days were so limited now, to filling in when the Homestead Cook Emily Banks was having time off. Emily was a lovely lady of forty years, very tall, and slim, with brown hair, and soft grey eyes.

Emily had been a great friend to Mel over the years, and was also a very good cook, and Mel regarded her highly. Ashton Banks, who is Emily's husband, was the cook for the property's hired hands. Ashton had his own galley, and mess in a huge area adjacent to the workers huts, which were allocated in the first paddock, opposite the creek.

Ashton was a tall man in stature, and his jet black hair without a hint of grey, was cut short back, and sides. His blue eyes seemed to always twinkle when he spoke. He was forty-one now, and he, and Emily had worked for The Coby's for fifteen years, so they were almost like family. They lived onsite on the property in a bungalow inside the house paddock, down towards the creek.

Mel was thinking how lucky they were to have such loyal workers living on Shallow Downs, but realistically she knew that they had all become their closest friends.

# JENNY MAC

## Chapter 7

The early morning breeze hit me in the face, and it bit with a vengeance. Winter threatened now, the cold air chilled me to the bone, and the frost upon the grass crunched under my boots as I walked on out to the inner stables. I buttoned my sheepskin coat, then pulled the hood up over my head to fend off the cold, trying to compete with the elements, and then, as a whim caught me, I paused for a moment to take in the beauty of the morning, and to greet the day. My eyes glanced over the paddocks, all covered in white now with the early fallen frost, and the leaves laden on the trees hung down to greet the ground. 'So beautiful' I thought. 'Almost pure.'

Colours seemed to combine the beautiful scenery with the stillness of the morning. It was a magic sight, and a great feeling.

I could never tire in experiencing all the wonderful countryside where we lived, and each different season had a beauty to behold. The hills, and the valleys, the giant gums, all a splendor to enjoy. Every new day was different, exciting, and nothing like the one before it. It was so great to be young, and alive with enthusiasm.

Looking back towards the Homestead, I noticed that the fires had obviously been lit in the fireplaces, as the chimneys in the big house were all billowing with smoke now. 'It would be nice, and warm inside when we came home.' I thought. How I loved to sit around the fires inside our home in winter. We had many a family gathering in the large living area of our house, where the stone fireplace took pride of place in the center of the wall. Father had laid slate on the floors all through the living areas which made it lovely, and cool in the hot weather, but in winter Mother had big mats scattered around the floors, and that gave it a lovely homely, cozy feeling as well as warmth. 'I loved our house!'

'We have so much fun in our home' I was thinking as I walked on. My Father arranged most of the things that I loved to do, like shooting competitions, and hunting trips, but we also went to dances, and he entertained at home, inviting lots of people over for big house parties.

He was also a very important figure in the town, and district, and our home was always busy. My thoughts receded abruptly as I reached the stable doors, and I went inside.

Sailor greeted me with a whinny, and nodded his handsome head towards me. His shiny black coat, glistened in the early light, and the white blaze on his forehead stood out like a bright star, the white socks on his hooves, a contrast to his body colour. He is a stallion with a great spirit, and bears the name I gave him as a colt. None of us had any way of knowing his potential then, but he had progressed into a very fast racing horse.

We all feel that he was appropriately named initially, because when he races, his hooves seem to sail over the ground, so the name suited him well. We both usually compete in the annual Gymkhana in Shallow Siding, and he's the fastest horse in the district. 'I just love to ride him!' He is gentle as a lamb with me, and nuzzles into my neck, and nudges my jacket. 'I often wonder is it me he loves, or the sweets that I have for him in my pockets! I would prefer to think the former option!'

Sailor does not usually like strangers, and he won't tolerate people trying to ride him, he has been known to throw anyone that tries to do so. 'I am the only one who can ride Sailor.'

"Hello handsome!" I say, as I give him a big cuddle, and plant a kiss on his velvet nose. He nudges me, and I nudge him back, then grabbing the saddle, blanket, and my bridle, I saddled up, and slid my rifle into the saddle sheath, and tied my pack to the saddle.

The rifle was a very special present to me for my last birthday from my Father. He made it up himself by sending for all the individual requirements like a handmade timber stock, barrel, magazine, bolt etcetera, and scope. It was a .22 caliber rifle with a telescopic sight, and as true as any gun I had used. He taught me at a young age how to shoot, and he liked to think that I had some protection out in the bush, so the rifle went with me everywhere at home, or in the bush, and I knew how to use it too.

I eased Sailor into a trot down the path towards the gate of the house paddock opposite the creek that runs through the property. I had two paddocks to cross to reach the top paddock, so I would follow the path along the creek until I got to the last paddock, and then cut across the property towards the hills. I knew where my Father would be so I planned to take a short cut across country. As I was passing the first bungalow I noticed Missus Banks walking outside to the wood pile so I turned Sailor off the path and headed over to her. "Good morning! Missus Banks, are you enjoying your day off?" I called as I reined in, jumping down to greet her.

"Good morning Jackie, I sure am! What a beautiful morning. It's very cold though, but I guess we're used to that here. I thought I'd get the fire going. Where are you off to so early? You know Jackie, you can call me Emily, you are old enough now!" she uttered. "Yes I know, but Mother says I have to respect my elders, and I rather like calling you Missus Banks, sounds better!" I said. "I am going up to meet Father at the top paddock, can I help you to carry the wood before I go?" I asked. "If you have that far to go Jackie you'd better keep going, don't let me hold you up I am used to getting the wood. I will be fine, thanks for the offer though!" she replied. "Ok, if you are sure then I will keep going!" I said, and climbed up onto Sailors back, gave a wave as I headed across to the path.

Once back on the track, I noticed young Deakan Hall cutting across the paddock heading towards the stables, then he starting running towards me. "Where ya goin Miss Jacqueline? Can I com with ya?" he asked, in a breathless rush of words, when he had caught up to me.

"Hello Deakan, how are you? No I am sorry, you can't come! I've got a long ride to go on, besides you have got work to do before school, haven't you?" I asked. "I always havta work!" he said.

"My Dad always says we havta earn our keep, but I

shouldn't havta work, an I don't ever get ta hav any fun.

You don't do work Miss Jacqueline, an ya hav lots of fun! I know ya do. I watch ya all the time. How come I can't do som things too?" he asked, screwing his face up in frustration, his dark eyes blazing in anger.

"Deakan, let me make myself quite clear to you here! I do a lot of work. Though I don't work for any wages. I just love to help my Father, and I am still studying my schoolwork at home, so I don't think I should have to be explaining myself to you, I think you are too young to understand, you had better speak to your Father about this! I have to go now, I have a long way to go!" I said as I gave Sailor a kick and trotted away. "Tis jus not fair!" he retorted.

Unsettled, I urged Sailor into a canter until I reached the creek, and tried to put the conversation with Deakan out of my mind, and recapture the good feelings I'd had earlier when I was in a happier mood. I reached the creek in no time, and settled Sailor into an easy pace along the straight stretch of path. A chilly breeze blew my hood off, my hair was blowing free, and my carefree attitude returned as I gloried in the surroundings, and the birdlife around.

A kookaburra called out laughing, and I laughed too. I noticed a group of kangaroos at the creek in the first paddock, probably had come down to drink early, they all scattered in different directions, as I rode past. Even though I knew what pests they were, damaging fences and grasses on our property. I still couldn't help but admire these true Australian animals, as I noticed how beautiful they were, but so splendid, and gracious in their escape, as they covered the ground so quickly with huge bounds, their great tail pumping at the earth, and supporting their flight in an unseemly effortless, and unique style.

My plan was to continue on towards the end of the second paddock. I knew of a place there that I could get down close to the creek to give Sailor a drink, and rest for a while. So we pressed on until finally I recognized tall grasses that grew along the bank of the creek, and a rough track winding down amongst the huge river gums.

I reined in, and climbed off Sailor's back to lead him down the narrow dirt track to the water's edge. I pulled my pack, and rifle off the saddle, and set them down, then tied the reins up so Sailor could walk freely. He moved towards the water to drink, so I sat down on a rock, and opened my pack for water, and food. 'Many thanks Mother!' I thought, as I pulled out a piece of cake, and a drink, and watched the water in the creek flow by.

Sailor smelt them before he seen them, I think. All at once his head flew up from the water with his nostrils flaring. He shivered, and he whinnied as he stamped his hooves. I dropped everything, and, as I rose to console him, I looked up into the deadliest eyes I had ever seen. I very slowly reached down for my rifle, slipped off the safety catch to quietly ease the bolt up to load a bullet.

# APRIL RAIN

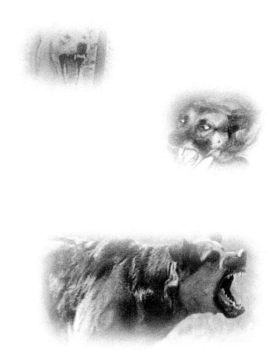

They emerged out of the long grass and halted on the edge of the sandy bank, two flanking the big male in front. I stood very still, and was petrified. My heart started thumping in my chest, but I couldn't look away from those vicious eyes of the monster before me. I guessed this larger beast in front was their leader, and no doubt the more dominant predator.

Saliva was dripping down its black gums, and the wild eyes were fixed on me standing at the water's edge. Its massive body stood as tall as a calf, hairs bristled on its black and tan coat, its intentions obvious when he opened his huge jaws in aggression, baring his massive fangs, and growled, with such a sound, that sent shivers up my spine. 'Feral dogs.' I thought, as I went numb. I am familiar with the markings of a true Australian Dingo, but these animals weren't dingoes, they were abandoned dogs, gone wild, the worst kind, and they were an ongoing problem in the district. Sheep Farmers especially, were having their sheep killed, and their horses, and other livestock attacked, and lately, cattle properties had lost calves also to these dogs.

Usually they were starved, and preyed on anything for food, but when in a frenzy, killed just for the fun of it. I stood staring at the three killers in front of me now.

Somehow I stayed remarkably calm, even though I could feel the adrenalin pumping through my veins.

I knew quickly though, that my rifle scope would not aid me here, as they were too close, so I needed the leader in closer. 'If I can just get him with a clean shot, then I may have a chance.' I thought. So I planted my feet solidly, and steeled myself to the waiting. I could sense Sailor's distress, but I didn't have time to look at what he was doing. *'Then the great dog came.'*

It bounded strongly across the short distance like a locomotive, its huge paws stretched out, and ploughed up the soft sand as it came charging towards me. The two stranglers hesitated, but then followed the leader eagerly, only several paces behind. Its growls pieced my brain, the face contorted in aggression, and then, from about eight feet, with me clearly as its target, it sprang.

## APRIL RAIN

I balanced, and brought my rifle up with my sights set on the gaping jaws, and slime, and fired into its throat. The bullet took it cleanly through open jaws, and the angle of the shot sent it on to shatter the back of its brain.

The feral dog was stone dead when it hit me, with such a jolt, that shook my whole body, and from the momentum of his huge frame, knocked the rifle from my hands into the sand, and me, flat on my backside in the water. I was shaken, but rolled the dog off me, and scrambling up to my feet, I lunged onto the sand, and grabbed my rifle. It was still intact, so I recovered the spent shell, and quickly loaded up another bullet ready to face the next attack.

'I could hear the crunch clearly from where I lay.'

Sailor was acting so crazy. I thought he would have raced off, but he was still there stamping his hooves, and whinnying. He kicked out wildly at the oncoming dog with his back legs, and his shoes connected with, and broke the dog's front leg, then the dog went down howling. Sailor then reared up high, and bringing his legs down, pounded the body of the dog with his steel clad hooves. I leaped immediately to my feet, as I could see the other dog slinking away now. Taking careful aim to get it in my sights, and directing my shot for the heart this time, just behind its shoulder, I pulled the trigger.

My shot rang out, and I watched as the bullet made its mark in the short hair of the dog's coat. The dog yelped loudly, then stumbled a bit, but ran on until it finally went down. 'It's over, over!' I thought, as my legs went to jelly, and I sank to the sand trembling with relief, as feelings of fear grabbed me in a vice. Shock, and realization hit me that my ordeal of terror was a real thing, like nothing I had ever experienced in my life before. 'Thank you Father for my training, and giving me determination.' I thought.

Sailor whinnied, so I forgot my own distress, and jumping up, I went to his aid. "Whoa! Boy, Whoa! I said, it's all finished! Settle down boy! Good boy, down boy!" I crooned to him. He stood down reluctantly as I closed in to smooth his shoulder. Still talking, I eased the knot from the reins to pull them over his head, as I patted his nose, and planted a kiss on his handsome face.

"You saved my life Sailor, thank you! I guess you do love me after all!" I said, as I continued to talk to him, and pat him, trying to calm him. Once he settled a little, a compulsive urge came over me to leave this revolting scene, so I quickly retrieved my pack from the sand then headed upstream, leading Sailor away from the dogs. I stopped only once along the creek bed to let him drink, and drank deeply myself from my water bottle. When I was finally sated, I tied my pack back on the saddle, and put my gun, covered in sand, into its sheath.

I guided Sailor along an old track, which was barely visible through the long grass but eventually led up to the path. My clothes were wet, and sandy, and my body shivered from the cold as I walked along beside Sailor, until finally I climbed up into the saddle, and we set off at a walk, to gradually pick up the pace after a while. I still had the last paddock to cross, so I veered across country for the last lap towards the hills to meet Father.

## Chapter 8

Clayton Coby watched as the stallion picked its way up the slope towards him. His daughter Jackie sat him proudly, gently guiding the big horse amongst the rocky terrain. Her long blond hair, to her waist now, was blowing in the wind, and a flash of those beautiful deep green eyes met his briefly, and he smiled. She smiled back with her brilliant smile.

'She is the only daughter I have left at the homestead now.' he thought. 'His two eldest daughters June, and Latisha were both married now, and lived in the city where they always wanted to be. They would all come back home for visits though, especially at Christmas time, and other holidays. His other daughter Lainey, had left home to start a job that she had wanted in another town, and when she was able, she would come to see them, and, she too would always love being home for Christmas, but Jackie was just happy at home. She was young, and vibrant, very intelligent, and honest, always called a spade a spade. But! he chuckled. 'She was also so very determined, knowing exactly what she wanted. Her interest in the property was her passion, her whole existence growing up.' he thought.

'Unlike her sisters who could not wait to leave home, and Shallow Siding, Jackie was always at his side to help with anything that had to be done, and asking questions, always asking questions. The bond between them was very special. He was so proud of her, and loved her undeniably. She could drive, ride, shoot, and tackled all the jobs required in running the property, better than most boys her age.'

'Jackie was positive with her views on everything, including the property, life, love, even at such a young age. He knew how much she loved their home, and that she could not imagine life being anywhere else in the world, but with her family.' he mused.

'Jackie would always be at Shallow Downs.' he was thinking. 'Even when Mel, and I have gone.' He felt absolutely sure about that. It made him feel comfortable, it was good to know that the work, and improvements they had done on the property, was all worthwhile, and would benefit her in the end. 'She would have a future here.' he thought.

Amidst the silence her voice startled him when he heard her calling out, interrupting his private thoughts.

"Morning Father! I'm here now, on my way up!"

Jacqueline was easing Sailor delicately across the top paddock hillside between the scattered rocks, to where her Father would be, but it was not hard to find him.

She reined in wanting to savour the moment, to pause a while, and indulge in the overwhelming reverence that she had towards this Father of hers.

He was a huge man, such a powerful man. 'Standing on the hillside, he looked like a giant who was blocking the only rays of sunshine that were daring to come out on this cold morning.' she thought. His massive broad shoulders, and physique, rippled with muscle, and on his deeply tanned, olive skin, she could detect the lines etched upon his handsome face. He had a certain way about him when his chin jutted out that indicated his dominance, his confidence, and stubbornness. 'He could definitely be very stubborn at times!' she thought.

'But it was his stature which took you unawares, as his whole demeanor oozed with a deep inner sense of pride.' Clayton Coby was a very proud man, honest, and straightforward, and it was very catching. All the Coby's were bred to be proud people.

'He is fifty-six now.' she thought. 'But just look at him, he is a tower of strength, and solid as a rock. His full head of wavy blond hair, now with only a few shades of grey, grew to his shirt collar, and fell across his tanned forehead, and into his deep green eyes.'

Jacqueline egged Sailor forward slowly, and while they climbed up the hillside she noticed her Father's green eyes watching her, and he smiled broadly. She smiled back, and called. "Morning Father! I'm here now, on my way up!" He waved, and called back.

"Good Morning Jackie! I am pleased you are finally here. I was wondering where you were, it is a bit cold this morning. How was your ride up? I have just made a wider opening in this fence so it'll be easier to get the cattle through, only twelve of them, so I sent Chip out to round up the strays, we can help him later!" Clayton said. 'Chip, our dog, a black, and white kelpie, is very smart rounding cattle.' "The fence is all trodden down, so we'll fix that later when they're all through!" he was saying, as I reached him, and dismounted. I tethered Sailor to a tree, then climbed into my Father's arms.

It felt so safe, and secure there, my guard collapsed. "Hey are you ok? You're trembling!" Father asked, with a concerned voice. "You look a little tired or something."

"Your hair is all full of sand, your clothes are a mess, and wet too! My god, is that blood I see?" "Ok! What's up Jackie, what has happened?" he asked. "Tell me all!"

Jacqueline wanted to savor the safeness of her Father's arms around her, and the familiar smell of his body for just a moment longer, as right now she felt like a little girl again, and she could feel the release coming.

The huge compression in her chest had bottled up inside her, and now felt like she was about to explode.

She thought she had her emotions under control until this moment, but now she started shaking, and sobbing uncontrollably, and the tears slid down her lovely face, as she looked up sadly to her Father.

"I'm sorry Father. I don't know what has come over me, I will be ok!" I said, as I continued to sob. "You will not be ok young lady, and don't you tell me otherwise! I know a delayed reaction when I see one, and I aim to find out what has brought this on!"

Clayton went to the Jeep, grabbed two blankets from the back, and spread one out under a gum tree. "Now you sit down there Jackie, I will get you a drink! Keep yourself warm!" he said, as he draped the other blanket around me. "Did Mother put any tea, and food in your pack?" he asked. "Yes Father!" I said. He then left, and grabbed Jacqueline's pack off the saddle, and looking down, he noticed the blood on Sailor's hooves, and legs.

He steeled himself, then walked slowly back, but not mentioning that to Jackie, she would have to tell him about that herself. 'My god, what has gone on here?' he thought, as he handed Jackie the water bottle. "Right Jackie!" he says. "We are going to settle down here, and have a nice cup of tea, and some food!" He opened the pack saying. "Good! Mother has made us sandwiches. Now Jackie, try, and calm down, have some food, and drink!" he said, as he passed me a sandwich of corn beef, and pickles, and then started pouring out our tea. "We will not talk until you are ready, but make no mistake young lady, you will not be leaving anything out, and we won't be leaving here until you have told me what happened to you earlier! I want to know everything! Is that quite clear?" he asked. "Yes Father!" I said softly, and proceeded to drink my tea, and eat a sandwich.

We sat for a long time, we had finished eating, and were talking about other things, and my senses seemed to clear. I asked about the cattle, and I told my Father of the roos I had seen earlier, and where they were. It was then that I decided I could not delay the inevitable, so I commenced to tell him what had happened to me.

Clayton listened very intently to Jackie relaying all the gruesome events which had played out in his daughters life this morning. He didn't interrupt or ask questions, but could not suppress the feelings he was getting, first of amazement, but then, total admiration, and huge pride for this small person before him, who was of his blood. 'What grit she has!' he thought, as he watched her reliving the horror she had been through.

His feelings suddenly began to turn to remorse then, and he was blaming himself for allowing her to become so physically involved in the lifestyle they led every day, and the exposure to all the potential dangers. He knew he had trained her from a young age in self survival, but he was starting to doubt his own judgement.

'He could have lost a huge part of his life today. His Daughter!' he was thinking.

Abruptly, Jacqueline stopped talking, and looked up at her Father. "That's it Father, that is the whole story. It's over now, and I feel much better. Shall we go, and round up the cattle now?" I asked, then proceeded to stand up. "Now you hold on a minute Jackie. It's my turn now! I can't tell you how sorry I am that you had to go through that ordeal. You are just the bravest young, or even older person I know, and I am so proud of you!"

"You are a true Coby! However, I cannot help feeling responsible for putting you in this dangerous situation. Maybe I have been too lenient in letting you do so much at such a young age, Jackie!" he stated.

"Father I can't believe you said that! You of all people! I will quote you!" I said, with a determined look in my eyes. "We live in the bush here Jackie! You have to be tough, and you need skills to survive!" you said. "How often have you said that to me? Well Father, you taught me all the skills, and how to be tough!" I said.

# APRIL RAIN

Jacqueline remembered learning to drive the Jeep, and shoot at age nine, and she was quick to remind her Father of this fact. "Besides Father! I think that I get my determination from you anyway!" I said, with a giggle. I love you deeply for teaching me all that, and I wouldn't want to be doing anything different now. That is why I survived today I guess, with a little help from Sailor!"

"So don't blame yourself for something that I love doing Father!"

Clayton loved to hear her laugh, and he laughed too. "Ok Jackie you win *This Time!*" he said, with a meaning.

"But we had better look after your rescuer, so he can live to fight another day!"

'Why do I always permit her do that to me?' pondered Clayton, as he got up to hug his Daughter closely. 'I give in to her all the time, and she has me wrapped around her little finger!' "Ok Jackie, let's go, and tend to Sailor, he needs to settle after his scare too." he said.

Father grabbed a bale of hay from out of the Jeep, and proceeded to pull it apart. I got the water bucket out of the back, and some rags, and we both walked over to Sailor. He gave us a whinny, and I patted his lovely head. 'He's been through a lot today as well.' I thought.

"I want to check his legs, and his hooves, Jackie!" My Father said. "Put your rifle in the Jeep! I will have to service that when we get home, it will have sand in it everywhere!" Ok! Father!" I said, as I pulled the rifle out of the sheath, made sure it was on safety, and walked over to the Jeep, and settled it in the gun rack, next to Father's gun, which was between the two front seats.

## JENNY MAC

As I headed back, I noticed Chip had all the cattle back in a group, and was just sitting there waiting.

'What a dog.' I thought. I called to tell Father. "He's a good boy, is my Chip!" he said, as he looked up, and I noticed that he was washing down Sailor's legs, and hooves. "No damage done here luckily!" he said, but we will change the shoes when we get back!" I walked over, undone the girth strap, pulled the saddle, and blanket off, unclipped the bridle, and left a halter on Sailor. Then I picked up everything to put it in the Jeep, grabbed a long rope out of the back, and went back, and tied one end to the halter, and then to the gum tree, and started washing Sailor down. "He's liking this Father! I said, as I rubbed him down, we can get the cattle now!"

"Just give Sailor some water Jackie, and I've got some hay for him, so we'll leave him now, and the cattle can wait too! There is something I want to show you, if you feel up to it! Are you feeling alright now?" Father asked.

"It is the real reason that I got you to come up here today Jackie!" Father said. "I am fine now Father, my clothes are almost dry, I am not so cold now, just feeling bruised!" I replied. "Ok, if you are sure then, but bring a blanket, and keep it wrapped around yourself Jackie to stay warm!" he said.

"Climb in the Jeep, and we'll head off, not far to go!" my Father said, as he resumed his mysterious manner, as his chin jutted out with that determined way he had.

'I was about to question him, but he beat me to it.'

"No questions Jackie! Have patience, and all will be revealed!" he said, smiling.

# APRIL RAIN

"But Father! … I was about to continue on, and he says. "No buts either, Jackie!"

So we climbed in the Jeep, and Father was looking very smug about something. I was busting to find out, I just had to know. "So where are we going Father?" I asked. "All in good time Jackie, I will tell you!" he said, as he started the motor, engaged the gears, and pulled off the track, heading out through the bush, and towards the highest hills.

The Jeep was set up for hunting, there was no roof, and a gun carriage sat between us. The windows pushed out for shooting. A large spotlight was centered above on the framework, smaller spotlights were bolted on the sides. There were no doors, so we were exposed to the wild elements of the morning, and the cold air gripped us as we moved. The breeze tossed my hair, my face was pinching from the cold, but it was exhilarating as I breathed in the fresh bush air with relish.

# JENNY MAC

Father drove slowly as he negotiated a way through the rocky terrain, and bush, still keeping the hillside in focus. "Might be a bit rough for a while Jackie till I cut the track I am looking for! How are you feeling now?" he asked. "I am fine Father, a few bumps won't hurt me, besides I am enjoying the countryside!" I replied.

I leaned back in the seat, and then pulled the blanket closely around myself for its warmth, and I looked out over the property as we climbed up. "It is just beautiful Father, I have never been this high up before!" I said.

"Yeah we are getting up much higher now Jackie, and yes it is such lovely country up this way. Can't say there is any better, and it is all ours Jackie! Many years, and a lot of blood, sweat, and tears we have spent here, but it's been worth it!" he said, with pride.

Finally Father found the small track he was looking for which led up the hillside, and as he turned onto it to follow it upwards, we drove onto much firmer ground until we could go no further.

"That is as far as we can go Jackie!" Father said, as he braked the Jeep, and pulled on the handbrake. "Are you up to a short walk?" "Yes Father, I have a few bruises, but walking will be better than sitting!" I said.

So then we walked up the gradual dirt trail until we finally topped the last rise. As our heads poked over the top of the hill, what we witnessed was the magnificence of the panorama spreading out before us.

I was astonished to see how breathtaking it was.

## APRIL RAIN

"My goodness, just look at it Father! How beautiful it is!" I said, in wonder. "Yes Jackie, this is another of our special places on Shallow Downs!" replied Father.

We could see all the paddocks defined for miles, and amidst it all, the different colours reflected spasmodically from the limited sunshine that streamed through the beautiful gum trees, and the early morning mist, rising high into the air.

Shallow Creek flowed swiftly, but took on another element too as it went idling through the paddocks, to seemingly provide another life form for a congregation of animals and the birdlife that gathered along its banks.

I had never seen it from up here before, and just to see how the creek wound its way through our Property was amazing to witness first-hand.

"Oh! Thank you for bringing me up here Father, it is the most glorious place!" I said, quite excited. "It sure is Jackie, but I want you to take a closer look at the distant trees!" Father said, as he pointed. "Do you know what it is you are actually seeing?" he asked.
"Is that our wattle plantation I see Father?" I asked. "Coby land Jackie! Our land, and yes! It most definitely is our wattle plantation Jackie!" he replied.

# JENNY MAC

## Chapter 9

My eyes squinted to the filtered light as I peered out over the distant hills, and caught site of the rows, and rows, of huge Wattle Trees, as far as the eye could see. Father's pride, and joy. "I see the trees Father, they are huge now, and it is a great view of the plantation from up here too!" I said.

"I wanted you to come up here today for two main reasons!" My Father said, as he looked into my eyes. "Well four, if you count the cattle, and the fence, but this is more important! The first! The mature wattle is almost ready to be cut, so that will be a very busy time, lots of things to organize. I wanted you to see it from up here first. I plan on having a Cutting of the Wattle Party to celebrate, so we will need to invite lots of town-folk, and property owners, and all their guests. Want it to be a big turnout Jackie, one that we will always remember. I will need your help with this. Maybe the invitations when the time is right, and think of some events we can hold to entertain everyone. We will have a proper meeting at home, and get some things down on paper!" "So what do you think?" he asked.

"I think it's a super idea Father, I'll definitely help in any way you need. It will be great Father, we could have a band too, and some horse events and … I was going to go on, when he stopped me. "Ok! Ok! Jackie, that mind of yours never stops. I will put you in charge of events when we do this, you can run things by me then! Knew I could rely on you!" Father said, as he smiled broadly.

"Now! The second thing. Let's sit down!" he said. We sat upon the grass overlooking the view, then Father seemed all at once, to adapt a different mood, as his chin jutted out with that dominant, stubborn, attitude. "Now! This conversation will be as serious as it gets Jackie, your Mother, and I have talked about this!"

We came to the same conclusion, so I have drawn up papers, that I intend sending to my lawyer in the near future, to set up trust funds for all you girls to receive at different times to be set out. The other girls will receive larger funds than you Jackie, because I have another option for you, I hope it is what you want.

Your funds will also be a half share in The Property, Homestead, all of it, when you turn eighteen. It will be effective from then!" Father said. If I hadn't been sitting, I think I would have fallen down. "You can't be serious Father!" I said, as the tears welled up in my eyes.

"This is yours, and Mothers Property, you've worked hard for it. Why would you want to give me half, why are you doing this Father?" I asked. "I thought you would be pleased!" he said. "I am pleased Father, I'm overcome with the unreality of it! I love this property, it is our home, only I don't understand why the need now? Why are you doing this now Father?" I asked.

"I've made up my mind Jackie! I have thought long about the future, and what it will hold. I want the Coby name to carry on at Shallow Downs always. So keep in mind Jackie for in your future. If, and when you marry. I would like your name to be a hyphenated name. Coby-someone? That is my only request to you!" he said. "Is that too much to ask from you, Jackie?" he asked, as he looked deeply into my eyes. "I will be proud to continue the Coby name Father! I am so pleased you thought of that. It is my best name after all. You have my word that I will always be a Coby!" I replied.

"Your word is good enough for me Jackie, thank you! Of all my girls, you are the only one who loves this place like I do, and let's face it now, I won't be around forever, and neither will your Mother. We want a direction so I am mapping out our own future. So dry those tears, this is a happy time, let us laugh!" he said, as he threw his head back into a bout of infectious laughter.

I climbed into his safe, loving arms, and we hugged, and we laughed. "Thank you Father! I will not let you down!" I said, and kissed his happy face. "I know you won't Jackie, and that's the reason I have to do this!" he said. "Ok, let's go now! We have a couple of jobs to do, so we will head back to the cattle, you have had a long enough day, and it's going to be slow going home!"

We walked down the slope to the Jeep, climbed in, and then set off. Chip was crouched, guarding the cattle, when we got back. Father got some water, and took out to him, then we herded up the cattle, and brought them through the opening in the fence.

In no time we had the fence mended, and I helped Father to secure the new netting, and then we strained the wires through the post holes.

As we were having our last cup of tea, and some food,

# JENNY MAC

Father made his decision, and spoke up. "You ride home in the Jeep too Jackie! Tie Sailor's rope to the back of the Jeep, and he will be able to follow us on a lead. I will only be driving slowly, so it will take us longer to get home, but much better for you in the long run! Also, when we reach the place at the creek where you had trouble this morning, let me know. I want to stop there!" he said.

"Ok Father! That's fine. I don't really think I could ride any more today anyway. I'm feeling a bit sore now! I will let you know when we get close to the place at the creek where I had stopped, but what are you going to do there?" I queried, as I looked up at him. "I just want to tidy up a few things there Jackie. You said the first dog fell onto you, and into the water. I want to get him out of there! Are you ready to go now?" he asked.

"I'll just give the animals a drink, then we can go!" I said, as I got up, and grabbed the water bucket to pour water for Sailor, and Chip. Untying the rope, I led Sailor to the bars welded on the back of the Jeep, and tied it tight. "Sorry Sailor!" I said, as I stroked his face. "I can't ride you home now, maybe some another time."

"Up boy!" Father called out to Chip, and the kelpie jumped over the tail-gate of the vehicle, and proceeded to go to his place on a ledge behind Father's seat, where he could lean out over the side. He was excited, he just reveled in going in the vehicle with Father, and he wouldn't move from there until he was told to get down.

My Father had trained him from a puppy, and the love between the Master, and his dog, had to be seen to be believed. They were best mates. We had other work dogs, but Chip was Father's favourite.

Then we packed our belongings into the Jeep, and climbed in. "It looks like we have everything Jackie!" Father said, as he scrutinized our surroundings before starting the engine, then engaging the gears, he started the Jeep off slowly, making his way among the boulders, towards the path along the fence line.

We would be going the long way home now. I looked back, and Sailor was moving along at a walk. 'It will be better when we make the path.' I thought. The sun was still trying to come out but the air was very cold, so I reached for my blanket, and cuddled it close to me.

By the time we had reached the creek at the second paddock, Father, and I, had covered all, but the final details for our future Cutting of the Wattle Party. It was up to me to do all the research on bookings needed, and to write up temporary invitations.

I was elated with importance, it was very exciting, and it was going to be a grand party, and celebration. I couldn't wait to get started on it.

Clayton had seen the crows settling from the last rise, but he waited till they drove closer, before saying anything. "We must be almost there by now Jackie! We have been driving along the creek for a while?" he said, as he looked at me. "Just up ahead there is a track going down to the creek Father! There!" I said, pointing to the long grasses by the road. "That's it!"

Clayton pulled the Jeep to a sudden halt, turned off the ignition, and engaged the handbrake. He grabbed a pair of gloves from under the dashboard, and climbed out. "Stay, Chip!" he said, and turned to Jackie, saying.

"Best if you stay here Jackie, I won't be long, maybe you could have a drink, and water the animals too!" He started to walk away through the long grasses, onto the rough track, then disappeared. "Ok Father!" I said, as I watched him go, and couldn't help but notice that his huge frame had to bend, and twist sideways to get down the narrow track, then he was out of sight.

Clayton found the first dead dog in the long grass. He toed the animal, taking note of the small bullet hole behind its shoulder.

'Good shooting.' he thought, as he put on his gloves, and dragged the dog to a clearing on the sand. There, he scooped out the sand to make a shallow hole, and rolled the dog in. Looking up, he at once noticed the mashed up frame of a dog on the sand, and the other in the edge of the water. He proceeded to drag them both across to the hole then went to pull out some long, leafy, branches from under the trees to completely cover them. Satisfied about his make shift work, he stood up. 'That should hold them for a while.' he thought, and he headed back to the Jeep.

At the top of the track, he picked up a stick, and at the edge of the long grass, he pushed it into the ground, and put his gloves over it, marking the spot.

Jacqueline got out of the Jeep when her Father had left, and while gathering the water tin, and buckets to give Sailor, and Chip a drink, the first stomach cramp hit her like a shockwave, severe enough to double her over.

## APRIL RAIN

She dropped the buckets, and sank to the ground.

'What was that.' she thought, as she sat on the ground in agony. After a short rest she rose again, and tried to ignore the dragging pain, as she continued on to water the animals, and then grabbing her water bottle from her pack, she sat back in the Jeep, pulled her blanket around herself, and had a drink. The pain was still there, it was something she had never experienced before, and now she was starting to think that she must have hurt herself somehow. She knew that she suffered a pretty severe jolt when the dog had hit her, and she had fallen backwards into the water, but when she inspected herself initially, she couldn't see anything, she was only very sore, it was much later the bruising had started to show.

'Oh please god!' she thought. I don't want to be sick, just make it go away. She looked up to see her Father returning so she tried earnestly to gather her composure, she didn't want to make a fuss in front of him.

Clayton climbed into the Jeep. "Ok all done for now Jackie, let's get on home!" he said as he reached over the back seat, grabbed his water bottle, and drank deeply, then he started the engine. "Are you alright Jackie?" he asked. "Just tired Father, I might have a sleep if that is ok?" I said, as I pulled up the blanket around my face and tried to suppress the dragging feeling in my body.

"That's a good idea, you've been through a lot today, here use this other blanket as a pillow." he said, while pulling the blanket from the back, and folded it under my head. "Thank you so much Father, wake me when we get home please!" I said.

## Chapter 10

Deakan Hall had just finished his work in the stables as his Father Axel Hall arrived in the pick-up truck to pick him up, and drive him into school. Deakan was in a very bad mood, he had stewed all morning about not being able to go with Miss Jacqueline, and it was eating away at him. 'I be almost ten years old now.' he thought. 'They all treat me like a baby.'

'Look at tha work I havta do here, it's not the sorta work a baby would do!' Deakan was a big boy for his age, and already muscles pushed at his tight fitting shirt, his threadbare jacket barely met at the front of his chest, and his old canvas pants were too small now for his growing frame. He took after his Mother in build, as she had been a very big woman, and like her, his skin was quite black, and his black hair hung down his back in a tangled mess.

"Are ya finished ya work Deak?" his Father called. "We hav to get goin, or you'll be late for school!"

Deakan pushed through the stable doors, slamming them back with force, and gave them a kick on the way out. "Nah, I not be goin ta school taday!" he informed his Father as he glared up angrily at him with eyes that were dark, and hostile.

"I've done nough work taday, an when am I gunna get ta have som fun hey? Couldn't go ridin with Miss Jacqueline taday either! So what's new? Damn Coby's!" he replied. "Ya will be goin to school taday Deak! If ya want to make anythin of yourself in the world, you'll need an education, an don't show disrespect for tha people who we work for here! What is wrong with ya?"

"Don't you realize that Clayton Coby is our boss, an a damn good one too! We hav a bungalow ta live in here, our food is supplied, an we both earn wages, isn't that nough for ya Deak?" Axel said, irritated with his Son.

"Ya always stick up for the Coby's, neva for me. I'm always in the wrong aren't I Dad! They've got everythin, an we hav nothin, an we neva will!" he said. "They have everythin because they hav worked damn hard ta get it Deak, an over many, many years, even before I arrived here Deak! It doesn't mean ya can share in what they hav, or do, just because ya live here!" replied Axel.

"Nothin here belongs ta ya or me Deak, we only work here, get that into your head, an the sooner ya do, the better, an leave Miss Jacqueline alone, she has her own life to live, and it doesn't include ya Deak! That's nough now! Get in the car!" said Axel.

Deakan kicked the car door, and his face pulled into an ugly grimace, as he spat the words out at his Father.

"No I won't git in tha car!" and he turned on his heels, and raced off down the track.

Axel Hall was not about to let his son get the upper hand. Deakan was getting too rebellious lately. So he decided to approach the problem that he had with Deakan, from a different angle. He turned the pick-up truck around, and drove down the track after him. He caught up with him, just as Deakan was approaching their bungalow, and Axel called out to him.

"Hey Deak, I hav a real great idea! Seein ya hav been

workin hard this mornin, ya deserve a little reward."

"How would ya like ta get a milkshake at tha Milk-bar in town, before ya go to school? There might be some of yor mates there! If we are early nough, you'll hav time ta talk for a while!" said Axel.

Deakan was having trouble controlling his emotions, but he wouldn't cry! He would never do that! Most of all, he would not let his Father see him crying!

He was angry mainly about his life, or the lack of it, and the Coby's. He was jealous of the Coby's, especially because they had so much, and he had so little.

He wanted to join in with what they all done at the property, but his Father keeps saying that he has to learn his place, that they live here only to work, and they were not to mix socially with the Boss, or his Family.

Deakan didn't understand this at all, and he hated it. 'I be born on this property too.' he thought. 'An I should be able ta do what I want ta do. Why can't I go to a party at the big house? An why aren't we ever invited? It's just not fair!' he stressed to himself.

He looked hard at his Dad sitting beside him in the truck, and this sudden new idea of his appealed to him. So he said, just as if nothing had happened. "Yeah Dad! That be good idea, I would like ta do that!"

Axel looked at him with a relieved look upon his face, then replied. "Ok then, ya had better get movin. Ya need ta go an have a wash, an change ya clothes, an I will be waitin for ya!" he said.

Deakan took off. Then in no time at all he was back climbing up onto the front seat beside his Dad. "Ready Dad!" he said. "Ya look good all cleaned up Deak." Axel said, as he put the truck into gear, and they started to move forward. "Ya know Deak, I can drive all ya kids to school, an pick ya up after, an if ya want ta go down an kick a football around after school with ya mates, I will take ya to the oval for a while if ya like!" Axel said.

"Wait up then Dad!" Deakan said. "I havta go an git me footy!"

Axel braked the pick-up truck, and Deakan flung the door back, and jumped out of the truck before it had stopped to land flat footed, and skidding in the dirt.

He raced inside, then in record time he was coming back running with eagerness, and with a football tucked firmly under his arm. He climbed up into the seat, and slammed the truck door.

"Ok I be ready now Dad, let's go!" he said, hiding the victorious smirk on his face.

# JENNY MAC

## Chapter 11

Clayton was all business when they arrived at the gate of the house paddock. He got out, and walked over to the bungalow nearest the creek.

"You there Axel?" he called. Axel Hall appeared at the doorway. "Yes Boss!" he answered.

"Hi Axel, I have a situation here! Do you know where Mick is?" Clayton asked. "I not sure boss, but they was talkin of goin ta the first paddock ta check some fencin this mornin!" he said.

"Get in the pick-up truck, quick as you like, and find him for me. Tell him to come to the Homestead straight away to see me, and bring two of his men with him!" Clayton said, as he started to walk away. "Ok Boss!" said Axel, as he started off towards the pick-up.

Clayton climbed into the Jeep, and drove towards the stables. He noticed that Jackie was still asleep. When he reached the stables, he pulled up, turned the ignition off, and climbed out. He went around the back, and patted Sailor, talking to him softly as he untied the rope, and inspected his legs, then led him off to the stables.

Roy Anson met him at the stable doors. Roy was the head stable hand, he worked at the Homestead stables.

"Morning Boss, what has happened here?" he asked. "Morning Roy, bit of trouble this morning, will tell you about it later, but right now I need you to look at Sailor."

"Wash him down, keep him warm, remove the shoes check his hooves, if ok, re-shoe him. Stable him inside with lots of straw, give him oats, and water." he said.

# JENNY MAC

"Will do Boss!" said Roy as he took Sailors lead, and walked away. "Thanks Roy!" Clayton called back, as he hurried to the Jeep. Jacqueline was awake, and sitting up. "We're home now Jackie!" Clayton muttered, as he looked at her. 'She looks terrible.' he thought. He was getting worried, she had been groaning in her sleep, and he had no idea what was wrong.

"Nearly home Jackie." he said as he drove up to the homestead to brake near the steps at the front verandah.

For a big man he was quite agile, as he jumped out of the Jeep, and hastened to Jackie's side of the Jeep. "I will carry you up Jackie!" he said.

"No Father, I will be ok!" I said, as a cramp hit me.

"Do not argue with me young lady!" he said, as he tenderly bundled me in his arms as if I was light as a feather, and started climbing up the steps. "Mel, are you there Mel? I need some help!" he called to Mother.

Mel watched closely as Clayton drove the Jeep up the driveway. 'He's got that stern faced worried look.' she thought. 'And Jackie is all wrapped up.' She hurried through to the front verandah even before she heard Clayton calling to her. "What is wrong Clayton?" she asked, as she came through the doors. "My goodness what is wrong with Jackie?" "I'm not sure!" he said.

"But I have a long story to tell. First though, we need to get her a bath, a warm bed, and a warm drink. Might have to get the doctor from town out to look at her, she's been groaning in her sleep so somethings up, it's not like Jackie." Immediately, Mother took control.

# APRIL RAIN

"Carry her to her room, I will meet you there when I find Mary." she said. Mel went into the house. "Mary, I need your help please! Mary where are you?" she called, with a hint of urgency in her voice.

"I be in tha laundry Missus, be comin straight away!" said Mary, when she had heard Mel call out. "Come up to Jackie's room, Mary!" Mother called back. Mary went quickly to Jackie's room, and knocked on the door.

"Come in Mary! Would you please run some really warm water for a bath for Jackie?" she asked.

Clayton could see he was in the way, and awkwardly, he retreated. "When you are sorted Mel, come down to the living room, we need to talk urgently!" he said.

"I will come up, and see you later on Jackie!" he said. "Thank you Father." I said. Clayton walked through the doors, and then softly closed them behind him. Jackie was sitting on the settee, and Mel sat down beside her.

"What is it Jackie, do you have pain, have you been hurt?" she asked. "I'm not really sure Mother," I said. "Though I did have a fall this morning."

Mary walked in then. "Hi Miss Jacqueline! What ya bin doin ta yourself?" she queried. "Let's get ya outer them clothes, an into tha warm tub!" and she proceeded to take Jackie's shoes, and socks off. "All is wet Missus, she be hav a chill I bet!" she said to Mel.

"Hi Mary, yes I fell in the water!" I replied. Mary, and Mel got Jacqueline up, and into the bathroom, they both undressed her, and eased her into the tub.

Jacqueline sunk down, and let the hot water envelop her. Mary started to wash her hair. "There be all sand here Missus?" she said, as she looked at Mel in question. "I don't know Mary! I had better go, and talk to Clayton now. Will you be ok now if I go down?" Mel asked.

"Yeah ya go Missus, I be scrub her clean, an dry her hair off, put some warm clothes on, an get her ta bed." said Mary. "Thank you Mary! I will be back in a short while." "Jackie, I am going down to talk with Father, are you ok for a while?" said Mel.

"Yes thank you Mother, the water is so good, I will be fine!" I replied. I could feel the heat easing all my sore spots, and my tummy.

Mel walked into the living room, and Clayton was sitting on the lounge in front of the fireplace. "I'm just going to make us a coffee Clayton, and while I'm doing that, I want to put some soup on to heat up for Jackie, luckily Emily made some yesterday. I won't be long." Mel said, as she walked on through to the kitchen. "Ok then Mel, be as quick as you like though!" Clayton replied.

Mel Coby returned to the living room, and placed their mugs of coffee on the center table. Clayton patted the joining seat beside himself, and she sat down with reservation, she had never seen her husband so concerned about anything before, and it worried her.

"Clayton, what has happened out there this morning? Did Jackie fall off Sailor, is that what this is about?" asked Mel. "No Mel, on the contrary, Sailor helped save her life! I will tell you the full story now." Clayton proceeded to tell Mel about Jackie, and the events that had taken place.

# APRIL RAIN

Mel was crying when he finished. "Oh my poor baby, thank god she is safe now, what an awful ordeal for her to go through. But I can't stop thinking how brave she was Clayton." Mel said. "She's got some steel in her that girl that's for sure!" said Clayton.

"I still don't understand though! Didn't you say that she rode to meet you, and that you still took her to the hilltop to show her the wattle, and even got the cattle in then fixed the fence? So didn't she have all her injuries then?" Mel queried. "That is the strange part Mel."

"She was in shock at first, and cold of course, but she was only sore, and then bruises came out, but she was ok until we stopped at the creek on the way back I think, because it was after that when she went to sleep that she was groaning in her sleep Mel. Now I feel responsible for this, I shouldn't let her do these things!" he said.

"What rubbish, Clayton Coby! Don't you dare stop Jackie from living her life how she wants to, she'd be like a duck out of water, and it is not your fault at all! I will hear no more of that talk!" "Things happen! We live in the bush here! I quote you!" she said. Clayton laughed.

"Looks like you both are ganging up on me!" he said, as Jackie's voice rang out. "Mother come quickly!"

Mel leapt off the chair, and hurried across the room. Then she raced up three steps to the bedrooms, and headed towards Jackie's room. As she opened the doors, and rushed in, she pulled up short, as Jackie was standing upon the mat in the middle of the room.

Tears were sliding down her beautiful face, and a look

of bewilderment in her lovely dark green eyes. Her hair was dried, and she was partly clothed, with socks, and slippers on her feet, a warm vest, and pajama coat.

But her underwear Mel noticed, was red with blood, running down her legs. "What is it Mother, what have I done to myself, what is wrong with me?" I pleaded.

Mel Coby had reared four daughters, and she felt confident that she knew what was wrong, but she wanted to make sure. "Mary get me a clean wet washer, and a dry one please, and another pair of undies." she said. "Ok Missus" said Mary. "It's alright Jackie, calm down, and I will check you out, but first let's get these undies off. She took the wet washer from Mary to clean Jackie down, and then she folded the dry one into a long pad, and put between her legs, and then put on her clean underwear. "Now Jackie I would like to check out your injuries, can you lie face down on the bed?" she asked.

"Yes Mother!" I said, and Mel took note of all the scratches up her legs as she got onto the bed. She noticed the huge purple bruising down her low back, and gently pressed it. Tell me now where the pain is coming from Jackie?" she asked. "There is no real pain in my back Mother, it's only really sore to touch, and stiff, and when I turn it is sore, and my shoulder hurts as well. "When I press here does it hurt your stomach?" "No Mother, my stomach is just sort of aching on its own." I replied. "Ok Jackie, turn over now." Mel said, and pressed Jackie's stomach about the same height as her low back bruise.

"Does that hurt Jackie?" Mel asked. "No Mother." I

replied. "What about here?" Mel pressed in the low abdomen where her uterus would be, as Jackie jumped.

"Yes Mother, that's it!" I said. "Ok, rest now, I want to have a word with Mary." Mel said, and she beckoned Mary to go with her to the bathroom. "Mary what are your thoughts?" Mel asked her.

"Me thinks it be moon blood Missus!" Mary said. "I thought you might say that Mary, because that is what I think too, but just to be sure, I am going to get the doctor out to check her! Can you stay in here tonight, I'll get a bed in for you?" Mel asked. "Yes Missus, but me sleep tha couch is ok. Me be here for Miss Jacqueline!" "Thank you Mary!" Mel said. "We will go back in now."

Mel walked into Jackie's bedroom. "Jackie, I feel almost positive that you haven't got any internal injury from your fall, but to be sure I will get the doctor out to check you. Mary, and I have discussed it, and we feel certain that the bleeding is your first menstruation, or your moon blood, as Mary calls it. Your sisters would have no doubt discussed that with you when they lived here, did they?" Mel asked.

"Yes Mother, I talked to Lainey about it long ago, but why does it have to be now?" I asked.

"Maybe it was brought on by the trauma that you had today, and your fall even, or maybe it's just coincidence. It was bound to happen at some time, you are a woman now Jackie, so I am going to treat you for that. I will get you something for pain, and give you some proper pads to wear, and show you how to wear them. Finish getting dressed now! I will be back, keep warm Jackie!" "Mary I have some soup heating in the kitchen, would you serve a bowl, and toast for Jackie? Bring that up please, and maybe a hot milo!" Mel asked. "Yes Missus!" said Mary.

Mary went out to the hallway, and down the steps to the living room. Clayton Coby stood up. "How is Jackie now Mary?" he asked, with concern in his deep voice. "Mornin Boss! Miss Jacqueline be ok, me thinks. Missus com ta talk ta ya soon! Me be gettin her soup an a warm drink!" "Thank you Mary, carry on then!" he said, and Mary walked on through to the kitchen.

Clayton watched her slim figure as she left him. 'Mary Higgs had been with them a long time.' he thought.

Orphaned at the age of seven, due to a car crash that claimed her parents, and she had been the only survivor. She was left alone, and homeless when Mel had found her. Mel had given her a room in their home at the back of the house, and trained her to be their housemaid.

Mary became very attached to Jacqueline when she was a baby, and as they grew older together, she had taken the responsibility of being her Nanny.

Mary Higgs was a full blood aboriginal girl with deep brown eyes, and dark curly hair. 'She would be about twenty now.' Clayton thought, and she had been a very loyal person to the Coby family. A knock at the front door aroused him, as the voice called out. "You there Boss?" It was Mick Jones, Clayton's overseer. Clayton rose from his seat, and walked to the front verandah.

"What's up Boss?" Mick asked. "Hi Mick, need you to

get two of your men to do a job for me."

We had some trouble this morning, now I've got three dead dogs down the creek bed, at the top end of the second paddock. I have marked a spot off the path with my gloves on a stick. What I want them to do is burn the carcasses where I dug a shallow hole to put them in. Tell them to take shovels as I want the hole bigger. I want them burnt in there on the sandy bank, where no trouble will start from the fire!" he said.

"They are just covered with bushes at the moment."

"Tell the boys to stay there until the carcasses are all burnt, and then cover them in with sand. I don't want the boars to come around the creek, and I don't want dead carcasses in the water, or on the bank. Make sure they do a good job, and report back to me when they are done. They can take my Jeep, there is plenty of water on board, might need to fuel up before they go, make sure they take a swag with blankets, in case to keep warm. They can go to the mess, and get some food in a tucker box, they should be back before dark." said Clayton.

"No problems." said Mick, turning to go, and then as afterthought, he asked. "Who killed the dogs Boss?"
"Jackie shot two of them Mick, and Sailor killed one!" Clayton said. Mick whistled through his front teeth.

"Wow that's a big call Boss! Is Jackie ok?" he asked. "I think so, I will hear more when I get back inside. Tell the boys, be as quick as they like. Oh, and by the way Mick, can you call by Jim's place, and tell him that school is cancelled for Jackie for a few days. Also Mick, my two rifles in the front seat of the Jeep, put them up on the verandah will you?" he said. "Leave it all to me Boss. I'll get the boys on their way now!" replied Mick. "Thanks Mick, appreciate it!" said Clayton, and went back inside.

Mel was waiting for him in the living room. "How is Jackie?" he asked, when he walked in, and sat down. "I think Jackie is going to be just fine Clayton, however I have called the doctor out to check her out. I examined her briefly, and have come to the conclusion that Jackie has no major problem occurring from her fall, apart from deep bruises, and scratches. She is very sore from that in her lower back, legs, and shoulder, but on the other hand, what I'm almost sure of is, that she is in the first day of her coming of age!" Clayton gaped.

"Her womanhood Clayton! Which is the cause of her pain, and now the bleeding. So your Daughter is not a child anymore!" she said, as she looked up at his gaping face. "I don't know what to say, or what to do to help Mel, are you sure?" Clayton asked.

This was one particular area that Clayton could not handle. Women's problems were always a mystery to him, and he rather left those things to Mel. "I'm very sure Clayton, but I believe the doctor will confirm it. Try not to treat Jackie any differently though, let her find her own way." Mel said kindly to him.

"Right then Mel, I trust your judgement. I will go up to talk to Jackie after the doctor has been. Oh! And by the way, I had Mick here earlier. I have asked him to send two of his boys out to burn the carcasses, so don't be alarmed if you see the smoke. I've also asked Mick to drop in at Jim's place to tell him Jackie won't be having lessons for a few days. What say we have lunch now? I'm famished!" Clayton said, as he looked at Mel with a relieved look on his face. "Ok Clayton, thanks for letting Jim know! I'll just check on Jackie first, and then we will eat. How about I get Mary to set up our lunch in the sunroom?" she asked. "Yes that would be good Mel!" he replied, as Mel got up, and hurried upstairs to Jackie's room, and went inside. "How is Jackie doing Mary?" she asked, as she went in. "Miss Jacqueline finish soup an drink, but she be shivering, so I put extra blankets on ha, but she still be in some pain there!" said Mary. "Good Mary, thank you, I'll take over now. It looks like it is just Clayton, and I for lunch, so we will eat in the sunroom, could you serve it in there please?" she asked. "Me go do that now Missus!" said Mary, as she picked up the tray. "Be back later Miss Jacqueline!" she said. I looked up to reply. "Fine, thanks for your help Mary." I said.

Mel sat on the bed beside Jackie, and asked. "How are you feeling Jackie, any better?" "I feel terrible Mother! I just can't handle this! Why does this have to happen now? I want to be the same as I've always been.

Now I'm starting to feel my young life disappearing, gone, changed in a heartbeat, and I'm not coping!" and she started to sob, big heartbreaking sobs that tore Mel apart. "Jackie! Jackie! You will still have your young life. That will never change! But life does change us all Jackie, as time goes on, and you will no doubt learn to adapt to those changes." Mel was devastated, her other daughters had never reacted like this, she was walking on eggshells here, not knowing how best to comfort her daughter, so she took her in her arms, and rocked her.

A knock on the door came, and she called out. "Who is it?" "It be me Missus." called Mary. "The doctor, he come!" "Thanks Mary, give us a minute, and then show him up please!" said Mel, as she hurried to the bathroom to get a wet face cloth. When she came back, she said to Jackie. "The doctor is here Jackie! So stop crying now!" she said, as she wiped her face with the wet cloth.

Mary greeted Doctor Jenkins at the entrance doors of the front verandah. "Please be ta com in Doctor Jenkins, folla me!" she said, and proceeded to lead him up to Jacqueline's room, and knocked on the door.

"Come in!" Mel called from inside, and moved to the door to greet the doctor. "Good morning Doctor Jenkins, thank you for coming out. Jackie had an accident this morning, a nasty fall, and also quite a stressful time, and now she has cramps, and bleeding. We want to make sure that she is not hurt seriously. Shall I leave you to talk to her about her symptoms?" asked Mel.

"Good morning Missus Coby! Yes, I would like to speak to Jacqueline initially, then I will do a thorough examination!" the doctor replied. "Thank you doctor! Clayton, and I will be in the sunroom, Mary will show you through when you have finished!" said Mel, as they left the room quietly, and went downstairs. "Just hold lunch for now Mary, the doctor may want to have lunch with us!" Mel said. "Ok I be do that Missus." said Mary.

Mel walked into the warm sunroom, such an excellent place to be during the hotter months with big windows, ceiling fans, and access through the double doors to the verandah, but now in winter with the open fire going, it was a delightful room in the house, with a full view of the landscaped property. Clayton had rekindled the fire, and had a nice blaze glowing in the recess.

"How is Jackie now Mel?" Clayton asked from where he sat in his favourite chair beside the fire. "I wish that I could be more positive Clayton!" Mel said, as she sat in the seat opposite. "But mentally Jackie is shattered, she is not reacting well at all, and not exactly welcoming her womanhood either!" "I'm grabbing at straws, as how to help her. I will need to have a long talk with her, maybe tomorrow, when she has settled down a bit." Mel said.

"This is not like Jackie at all, Mel!" Clayton said. "No, I know it isn't Clayton. I don't think she has got over the shock yet, or it could be that she has had such a rough day, and it is all too much for her." replied Mel.

Mary ushered the doctor towards the sunroom, and then knocked on the door. "Come in Mary!" called Mel. Clayton, and Mel rose to greet the doctor as he walked in, and they shook hands. "Would ya like to sit here doctor?" asked Mary, as she showed him a window seat.

"Thank you Mary, that will be fine." replied Doctor Jenkins. "Would you like to stay with us for lunch doctor?" asked Mel. "No thanks Missus Coby, I can't stay too long, but I won't say no to a cuppa!" he said. "I be make tha tea then Missus, an bring it in." said Mary.

# JENNY MAC

"Thank you Mary!" Mel replied, as she turned to speak to the doctor. "So tell us Doctor Jenkins, how is Jackie now?" she asked.

Doctor Jon Jenkins was a young man of thirty-eight years, his slight build enhanced the cut of his dark grey wool suit which he wore over a light blue shirt. He had sandy colored hair, and his clear brown eyes were encased by the spectacles propped on his nose. He had opened a small medical practice in town when he moved to the Country, and with a new vision for the area, was planning to build a hospital in Shallow Siding. He was waiting for his plans to be approved, and a government grant to come through. He had proved himself to be a caring doctor to the locals, and he liked the town.

A genuine smile escaped his lips as looked into the concerned faces of Clayton, and Mel Coby. "Jacqueline, and I have had a long talk, which was very enlightening, and I feel she is going to be just fine in the near future Mister, and Missus Coby! After my examination, I find that apart from her being under some sort of stress, and suffering a bout of chills, her injuries are superficial, not internal, so in time all the bruising, and soreness will disappear. I have taped up her shoulder, she seems to have given that a fair whack, it's not dislocated, but I felt she would be more comfortable if it was positioned in the correct place for a while. You could leave that tape on for a few days!" he said. "The only other complaint, of which you are obviously aware Missus Coby, is that Jacqueline is menstruating. I'm guessing this is her first time, and I think she is more stressed about that than her injuries, no doubt you can help her there. I have given her a sedative, so she will sleep for quite a while, keep her very warm, and I have left some pain tablets for her beside her bed." he said. "Thank you Doctor!" said Mel.

"Yes thank you Doctor!" said Clayton. "We appreciate you coming out, and all your help!" Just then, Mary knocked on the door. "Come in Mary!" called Mel, and Mary brought in the tray, and set it on the table. "Thank you Mary I will pour," said Mel getting up. They chatted as the tea was served, then the doctor looked at them both, and said. "I would like to say something if I may!"

"Of course doctor." said Mel. "I would like you both to know that Jacqueline is a very brave person, you must be very proud of her! She told me what happened to her today, and quite frankly I don't think I could have done that myself, what a spirit she has! Believe me when I tell you, this new problem she has of becoming a woman, won't last, she is too determined for that to get in her way. She will be a very proud, strong woman!" he said, getting up to shake their hands. "I must get back now, thank you for your hospitality, call me if you need me!"

"Thank you for your advice Doctor." said Mel, and Clayton rose. "Thank you Doctor, I'll walk you out!" he said, and they both left together. "So tell me more about your plans for the hospital Doctor Jenkins. What do you need to get it all organized, maybe I can be of some help!" said Clayton, as they reached the front verandah.

When Mel walked through to the living room, they were still out there talking.

# JENNY MAC

## Chapter 12

Jacqueline Coby sat curled up on the window seat that overlooked their property during the pre-dawn, semi-darkness of her room. A bedspread she had taken off her bed was wrapped around her tightly in an attempt to combat her bouts of shivering, and there was the pain, the continuous pain, no one had warned her of that.

Three days she had spent there since her harrowing ordeal at the creek, shunning the real world that she could not yet face, not wanting to leave the safety, and the seclusion of her room.

She could not believe what was happening to her, or come to terms with it either. Suddenly, for the first time in all her life, she was experiencing the first feelings of doom overcoming her, and she was simply drowning in such unfamiliar territory. 'What was she supposed to do now?' she wondered. Her body had cheated her. 'How was she expected to react now?' She wasn't ready for this change at all. She knew nothing about being a woman, but she also knew that becoming a woman was meant to be a very special thing, her Mother had explained that to her in detail, she recalled.

Jacqueline could still hear her Mother's softly spoken words uttering repeatedly in her head when she had whispered to her in the darkness one night. "Jackie!" My Mother said. "Life is just not all about being a young person, no one stays young forever. It is about growing up, learning, coming to terms with all the changes, and adapting to them, and by doing that, you will experience a change like no other, by finally becoming the complete person, and adult, that you will be, and only you Jackie can dictate who that person is going to be, from now on into your future!"

"You have to be your own person Jackie! Find your own way, and you don't have to cease doing all those things you love to do Jackie, because that is you Jackie, all a big part of you that we all love so dearly. Your life is not ending, it is just beginning! Just go about things in a more mature way, accept what life offers you!"

"You don't realize now, but you will as time goes on, that you have been given a gift by being a woman, you have to work your way through it until you find that woman who you want to be. However, you do need to build confidence in yourself Jackie, but let me tell you a secret young lady."

"You are going to be the most beautiful, and desirable woman this town, or country has ever seen!"

"You know you can produce life now Jackie, and that is not to be taken lightly. It is a very delicate situation, so you have to look ahead in your mind, and realize that if, and when you want to marry one day that you will have the most precious gift to give your husband, and that is your virginity.

I have been strict with all the girls in that respect Jackie, and I aim to be the same with you! I think you know Jackie that pride, is a huge factor with your Father, and he would frown on any discredit to his name, or your name, for that matter so as a Coby you're expected to do things the right way. I hope you will understand, and respect that! Be assured though, if at any time you are in a situation that you can't handle, then come to me Jackie, and we will talk. I have a lot of knowledge to share, and please believe me! 'There is always a way!' Doesn't Father always say that?" she said, as she laughed, and for the first time in days, I laughed with her, or I would have cried.

So I sat huddled in my room, my mind in a turmoil, thinking of a million things, and my body in a no better state, but my Mother's words calming, and reassuring were bringing some light to my problem, and slowly but surely my determination was starting to reappear.

Mother was right, she usually was. I can beat this. I had just experienced the worst day of my life, one I would never forget, but now it was time to face reality.

I just have to get used to this new person who has taken over my life, and body. But she had better like riding, shooting, and hunting, besides I have to learn how to run this Property, and I also have organizing to do! 'What am I doing wasting time here?' I thought.

I threw the coverlet off me to the floor, and jumped up. Racing to my door, I opened it, then called out into the hallway. "Mary are you up? Can you come up here please?" "I want to go down for breakfast this morning!"

"Yes Miss Jacqueline, I be down the hall at tha linen press, I be comin up now!" I heard her call. "Come in Mary!" I called, when I heard her knocking on the door, and Mary walked into the room amongst the flurry of bedclothes, linen, and clothes strewn all around. "What be happenin Miss Jacqueline?" Mary asked me, as she started picking up my things off the floor. Jacqueline looked at her with her best smile on her face, saying.

"This morning is a special day Mary! I am going to bathe, then I will need my riding clothes, and my green jacket. I am going to have breakfast with Mother, and Father, and then I am going riding!"

"That be fine news Miss Jacqueline, I be run ya bath for ya, and while ya do that, I be make ya bed, an find ya clothes." Mary said as a big smile spread across her face, relieved that the crisis was over. "Thank you Mary!" I said, as I rushed to the bathroom.

Jacqueline walked lightly down the steps, and out into the kitchen. She wore her favourite green duffle jacket over a camel coloured vest, with a white long sleeved shirt underneath. Her camel coloured jodhpurs hugged her figure, and her green eyes sparkled.

"Good morning Missus Banks!" I said, as I walked inside. "Oh! Good morning Jackie! You look so beautiful this morning, are you going out riding?" asked Emily. "Thank you for the compliment Missus Banks, and yes I am going riding after breakfast! Is Mother, and Father down yet?" I asked. "They are in the sunroom Jackie."

"They are having bacon, eggs, and pancakes. Would you like the same?" she asked. "Yes thank you, Missus Banks, that sounds good, I am hungry this morning!" I said, as I walked out. Emily watched her go. 'Wow! She is going to be a beautiful woman that girl.' she thought. She knew about Jackie's problems, as Mel had confided with her. 'Looks like the problem is solved.' she thought.

Mel, and Clayton Coby were both sitting in their favourite chairs, and looked up when Jacqueline walked in. "Oh good morning Jackie! So good to see you up, are you joining us for breakfast?" asked Mel, with a twinkle in her eye. "Yes Mother, I am! Good morning! Good morning Father!" I said, then I kissed them both on their cheeks. "Good morning Jackie!" said Clayton. "Are you going riding after breakfast?" he asked.

"Yes Father." I replied. "Good, then I will come with you!" Clayton replied. "I want to talk to you about some organizing!" "What organizing Father? Do you mean the Cutting of The Wattle Party?" I asked.

"No Jackie!" he said. "I have had a new brainstorm. It came to me when the young Doctor was here the other day. We spoke about it!" 'Not another brainstorm' I thought. 'Does this Father of mine ever sit still?' "What is it Father?" I asked. "I am running a fund raiser, to get funds, and equipment for the new hospital. A shooting expo, held two weeks from Sunday, a competition, but an exhibition as well, and fun for all the families. I have organized teams. Five Outback Property Owners have confirmed each with one team member who will join our team. So twelve shooters from the Outback Properties, verses The Town, and Country of twelve shooters. The venue is the rifle range, over the river, the other side of Shallow Siding. I will need you to organize some events for the children. Maybe some horse rides? I know the Bells have Shetland ponies out at their place, so maybe we can get someone from over there to organize that! Also, maybe some games, or something? I will leave that up to you!" he said, then added.

"I have spoken to members of the Town Committee, they will be arranging donated food, to be sold at the stalls. I want lots of stalls! I have sent word by the mail driver to other properties, so we could expect a lot of people to come in. I also have a big barbeque lunch in mind, so will need people to cook. All proceeds for the day will go as a donation to the new hospital fund. What do you think of that? Are you going to be on my team Jackie?" he asked. "You can bet I am Father! It is the most super idea! Wherever do these ideas come from?" I asked, looking up at him with pride. "If there is a will, my Daughter!" 'There is always a way!' said Father, and he laughed, then Mother, and I laughed with him.

So the magic of Clayton Coby unfolded, and when the big day arrived for the Hospital Fund Raiser all was in place, and arranged in Father's usual style. 'More is always better then less!' he says. Father had set up his tents, and marquee, and he also donated the meat for the bar-be-que. Henry Ball from the rifle club had arranged seating, supplied the set ups for shooting, and was also providing ice, access to fridges, and power. The town committee were bringing salads, and all the town ladies were baking. Breads were donated from the bakery and my arrangements catered for all the children.

## Chapter 13

Sunshine was bursting out amongst the gum trees, trying to materialize in spite of the cold foggy early morning. Fallen frost was melting, and seeped into the lawns, and gardens. There was a crisp chill to the light breeze which blew into our faces, as we walked laden with our goodies, down the steps of the Homestead, and out to Father's Ford Sedan where we loaded everything into the boot. Father carefully laid our rifles, lovingly prepared for the event, and packed in their cases, into the boot beside his ammunition case. Father's Ford was his town car when roads permitted, and he was a man of importance today, a man on a mission.

'How privileged I am to be his Daughter.' I was thinking, as I watched him walk around the car to open the doors, and my heart filled with such pride for this wonderful man who was my Father. He was decked out in his favourite shooting breeches, and black boots. The collar of his black shirt came out over his open padded vest, and he wore a black sports cap. His massive physique was contained exquisitely in the well-made clothes which he wore. "Ok everyone, let's get this show on the road. Climb aboard!" he said, as he sat in behind the wheel. "You look spiffy Father! I think you've got the winning clothes on!" I said, as I climbed in the car.

"Providing spiffy is a good thing Jackie, thank you! You, and Mother look pretty good to me too!" he said, as he laughed. We laughed, and replied our thanks.

I noticed Mother's tailor-made wool slack-suit of blue-grey, brought out the deep colours in her eyes. Teamed with a grey silk blouse, and a long yellow scarf, she looked just amazing. Being meticulous, and daring, earlier with my dress, I wore purple jodhpurs, black boots, black silk shirt, a purple, and black vest, and my hair braided in purple, and green ribbons.

We travelled the seven miles to Shallow River. It was going to be a beautiful day I predicted as I looked out the side window at the countryside flashing past, and witnessed a transformation taking place from the grey sky slowly clearing, and making way for the brightness materializing, as the sun broke through in its brilliance, to now transform the day. 'Excellent shooting weather.' I thought, as we crossed the bridge at Shallow Siding, and travelled to a turn-off about a mile down the dirt road, where the old well-worn sign read. 'Rifle Range.'

Father turned off, and followed the track among the bushes, and gum trees. We had made good time, though it was not long after daybreak when we had left. Father was hoping to be early, as he had a lot of organizing to do. We could hear the music coming from the direction of the rifle range complex as we climbed the last rise, and drove on down the hill, and through the car park.

The Clowns met us at the gate. Father braked, and wound the window down. "Good morning Mister Coby!" said a white faced Clown, with green hair, and a bright red nose. "Lovely day! We are taking any gate donations that you might like to give us, and all for the Hospital!" he said, while displaying an elongated smile.

# APRIL RAIN

Father laughed. "Good to see you doing a good job, keep it up! We want to raise as much as we can today! Then pulling out his wallet, he stuffed a wad of notes in the Clowns fist. I'm just going to unload, I will come back, and park the car!" he said. "Thanks heaps Mister Coby!" the Clown said, gaping at his fist, as Father drove on in.

"Your idea Jackie?" Father asked as he drove on. "Yes Father!" I replied. "A good one too, well done!" he said.

"That was very clever Jackie!" said Mother. "Thank you Mother, and Father!" I said. "Ok ladies! Plan A. First things first, I need to check the spits, and make sure that the meat is on, and cooking. I brought in several large sides of beef, and they will take a while to cook. I've asked Henry to light the fire in the pit early so it will burn down to coals, and then load all the spits, so I'll just swing by there first, and then we can unload our gear!" As we drove through I could see all the tents Father had set up. The big Marquee in the center, would be used for a food court, and there were already chairs, benches, and tables scattered around, even under the gum trees.

Several other tents that were used as stalls each had balloons tied to posts with colourful banners displaying their wares for sale. Music played amidst all the stalls of home bakery, food produce, second hand stalls, books, homewares, pottery, and paintings. A huge drinks tent, and two stalls that I had provided for the children. One, a knock-um-down stall, the other a pin-the- tail-on the-donkey. Someone had set up swings, and slides as well, and four Shetland ponies already stood saddled out in a separate paddock. An open booth that stood out alone, had a big banner which read.

*... WELCOME...Shallow Siding Hospital Fund Raiser.*
*PLEASE DONATE HERE.*

People were everywhere busying themselves with the unloading, and setting up. It was going to be a Gala Event, I was so excited. "Look Father!" I said. "They've set up the shooting range!" There was two big banners in bold red letters set apart from each other.

On one side reading *THE TOWN AND COUNTRY TEAM*
On the other side *THE OUTBACK PROPERTIES TEAM*

Three targets were set up on each side out on the range.

"Sure looks good, it's going to be a great day!" said Father, as he stopped at the rifle club. "Won't be long." he said, and got out, and went inside.

My Fathers face told the tale, as he walked back to the car grinning from ear to ear. "Everything is working like clockwork there!" he said, as he opened the door, and got in the car. "Emily, and Ashton came out here early this morning, and they have taken over. They will be doing all the cooking, and running the Marquee all day. Thanks for organizing that Mel!" Clayton said.

"Well I aim to please, and besides Emily, and Ashton were over the moon about the idea, and were only too pleased to help out, and to be a part of it all." Mother replied. "That is good, now one more important thing first!" Father muttered to us as he drove off.

"We braked opposite the open Donation Booth, and Father got out with cheque-book in hand, and walked over. He proceeded to write a cheque, and then gave it to the person there. We could hear them thanking him from where we were sitting. Father came back towards the car looking very pleased with himself, as he put the receipt in his wallet, and got in. "Ok, Jackie. I'll drop you off so you can check on the people that you have arranging the stalls, and over at the horse rides. I will help Mother unload all her things, and unload our shooting gear, so I can go to park the car! Then we will be at the rifle range, so meet us back there in about an hour."

"I have arranged for Henry to meet us back there to give us a rundown on everything!" said Father. "I prefer to go over to the horses first then Father, just to make sure they have everything they need, I will walk back. I have two boxes in the boot for my stalls, would you drop them off for me please?" I asked. "Right then!" said Father, and he drove to the far paddock, and I got out.

"See you both soon." I said. "Jackie, I put some hay in the shed let them know that it is there." he said. "I will Father." I said.

They were all organized in the horse paddock, the younger Bell boys were organizing the rides, and had replacement people to be on stand by for the afternoon. Banners flapped in the breeze, and a shade tent had been set up for the parents to sit. I checked on the horses, and told them that there was hay in the shed. "If you need anything, I will be at the rifle range!" I said to the eldest boy. "Thanks Jackie!" he said. "Hope you shoot well." "I will be trying Frankie, I have to get over there now, have a good day!" I said, as I walked out through the gate.

Music was belting out a tune as I walked towards the tented areas. I looked across, and noticed droves of people, all loaded up with chairs, blankets, and boxes, were now congested at the main entrance gate, and were chatting, and laughing with the Clowns. 'Father has left no stone unturned, he's asked everyone' I thought to myself, as I reached the tents. 'What a day it will be.' As I walked into the tents, the girls all fussed, anxious to show me what they had done with the equipment that I got Father to drop off for me. They had done a really good job, and I said so. They both were thankful for the compliment I paid them. "Thank you so much Jackie!" said Del Jones, and her Sister Joy chimed in. "I can't wait to start Jackie!" she said all excited. "I hope you have someone lined up to help after lunch?" I asked. "Yes!" They both replied. "Mother has arranged that." said Del.

"Alright I will have to get to the range now, good luck today girls!" I said. "Good luck for you today Jackie!" said Del. "Hope you shoot well." Joy said. "Thank you girls, enjoy your day." I said, then I walked outside. I weaved my way through the multitude, speaking as I went to different people, and as I got closer to the rifle range, I looked for Father. It wasn't hard to find him, as he stood towering above the rest, so I moved on through the crowd towards him. He waved to me pressing his finger to his lips, and I realized what was happening as I noticed Henry Ball standing on the small dais with a microphone in his hand, ready to speak. One, two, three testing, he said. "Good Morning all, and welcome to the Rifle Club, and to Shallow Siding Hospital Fund Raiser. Attention please: This is the very first call for ALL COMPETITORS, ALL COMPETITORS! Please be at the dais for your shooting order, and your briefing in half an hour. Thank you!" he said, and he climbed down, and come over to where we were standing.

"Good morning Mel, Jackie." he said, extending his hand to both of us. We all shook hands, and I spoke up first. "Good morning to you Mister Ball." I said. "Good morning Henry, everything is looking so grand I can't believe it has happened in such a short time!" said Mother. "Well Mel you can thank your husband for that.

He has had his nose down to the grindstone for weeks now. It's all on his shoulders, and if I may say so, that's pretty big!" he said laughing. We all laughed as he took father's hand in a handshake. "Morning Clayton, don't mind the jest! Business now, what I'd like you to do if that is ok, before I give the briefing, is say a few words if you would? It's your baby you know!" he asked, looking up at Father. "I will be honoured Henry, and good luck today!" Father said. Mister Ball laughed. "I might need that Clayton. Helena, and I are teamed up against you, and Jackie today. I will give you your cards now for your shooting order. You, and Jackie are on target two, shooting order seven, and eight, so your team members five and six are in front of you. I will explain more in the brief." he said. Amidst our conversation, the loud music, and the general chatter all around us, I heard my named being called. I turned towards the loud voices which rang out. Jackie! Jackie! Jackie! My very dearest friends were heading towards me through the great wall of people, waving as they come. The first to burst through, and reach me was Anne Giles. "Oh, Hi Jackie, isn't it all quite marvelous, you look positively chic today. I can't wait to shoot today! Isn't it so exciting?" she said quite breathless. "Hi Anne, you'd better slow down, or you won't be able to shoot, but you are right it is a magic day, and it is exciting, thank you for the compliment, but you look really smart yourself today Anne, and I just love your outfit!" "Thank you Jackie!" Anne replied, as her big brown eyes lit up. She was dressed in green breeches, a two tone green shirt, white boots, and green, and white vest. "The spectators will hardly miss the lady shooters today adorned in all the bright colours we are wearing. Look at Rebecca, and Helena!" I added. We looked up as the other two girls joined us in a fit of giggles, they had heard what I just said, and so we all laughed together.

"Hi Jackie, good to see you, it's been a while, it will be good to catch up, and you are right, they won't miss me today!" said Helena, who was dressed in red breeches, black, and red shirt, black boots, and black duffle. "Hi Jackie!" said Rebecca she wore orange pants, a cream, and orange shirt, cream boots, and an orange vest. "Hi Helena, Hi Rebecca. You both look marvelous, it is so good to see you all." I said.

"We will have a great... My words trailed off as I was interrupted by the voice on the microphone, and we moved closer to my Father, so that we could see what was happening. Henry Ball was on the dais, he was a thin man of medium build with black hair, and his blue eyes twinkled as he began to speak. "Good Morning everyone, a very big welcome to you all, and to Shallow Siding's Hospital Fund Raising Day!" Everyone clapped.

## APRIL RAIN

"*ATTENTION TO ALL COMPETITORS*. Please make your way towards the dais now, I will be giving you a brief shortly, then I will be handing out your shooting orders.

In the meantime it gives me great pleasure in handing over the microphone to a well-known identity to you all here. Someone who has had the foresight for the great necessity in holding a Hospital Fund Raiser for Shallow Siding, and has done something about it. His tenacity is the result of bringing all this about, and he is the sole instigator of making this great event happen today.

I give you Clayton Coby!" said Henry, and the crowd erupted with applause.

Father climbed the dais, then stood proudly as he reached out to the crowd, and spoke. "Greetings everyone! Thank you so much for making this event possible, without your support it would be impossible.

All of you here should be commended for its success, and I thank you all for coming out in force today. Let us make this a memorable day, and one that will go down in history! Enjoy your day, but remember our purpose. We are here for a cause that will benefit Shallow Siding, on into the future so give generously today, and visit the Donation Booth, as quick as you like! Thank you!" said Father, and he stepped down off the dais to thunderous applause from the crowd. "Well-spoken Clayton!" said Henry Ball, clapping as he stepped up onto the dais to speak into the microphone. "Thank you Clayton! A big hand for Clayton Coby everyone please!" he said. They all clapped, and cheered to show their appreciation.

# JENNY MAC

## Chapter 14

Reagan Chase was trying to make a way through the crowd as he headed towards the front of the dais. When he looked up to see ahead, and maneuver a path towards it, he abruptly stopped short, and his feet were just glued to the spot as his eyes, unable to be torn away, rested on the girl beside Clayton Coby.

'My goodness, but she is just so beautiful.' he thought. Immediately though, he was cheated of the vision, as the big man moved in front of her, and blocked his sight. 'Almost like a cloud blotting out the sun.' were Reagan's thoughts, as he watched Clayton Coby step up onto the dais, then commenced speaking into the microphone.

'My goodness but he is huge.' he thought, for the few seconds it took Clayton to move clear, until then again Reagan's eyes fixed upon the girl. 'So elegant, so proud.' Were his immediate thoughts about her, but his feelings were enhanced entirely by the look on her beautiful face, as he watched her standing poised by the dais, the sun shining through the golden tresses of her long braids, her outfit hugging her slim young body of perfection.

A transformation was taking place in her deep green eyes that he could see quite clearly shadowed by thick eyelashes. They were misting over now, as he witnessed a reverence in her face like no other he had seen before, as she looked up to the man now speaking.

His heart skipped a beat. His guilt seemed to shame him for intruding on this special moment of hers, but he could not tear his eyes away, he was mesmerized. He just had to meet her today. 'I wonder what her name is?' he thought. 'Maybe she is Clayton Coby's Daughter, for she seems to be so moved by his speech.'

Reagan was jolted back into reality once again when Clayton Coby resumed his former place beside the girl, and the other man spoke out. "No doubt Clayton was very quick to the point, as I am going to be also! Attention!" Henry Ball called to the crowd to continue.

"As you will see on the range, there are three targets on each side separating The Town and Country Team, from the opposing team The Outback Properties Team. For those who miss my brief I have shooting orders, and target areas printed on a sheet, for each side.

There will be three shooting distances today. The first being 150 yards 200 yards and after lunch 250 yards and an exhibition shoot. The targets are circular with five rings, the inner bull 10 points, the outer bull 5 points, the third ring 4 points, the fourth ring 3 points, and the fifth ring 2 points, the outer is white, and will only score one point. So a possible score of 50 points each competitor.

Five shots each competitor, targets will be changed, and scored after ten shots, or after the second person. An example for order is Target 1: order 1 + 2 and 3 + 4***
Target 2: order 5 + 6 and 7 + 8***
Target 3: order 9 + 10 and 11 + 12*** Please keep the same shooting order throughout the day.

I have scorers allocated for each team, and I will

endeavour to keep you all informed during the day on an update of the scores. There you go, as clear as mud! I declare this contest open. Enjoy the competition today, and give generously to our cause. Lunch today will be provided in the large marque after the second round of the competition, approximately about 1pm. The break will continue till 2.30pm, and then competition resumes.

Would all competitors now go to their target areas? Thank you!" said Henry, and he proceeded to call names for shooting orders.

Everyone was dispersing in all directions, the rush was on to try, and obtain the best possible vantage position they could get for viewing the competition, and as Reagan lined up amongst the shooters, he searched for the girl, but she had vanished in the crowd.

"Reagan Chase?" someone called out. "Yeah that's me!" he said, and moved forward to collect his card.

"Target one, shooting order number two!" the voice said. "Thank you!" he said, and moved away. 'I'll just go to find her and introduce myself.' he was thinking, when he was tapped on the shoulder. "All set Reagan?" asked Richard Chase. "We have to move, we are first off!"

Richard Chase was a solid built man though he was above average height, and his muscular body was well toned. He was a man of forty-two years, and his auburn coloured hair fell all about his face as he looked at his Nephew with his deep green eyes. Reagan Chase looked absently at his shooting card. 'Damn it!' he thought. 'We would have to be first off!' but to his Uncle, he said.

"Let's do it Uncle Richard. I am all set! I think this is going to be a memorable day, in more ways than one. I can just feel it!" Reagan replied.

"Don't get over confident Reagan or you will miss the first target. We are on The Outback Properties Team you know! We have got many talented shooters on our side, best we work as a team. Let's just concentrate first, and ease ourselves into it!" said Richard. "Yes that seems a good plan!" said Reagan, but not exactly talking about the shooting, he had other things on his mind now. "If you want to look at all the team's targets, and shooting orders, I have a sheet here!" Richard said, handing it over. Just the one name, 'Coby.' Stood out, and grabbed Reagan's attention. 'Jacqueline, nice name. Looks like I'll have to wait till after she shoots.' he thought.

Jacqueline, and Clayton Coby arrived at target two, and set up an area close by under the gums for their rifles and equipment. Clayton placed some chairs down. "Is that where you want to be Mel?" he asked. "That is fine thank you Clayton, I have a view of all the targets from here, good luck to both of you!" said Mel. "Thank you Mother!" I replied. "Yes, thanks Mel! We've got a good team. Here are two of our team mates now!" he said.

Sim, and Arthur Bell piled their things into a heap, and moved forward to shake hands. "Good morning Mel, Jackie! Hi Clayton, how are you all? What a turn out today, you've done a good thing here Clayton!" said Sim Bell. "Morning Mister, and Missus Coby, Hi Jackie, good to see you all again!" said Arthur. Clayton shook their hands in earnest. "It is good to see you Sim, and Arthur. Yes Sim it is going to be a big day I think, I hope, and thank you!" he said. "Good morning Sim, Arthur!" said Mel. "Hello Mister Bell, hello Arthur. Best of luck with your shooting today! Also, thank you Mister Bell for the Shetland ponies. I have been over to check on your sons, and they are doing a great job, they have a lot of interest over there!" I said. "That's really good to hear Jackie! I am only too pleased that I could help you out. Good luck today Jackie!" said Sim. "Thank you Mister Bell, I will be trying my best!" I replied.

"Ok Arthur, let's get our gear sorted, we're first off, we've got to make a start for the team!" said Sim, as he picked up his rifles, and moved on towards the huge mound of the shooting bay. "Ok Dad!" said Arthur, as he picked up their things, and followed.

From the shooting positions, and in line of all targets, mounds of earth raised up, making a statement of the professionalism of the rifle range team with their set up.

Tarpaulins pegged the earth over the mounds adding comfort, and protection for their clothes, rifle brackets sat at hand for those who required them. Complying with the rules, the mandatory position of shooting for everyone in the competition was the prone position.

Father looked at me. "We had better get ready too Jackie, what rifle are you using for the 150 yards?" he asked. "I think I prefer the .22 for the shorter distance, what do you suggest?" I asked. "A good choice I think!

There is a slight breeze this morning, but down-wind at the moment, but keep in mind it will probably change today. Keep an eye on the wind Jackie!" Father advised. "Thank you, I will Father! I'll check the rifle!" I said, as I undone the rifle case.

Reagan took a quick look over to target two, trying to get a fix on the girl's position just before he was to shoot, as he was next in line after his Uncle. Jacqueline sat eloquently on a rug on the ground, her concentration intense, as she polished her .22 rifle, and scope, and then with perfection she proceeded to fill the magazine with bullets, then engaged the safety catch. Bright sunlight streamed through her golden hair. She looked positively alive with happiness, as she looked up, then laughed, showing her pearly white teeth, and her eyes sparkled at the lady sitting in the chair. 'That must be her Mother.' Reagan thought.

Richard interrupted his thoughts. "Your turn Reagan! I scored eighteen points, I hope you can do better!" said Richard. "I will try Uncle." said Reagan, as he picked up his rifle, and walked to the mound. By the time he had returned scoring only thirteen points, he noticed Clayton Coby was ready to shoot. 'Jacqueline will be next.' He realized. "I am just going for a walk Uncle, I will be back soon!" he said.

He stood at the back under the gum trees watching her outstanding performance. Such exuberance that she unintentionally applied to her shooting was just a treat to watch, and Reagan Chase could barely believe the professionalism, and the obvious grace she possessed for one so young. 'She had fired three shots, but already his paltry score was beaten.' he noticed.

'She was not only beautiful, but very talented, and so vibrant, and full of life, a real Country girl.' he thought.

His obsession to meet her was his priority now, and in the forefront of his mind, as he moved slowly down the embankment towards the shooting mound. 'I just hope I don't mess this up.' he thought to himself, as he walked up to her.

Jacqueline lay upon the ground in the prone position propped up on her elbows. Her face was intent, her rifle lay by her side, and the sun gleamed through the golden braids of her hair. She had just fired her last shot, and was waiting for her scores when Reagan Chase squatted down beside her. She started, as she sensed his presence.

"Nice shooting! I am pleased I am on your side! You had better remind me always to do that!" said Reagan, as he laughed. Jacqueline turned her body to front the intrusion from the voice that had startled her, and with a puzzled look on her face she looked upwards. A shiver went down her spine as the intruder looked deeply into her dark green eyes, and smiled.

Jacqueline stared, at a loss for words as she looked at the handsome face confronting her. His searching, deep green eyes, seemed to pierce into her soul, and his voice, so gentle, but yet so tantalizing left her breathless, and her heart missed a beat as the new feelings stirred inside like she had never experienced before, and crept into the pit of her stomach. 'He is just so beautiful.' she thought. His smile now emphasized full lips, a strong pronounced jawline on his tanned face, and the sunlight revealed hints of auburn in his wavy black hair, which fell loosely to his shirt collar.

"Hello there! I just wanted to introduce myself seeing we are on the same shooting team! I am Reagan Chase." he said, as he smiled broadly.

Jacqueline was left speechless, and surprisingly, she felt a little unsteady, and the face seemed to float before her. 'Whatever is wrong with you?' she asked herself determinedly as she tried to compose herself quickly for her reply? "Hello I am Jacqueline Coby! I am pleased to meet you. 'Reagan?' was it, and who might Reagan be?" I asked, as I smiled back at him, and held out my hand.

Reagan took her hand in his, and found that her hand felt like velvet, and he didn't want to give it back, so he continued holding it and the handshake soon came a caress as he stood there smiling. "Well, Reagan Chase is my name Jacqueline. I am competing here also in the shoot today on The Outback Properties Team with my Uncle, Richard Chase. Originally I came out from the city, but moved to the Country a few months back, and now I live out on Ainsley Downs. I am very pleased to meet you too Jacqueline!" he replied.

"I see! I do know your Uncle, Richard Chase, and the property Ainsley Downs!" I said. Then for no reason, I laughed, as I added. "So what is it again that you said I always have to remind you to do Reagan?" I asked him.

"Why! To always be on your side of course!" he said.

We both smiled, and laughed together at the joke.

"I wouldn't like to be on the opposite side! Not ever!" Reagan said seriously.

'He is just so sure of himself.' I thought to myself, as I realized that he was still holding my hand, and at once I became very embarrassed, but I could not suppress the feelings multiplying inside me.

Jacqueline eased her hand from his grip. She could feel her face flushing, not something she was used to, and it unsettled her, so she made to get up, but he put his hand out again to steady her.

Not really knowing what she should do Jacqueline consented to his help as she rose up. For that brief time their bodies touched, sending a shock through her.

She felt the strength in his arms, and his hard young body very so close to hers. They stood together for that moment, lost in each other's eyes, and the air between them was electric.

Jacqueline simply had to turn her head away, and to release his grip again. "Thank you for your help Reagan, but I must go now! Father will be waiting for me!" I said, trying to meet his eyes.

"The pleasure has been all mine Jacqueline Coby! It has been great to meet you, but I had better get back to the team now too, it must be time for the 200 target to go up. Could I ask if you would like to join me for lunch in the break, it would be really good to get to know you some more?" he asked, with a cheeky, irresistible grin.

"I'm not sure if I can Reagan! I should have lunch with

Mother, and Father. We came here together, and I think that it would be expected of me. Besides we are bound to have other people come over to see us in the break!" I replied.

"What if I ask their permission then, and if they agree would you lunch with me then. Please Jacqueline?" he asked, in earnest. My heart was saying yes as it melted when I looked into his eyes, but I was torn between my duty, and these newly felt feelings.

"I guess I could have lunch with you if it is alright with Mother, and Father!" I answered. "Excellent! I will ask your Father now, he seems to be coming our way!" said Reagan in surprise, as he then noticed the big man's fierce scowl, as he came towards them.

Clayton Coby had just completed his first round of shooting, and he walked up to where Mel sat under the gum trees. "Well done Clayton!" she said. "Yes I am happy with that score first up, we will have to get better though." he said. "Would you like some morning tea Clayton?" Mel asked.

"Yes that would be perfect thanks Mel, how about you organize that for when Jackie is finished. I just want to go to talk to a few people first. I haven't had a chance to say hello, and thank all the shooters for coming, so I will do that now while I have a chance. I won't be too long." he replied. "That is a good idea Clayton! You go, and do that then, and I will have everything ready when you come back." said Mel, and Clayton walked off down towards the shooting areas.

Mel had everything ready when Clayton came back, and sunk into the camp chair. She handed him his tea. "Thank you Mel! Everyone is having a great time.

It is the best thing I have done for a long while, a very good day, and they are all geared up with the shooting competition too!" he stated. "Yes Clayton, a magic day, you have done a good thing, I am really enjoying it too." Mel replied.

"Jackie had fired three shots when I past her so she should not be too long now. She is shooting well, and is becoming quite a serious competitor!" Clayton said, as he looked down towards the target area. "Oh see, she has just finished, we should have her score come up in a minute." he said, searching for the scorer. "Yes I have noticed that Clayton, she just loves shooting." said Mel.

Clayton jumped up when her score was put up. "She scored twenty points in her first shoot Mel, a real great effort!" he said, as he looked for Jackie with pride. "Yes that is very good, and you had twenty-five points, so a good start to the day Clayton!" Mel said, as she looked up to his now stern face. "What is it Clayton?" Mel said following the direction of his eyes. "I am not sure Mel, but I aim to find out! Who is that talking to Jackie? Look he is holding her hand now! I am going down there!" he said, his frown becoming quite fierce. "Wait!" said Mel.

However Clayton already was moving away quite quickly, and smoothly, for a big man his size, but he had the protective armor of parenthood weighing heavily on his shoulders, his face set for battle. He was not happy seeing some stranger touching his Daughter.

A new unfamiliar fear seemed to hit him, and nag his stomach. 'Was it purely protection though?' he asked himself. 'Or pure jealousy.' Jackie was his youngest, and he always had her undivided attention, and respect. He wanted to hold on to that for a while.

'I know it will change though, it has to! It is bound to happen sometime in the future, but why so soon?' he argued with himself. But Clayton knew Jackie so well, and he had the answer. 'He had never ever before seen that certain type of look that made her eyes come alive, until just now, when she was looking at this young boy.'

I looked up, and watched Father as he approached us. 'He has that look.' I thought. 'And I know that look.' 'Reagan is going to be in for a little education I think!

This should be very interesting indeed!' I put a hand to my mouth to hide the half smile that crossed my lips, although it didn't go undetected from Reagan. "What is it Jacqueline, what is so funny?" Reagan asked. "I think you are about to find out Reagan! I am so sorry!" I said.

Clayton Coby towered over Reagan with his look of seriousness gracing his face, his scowl was fierce enough to frighten anyone away, but Reagan Chase stood his ground. "My name is Clayton Coby!" said Clayton, as he glared down at Reagan. "This young lady happens to be my youngest Daughter, Jacqueline Coby, and if I recall, I don't believe we have ever met you young fellow. Who are you, and where are you from?" he asked.

## Chapter 15

My name is Reagan Chase Sir. I have only just met Jacqueline, we are on the same shooting team. I was wondering if... Clayton couldn't help but notice his polite manners, and his obvious good looks, but he cut him off anyway. "We are Coby's young man, and we do things a certain way! My way! Respect is a very big issue with me, especially when it comes to my Daughters, and I won't have some stranger walking up to my Daughter, and speaking to her in an underhand, and inappropriate way!" "I wasn't being... "Don't interrupt me when I am speaking, I know exactly what you were doing, and I haven't finished with you yet. If you would like to speak to my Daughter in the future, you may come, and meet with my wife, and myself first! Do you understand me, and do I make myself quite clear?" Clayton stated in a gruff voice. Reagan's jaw dropped. He was not used to this sort of grueling, not even from his own Father. 'Boy, what a hard task master he is.' he thought, as he looked up to Clayton's face, and into his angry eyes.

"I understand perfectly Mister Coby, and it is quite clear Sir! I must apologize. I am so sorry Jacqueline!" he said. "Thank you Reagan!" I said, as my face flushed.

"I don't mean to be rude Sir, but I am first off for the next shoot, can I go now? My Uncle will be looking for me, and once again, I am sorry!" Reagan said.

"Yes that is all Reagan. I will accept your apology for now, and you may leave." said Clayton. "Thank you Sir, goodbye for now." then he faced Jacqueline to say. "It was nice talking to you Jacqueline!" "You too Reagan." I replied, and I watched him walk away. "That was a bit harsh Father!" I muttered, as I looked up into his face.

"Trust me now Jackie! We will soon see what this boy is made of, and also, if he will show true mettle!" replied Clayton confidently.

Reagan walked slowly back to his target area feeling quite dejected. 'I have really made a mess of that meeting then.' he thought. 'Whatever was I thinking? It will be different next time, and there will be a next time! Of that he was certain!' "Why so glum, Reagan?" asked his Uncle Richard, as he walked up to him.

"If you want the honest truth Uncle. Well, I have just met this wonderful girl, someone I would really love to get to know, and I wanted to have lunch with her today in the break. I guess I went about it all wrong because her Father came down on me like a ton of bricks. He said I should have gone over, and introduced myself to him, and his wife, and Daughter initially. He even said I was disrespectful, and more!" said Reagan.

"Who is this dominating Father then?" Richard asked. "Clayton Coby!" replied Reagan. "Then you need say no more Reagan, just trust you to go to the top of the tree. Clayton Coby is big fish in this Outback Country! A very proud man, and he is the straightest man I know, a good honest man, but likes things to be done in the correct manner, and yes, he does deserve the respect he asks, he has earnt that. He is a great business man, and he has set a huge example for property owners in these parts to follow. Did you know also that he is the sole person responsible for this day today?" asked Richard.

"I'm sorry Uncle, but no! I didn't know any of that. I certainly didn't mean any disrespect, I just didn't think. It's just that I had to meet that girl!" he said.

"Then this is what we will do Reagan, we are here to shoot, so let's get stuck into that for the next target, then in the break, we will both go to visit the Coby's together.

What do you think of that idea?" he asked. "Thank you so much Uncle that is a better idea. I would be in deep water on my own." he replied. "Clayton's bark is worse than his bite you'll find!" replied Richard.

They all heard the loud speaker blaring out across the field. "Attention all competitors! Please go to your shooting areas for the second round of the competition. Distance will be 200 yards. Good luck, the competition is very close. Scores for the first round are. The Town and Country Team 171, and everyone clapped. For The Outback Properties Team 180, and a huge roar went up.

"Well we are ahead for now!" said Clayton, as he sat back in the chair under the gum trees. "Which rifle do want this time Jackie?" he asked. "I think I might use the .303/25 Father, the wind is still with us but it is stronger, what do you suggest?" I asked. "Sounds good to me, I am going to do the same. You scored well the first shoot Jackie, well done!" "Thank you Father, yes I will use the .303 rifle I think!" "Are you enjoying yourself Mother?" I asked. "I certainly am Jackie. After all, I am with two of my favourite people, the competition is very exciting, and so entertaining!" said Mel.

"Clayton before you, and Jackie go out to shoot again, would you like me to arrange lunch to be brought down here? It is rather pleasant under the gum trees. I'm sure Ashton would arrange it for us?" Mel asked, looking up at him. "That is a great idea Mel, can I leave you with that then? Better tell Ashton to cater for extra, in case we have guests though, you never know who might turn up!" Clayton replied. "You just leave it all to me, I will go to do that now!" said Mel, as she gave him a special smile, and got up.

"Then I'll be certain to leave it in your capable hands my lady! "As quick as you like though!" said Clayton with a chuckle, as he watched his wife walk away, and disappear through the crowd. As he looked down to the shooting range, he noticed Doctor Jon Jenkins was on his way towards them.

Jon Jenkins was waiting his chance to have a private word with Clayton, so he started walking to where they were sitting. "Good morning Mister Coby, and Jacqueline!" he said, as he got within earshot of them. "Doctor Jenkins good to see you, come on up!' said Clayton rising from his chair to shake the Doctor's hand.

"Please call me Jon, Mister Coby!" he said, as they shook hands. "Only if you insist Jon. You can call me Clayton!" he said. The doctor then spoke to Jacqueline.

"I must say you look marvelous Jacqueline, you have recuperated nicely I see!" he said. "Hello Doctor Jenkins, yes I am much better now thank you!" I replied.

The doctor turned to address Clayton, and said. "I wanted to be one of the first to speak to you, and thank you personally Clayton for the huge effort you have put in towards today. It is a huge success, probably the best fund raiser ever held here, and I really can't find enough words to express my true gratitude. However, I do have some very exciting news to share with you!" said the Doctor.

"Thank you Jon, I am only too pleased to be of help, but what is this exciting news though?" asked Clayton.

"Building plans for the hospital have been approved, and I have just received word that my grant has been accepted. Prematurely I think, as there was an outside influence to help my application. I am only guessing you know about that? So now Shallow Siding will have a Hospital!" Jon, and Clayton laughed. "There is always a way Jon! That is the best news, especially today! Would you make an announcement of that later?" he asked.

"I will do more than that. I would like to name The Hospital after you Clayton!" offered Jon. "Now hold on Jon, not The Hospital. I haven't done this alone, but I will settle for my name on a wing if you agree?" Clayton replied. "Deal!" said Jon, and they shook hands.

Completion, and the finalization of the second round in the Competition finally happened amidst a huge conglomeration of people laughing, and talking, as they headed towards the big marque for their lunch break. Music once again was blaring out, and a sense of gaiety had gripped them all, but the loud speaker overrode the noise by catching everyone's attention with the latest announcement. "Attention all! Enjoy your break. I have the results at hand for the second round 200 yards shoot, and the Competition is full on. The Town and Country Team 214, People cheered. The Outback Properties Team 224. They all clapped loudly. So The Outback Properties Team has crept ahead by 19 points. Competitors please make sure you are at target areas for the final round at 2.30pm. An exhibition shoot will be at 4pm Thank you!"

At Clayton Coby's makeshift camp, everything was happening in the usual Coby style, and Clayton, and Jacqueline arrived to see that Mel Coby already had scattered tables, and chairs around the gum trees, trestle tables also were set up, groaning with the abundant food that she was now fussing over, and preparing for guests.

"Mother, this all looks wonderful!" I said, as I joined her. "Can I help with anything? I asked. "Yes, great job Mel!" said Clayton as he sank into one of the camp chairs. "Hello you two! I have everything under control thank you Jackie, there is only one thing though. Could you please allocate tables for the younger people, and make sure your friends, and any others are catered for!" said Mother. "That is good idea Mother, leave that to me!" I said.

"Clayton, I have eskys with ice and full of all sorts of drinks so if you would like to do the honors we can toast your good scores!" said my Mother, as she looked up to Father's face to smile, but Father was looking elsewhere. I noticed his face become somewhat transformed.

## APRIL RAIN

Firstly with bewilderment, then it became a knowing look, and a personal sense of achievement, I guess, but also a look of respect, and admiration. I just knew him so well. We had sat in the camp chairs to reminisce the shoot, and our scores for the day so far, but the look on his face urged me to follow his eyes to the source of that look, and I knew in an instant, what he had been trying to achieve earlier. 'There were just so many ways to my Father that never ever ceased to amaze me.' I thought.

He immediately started to chuckle. "Well, well, well!" he said, through a bout of his mirth. "The young suitor returns, and look, he has even brought the cavalry with him!" said Father as his huge grin spread across his face.

"Whatever are you babbling on about now Clayton?" asked Mother. "I will have to fill you in later Mel, but right now, it looks like we have guests!" replied Father, as he stood to greet them.

"Richard! It is good to see you! Whatever have you been doing down there, looks like you need to practice up on your shooting!" Father said, as he laughed. "Good morning Clayton, haven't seen you for a while, but yes the shooting is ordinary but we are getting better, saving the best for last!" Richard Chase replied laughing.

"Good morning Mel! Jacqueline! I have someone that I would like to introduce to you all. My nephew Reagan has been staying with me for a few months now, he has come all the way from the city. His Father would like him to learn all the aspects of how to run the property, and introduce Reagan to Country life!" said Richard.

"Reagan, I would very much like you to meet Missus Mel Coby! Her Daughter Jacqueline Coby, and Mister Clayton Coby. Owners of the property Shallow Downs, not far from our property!" he said.

Reagan stepped forward, and politely addressed the ladies first. His heart was pounding, his mouth dry, and he was quite nervous, but he was so determined to make a good impression this time. But he was still not too sure about Mister Clayton Coby.

"I am very pleased to meet you Missus Coby! I hope that you are enjoying the competition so far?" he asked, as they shook hands. "Thank you for asking Reagan. I am enjoying the day immensely, and I am pleased to meet you also. How do you like living in the Country now Reagan?" Mother asked. "Well I haven't seen much yet Missus Coby, only our property, and Uncle Richard always has a lot of work for us to do, so we just keep busy I guess!" he replied. "Well we will have to change that, and invite you over some time soon. It is time you socialized, and made some new friends."

"Shame on you Richard, this young man needs a life you know!" said Mother. "Yes Mel, thank you for your advice, but I do realize that!" We just haven't had the time to socialize yet." replied Richard.

"Reagan I'd like you to meet our youngest Daughter Jacqueline! She has a lot of friends, so I am certain that you will get to meet some people today." Mother said. "Thank you Missus Coby." Reagan said, as he stepped towards Jacqueline, and shook her hand. "Hello again Jacqueline! I want you to know that I am really pleased to meet you, and your parents properly this time. I hope we can start over? I guess your Father was right after all!" he said, as he smiled. My heart melted, and I could hardly get the reply out. "He usually is Reagan, and we will start over, it is good to see you again!" I said. "Very nice shooting today Jacqueline, maybe you could be my coach?" he asked, and then we both laughed as I replied.

"I could certainly try Reagan!" Reagan then turned to address Clayton Coby who stood waiting.

Clayton Coby had heard everything that was said, and he was waiting for his chance to speak to Reagan, when the young man addressed him. Reagan looked up into the big man's eyes, the fear evident on his young handsome face, but with determination he held out his hand to Clayton Coby, and said. "I am very pleased to meet you Mister Coby, and Sir I just wanted…Clayton could not prolong the boy's agony much longer, so he interrupted him once again. "Reagan we all often make mistakes in life, learn from them. It is what we do with the rest of our life, is what counts! It is what makes a man Reagan. I am pleased to meet you Reagan, and shall we start over too?" Clayton asked, as he smiled.

Reagan could not believe what he just heard "Yes Sir, Mister Coby! We certainly can, and thank you Sir."

"Though I must say you were right all along!" replied Reagan, and they both laughed together. "So tell me

Reagan, how is Klim these days? How is the city life treating him?" asked Clayton. Reagan was at once taken aback. "You know my Father Mister Coby?" he asked.

"Yes Reagan I do! Klim, and I go way back. If you become half the man your Father is, you will be doing well. Learn from your peers Reagan!" he said. "I will remember that!" said Reagan. "Father is keeping well, but I secretly think he would prefer to be back in the Country. I think that is why he wanted me to have the experience, and a chance to choose where I would like to be!" Reagan replied.

Clayton knew why Klim Chase left the Country. He met a city girl who wouldn't live out here, but he married her anyway, and they had moved to the city. He eventually owned two companies there, but leaving his own property Ainsley Downs, to be run by his brother Richard. "Then choose wisely Reagan!" Clayton said as Mel stepped forward to join the conversation saying.

"Excuse me Clayton, but we really should be getting lunch now, people are starting to head this way!" she said. "Then we had better move my lady, and take care of our guests!" Clayton replied. "Richard, would you, and Reagan like to join us all for lunch?" he asked.

"Thank you Clayton, we would like that very much!" replied Richard. "In that case Richard, would you help me to get some drinks organized?" Clayton asked. "Sure thing Clayton!" Richard replied, and they both walked off together chatting.

"Jackie, maybe Reagan can help you with your tables

now, and don't forget to introduce him to everyone at lunch!" said Mother. "I will see that he does that Mother, and I will be the perfect hostess, you will see, and thank you Mother!" I replied.

I was so pleased that everything was working out that I almost laughed out loud, as I looked at Reagan, and he looked at me, the relief we seemingly shared was so evident in our eyes, but then was immediately replaced with a sense of freedom that overcome us, the joy of just being young, and alone together at last, was intense.

I had never felt so happy, and so carefree. "Come on Reagan, let's see who can set the best table. Coby style!" I said, as I pulled him along laughing. "I will have you know young lady that I have won prizes for the best table setting!" he said, as he laughed with me.

Almost at once we were inundated with people as they arrived at out site. This is another of Father's little surprises I guessed, as I realized he had invited all the shooters from both teams to join us for lunch, no wonder he wanted Mother to arrange extra food. I was very busy introducing Reagan to all my friends, then he got one of the boys to help him get the drinks for everyone.

We had twelve people at our tables. Reagan Chase, myself, and the others were a special group of people I had grown up with, we were all close in our ages, and they were my very dearest friends.

George Worthington, Anne Giles, Bob Jones, Helena Ball, and Arthur Bell, Mitchell Stringer, Matt Sole, Cliff Gibbons, Sonny Peet, and Rebecca Strickland, were all here, and everyone was in a great jovial mood, and all of us talking a mile a minute. Reagan was really enjoying himself immensely, but when our eyes met from time to time, there was a look in his eyes that I loved so much, and my whole being was in a turmoil, and alive with emotion. I felt like we were alone amongst the crowd as we smiled at each other.

"Where did the dreamboat come from?" asked Anne, when she had pulled me aside to talk to me. "I think he likes you Jackie, he has eyes only for you, and, if I may say so, I think you like him too!" "Do you really think so Anne, is it that obvious?" "From where I'm standing, it sure is Jackie!" she said. "I have only just met him today Anne, but already I feel like I have known him forever, he is really very nice, and I would like to get to know him some more!" I said. "I have a feeling, somehow that will happen Jackie!" said Anne. "Reagan comes from the city, and he is living at Ainsley Downs with his Uncle Richard who is teaching him how to run their property!" I replied. "Well he's not too far away, is he then!" said Anne, with a giggle, and we both laughed together.

Lunch went all too quickly, and came to an abrupt halt when we were alerted by the announcement on the loud speakers. "All competitors to their shooting areas now for the final round 250 yards. Thank you!" Everyone thanked Mother, Father, and myself and they prepared to disperse to their prospective target areas.

"Just a moment all!" called Father. "Make sure you all come back here after the exhibition shoot, as we are going to celebrate then, and the party will continue on into the night. We've got plenty of food, and drink, and we have music here, so let's enjoy this day!" Everyone was in a joyful mood, and they cheered in appreciation. They all left saying. "We will Clayton, and thank you!"

So we all competed in the last shoot, and when the final shot was fired a huge cheer went up from the spectators. Henry Ball took the microphone to make the final announcement.

"Attention all! The scores for the final round are in. Town and Country Team 250 and a final total of 635 points. The Outback Country Team 260 and a final total of 664 ahead by 29 points, and they are the winners of the Competition!" "The best score of the day, and a worthy winner, is Clayton Coby 82 points. Come on up Clayton, and Congratulations!" he said.

Father climbed to the dais as they shook hands, and everyone clapped, and cheered loudly. "Thank you! I can't remember when I have enjoyed myself so much, it has been a great day, but it is not over yet. I would like to offer a special thank you to all of you though for your attendance today, and your donations which have made the day so successful, everyone has had a marvelous time!" "Now I want to introduce you to someone here who has some great news that he has to share with you all, and he would like to speak to everyone, so I give you Doctor Jon Jenkins!" said Father, as he then handed the microphone to the Doctor, and stepped down.

"Good afternoon all, today has been just exceptional. Sport played in true spirit, a fund raiser like no other, it has been a great event, and I wish to personally thank Clayton Coby for his organization of this event. My exciting news is for all of you folk from Shallow Siding, surrounding areas, and from all The Outback Properties.

I have much pleasure in announcing that all approvals have come through for the building of The Hospital, and also with the money raised here, we will have The Hospital built in the very near future!" Huge cheers went up, people shouted, clapped, and it took a while before the Doctor could continue. "I would also like to say it has also been decided that a wing of The Hospital will be named in honour of Clayton Coby for his huge involvement in the whole process. Thank you Clayton, thank you all!" he said, stepping down to the applause.

Henry Ball took the microphone, and spoke out. "We have a short exhibition shoot now, five shots per person, and the people giving the exhibition are the four highest scorers from the shoot today.
*Congratulations to these competitors.*
Clayton Coby, and Jacqueline Coby.
Jeffery Stringer, and Mitchell Stringer.
Would you all please go to the allocated target areas to commence The Exhibition Shoot, thank you!"

"Enjoy the show everyone!" he said.

# APRIL RAIN

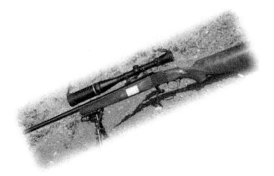

## JENNY MAC

Mitchell Stringer was deep in thought as he walked with his Father, and followed the Coby's to the shooting areas. 'What is so different about Jackie today?' he questioned himself, but something has changed, and I can't quite put my finger on it.

Mitch was a good looking boy. His sandy, almost sun-bleached hair fell about his face to his shirt collar, and his deep blue eyes seemed to twinkle, and light up in his deeply tanned face. He looked a bit lanky in his tall lean frame, but he was starting to fill out now with evidence of muscle in his arms, and legs. He regarded Jackie as one of his very best friends, they had always been close, and comfortable around each other. The both of them had been schooled in Shallow Siding, and had grown up together, they were the same age to the month.

He had noticed at the lunch break, that the new boy from the city was showing Jackie a lot of attention, and that made him feel uneasy, and quite envious, almost jealous. Maybe he had taken too much for granted in just assuming when the time was right that the two of them, Jackie, and himself, would get together as a couple. He was shattered to think that he had not seen the signs sooner, and he could not believe it. He thought they had plenty of time yet. Mitchell was feeling like he had left his unsaid feelings too late.

Looking at her now, as if for the very first time, his thoughts roamed as she was speaking to her Father. 'She is just so beautiful, well I guess she has always been that, and talented too, but not only that, she is such a lovely person, always has been. Well I am not going to give up on you yet Jacqueline Coby!' he promised himself.

However these new thoughts, and persistent uneasy feelings that he was now experiencing, crept up, and overwhelmed him, and for some unknown reason, inside, he had a deep feeling of regret.

"Congratulations Father!" I said, as I looked up into his eyes. "Remember I said to you this morning that you had the winning clothes on! I guess I was right!" Father laughed. "You shot really well today Father, and it is such great news about the hospital wing being named in your honour. I really am so very proud of you!" I said.

"You need Congratulating too Jackie! I am so proud of you as well. Scores of 20, 24, 27, that is a mean feat in itself, and the simple fact that you are in the exhibition shoot, suggests that you shot extremely well today also. So well done, and you have to be proud of yourself for that!" Father replied. "Thank you Father. I am proud of myself. I just felt so different today I guess!" I replied.

"What do you mean Jackie, different in what way?" Father asked. "It's just that I felt my nerves were steeled today, or something! I was so very solid all day, totally confident, and calm, I think my skills improved because of that. It is only just a guess, but the only reason I can think of for improving my expertise, and performance in shooting today, is from the real life experience I had at the creek just past when I was attacked by the dogs. I remember the feelings quite clearly now. It was almost as if I was transported to a fixed line of thinking that day, and I was extremely focused, and calm!" Does that make sense Father?" I asked. "It makes very good sense to me Jackie, and I think you are absolutely right. It is good that the experience has helped you in that respect, it is always a bonus to turn a negative into a positive and you have done that!" he said.

"Do you really think so Father?" I asked. "I sure do Jackie!" replied Father. "Thank you so much, I will hold on to those thoughts!" I said. Our conversation ended as Jeffery, and Mitchell Stringer walked up to join us, and Father faced them both to speak.

"Well! Congratulations are in order for you Jeffery, and Mitch, well done to both of you today!" said Father.

"Thank you Clayton, and Congratulations goes to you too, not only for your shooting, but I am pleased to hear about the honour that they have bestowed upon you by allocating a wing of the hospital to be in your name! That is just great news." said Jeffery. "Thanks Jeffery." Clayton replied. "Thank you Mister Coby and I must congratulate you also!" said Mitchell.

Mitch looked at me with that big grin on his face. "Knew you could do it Jackie!" he said. "A great competition shoot! You really shot well today, so My Congratulations!" "Thank you Mitch, it was a lot of fun today, and Congratulations to you too, you shot well also, well done!" I replied, as I looked up at his face, and returned his smile. "Thank you Jackie." said Mitch, as he smiled at me again. "Congratulations Mister Stringer, well done today!" I said, as I held out my hand. We shook hands and he said. "Thank you Jackie, you have exceeded our expectations today young lady, well done, a great effort!" "Thank you Mister Stringer!" I said.

"Ok let's do this, and then we can all celebrate! Good shooting everyone!" said Father, and then we all readied ourselves for the shoot.

So when the golden sun lost its brilliance as it filtered through the trees, and started it's descent from the sky, it was all over. The shooting competition was completed, and the hospital fund raiser a total success, and a host of well-wishers swamped us to express their gratitude, and congratulate us, as the night air closed in upon us all.

Huge fires were being lit, lanterns were erected in the trees, the music blared out across the field, and amidst The Coby Camp everyone was busy setting up with the host of food, and drinks that were arriving, and all the shooters converged for the final celebration.

Reagan Chase walked slowly towards me, my knees felt weak just with the very sight of him, and we smiled at each other. For some unknown reason he had a massive effect on me. My stomach was full of butterflies, and anxiety overcome me as he moved close to me.

"You were wonderful out there!" he said. "Was there anyone else out there shooting? I must admit though, I have become a bit bias, and I only had eyes for you!" he admitted laughing. "Seriously though Jacqueline, you really are very good to watch, such concentration, and determination, like you are in your own little world. I can see that you like shooting a lot." he said.

"Yes I do Reagan! I guess shooting is a huge passion of mine, and thank you Reagan for your kind words!" I replied laughing. "You do have a way with words!" I said. "I try!" replied Reagan, as he grabbed my hand. I looked down at our entwined hands. "The last time you done that, you got into serious trouble I recall!" I said, as I looked up into his beautiful eyes, and he smiled.

"Can we walk then Jacqueline? I would like to learn all about your other passions, just by talking to you, and getting to know you. Besides, who knows when I will see you again!" he replied.

This unfriendly thought hit me so hard, I just wanted to push it right out of my mind. "Let us walk then Reagan, I think that would be nice!" I replied instantly.

So in the semi-darkness we wandered hand in hand, and we talked like our very life depended on it, both of us consumed with the need to search the inner depths of each other's minds, and trying to justify the reason for our short-lived feelings for each other, and we were in awe of our new discoveries.

Our similarities were so amazing, just like looking to a mirror image with its reflection revealing a closeness, an uncanny likeness, and affinity between us.

"Let's sit here Jacqueline!" said Reagan, after we had walked a distance from our camp, and had come upon seats now deserted that had previously been occupied by spectators. We sat down, and suddenly I witnessed a side of Reagan that I had not yet seen. He pulled me closer to him and I could see by the look on his face the importance of what he was about to say, as he held both my hands in his, and very passionately he looked deeply into my eyes.

"I have a very serious confession to make Jacqueline! From the very first moment I saw you, on impulse, I just had to meet you. I couldn't concentrate on anything else, as you were constantly on my mind. Believe me, I have never felt this way before, and I have never met anyone quite like you! These feelings that I have for you are real Jacqueline. I am completely head over heels in love with you already, and you may think that strange now, as we have just met. We are both still young, but we can take our time, and we will have a long future together if you feel the same about me, as I do about you. But for the present time I would like to ask you very prematurely to please be my girl?" he asked. Then added, with a laugh.

"After I have checked with your Father of course!"

I smiled at his jest, but I wasn't even alarmed at his question. My body seemed to sway naturally towards him as he took me gently in his arms, and his kiss was intense with desire, but so tender, as the initial shock of my first kiss reverberated right through my body, to the core of my soul. "Yes please Reagan!" I replied softly.

I guess without any doubt, I fell in love with Reagan Chase that day, and my captured heart fluttered like the flight of a wounded bird. I was drinking in his love, and reveling in the excitement of my own feelings, my body possessed with my new found love.

*'We would be together always!' I thought.*

# JENNY MAC

*The Outback Gardens Bush Camp... Shallow River.
The year 1996*

## Chapter 16

Royce, and Riana Charmers lounged upon the camp chairs inside the huge common tent at The Outback Gardens Property. At the break of dawn they ventured out to walk along the river, and the early morning mist cloaked the trees, and blanketed the river like a thick heavy cloud searching to soak up the scenery. Visibility was very limited, making the scene quite eerie-like, but the silence, and stillness of the morning was unerringly complete. They returned with a sense of calm, and were waiting for their breakfast to be cooked on an open fire, Outback Style, by their cook Joe.

"Can you just believe this place Royce?" said Riana. "I haven't been so relaxed for as long as I can remember. They say that it's tough living in the country, but I'm thinking our city life is worse! What do you think?" "I am impressed Riana, and you are right, it is relaxing. I guess we live a fast life in the city, always a schedule to keep, traffic to battle with, and our work to do, but it is home, and that is where the heart is I guess. It is nice to get away for a while though, best idea we've ever come up with for a holiday!"

"I can't believe the boss himself actually picked us up off the train, and gave us a Country welcome, how was that for service? He's a nice guy Pete, really down to earth, and knows his business well, and did you notice how he treated the animals? So calm, and gentle, almost like they were his pets, and you could see plainly that the animals loved him too. I really do appreciate having seen that first hand, quite unique." Royce said. "Me too!" said Riana.

"Yesterday was so special!" said Riana. "Our first day at The Outback Gardens, and we have done so much already! I slept like a baby last night, not bad for bush beds! What about you Royce?"
"I never moved all night Riana it was a very long day!" he replied.

They had arrived to all the splendor of The unique Outback Gardens Bush Camp Site, and had found it very hard to comprehend the size, and style of the whole place. It was like nothing anyone had seen before, and the excitement between them all was mounting, as they climbed out of the vehicle.

Pete had started unloading their belongings from the vehicle, and they were immediately joined by Joe Jeffries and Susan Hind who had come out to help them unload, and introduce themselves. Pete offered the formalities. "Joe, and Susan. This is Royce, and Riana Chalmers, and Col, and Fiona Selmy. And my guests, please meet Joe Jeffries my cook here, and Susan Hind his assistant, and your tents organizer, and they will both be looking after you all.

Everyone shook hands. "Nice to meet you folk, said Joe. Hope you enjoy your stay with us, and if you want anything just yell!" he said. They all laughed, and said. "Thank you Joe!" "Welcome to The Outback Gardens everyone, everything is ready for you!" said Susan. "If you would like to follow me, I will take you on a short tour of the camp area, and show you to your sleeping tents, and amenities that we have here, if you would like to freshen up. Joe is preparing a welcome treat when you are ready." said Susan. They all offered replies.

"Hello Susan, and thank you Susan." and they picked up their luggage to follow her.

"This is the galley, and cooking areas." said Susan. "You might want to set your belongings down there, she pointed to an area, and I will show you around here first." The huge three semi-sided galley clad in rushes, had an elevated thatched roof, and adjoined the tented dining area where tables were set up like a restaurant.

Although there was a cooking area, and camp fires outside, the inside of the galley existed of a very up-to-date bar-be-que area, and ovens. Just adjacent to the galley in a screened-off area, was an outside cooking area where huge pots of water steamed on the fires.

There were billys, camp ovens, pots, and pans, and a huge serving bench, where underneath accommodated serving plates, and cutlery. Joe was busying himself at the campfire preparing their welcome ritual of billy tea, and a bush style damper.

Their tour continued. Standing quite central, taking pride of place, and separating the scattered living tents, was the massive Common Tent. Prepared campfires were ready to light outside, and inside was all the sitting comforts on a grass matting floor.

"My goodness!" said Fiona. "Have you ever seen the like?" "Yes I know what you mean!" replied Riana. "I will take you over to your tents now so that you can put your belongings inside." said Susan. So they all followed her in earnest.

"This is your tent Riana, and Royce!" she said as she stopped outside the large tent nestled amongst the gum trees. "You will find there is a wash basin on top of the sideboard, and linen, and toiletries beside it inside the cupboard, and if you need warm water at any time Joe always has a huge pot of water on the fire outside, so you can just ask anyone here." "Thank you so much Susan!" said Riana. "I will just take Fiona, and Col to their tent now, if you would like to meet us over at the back of the tents, I will show you the amenities." said Susan. "Thank you Susan." replied Royce.

Riana had noticed at once when she walked into their large living tent, that the floor area was completely covered with grass matting, she couldn't wait to check out everything in there. "Look Royce, will you look at that bed." she said. "Yeah, looks good to me!" said Royce. It was a huge bed, all made up with beautiful linen, fluffy pillows, and a feather down quilt. To each bedside stood small timber tables topped with three chunky candles cradled in their holders. Two gas lights hung up on hooks, which attached to a timber stand that stood in one corner, and a mirror, set in a timber frame stood in the opposite corner. One single electric light shade, made out of what looked like a nest of sticks, fell from the center of the ceiling, and was operated with a pull cord she noted.

Atop the timber sideboard sat a wash basin, and jug, and when Riana opened the doors, there was absolutely everything in there that they would need, even a small section for their clothes. At two points on the canvas walls, containers hung from the ceiling concealing the two citronella candles nestled inside, and a small table, and two camp chairs stood against the blank wall.

"Oh this is just lovely." said Riana. "I want to extend my stay already Royce!" she said, as she looked up at him. "One day at a time Riana, then we will decide, we had better get out back now though, they will be waiting for us." said Royce.

They noticed two huts standing apart from a central larger hut. The construction was a sloping thatched roof building, each side being mid height, clad in rushes with push in doors at the front, and they could see the shower heads through each top section. In the central hut was a laundry, and toilets. "Oh how quaint is that!" said Riana. They moved on and entered the much bigger building opposite of the same thatching, and rushes, but fully enclosed, on the inside stood the biggest hip bath Riana had ever seen, big enough for two people, a wash basin was set in a bench, and toilets. "Wow!" said Riana. "Look Royce I can see a water heater too!"

Susan immediately went to carry some warm water over for the two couples to use in their living tents, and when she returned, she said. "When everyone is ready, I will meet you all over at the main campfire. Joe has everything ready, and Pete is there. No doubt we will have a small welcome meeting." she told them.

# JENNY MAC

Joe had everything laid out for them on the trestle tables when they arrived at the camp fire site. Camp chairs were around the fire in a laid back, outback style.

"Oh good you are all here, dig in and help yourselves, I've made you the best bush style damper, and billy tea you will ever have, or so they tell me!" laughed Joe.

"Thank you Joe!" said Riana. "We all appreciate that." "Yes thank you Joe." they all replied, as they started to help themselves at the table.

"Hi everyone!" said Pete. "Did you have a good tour? I hope you like our place here, and a very big welcome to you all!" "Oh it is just fabulous here, and Susan has shown us around the camping area, thank you Pete!" said Fiona. "Yeah very nice place." said Col. "Everything is tops!" "Looks like a really relaxing place you have here Pete. You've put in a lot of work in here from what I can see, it exceeds all our expectations, and already Riana wants to extend our stay!" Royce said. "Yes, my Father, and I have done a lot of work here over the years, you will meet him this afternoon, he is coming over to dine with us tonight." said Pete.

"For today though, I have a big day planned for you all. My camels are being prepared, and I have a trail ride organized, we will be gone most of the day so Joe will be coming with us to provide morning tea, and lunch. We will leave after breakfast. In the meantime, I will show you the rest of the camp, and take you down to meet the staff, and animals. We will head down there when you are ready!" said Pete.

## APRIL RAIN

As they got up to leave, Pete said. "We might walk, it's not far, and it will give you a chance to stretch out a bit!" So they walked along the track through the camp area amidst the magnificent gum trees, and were admiring the well kept premises along the way. "Tim is our ground-sperson here!" Pete said, as if reading their thoughts. He is Joe's Son, you will meet him at some point when he is free, and you will meet his sisters this afternoon. They will be serving you in the dining area, and will also look after your tents, linen etc. They are also housemaids at the homestead." Pete said.

There stood six other camp tents in the complex with similar amenities, and all were occupied they noticed as they passed. Pete paused beside a separate shed. "Just wanted to show you our storage shed, lots of things in here, and we keep all the fishing equipment, and the oars for the canoes stored here if you want them at any time!" he said.

Moving on they finally arrived at the large holding yard where the tethered camels were being tended to by three workers, and big saddles were being brought out.

"Ok everyone, come and meet my staff first, then you can get to know my animals!" said Pete.

Sam Hind was the first person to approach them. "Hi everyone, I'm Sam. Welcome to The Outback Gardens!" and immediately held out his hand. "Sam, this is Riana and Royce Chalmers." said Pete. "Pleased to meet you Sam." they said, as they all shook hands. "Also meet Fiona, and Col Selmy!" said Pete. "Hi Sam!" said Fiona and Col. Then they were joined by two other workers, and Pete introduced them all around. "Meet Jimmy, and Hank everyone, and guys, meet Riana, and Royce, and Fiona and Col!" They greeted each other as Pete turned to talk to Sam.

"Did you get my bag Sam?" he asked. "Yeah! I will get it for you now Pete!" he said, and he walked off.

When Sam returned, and handed Pete the bag, Pete opened the gate saying. "Ladies first, come on through, and meet the camels, and this is for you all to bring in!"

He handed the bag to Riana. "I will go in first, and when I signal, you all can come over!" said Pete. Riana opened the bag. "What is this for Pete?" she asked. "For the camels, it's alfalfa, the camels love it!" said Pete, as he laughed.

They watched as Pete approached the camels, calling to each one by name. There were six of them, and once they heard him call, and were aware of his presence, there was some shuffling for his attention, and some of them groaned in utter pleasure just to be near him, and others just looked at him with love-struck eyes with their long eyelashes batting at him. "Oh will you look at that!" said Riana. "They love him!" Everyone was very interested with the interaction that they were witnessing between the animals, and the man, and all at once they expressed their opinions to each other.

Pete went to each camel to caress them, and saying "Jhu Jhu" when he held their halter rope, then each camel couched on his command, and sat down as he went on down along the line.

Pete signaled to them, and they all went over to him.

## APRIL RAIN

"If you would all get some feed now, and we will start with Marylou." said Pete, and as they all petted the camels, and fed them the alfalfa Pete was saying their names. "This is Al Capone, this is Mable, this is Archie, this is Cybil, and finally Clover!" "They seem to be very well behaved." said Fiona. "Yes I have trained them all myself, they are all great animals!" said Pete. "You will all enjoy today! Well we all better get back now, Joe will have your breakfast ready, and after that we will get organized to move out. I will leave it all up to you Sam!" Pete said. "We will be ready Pete!" said Sam.

*The Outback Bush Camp ... Camel ride ...*

## Chapter 17

Simulating a string of pearls, was the rope line linking them together, as they moved out from The Outback Bush Camp mounted on the six camels, to head towards the hills on a well-used sandy track which weaved its way amongst the huge river gums.

Leading the entourage, was the imposing figure of Pete Stringer, as he sat atop his lead camel Al Capone. His khaki bush trousers were hugging his lean hips, his cut out shirt sleeves exposing his huge muscled arms which rippled as he moved, and his country bush hat sat at a jaunty angle over his deep blue eyes.

To the rear came Joe on his mount Archie. Because of the heavy load that he was toting, Joe rode on a specially made one seated camel saddle with a deep forward seat set over the camel's front shoulders, encased in iron bars at the front, and back, and the sides and rear, giving him exceptional stability, and control. The back section of the saddle was set up for packing large amounts of supplies for long treks to The Outback.

In the center, the tourists trailed along upon the other camels seated on the back end of double seated padded saddles which offered them a comfortable ride. Their saddles were designed with the center sitting just above the camel's hump with a thick pad resting on the camel's flank, and two pads on the front shoulders and iron bars at the front, center, and back, there were stirrup irons for the feet, and places to hang their belongings in front.

Joe had instructed them as his usual routine prior to setting out on their travel, about the attire they should wear, and things they may need. He had supplied them with their own personal water bottles so they were all well-equipped. They leaned back swaying to the gait of the camels as they padded along the track.

Riana was finding it really hard to concentrate on the close surroundings as she was meant to be doing, but the sight of Pete Stringer on the camel in front of her was seeking all her attention, and she could hardly keep her eyes off him.

My goodness, she thought to herself, but he is a hunk of a man that's for sure. There was something about the raw country look of him that stirred her feelings, and she couldn't wait for them to stop so she could talk to him, so she decided to do the alternative. "Hey Pete!" she called. "I am liking your property well enough, the scenery here is amazing. You must think yourself lucky living here, and owning all this!" she said. Pete turned half way around to face her, and his smile was huge.

"Yes Riana, this is beautiful land, we all love it here, but the best is yet to come when we get closer to the hills there!" and he pointed, as he replied. "So what is up there?" asked Riana. "That would be telling!" said Pete, as he laughed. Fiona tried to enter the conversation even though she was on the camel behind Riana. "Come on Pete, let us know what is up there, and how long before we get there!" she called.

"Patience is a virtue Fiona, all will be revealed!" Pete

replied. "Yes, you always say that Pete." called Fiona.

"Ok Fiona, we will travel for about an hour, then we will be stopping for morning tea, and then you will see! Maybe if you are interested in looking, we have put the horses in the top paddock this morning, so we will pass them shortly on the way." called Pete. "Oh good, thank you Pete, I will do just that!" Fiona called back. 'Thank goodness for that' thought Pete. "Thank you Pete you have been most helpful." Riana said, as he was turning back to face the front. "No problems Riana, enjoy your ride ladies." he said, as they resumed their trek.

The quietness of the morning slowly engulfed them, and the only disturbance from the padding of the camel's feet was the call of the kookaburra's laughing in the distance. Overhead the galah's flitted from tree to tree, and bush parrots seemed to set the low bushes alive with the colours of their plumage as they settled in amongst the foliage. However, a large flock of black cockatoos startled them all, when they screeched loudly, desperate in their flight high above them, in search for another group of gum trees.

"Oh look. There are the horses!" called Fiona. "How come all the black horses are separated from the rest Pete? You said that you only had six horses, and when are we going to get to ride some of them?" she asked.

'Oh! Here we go again' thought Pete, as he turned around to reply to her endless questions.

"Yes Fiona, I do have only six horses, they are used solely for the Outback Camp guests, and all the black horses are Father's breeding stock, that is why they are separated from the others. But don't ask me details, he just likes black horses I guess!" said Pete. "If you can contain yourself until tomorrow, I am planning to have the horses brought in for after lunch, and we will discuss that more tonight!" he replied. "Oh I see. Thank you Pete." said Fiona.

They continued along in silence until a small bridge emerged, then Pete led them out onto the planked pathway of the bridge which crossed a beautiful rock pool, so clear, that they could see to the very bottom.

Over the opposite side, and from the colourful cliffs above, a waterfall cascaded down into the pool, blinding white in the sunlight, and tumbled into huge sprays on its entry into the pool, then gushing from the rock pool, the water surged over the edge of the great rocks down below on its way to the river.

Pete led them off the bridge to a sandy stretch along the edge of the rock pool where the sun streamed down through the river gums, then he jumped down, and started the process of couching all the camels.

"Ok everyone you can dismount now, we are going to have morning tea here, if anyone wants to swim it is just great in there, we will have a two hour break!" he said.

Riana was the first to dismount, and then she walked slowly up to Pete, and she moved her hand up to the muscles of his arm. "So lovely here Pete!" she said, as she squeezed his biceps, and left her hand lingering on his arm. Pete slowly removed her hand, and his eyes darkened with annoyance as he looked into her hazel eyes, but he kept his tongue controlled, saying. "Yes it is real lovely place Riana, but please remember one thing! Somethings are approachable but others aren't! Do you understand me?" he asked. "I think so!" said Riana.

Royce was dismounting, and he looked up just as Riana, and Pete were speaking. 'What is that all about' he wondered, as he jumped down to the ground! "I will give you a hand there Joe!" he said, and together they unpacked the stores from the camel, and then went to gather wood for the fire. Joe had a camp set up in no time, a tarpaulin was stretched out between the trees for shade, camp chairs set around, a fire was blazing, and the billy set up above it.

Fiona was already testing the water. "Who is coming in for a swim?" she asked. "The water is so wonderful!" Everyone was all for having a swim, and Joe had erected a change area for their privacy, and provided towels for everyone. "Thank you so much Joe!" said Fiona, after she had changed clothes, and then headed for the water.

"That's ok Fiona!" he said. They all had so much fun in the rock pool, but all too soon Joe was calling them out for morning tea.

With all the finesse of a bush cook, Joe had laid out a buffet for them, there were scones, and pikelets with jam, mince savoury puffs made in the camp oven and of course, his billy tea. "Wow Joe, this is quite a morning tea!" said Royce, as he tucked in. "Sure is!" said Col. "I don't get this sort of food at home!" he stated, as he looked at Fiona. Fiona laughed. "Sorry Col!" she said.

"I will have to get Joe's recipes!" "Yes thank you Joe for going to so much trouble, but I am famished after the camel ride, and the swim!" said Riana. "No problems!" said Joe, as he laughed at them all. "Dig in we have a long way to go yet, you will need your strength before the day is out!"

Their morning was full of friendly banter as Pete, and Joe were full of tales to tell, and everyone was enjoying it immensely. Only Riana was having guilty feelings. 'I will have to speak to Pete, I have made a huge mistake.' she thought to herself.

His voice startled her, and he clapped his hands, as he said. "Ok everyone, ladies first! Back into the riding gear. Let's get packed up, and ready to leave in fifteen minutes! I will tend to the camels Joe!" "Ok boss!" said Joe, and he started packing up, and putting the fire out. Col and Royce helped him, and Riana and Fiona went to change their clothes. When Riana came out fully clothed, the men were still busy, so she walked casually down to where Pete was fussing with his camels.

"Pete can I have a word?" she asked. Pete stood up, and looked down into her eyes. "What is it Riana?" he asked. "I'm terribly sorry Pete I really want to apologize. I hope you can forgive me as I have made an awful mistake!" she said. "No harm done Riana, all forgiven, it's best not to mix business with pleasure!" he said.

Riana replied with a giggle. "Thank you Pete, I will be on my best behaviour, you will see!" "I hope so

Riana, you don't need to spoil your holiday." Pete said.

"That is food for thought, I think!" said Riana, with another giggle and a cheeky smile. He just looked at her, and had to laugh. 'This one is definitely a problem child' he thought to himself, and they both laughed together.

"What are you two laughing at?" asked Fiona, as she walked up to them.

"Oh just something Riana said Fiona, she is a bit like you, and asks too many questions!" said Pete, as he smiled at Riana, and then Fiona. The others joined them then, and Joe spoke to Pete. "All ready boss!" "Ok then let's move out, we will be taking the river road this time, a bit longer travel, about one, and a half hours, but you will find it is worth it. We will stop for lunch at the river." said Pete. "Everyone climb aboard."

Very tentatively Pete led them down the hillside onto a small trail where the countryside changed again. Thick scrub lined the track, and river gums now shared their space, and were joined by paperbarks, blackbutts, wattle trees, and other native plants, but the mulga trees amassed along the creek overwhelmed them with their distinctive smell. It was real bush country now, and as they passed through the bush, the small wildlife scattered everywhere.

They saw rabbits, lizards, and snakes, then a huge wombat ambled along in front of them, and crossed the track. Pete halted his hand pointing up to the eucalyptus tree. Deep in the fork of a big gum tree a mother Koala sat uninterested in their approach as she munched on the gum leaves with her baby clinging to her back. Pete could hear the girls calling out at each surprise, but were too busy to communicate, enthralled in the adventure.

Quite suddenly though, as the dense bushland had appeared, it ended abruptly, as the countryside took on another aspect of wide open plains, clay pans, and scattered river gums. Looking further ahead they could see a course of the river mapped out before them across the property, its banks lined with the weeping willows bowing their heads, and branches to the running water.

As they crossed the grassland they disturbed all the wildlife. Kangaroos darted about, and bounded away pounding the earth in their anxious flight to escape, and the emus ran in full flight. They arrived at the river, and connected with a sandy trail which followed the path of the river, and as they followed it along, the abundant birdlife was everywhere, and out on the water the water hens, and wood ducks, were in a paradise of their own. Two black swans flew down, and glided onto the water in a perfect landing.

After about twenty minutes riding, they noticed that the river had widened. Sandy banks were much more prominent now, like a playground in the sun, and the huge river gums stood up proudly. Pete halted with his hand up. As he couched his camel, he went along the line to couch the other camels, and he said. "We can dismount now people, we are spending two hours here for a lunch break. You can swim, or if you want, Joe has all the gear for fishing, and some earth worms for bait."

# JENNY MAC

"That ride was just amazing Pete!" said Riana. "You live in paradise here, it is just so beautiful Pete! Fiona said. I can't say when I have enjoyed myself more!"

"Pleased you liked it ladies, just let Joe know what your requirements are for here, and he will set it up for you." Pete replied. Joe was busy setting up his camp, and Royce, and Col helped him gather the wood to start the fire.

"This is a great place here Joe, so much to see and that ride was fabulous, you must love living here." Royce said. "Wouldn't want to be anywhere else Royce, my heart is in the Country." said Joe. "You do a great job if I might say so Joe!" said Col. "Thanks Col, but I love my work, and all the people around me!" he replied. Joe unpacked the fishing lines, and equipment, and set it aside. "I have made up some throw out lines, if anyone wants to have a fish, go for it, bait is in the tin. I will start making lunch now." he said.

"Thank you Joe." said Royce. "We just might catch something for dinner." he said. Col helped him to carry everything down the sandy bank to the river, and the two women joined them. Many jests were shared as the inexperienced fishermen tried to catch a fish, and when they did, the two women squealed so loud with delight, Pete had to go down to see what was happening.

"We've caught a fish Pete, a big one too" said Fiona. "What an unlucky fish, I will go, and get a hessian bag. We will keep it alive until we are ready to leave!" said Pete. Joe was already coming down with the bag, and he put the fish inside, sat it in the water, and staked the bag.

"That should hold him." he said. "I will be going home after lunch, so anything you catch I can get back quickly, we are only twenty minutes from home here." he added. "Oh I didn't realize we were close to the Bush Camp Joe!" said Riana. "Yes it is deceiving but you don't realize we have done a big loop today, so it is not too far home now." replied Joe.

Joe put on quite a display for lunch. He had brought with him fresh produce from the gardens to make up salads, and he made omelettes, and damper bread on the open fire, and of course billy tea. When he called them, all they were amazed with his talents.

Pete revelled in the bush, he was enjoying the day as much as his guests, and as they sat around the fire, and ate lunch he found the conversation was enjoyable, and they were all in a great mood, and a bond was being formed between them all.

"I hate to be the one to break up a party." Pete said. "But we have to leave in twenty minutes. Joe will be going back alone. My Father is joining us for dinner tonight so Joe has some preparation to do when he gets back, and I will be leading you all home, no doubt you will all need a rest when you get back before dinner.

When Joe was all packed up, and everything was in readiness to travel, he set off at a loping trot, and the others climbed up on their camels, and they set off at a more sedate pace.

So it was about mid-afternoon when the weary trail riders returned to The Outback Bush Camp. The day had exceeded all their expectations, and as Pete coached the camels, they were so pleased to see that he had a vehicle there at the yards to take them back to the tents.

"Thank you so much for today Pete, it was the best day ever!" said Riana. "Yes I agree Pete, thank you, I had a wonderful time!" added Fiona. Royce, and Col shook Pete's hand, and thanked him also. "It was my pleasure!" said Pete, as they climbed into the land rover.

As Pete drove along, he said. "We will meet for drinks in the common tent tonight at five-thirty, then dinner will be served at six!"

Mitchell Stringer arrived early, and he brought with him his employees Marie who was eighteen now, a slim girl with red hair, and freckles, and bright blue eyes, and Sandy was sixteen, she was quite short, and had auburn hair, and blue eyes, they were both serving in the dining tent, and they were Joe and May Jefferies daughters. "Hi everyone!" Mitchell called, as he walked into the galley.

Pete was talking to Joe when his Father walked in. "Father! Hi, come on in. Our guests should be over soon." he said. "Hi Marie, Hi Sandy. You can start setting up the dining tent now girls." Pete said.

"Ok Boss!" said the girls together." "I will give you a hand Pete!" said Mitchell. "How are you Joe, how did your day go today?" he asked. "Yeah good boss, we all had a great time, the girls caught two fish so I am going to surprise them with fish cocktails for entrees' later!" Joe said. "Sounds good Joe, I will look forward to that also." Mitchell replied.

"How are you Pete, sounds like today was a success, what can I help you with?" Mitchell asked. "I'm good Father, a great day. I just want to put some drinks on ice, and then Marie, and Sandy can take over then!" he said.

"Right, let's get to it then, so we can relax!" replied Mitchell. When all was completed, they lounged in the common tent, and chatted, and in a short time the guests arrived. Pete raised himself off the chair to meet them, and said. "Come on in everyone, and meet my Father, Mitchell Stringer. Father please meet Riana, and Royce Chalmers, and Fiona, and Col Selmy."

They all shook hands, and then seated themselves. "We have heard a lot about you from Pete!" said Royce. "You have a lovely place here Mister Stringer!" Riana was looking hard at Mitchell when he spoke. "I hope it is all good things you have heard Royce, but please everyone, call me Mitch!" he said. 'Such a handsome man' thought Riana. 'Like Father, like Son! Both oozing country.' "Pleased to meet you Mitch, we are really enjoying it here!" said Riana, as she smiled. "Hi Mitch, great place!" said Col, as Fiona spoke up. "Hi Mitch, she said. I saw your beautiful horses today. Also, could you tell me who paints the signs for your property?"

Everyone laughed, and Pete said. "Don't mind Fiona Father, she likes to ask a lot of questions!" "That is not a problem!" said Mitchell. I am only too pleased to answer your questions Fiona!"

"My horses are a special hobby of mine. I have been breeding them for many years now, but this is the best stock I ever had. I am pleased that you asked about the paintings on the signs. They are only a couple out of many around Shallow Siding. When you go into town you will no doubt see this man's work in various places, though he only does small jobs these days, he is getting on in age but he is an active old blighter, a pensioner, but he makes good money from his paintings. He is also an active member of the Entertainment Committee, he does the artwork for our events.

"Oh how interesting!" said Fiona. "Thank you Mitch, I will look out for the art work when we go to town!"

"You are welcome Fiona, by the way everyone, I have a big morning organized for you all after breakfast. A tour of the Homestead, and The Gardens, morning tea, and then you can play tennis. We are going to have a bar-be-que lunch out on the lawns." Mitchell replied.

"Oh, that sounds wonderful!" said Riana. "It sure does!" said Fiona.

Marie excused herself to say. "Dinner will be served now in the dining tent!" So they all moved, and were served drinks, and entrées by Marie, and Sandy.

Joe called out. "Just to let you know ladies that you are eating the fish you caught today, thought you might like the special treat." he said.

"Thank you Joe." they all replied. "How thoughtful!" said Riana. Dinner was a huge success. Joe had made a traditional baked dinner. Legs of lamb, sides of beef, produce baked from the gardens, and a special sweet. So as the night closed in around them they sat, and talked long into the night.

## APRIL RAIN

Heavy fog hung very low among the gum trees, the morning was cool, but there was a calmness in the air as Col, and Fiona joined Royce, and Riana in the huge Common Tent. It was their second day at The Outback Gardens. "Good morning Riana, and Royce." said Fiona as she sank into the camp chair. "Morning you two!" said Col, as he joined her. "Good morning Fiona, morning Col!" Riana, and Royce replied.

"We just went for a walk down to the stables, Riana, you won't believe what is going on down there in the paddocks!" Fiona said. "What do you mean Fiona?" asked Riana. "Well the men have all the horses in, and they are building jumps, and making a course out in the paddock. Looks like I have stumbled on one of Pete's surprises!" she said. "Well I never!" said Riana. "Pete thinks of everything, just keep it to ourselves though. Is everyone agreed? We don't want to spoil his surprise, since you have been at him ever since we got here to ride the horses." said Riana. "Yes all agreed!" they all said.

"We have just been down to the river." said Royce. "It is amazing down there in the early morning, this place is really something!"

"I am still getting over yesterday." said Col. "What a day it was, and by the looks of it today is not going to be any easier either!" he laughed.

"Morning all!" called Joe. "Breakfast is ready now, and Pete will be coming to collect you after that to go to The Homestead." he said.

"Good morning Joe, thank you!" they all said, as they moved inside to eat. They were just finishing breakfast when Pete arrived to pick them up. "Morning all! Big day today, I hope you are all up to it!" said Pete, with a laugh. "Good morning Pete!" they all replied in unison. "We are all ready!" said Riana. "Yes ready!" the others chimed in as they walked to the land rover to climb in.

Mitchell Stringer was waiting with his staff on the lawns when they drove up the road towards the Homestead.

Riana could not help noticing what an attractive man he was. 'His presence is quite overpowering, he is a real cowboy' she thought, as she looked through the window of the vehicle. When they slowed to stop, and climbed out of the vehicle, he greeted them all with a handshake. "Welcome to The Homestead, and The Market Gardens everyone. You have met Marie, and Sandy, this is May, their mother, and my cook here." drawled Mitchell.

"May! I would like you to meet our guests. Riana, and Royce Chalmers, and Fiona, and Col Selmy." "Good morning everyone I hope you enjoy your tour with us." replied May. "Pleased to meet you May, and good morning girls." said Riana. They all shook hands." and May added. "We will have morning tea on the lawns after a tour of the Homestead, and Gardens, and then you can play tennis till lunch." she said.

Mitchell Stringer was quite obviously the perfect host, as he proceeded to show them around. "I will show you all downstairs first. Come with me." he said. Under the house was a full kitchen area, and a bathroom area with showers, but he was very particular in showing them his greenhouse which housed orchids of many different varieties. On the lawns, tables, and chairs were set out amongst the gardens where a wide variety of bush plants grew, and bloomed, and the beautiful gum trees were scattered on the lawns providing shade. There was a bar-be-que area, and a swimming pool at the end of the garden, and two clay tennis courts set to one side.

"Amazing place!" Fiona said, and everyone voiced their opinions. "Upstairs now." said Mitchell, as he led them to a set of external steps.

The Homestead left nothing to their imagination, as they walked through experiencing the grand house.

The décor was in Heritage style, with double doors opening out to wide verandas, where the view of the property, the river, and The Market Gardens, all lay before them. "Right everyone, we will go down to the Gardens now, and you can select, and pick whatever you would like to add to lunch." said Mitchell.

Pete met them on the lawns for morning tea, and they were all full of chatter. "I might join you for tennis, and then a swim if you are all up to it before lunch, we have some spare bathing costumes, and towels downstairs in the bathroom area, so you can change there." said Pete.

"I am arranging lunch a little earlier today, as I have a special surprise for you all." he said. "Oh really Pete, whatever could that be?" asked Fiona, as she looked to the others with a knowing look. "Patience Fiona!" said Pete, as he laughed. "You always say that Pete!" she said, and she laughed with him. "So let's see how good you are on the tennis court. We will have to show this country man something!" she said. But as usual Pete excelled, no-one could better his talents.

After some time May called them for the bar-be-que lunch she had prepared, so they left the pool to change, then joined Mitchell on the lawns. They sat chatting, and laughed, as they reminisced about good shots that were played and proceeded to tell Mitchell of their frustration in trying to beat his son. "I think I know exactly what you mean!" said Mitchell laughing. "Pete is a hard man to toss!" All too soon Pete was urging them to leave.

"Ok people, time to go!" said Pete. "We can't waste this good day!" So they thanked Mitchell, and May for the lovely time, and they all went to the rover.

Fiona could see the jumps out in the paddocks, the set up was second to none. "Oh Pete, thank you so much, this is going to be so much fun!" she said. "Thank you Fiona! The course goes over two paddocks then down to the river, and back. A bit of a challenge, but I am sure you are all up to it." he replied. "We sure are!" said Riana. "Good stuff said Col!" and Royce agreed.

So after the final rules, and directions, straws were picked for their riding positions. Col was drawn first so they all settled down to watch his ride. Pete was timing everyone, and the competition was fierce, but when Pete took Sebastian out for his turn, they all just sat, and watched in awe of his talent, and clapped for him on his final run. Riana watched him mastering horse, and the course, and she could not still the feelings she felt for this

## APRIL RAIN

Country Cowboy. 'He is unbeatable, unstoppable!' she thought, in admiration.

Darkness closed quickly, the cool night air making its presence felt, so they packed up to return to their tents in preparation for dinner. When they all met back at the galley, the campfires had been lit, and they lounged around the warmth of the fires, and chatted.

"That was the just the best day ever Pete, thank you so much!" said Fiona. "Yes, thank you Pete, you are so amazing, not one of us can beat you at anything!" said Riana. "Yeah a lot of fun!" said Royce. "We will get you at something yet!" said Col, as he laughed. Pete laughed.

"I'm pleased you all had a good time, but tomorrow I have something special for Royce! His request! I have organized access from property owners, and have our licences prepared, so we are all going on a roo shooting hunt! We will discuss the final details at breakfast." he said. "That's great!" said Royce. Thank you Pete. "You are the best Pete!" they all said in unison.

*'Roo shooting Hunt'*

## Chapter 18

Daybreak came during the still of morning. Birds flitting throughout the trees were an only threat to the silence, and there was a calmness as the clouds hung low, the air was cool, but amidst the fog, sunshine was bursting through in its brilliance threatening to disperse the early mist, and warm the air.

From the depths of the stillness, the breakfast gong was deafening, and shattered the serenity of the camp.

Everyone woke immediately to the din of it, and were up, and out around the fires in no time. Pete was waiting at the camp fire for them.

"Good morning all, sorry about the early start, but we have a different format today, so while we eat breakfast we will discuss our hunting trip for tonight." Pete said. "Good morning Pete." they all replied. "Good morning folk, breakfast is ready!" said Joe. "Good morning, thank you Joe!" they all replied, as they moved to the dining tent where the buffet was all set out for them.

"First things first! I need to know who will be coming out shooting tonight?" said Pete. "Obviously Royce! What about you Col?" he asked. "Yeah, count me in Pete!" said Col. "Ok good, what about you ladies then? "Fiona?" Pete asked. "Oh definitely Pete, count me in!" said Fiona. "Fiona, I want you to know that we will be killing kangaroos, so there will be shooting, and blood, and we will be skinning the roos if you all want to keep the skins!" Pete stated.

Fiona had an exasperated look as she looked up to meet

## APRIL RAIN

Pete's eyes. "I'll have you know Pete Stringer that I am inquisitive, not squeamish. Of course I am going!" she replied. Pete laughed. "Ok Fiona!" he said as he held up his hands to her in defense. "What about you Riana?" he asked. "Need I reply to that Pete? Of course I will be going!" she said. "Right then! Rules now! Early lunch, so make sure you sleep all day, we will be out all night, so dress warm, a meal at 4pm leave at 4.30pm." he said.

They travelled about ten miles to their venue. Light was fading fast as they entered the property, and the coolness of the evening crept inside the specially designed hunting vehicle which had no doors, and a collapsible front windshield, with specially made bars across to shoot from. Three spotlights were set up, one on either side of the vehicle, and one centered on the cabin roof. There was seating for five people, and the back of the vehicle was extended for extra loading.

As they approached the homestead, Pete braked, and stopped. "I just need to see the property owner to let them know we are here, and get some directions. I won't be long!" he said, as he climbed out of the vehicle. The property owner met him at the gate, they shook hands then immediately they both squatted, and he started drawing a mud map on the ground. "Come in for a cuppa!" Jim offered when they were both satisfied, and had walked over to the vehicle. Pete introduced him to everyone, but they declined the offer to go in. "We've just eaten." said Pete in response. "And I'm guessing everyone is anxious to get going, thanks anyway Jim!"

he said. "Ok that's fine, maybe next time!" Jim replied, as Pete climbed in, and started the engine, and waved as he drove off.

As they left the homestead Pete directed the vehicle onto a smaller dirt track which headed in a different direction. Darkness was closing in now, and he turned the headlights, and spots on as they drove through the changing countryside, where thick scrub lined the edge of the track, and the enormous trees towered overhead.

They were deep in the heart of the bush now, in thick scrub, and the excitement was building in the back seat. Fiona couldn't help herself as she asked. "What do we do if we see a roo Pete? Should we tell you?"

"That would be a good idea Fiona!" Pete replied, with a laugh. "There will be times we can't see them, but you will be able to!" "Ok thank you Pete." replied Fiona. "I will use the spotlight on my side, and the central one. Royce will be using the other. Royce if you haven't used a spot before, when we see a roo sitting, hold the spot right in its eyes, but if they are hopping, shine the spot out in front, and they will stop!" said Pete. "Thanks for that info Pete, I'll do my best." said Royce.

They didn't have any trouble finding roos, and Pete was able to give everyone an opportunity to shoot, and when they reached their quota he pulled up, and they unloaded their kill for skinning.

Fiona watched with intensity as Pete proceeded to skin the Kangaroo's, explaining the proper procedure as he went. His razor sharp knife made the cuts with ease as he ringed above the hands, and feet, and the great tail, to leave a four inch butt from the body. The first incision to the stomach, and the teasing of separating skin from the tissue along each side, the legs, and arms was quite delicate, before he turned the body pushing his foot into it, and pulled hard to pull the skin off first the legs, up through the body, and then the arms, to the butt of its ears, where he cut it off, and rolled the skin with care.

"Pete, could I have a go a skinning one?" asked Fiona. "I have been watching closely!" "Yes, sure Fiona, just select the one you want!" Pete said, as he pulled a knife from his sheath. "Be careful it's sharp, better put these gloves on in case you cut yourself."

"Thank you Pete!" said Fiona, as she moved amongst the roos to choose, and selected a red buck. She steeled herself in preparation stooping over it, but as she lifted its leg to make the first incision, she jumped back yelling in horror, as in one movement the big roo came groggily to its feet, and stood erect, and snarling at her.

"Pete! Help! It's still alive!" Fiona screamed out in fright. Everyone stood mesmerized, simply stricken with panic, but Pete was alert, and quick into action, as he reacted. Taking three massive strides to reach the back of the vehicle, while firing orders as he went, he grabbed a double-headed steel mallet from the vehicle.

Roughly he pushed Fiona behind him, and then stood facing the wounded Kangaroo. "Get in the rover quick everyone! Col, turn the spotlight on its head! Royce get my gun out ready to hand to me. It's loaded, on safety, don't attempt to shoot it yourself!" he said, as his voice suddenly became quite ragged, the beads of perspiration appeared on his brow. The spotlight flashed at the bucks head, and in its brightness the wounded Kangaroo stood dazzled, swaying, and growling in pain.

Pete lost no time at all. He moved forward, carefully weighing the weight of the mallet, his muscles rippling in the smooth swinging action as he aimed for his throw.

Like a projectile, the steel mallet flew through the air, and the loud crack pierced the stillness around them, as it made its mark in the roo's forehead. The kangaroo fell dead, and senseless to the ground at Pete's feet.

Riana sat quite dumbfounded by this bushman who travelled by the stars at night, and whose shooting was an exhibition. 'He excels at everything so effortlessly.' And just now, she witnessed his quick wit, and action in the face of danger. 'What a man!' she thought.

Pete turned around quickly to Fiona. "Are you alright Fiona?" he asked. "Thank you Pete, I will be fine." said Fiona shakily. "Is everyone else ok?" he asked. "We are now, thanks to you Pete!" said Riana. "Yes, all good." Royce, and Col replied in shock. "Ok good! I will skin this one, then we will head home. We have to peg the skins out early in the morning so they will dry in time. Fiona, and Col, they are leaving the day after." said Pete.

Late afternoon the following day, darkness engulfed them, and they all helped pulling up the last of the roo-skins. The changing sky became so ominous as the huge banks of dark cloud was threatening to blot out the remaining sunshine. Thunder rolled across the sky, and clapped all around them as they all made a dash for the vehicle, and Pete drove them back to the campsite.

Lightning struck white across the heavens, then the skies opened up, the cold wind became fierce, and wild, and then the rain came. Unrelenting, and unforgiving as it swamped the camp, and pounding the camp site with sheets of white water in a torrential downpour.

Joe had put some fire pits inside the dining tent, and common area, and they sat around the fires waiting for their dinner as the rain continued into the night. "We only just got our shooting trip in!" said Royce. "When it rains here, it really rains. Thank you Pete for arranging that, it is something I will always remember!"

"Yes thanks so much Pete! You are a true professional bushman!" Riana said in admiration. "Thank you Riana, and Royce." Pete said. "Pete I also want to thank you for everything!" said Col. "We would love to stay on like Royce, and Riana, but we have to get back to reality!" "Thank you Col, it's been a pleasure having you both!" said Pete. "I can't believe our stay has come to an end Pete, thank you so much. I can't begin to tell you how much fun I have had. I will always remember you!" said Fiona, as a tear slid down her cheek. "Not quite over yet Fiona, you can say your goodbyes tomorrow. Riana, and Royce will be coming with us very early in the morning for a town tour before the train leaves tomorrow." said Pete. "Oh Pete, you think of everything." said Fiona.

"Oh great! Thank you so much Pete." said Riana. "I aim to please!" said Pete with a grin.

# JENNY MAC

*The Historic Railway Station ... Shallow Siding ... 1996*

## Chapter 19

Jacqueline Coby was feeling quite uneasy as she waited on the platform, but was instantly relieved when the friendly face of Sam Hind appeared before her, and he stopped to speak to her.

"Hello again Jacqueline! Sorry about the wait, you seem to be awfully lonely here by yourself, are you sure you wouldn't like a coffee or something?" Sam asked. "Hello Sam! Thank you for asking, but I am fine, I may get something later. It looks like you are kept busy here Sam, is there any update on the train?" asked Jacqueline.

"Not yet Jacqueline, but Jake is starting to think that something may have broken down, he is about to try and contact some people. He has given me instructions to take some messages out the front to a couple of the station hands, so I had better move!" he said.

"Did you say his name was Jake, Sam?" "Jake who may I ask?" Jacqueline queried. "Why! Jake Hardy, he's the Station Master here Jacqueline!" Sam said. Jacqueline could not believe his reply, and the memories began to swamp her. "I think I may know him Sam!" she replied. "Oh really what a coincidence, fancy meeting someone you know way out here. I will let him know that when I go back inside, but right now I have to go!" said Sam.

"Thank you Sam!" Jacqueline replied absently, as Sam waved goodbye, and walked away.

Jake was on his hands, and knees on the floor behind the office counter when Sam returned. "Where are you Jake? I have handed out your messages to the people you wanted, they will carry out your instructions!" Sam called. "I'm just here Sam, no need to yell I can hear you Sam, and thank you." replied Jake. "What are you doing down there Jake?" he asked. "I am trying to find some more string, and tape." said Jake. "There is some in the cupboard on the back wall Jake." Sam said. "Oh! By the way, before I forget to tell you. There is someone on the platform who thinks they may know you. A stranger, and a lady too!" replied Sam, pleased with his statement.

"What lady?" asked Jake, with a grunt, as he tried to get up. "The good looking one on her own at the end of the platform, her name is Jacqueline Coby!" said Sam.

There was no reply from Jake, and slowly from the depths his flushed face rose above the counter, his eyes were puffy as they widened in astonishment, while his gaping mouth was at a loss for words. "Are you ok Jake?" asked Sam with concern.

Jake's dry mouth croaked a reply. "Who did you say the lady was Sam?" he asked. "She told me her name is Jacqueline Coby! What is wrong Jake?" asked Sam.

Jake was disorientated, and slumped into a chair. 'It can't be!' he thought to himself. 'Not after all these years, it just can't be her. No one knew what had happened to Jacqueline Coby!' he stressed. Sam was worried, and he left to get some water. "Here Jake drink this!" he said.

Jake grabbed eagerly for the glass to drink deeply, then a thought occurred to him. "Anne, where is Anne?" he mumbled. "She went home Jake, you were speaking to her just before she left, remember!" said Sam. "Yes of course! I'm sorry Sam. I have had a shock, but I feel ok now, I must go out to see her. Hold the fort please Sam. I will explain later!" Jake said. "Yeah sure Jake!" said Sam.

He rose heavily from his seat, and strode out towards the front doors, and disappeared out onto the platform. As he walked along the platform in a daze, his mind was running wild. 'It was so long ago' he thought. 'So many unanswered questions, what should he say.' He was at a loss. Then the lady lifted her head, and the unmistakable deep, green eyes were watching him walk towards her. Jake knew that his earlier confusion was justified, when his recollection had failed him, to recognize her before.

*'It was indeed Jacqueline Coby.'*

Jacqueline watched the Station Master walking towards her. 'I would have passed him by on the street without recognition.' she thought. 'He looks so different now, except for those eyes, his warm, friendly, brown eyes.' She searched his eyes for a sign of any bitterness, but found none. Only kindness, and tenderness.

"My god! It is really you Jacqueline!" Jake said, his voice shaky, as he held out his hand. Jacqueline took his hand, and rose to greet him. "Yes Jake, it is really me!" she replied. He pulled her towards him, and then they hugged fiercely, and a tear slid down her beautiful face as the realization finally registered to her what she had been missing in her life. Friendship, true unconditional friendship, and it felt good.

"Enough!" said Jacqueline, wiping her tears briskly aside. "Sit with me Jake?" she asked. Jake sat beside her, and took her hand. "It's been far too long Jacqueline, too many lost years, but welcome home." he said tenderly.

I have a million questions, though they can all wait I guess. Just know that we feared for you, and missed you terribly in our grief!" muttered Jake.

"Thank you!" Jacqueline's voice was husky now. "I am so very sorry Jake! If I had a choice, or a way out, I would never have acted like I did! Please forgive me?" Jacqueline pleaded with her eyes, her voice broken.

"Nothing to forgive Jacqueline. At least you are home safe now once again!" he replied. "Jake, did you marry Anne?" Jacqueline asked. "Sure did!" replied Jake. "Best thing I ever done, she is one person who won't wait one minute to see you once I tell her you are home!"

"We were both so sorry to hear about … Jacqueline stopped him. "Not now Jake please! Not here. Please tell Anne I will come to her, I have much to tell you both!"

"Ok Jacqueline, I will ring her to tell her you are home though, and tell her your wishes." Jake said. "I should go to do that now before someone else does!" he said, as he rose to leave. "Jake!" called Jacqueline, and he turned back. "Thank you!" she said, her eyes brimming with tears. "It will be fine Jacqueline, you will see!" he said.

Jacqueline pressed her fingers to her temples.
Casting her mind back over the years.

*'Much to tell but where to start?' she thought.*

## APRIL RAIN

'On looking back reliving events of my past life'
I found that the happiest times were the easiest to recall when I was young, full of life, and so in love with my soul mate. *'Reagan Chase.'*

'However my living nightmare was the darker side of my life that was very difficult to relate as it stayed deeply suppressed within me in a state of rebellion as I struggled to come to terms with it.'
  *'I have to tell them, I owe them an explanation.'*
  *I thought 'That is why I am here.'*

*So my thoughts drifted back in recollection.*

# JENNY MAC

# APRIL RAIN

## Chapter 20
*Cutting of the Wattle ... Garden Party ... Year 1961 ...*

We witnessed all the brilliant colours of the dawn breaking from the sunroom of our house, as the great orb rose in all its glory, and broke through to scatter the last bank of clouds with its presence. The sky brightened, and cleared instantly, to become the deepest blue I had ever seen. Proof was evident as it came with a blessing, and a promise of a magic day.

There was a buzz of activity all around the property, workmen were setting up tents around a huge marquee which took pride of place at the center of the action, fire pits were being tended to, and large sides of beef were already being placed on the spits to cook. Seating, and trestle tables were being set up in tented areas, or on the lawns where shade was provided from the huge gum trees. As the majority of our guests were staying over for the two day events, make-shift toilets, and showers were erected in the camping areas.

*"And now it begins!"* stated Father, as he looked out over his property with pride. "I am so very proud of you Jackie! You have done such a marvelous job with all the organization, but it is not over yet!" "Yes I know Father, and thank you, but I was only the assistant!" I replied, with a giggle. "Yes but a damn good one!" he laughed.

We had in store a gala event. A new sensation for our invited guests, and our celebration would be something that people would always remember around Shallow Siding for many years to come.

## JENNY MAC

I suddenly felt overcome with a deep sense of pride at what I had achieved personally. For the first time, I had stepped into a new role on a much larger scale, working beside Father learning more about organization, and the whole business side of running the property, and of course, his pet hobby, the entertainment. Father reveled in entertaining his business associates, and friends.

Many months of preparation, and hard work had taken place in arranging this event, I recalled, as I made my way through the house to the steps, which led out to the lawns, and gardens. Now it is time to enjoy the fruits of our labour.

Everything had eventuated from one special meeting called by Father, and was to be held in the sunroom of our house. Mary had arranged the pencils, and paper at every place setting for ten people. As the friends, who were an essential part of our plans for success, arrived at the front verandah for the meeting, Mary escorted them all through. Emily Banks was in the kitchen preparing a luncheon for everyone, as we expected the meeting to cover some many hours.

Mother, and Father took their places and as I watched from my seat next to Father, he rose to greet everyone.

His presence was so overpowering, his chin jutted out oozing his dominance, and self- pride, but the look in his eyes was of pure excitement as he spoke.

"Good morning to you all, welcome! Thank you for coming!" he started. "Good Morning Clayton!" everyone replied, and Father added. "No need for me to tell you all what this means to me, and as you all know I have been waiting for some rain before I cut the wattle to make the process easier. However I think the bark will be easy to strip now, so it is time to cut, and our quick movements are needed. 'I guess that I have been lucky!' Father said, and everyone laughed. We will have a lot of organizing to do, and a huge party to arrange for the celebration! I hope I can rely on all of you for your help, who is in favour?" Father asked. There was a show of hands as everyone committed. "Good, thank you all, let us proceed. Mel, can you ask Emily, and Mary to join us please, they are involved too." he said.

When everyone was seated Father resumed talking again. "Ok everyone listen up. I will be splitting this all into areas, and appointing one of you people to be in charge of those areas. When I call your name, we will discuss your role, and also any questions you have."

"Make specific notes for yourselves on the paper provided! All clear?" he asked. "Yes Clayton all good!" everyone chimed in.

"Right then! We will commence with the cutting first. I will be hands on for the cutting, my responsibility will be to section off the mature trees to be cut, arrange all transport for them, the bark, and a timber mill, and refinement center to send them to. I plan to hire over one hundred people for the cutting, bark stripping, and extra staff that I will require during the cutting. I will be arranging their positions, and pay structures. Because of the huge numbers, the workers will have their own wind up party at the completion of the cutting, and they will be packed up, and gone from here by the time we have our celebration here at the homestead, where I will be holding an invitation only, two day event for my invited guests."

"Mick Jones!" Father called out. "Yes Boss? Good morning Mel, Jackie, everyone." he said. We all replied to Mick, and Father went on. "Big job for you Mick, as overseer your role is major, and consists of the cutting, and the events for the entertainment at our party. Make a note of that. I want you to utilize our existing staff as your back up team to maintain a consistent flow in the cutting, and they are to supervise all the breaks, meal hours etc., Happy workers are good workers Mick. The cutters I hire will be doing the cutting, and the stripping, so get your team to clear the tracks down the sides of the wattle so the trucks can be loaded. Send the bark to the drying shed when it is stripped, and the trees will be loaded onto a semi-trailer, check all machinery, and tow ropes etc., Also Mick, for our party we will hold camp drafting, and horse races so I need the cattle, and horses brought in, and get some good riders to put on a show for the guests! Any questions?" asked Father.

Everyone watched as Mick's face paled under the instructions Father put forward, then surprisingly he started to laugh, as did everyone, and in his mirth he shook his head saying. "No doubt about you Boss! You don't leave a stone unturned, but I'm up to it. I will do the best job I can for you. Questions! I don't have any, I think you have covered it all. I will know where to come if I need advice!" said Mick. "Thanks Mick, good man!" said Father.

"Jeffery, Mitchell Stringer, and Roy Anson!" Father called. "Yes Clayton!" they all replied. "Jeffery, and Mitch have offered their services to help with the horse events for the party, so I've teamed them with Roy."

"Jeffery, I will have a room for you both to share in the house!" Father said. "Thank you Clayton!" replied Jeffery. "Might be better Roy if you use the outer stables for events, none of my horses from the inner stables will be used. You will be in total control of the upkeep of all the horse's requirements, utilize our existing staff, if you need more men, just let me know." "Jeffery, if you could arrange a timetable for events, morning, and afternoon for the two days, we will have some camp drafting, short course horse racing, and of course the mile race."

"You will need to map out a course, it will be your sole responsibility to arrange the events, the timetables, the riders, and the announcements, and also the prizes. I will give you a list for the prizemoney when the time comes, any questions?" Father asked. "No, all good!" said Jeffery, and Roy.

"I have only one question, Mister Coby!" Mitch spoke out. "Aren't you entering Sailor in the racing this time?" "It appears not Mitch!" said Father.

They all looked at me, but said nothing, so Father continued on. "Ashton and Emily Banks and Mary!" "Yes Clayton!" The Bank's replied. "Yes boss!" replied

Mary. "No doubt your jobs will be enormous. Ashton, total charge of staff in your galley for the cutting for all meals, let me know how many more staff you need. For the breaks, Emily can take over cakes, scones etc., and for the workers party set out down at the huts, I would like you all to work down there, a big feast, drinks, and some music."

"Emily, for my guests on the lawns, I want you, and Ashton to work together. You are in charge of the house kitchen, Ashton in charge of the spits. Use our staff here, but let me know how many extras you need, and just remember serve plenty of food including morning, and afternoon teas on the lawns, and I want you both to compile a list of stores needed. Mary, you are in charge of the wait staff on the lawns. Any questions?" asked Father. "Are ya sure 'bout that Boss?" asked Mary. "Yes Mary, quite sure!" said Father. "Thank ya Boss!" she said. "We are fine Clayton!" said Emily, and Ashton.

"Jackie!" "Yes Father!" I replied. "Get your pencil ready, yours is a huge list. Firstly, I have advertised through the bigger town's newspapers for workers for the cutting, and bark stripping of the wattle, if you could take over the communication for those, and get some numbers back to me. Invitations to my guests, I will get a list to you, if you could do that please. Also I will need to know who confirms, and if they are staying over."

"I will need some flyers made up to put around town for hiring cutters, and staff for the kitchen, and grounds, they could also be included in the invitations, we should be able to pick up a host of interested workers." he said.

"I also would like a billboard made up for the front entrance! Has anyone any ideas on that?" Father asked.

Emily Banks immediately remembered when just recently Axel Hall had arrived knocking at her door.

It was her birthday, and Axel very sheepishly offered her a gift that he had made. It was a black, and white sketch of the creek, and the landscape at Shallow Downs framed in old timber that he had found, but very nicely sanded, and stained. She remembered how modest he was when she commented on the talent he had, and thanked him for the gift. "I will cherish this always!" she had said.

So now she spoke out as she looked up at Clayton. "Clayton you might be interested to know that Axel Hall does really good art work, and sketches, I could show you one that he made for me if you like." said Emily.

"Thank you Emily! That is a real surprise!" "Have a talk to Axel, and have a look at his work Jackie, see what you think!" said Father. "I will go over, and see him Father!" I replied. "Finally Jackie, we need to hire a good band for the two days, you had better get that booked early. I will give you an exact date in a week. Any other type of entertainment that you think is required, I will leave up to you. Also Jackie, if you could arrange some music for the workers party please that would be good!" Any questions?" Father asked.

"No Father, I'm fine." I replied.

"Right then that wraps it up for now, I will get some exact dates back to you all within the week. Let us have lunch, and we can all get back to work, and once again, thank you all!" said Father.

Lunch was served amidst the friendly chatter as ideas were tossed around the table. Everyone realized the huge task that was put before them all, and they were all excited to be a big part of it. When lunch was over they started to disperse one by one until only Jeffery Stringer, and Mitchell Stringer remained, and Jeffery spoke up.

"Clayton, if it is fine with you, I might drive around that first paddock while I am here. I want to visualize where the best place would be for the mile race, might give me a few ideas." "Sure Jeffery, good idea!" replied Father. "Excuse me Father, Mister Stringer, Mitch, but I must go over to see Axel now, so I will see you all later." I said, as I got up to leave. "Good idea Jackie, see if you can look at Axel's work!" said Father. "I will father." I replied. "Goodbye Jackie!" said Jeffery Stringer, and Mitch replied absently. "Yes, see you Jackie."

As I reached the front verandah I paused as I heard Mitch call to me. "Wait up Jackie!" he was calling, as he hurried to catch up to me. "What is it Mitch?" I asked.

"There is something I have to ask you, can we talk for a while?" he asked. "Sure Mitch, take a seat." I said, as I sat down on the verandah settee, and Mitch sat in the chair opposite me. "What is it you want to ask me Mitch?" I asked. "Well Jackie, it's about Sailor!" he said, with real concern. "What about Sailor, Mitch?" I asked.

"I can't believe you aren't riding Sailor in the big race!

I just wanted to know why?" he asked. "Oh that!" I tried to pass it off with a laugh, which didn't convince Mitch, he knew me so well. "Yes that!" he said. "Well Mitch, you may have noticed I have a lot to do for Father, and we have lots of guests to look after. Besides it is time I started acting like a lady! Don't you think?" I asked.

As I looked up into his handsome face, I witnessed a transformation in his features. Something clouded his deep blue eyes, and his face seemed almost to have a look of bewilderment, but something else was there too, a tenderness overcome him to soften his voice, and I will always remember the words he said to me.

"Jacqueline Coby, if there was ever another girl more of a lady than you, then that would surprise me. You are a lady always no matter what you do, so don't lose track of who you are Jackie! You should ride Sailor, like you always have!" he said.

I was so taken by surprise that my reply felt shaky. "I can't this time Mitch. I am committed, but there will be other times!" "I hope so! Is that a promise!" he asked. "It is a promise Mitch!" I said.

Then as an afterthought, he added. "Well how about you let me ride Sailor for you Jackie?" "Mitch! A great idea, but somehow I don't think Sailor will allow you to do that!" I replied, with a giggle. "So let's go, and find out then, shall we?" Mitch asked, with a wide grin.

"That, I would love to see Mitch!" I said, and laughed as I pulled him up. "Let's go then." I said.

# JENNY MAC

APRIL RAIN

## Chapter 21

Sailor was in the first paddock. He whinnied, and tossed his beautiful head in the air when he heard me calling him, then he reared up high, stretching, and pawing at the sky with his hooves, then came down fast with his long mane flowing in the breeze, and pranced towards me where I stood beside Mitch at the gate of the holding yard. "You are a show off!" I said, as he came to suddenly to a halt, and moved in close to nudge me, and nuzzle my jacket.

I placed my hand on his velvet nose, and stroked him lovingly, and thrilled to the smell of him as I kissed him there. He snorted, it was his usual way of telling me that he liked that, and I laughed. "I can see this is going to be a huge task!" said Mitch, as he moved closer.

Ever so gently Mitch reached out to Sailor with the back of his hand towards his forehead, and stroked him softly. He whispered to him as he moved his hand down towards the smoothness of his velvet muzzle, leaving it there so Sailor could smell him, and at the same time in a smooth stroking action, his other hand crept out along his neck. 'It was a very good start' I thought, as Sailor snorted his approval. Mitch looked at me to say. "I want you to move outside the yard now Jackie so I can to try some things!" So I walked out though the gate, closing it as I went, and climbed up onto the railings.

Mitch turned to Sailor, whispering to him in a voice so soft, I could barely hear his words. Sailor was alerted, and stood still as Mitch inched his way towards him, with his hand outstretched. Sailor backed off, and Mitch stopped, turned his back on him, and walked away, and Sailor took a step forward.

The cat, and mouse game continued on as Mitch continuously whispered to him, and he moved in closer. I was so amazed with the patience that Mitch had as he persisted, until finally Sailor permitted him to touch him.

A closeness evolved between the two as Sailor tossed his head. Mitch grabbed his mane pulling his head down to caress him with the tenderness of a lover, and ran a hand down his leg to lift his hoof, replacing it as he patted his chest. In the same movement he stroked his back as he grabbed his mane, and was on Sailors back in one agile movement. Sailor shivered.

Mitch looked over to me laughing. "Well that was eas...ee!" he called, as he was airborne. Landing with the gracefulness of a cat, and rolling back onto his feet, he was back on Sailors back before I could ask how he was.

It was a battle of wills but after the third throw, Mitch said. "Get me a bridle please Jackie!" So I went to get it but giggled as I handed it over. At that time, I relished in seeing a side of Mitch that he had kept to himself. 'I've known him all my life, our bond is special.' I thought, then realization hit me that Mitch was grown up, almost a man now. Unlike Reagan, who was much older so self-assured, and positive! Mitch was still feeling his way!

Meticulous in his actions Mitch persevered, and went

through the whole process again until he had the bridle on, then he called. "Open the gates Jackie!" I swung the gates wide as he jumped on Sailors bare back, and then goaded him into a full gallop, on out towards the open paddocks. I waited endlessly, then finally I noticed the two bedraggled figures coming back, both were lathered in sweat, and just completely exhausted. Although as I watched with great pride for Mitch, and his efforts, I couldn't help but notice with a pang of jealously as he dismounted to hug my horse, that they were one. Mitch Stringer had won him over. "Well done Mitch, you were amazing!" I said laughing. "Thank you Jackie, but you had better get him seen to, we've had a big workout!" he said. "I will do that now!" I replied.

Jacqueline, and Mitch left Sailor over at the stables in the care of Roy Anson, and they headed back towards the homestead chatting as they walked. Jacqueline was quite puzzled by everything that had taken place, she sensed a change in Mitch she had not noticed before.

"You know what I think Mitch?" I queried, looking up at him. "What's that Jackie?" he asked. "You have such a real special way with horses! You have surprised me immensely today, wherever did you learn all those skills? I think you have a huge talent, a gift! Maybe that might be your calling in the future!" I stated.

Mitch laughed, and replied. "Thank you Jackie, I do spend lots of time with our horses at home, so I guess I have learnt a bit. As to the future, who knows? But the thought has crossed my mind!" *"I think I'll call you the horse whisperer!*" I replied with a giggle. Mitch laughed at that, joining me in my joke. Then he got serious.

"Jackie, I would like to enter Sailor in the mile race if you agree, and I would also like to ask your Father's permission as well, so what do you think?" he asked. "I looked into his blue eyes as I said. "Mitch, I cannot think of another person who I'd like to ride Sailor more than you. You do have my blessing, and besides no-one else could ride him!" I said, with a giggle. Mitch laughed. "Thank you Jackie I'll take care of him, and come out to practice every day. You could come out and watch us!" Mitch said. "I may do that Mitch, a good idea! Oh look Mitch, Father is on the verandah, we can talk to him now!" I said. "Good idea! Then I should go, and help Father!" said Mitch. We topped the verandah, and Mitch told Father what we had done, and asked if he could ride Sailor in the race. Father laughed out loud, as he said. "Good job Mitch, if you rode Sailor, I take my hat off to you, well done! Of course you can ride him!"

Reagan Chase arrived in a swirl of dust as he drove the land rover up the driveway of the homestead, and braked in the shade of a huge Jacaranda tree at the front entrance. We watched from the verandah as he walked towards the house.

His dark hair fell free when he lifted up his hat, the sunshine picking out the hint of auburn. His deep green eyes sparkled, as he flashed his magic smile at us, and climbed the stairs. *'He is so beautiful!'* I thought.

"Good afternoon all! Special meeting is it?" he asked.

# APRIL RAIN

"Hello Mister Coby, Mitch!" he said, as he held out a hand to them. "Hello Jacqueline it is so good to see you." he said, as he smiled down at me. "Hello Reagan, what a surprise. I thought that you said you would be busy this week?" I asked. "Yes well I have been, but I was close by working on our windmill so I thought I would come and say hello!" he said. "Hello Reagan, good to see you!" Father replied. "Well I guess we are having a type of meeting! Mitch here has just mastered the stallion, so he is going to ride him in the big race!" Father replied.

"Well done Mitch, a mean feat that was!" he said. "Yes! It wasn't easy Reagan!" said Mitch, as he rose.

"Excuse me everyone, I've promised Father I'd help to mark out the race track, I'll catch you all later!" he said. "Bye Mitch!" we all replied.

"Well I must go to see Axel, would you come with me Reagan?" I asked. "You bet!" he replied. So we walked across the paddock, and I thrilled to Reagan's touch as he put an arm around me. It was so good to see him, and we chatted, and laughed out loud, but our laughter was cut short as we approached the bungalow and heard the shouting. "What is going on here Jackie?" Reagan asked, as we reached the front steps. "I am not sure Reagan, but I guess we will find out soon enough now we are here!" I said, as I knocked loudly on the front door.

Axel Hall sat out the back of his bungalow at a makeshift table that he had made out of scrap timber, and the top was elevated so that he could place paper on it at eye view. He was working on a new experiment.

# JENNY MAC

Initially the special interest that was sparked in him started by chance, when he commenced working with charcoal that he retrieved from his outback fire, and he had walked around the property retrieving all types of leaves, that he sketched onto old tins, until he had all the images to perfection. Since then he had progressed to pencils, and proper paper, which was his first purchase when he had saved enough money. He was attempting something harder now, and he was excited about it.

"What! ya still at that?" yelled Deakan, as he framed the back door, then jumped down the steps into the dirt.

"Always wastin time on that rubbish, look at all yor tin cans!" he said, as he gave some a kick. "An all these old leaves!" he brushed them angrily to the ground.

"What's the point of it all Dad, ya crazy?" he asked.

Axel quickly jumped up off his seat in anger, he was getting tired of his son's outbursts, and as he stood up, he noted that they were the same height now, and Deakan was just developing far too quickly for his own good. He had become defiant, disrespectful and abusive, he had a horrible, violent temper, and was a real bully.

"Pick up me leaves there Deakan, an me tins, they be important to me work, an I'll not have ya interfering!" said Axel. "What work? Ya be workin for The Coby's old man, or hav ya forgotten, an I aint pickin um up!" yelled Deakan. "It is me intrest, ya will pick um up Deakan or I be reporting ya to the Boss, ya won't be so smart if ya hav no work, an then ya will have no money ta spend." Axel yelled back, as he heard a knock on his front door.

# APRIL RAIN

Deakan Hall filled the doorway, and the door was flung back from my reach. "Well if it's not Miss Jacqueline Coby come ta visit us, an the boyfriend too, Mister Reagan Chase!" he slurred, leering at us with an angry, and screwed up face. "Slumin taday are ya Miss Jacqueline, well what ya want then?" he asked rudely.

Reagan topped the steps in two strides, he had heard enough. He towered over Deakan, and glared at him as he spoke. "Do not ever speak to Jacqueline like that again Deakan! Do you hear me?" he stated angrily. "If Clayton Coby heard how disrespectful you are being to his daughter, I know that his disapproval would be so evident that you would experience the full force of his wrath. Now you just step aside, Jacqueline has been sent here by her Father, and she would like to speak to Axel thank you!" Reagan said, his voice full with authority.

Deakan was about to retaliate but his Father spoke up quickly. "Stop it Deak, leave us now!" he turned to face us both with a sad look upon his face. "I am sorry Miss Jacqueline, and so sorry Reagan." he apologized. "Please come inside!" he said.

As we followed Axel into his modest front room, we heard the loud bang as the front door slammed shut and the timbers rattled, shaking the bungalow with force.

"What is going on Axel?" asked Reagan. "Reagan, I be so embarrassed, but the truth is now I hav lost control of Deakan. He just be so angry all the time, an I don't know what ta do, he don't listen ta me anymore!" Axel replied.

"Well I know what to do Axel. I'm sorry, but I will be

reporting Deakan's behaviour to Mister Coby!" said Reagan kindly. "Ya do whatever ya havta do Reagan, I hav tried, but I don't know what else ta do. He is getting worse an he frightens me with his temper. I am so sorry Miss Jacqueline!" said Axel.

"Thank you Axel, though it is no fault of yours. But maybe you should have brought this problem to my Fathers attention long before if you are having trouble!" I replied. "Yeah should hav. It be on me mind a lot, jus too shamed!" he said. "My Father has asked me to come to speak to you Axel. As you know we are arranging a Garden Party at the big house for Father's guests after the cutting of the wattle. Missus Banks has told us that you do very good art work, and Father would like me to look at your work if that is possible Axel?" I asked.

At the mention of his art work, Axel's face lit up like a neon sign, and he jumped up quickly. "Come Miss Jacqueline, come Reagan! I will show ya, is out the back!" he beckoned, and led the way to his makeshift art area where he then proceeded to haul out a very large tin from underneath his table. "Is only my drawins, an only in black an white!" he said, almost apologetically as he lifted them gently from the tin. Then one at a time, he spread them out across the table.

What we saw before us was unbelievable, and just too hard to comprehend. Axel had managed to capture on paper the very life, and essence of our property with his black, and white drawings. There were animals, and the flowing creek, wattle trees, and the landscape sketches, a true showcase of Outback Australia. I gasped, and my eyes locked on Reagan's, and his dumbfounded face.

"My goodness Axel, these are really good sketches! Do you know how very good you are?" I asked. "Really? Miss Jacqueline, are ya sure?" he asked in doubt. "There is no doubt about it Axel, you have a real talent!" I said.

"Don't you think so Reagan?" I asked. "Axel, believe me when I tell you that I have never seen work as good as this. My Uncle Richard is an avid lover of good art. I am betting he will be one of your first customers when I tell him!" Reagan replied. "That would be after Shallow Downs, Reagan!" I giggled in reply.

"Axel Hall! I would formally like to hire you as our artist for Shallow Downs! Are you interested in that?" I asked. "Am intrested a lot Miss Jacqueline if ya think I be good'n'ough!" he said. "You sure are Axel."

"Firstly though, I will need some flyers for around town, just mainly advertising, with a small amount of artwork. I will get some wording back to you, and how many you need to do!" I said.

"The main job for you however, will be to create some artwork on a large welcome sign at the front entrance for the Garden Party to celebrate the cutting of the wattle. If you could draw up a rough sketch as to what you would like to paint, and show it to me for approval, then I will buy all the coloured paint you will need, and brushes, easels etc., material, and timber for a frame! Father will pay you accordingly Axel! What do you think?" I asked.

"Me thinks tis the best thing that's happened to me in

me life Miss Jacqueline, only I hav one problem! I hav never painted with real paint or colour! Axel replied with a dejected look on his face. "Don't you worry about that Axel, you will be fine. I will buy you a colour wheel, and then show you how to mix colours, and after some practice, you will be showing me I don't doubt!" I said laughing. "Thank ya Miss Jacqueline, I'll do me best work for ya!" he said.

Jacqueline looked at the weather-beaten face of Axel Hall, and his wiry physique seemed to lift in pride. 'Such a modest reserved and polite person!' she thought to herself. 'He doesn't deserve the treatment he is getting from his son!' His excitement was so evident when he flashed a smile that lit up his elated face. His long hair fell into his dark eyes which misted over, and a tear slid down his cheek. Jacqueline felt so happy for him. "I know you will do good work Axel. I think it may be the first job of many for you!" I said. "Thank ya so much Miss Jacqueline, I won't let ya an the Boss down!" he replied. "Thank you Axel but we must go now, keep in touch, and I imagine you can expect a visit from Father!" I said. "Yes Miss Jacqueline!" Axel said, as we walked to the front door.

We strolled across the paddocks heading towards the stables where I noticed Father outside talking to Roy Anson, he was about to get in the Jeep, so I called to him. "Father! Wait!" He looked up, and waved to us. "Father, I have hired Axel for the sign, and the flyers. Wait till you see his work, it's unbelievable!" I said as we joined him. "That is just great news Jackie, well done!" Father replied. Reagan cleared his throat ready to speak.

"Mister Coby, there is something that you must know, and I do not think you will be very happy about what I am about to tell you either!" he said.

Fathers face flushed, his eyes darkened in annoyance as he listened to Reagan telling him about Deakan's behaviour, not only to us, but to his Father too. "Well I will sort this out quick smart!" Father replied, as a fierce scowl set on his face. "Jackie, go home with Reagan now, I will go over to see Axel, and take the young boy with me for a talk, thank you both for telling me!" Father said as he called out to Roy. Roy poked his head out from the stable doors. "Yes Boss?" he asked. "Send young Deakan out to see me Roy!" he stated. "Ok Boss, he's working inside." said Roy. "We will go now Father!" I said. "See you Mister Coby!" said Reagan. "Ok then!" Father said.

As I looked back I could see Deakan walking out from the stable doors. Father at once pointed to the spare seat in the Jeep, and with his face set like stone, he climbed into the driver's seat himself beside him.

His overpowering frame made Deakan Hall look like a dwarf, but it was his booming voice that startled me as it seemed to even raise above the engine as he started it, and I could almost guess what kind of dressing down Deakan Hall was getting from my Father.

# JENNY MAC

## Garden PARTY

*'The Year'* ... 1961 ...

## Chapter 22

I stood poised on the steps leading down to the lawns where I was to greet our guests, and my eyes drifted over all the early activity, and came to rest on a solitary figure amidst the early arrivals who slowly progressed through the front portals entrance to the Shallow Downs Homestead to head towards the lawns, and the cutting of the wattle Celebration Party. Suddenly able to break free from the press of all the people, he started to stride out across the lawns straight towards me, and I felt I was seeing him for the first time. Not someone I had known all my life, who I shared a close bond with as we grew up, to become one of my very best friends.

*'He is the epitome of Country life, a real Cowboy.'*

I thought, as I watched his tall lean frame dressed in riding leathers stretching out to expose such strong leg muscles with each movement he made.

His arms worked beneath the cut-out sleeves of his shirt, and his muscled biceps rippled as he balanced a saddle upon his shoulders. A country style cowboy hat seemed to complete the outfit, and sat at a jaunty angle over his deep blue eyes, but something about the look in those eyes sent a shiver through me as they seemed to light up as he looked up at me. His white teeth flashed against the tanned face as his mouth widened to a huge grin when he waved. My intake of breath seemed almost dormant as I gasped, and with relief I exhaled, and was barely able to recover in time to answer him.

"Hey Jackie come down, and see what I've got!" he

called, and I walked down the steps.

"Wow. You look stunning this morning Jackie! I guess my prize is going to be much sweeter, and well worth the wait! I will have to work my butt off to stake my claim!" he said. "Whatever are you rambling on about Mitch. What prize are you raving on about, and what is with the saddle?" I asked, with a giggle.

Mitch looked at me long, and hard, then laughed as he said. "Why, the prize is you Jackie!" I was not too sure where this conversation of ours was going. I knew he was teasing, and I giggled as I replied. "Please explain Cowboy?"

"That's just it, you've hit the nail on the head. For two days I will be a Cowboy fighting to win the prize, only difference is, if I win I will forfeit my prize money to a charity for a dance with you!" "Do I have a deal?" he asked, as he looked deeply into my eyes. "Well I guess when you put it that way Mitch, how can I refuse?" I replied. "Great!" he said, as a huge grin spread across his face. "Now this is my surprise!" he said, as he pulled the saddle off his shoulder. "Wow! What a beautiful saddle Mitch!" I said, as I took particular notice of the detail in the leatherwork, and then the big letters J.C. handwritten in gold. "It's amazing!" "I am pleased you like it Jackie, I had it made especially for you, it's yours, but I would like to use it in the big race if I could, it is made for racing, but I would rather see you use it in the future!" he said with meaning.

"Really Mitch? You had this made for me? How very

sweet of you, I can't seem to find the words to express my gratitude, only to thank you! I will cherish it always, and of course I will use it!" My reply was rather husky, and I looked up to his face. "Come on now Jackie it's only a saddle!" he said "Let's not get all sentimental, we have work to do!" he said, as he laughed, and I laughed with him. "I guess you are right there Mitch. Good luck with your events, I will be watching."

"Oh! By the way Mitch, what was all the confusion at the entrance when you arrived?" "Thank you Jackie! The confusion? Oh! Everyone was milling around admiring the sign that Axel painted, looks like it's a big hit with the guests. Your Father will be pleased." he replied.

Axel Hall was beside himself with pleasure as he sat at his new easel applying the finishing touches to his painting for the front entrance sign at Clayton Coby's Garden Party, a celebration event for the cutting of the wattle. Axel just felt such an enormous new sense of achievement, and pride. He had almost completed this new task, and he was so very proud of it.

True to her word Jacqueline Coby had left no stone unturned. She ordered the timber, and metal required, even nails, and a new carpenter set. There were different coloured paints to mix, even an easel and a colour wheel which she had shown him how to use so he could make his own colours, and she had personally taken the horse, and wagon to town to pick it all up, and delivered it all to him. He savoured the memory of showing Jacqueline his sketch for approval, and her reaction to what he had come up with. "Oh! Yes please Axel. This will be just absolutely marvelous, you are a genius, please go ahead! Father will just love it!" Jacqueline had said.

His vision was of flowering wattle trees out in the foreground, something he had studied intimately, the bright yellow standing out to attract the eyes, and guide the viewer to the center, which was a window into his painting of The Garden Party with people and tents, and activity everywhere, and horses being ridden along the track beside the railings. *The painting depicted a Gala Event.* Axel nearly fell from his stool as the voice spoke out behind him.

"Tis good Dad!" said Deakan loudly, and Axel turned around to face him thinking he must have heard wrong, as his son's behaviour had been anything but friendly towards him lately. "What was that ya said Deak?" he asked. "The paintin, tis good!" Deakan said. "Thank ya Deak, it's good to hav some support." said Axel.

Deakan lounged in the doorway, the usual sneer missing from his face as he smiled down at his Dad. *'The ol fool.'* he thought. 'Paintin's good, but I'd love ta smash it. Damn Coby's an their fancy Garden Party, I'd love ta mash that too.' he thought.

Deakan had come to realize that he needed his Dad, for now anyway, so he deviously adopted a deception plan to fool his old man into thinking he was repentant, so he could get what he wanted, but only while it suited him to do so.

Clayton Coby had made it very clear to him what his

position on Shallow Downs was now, and Deakan was skating on thin ice. Clayton had really raked him over the coals, giving him such a grueling and displaying his full wrath as he told him in no uncertain terms that he would give no quarter, at his next outburst or disrespect to anyone here at Shallow Downs, he would have him thrown off the property.

'That was somethin I would never forget, not ever.' he thought. 'Damn Clayton Coby, built like a mountin, an he throws his big weight around too. Who does he think he is, talkin to me like that?' 'Neva mind Clayton Coby your day will come. I'll get even, and somehow, some way, I'll get back at ya.' he thought. 'An I won't forget the precious Daughter either, or Mista Reagan Chase! The two that told tales about me to ya.'

*'I'll get even with them too.'*

He seethed inside, and he had to dig deep to suppress his anger which was at boiling point as he faced his Dad. "Would ya like to help me set up the sign at the entrance when it's fished Deakan?" his Dad was saying. "I should be finished this taday, maybe we can do that tomorra?" Axel asked with a hopeful look on his face. "Yeah sure Dad, whatever ya want!" Deakan replied absently, still trying to contain himself, and get in control.

B lissful chaos was the way to describe our Garden Party. Even though the first rays of sunshine were peeping over the hills and filtering through the trees, the atmosphere was already electric, and people arrived in droves now, some with their bedrolls, and others toting pillows, and personal items. As I walked amongst them, I found it impossible to greet them all so I decided to let them settle, wait for everyone to arrive, then greet them all from the microphone being set up on the small stage.

Everything was in order I noticed, as I made my way through the press of people in the pavilion, and I crossed the floorboards which was set up as the dance floor. All other tents were erected, pit fires ready to light for the night, tables, and seating arranged, the band was setting up, and tuning their equipment at one end of the pavilion where the huge chalk board stood out proudly marking the chain of events on offer, and timetables for over the two days. All the staff were busying themselves with their various jobs, and the cooking spits already in full operation as sides of beef rotated slowly above the coals, teasing the sense of smell with the aroma.

I noticed Father entering the tent at the other end, and we met at the stage. "It all looks good Jackie, I will just say a few words, and then you can take over, you have done a great job!" he said. "Thank you Father, it has been a pleasure!" I replied, and Father stepped out onto the stage. "Good morning everyone, I hope you all enjoy your two days of celebration here for the Cutting of the Wattle, welcome to Shallow Downs!" Father said, as he spoke into the microphone. "I will now let my Daughter Jacqueline explain the events we have in store for you, she has organized all your entertainment, thank you for coming, and enjoy!" he said.

Everyone clapped, and cheered very loudly as I took

# APRIL RAIN

Fathers place. "Welcome to our Garden Party everyone!"

"Firstly, those of you who are staying over, your tents are ready, just check the information on the chalk board over there, I pointed, and you will find which one you are allocated to. I also have a list there of all events, and the timetables for over the two days, and to keep you all amused I have arranged some games for in between the horse races, and the camp drafting.

So if anyone is interested in entering these events, just write your name on the sheets provided. For some fun, I have organized either a tennis round robin, or a euchre tournament, croquet, and darts. Morning, and Afternoon tea will be served throughout the lawns, lunch will be provided in the pavilion. In the evening the band will be playing, well actually, they will be playing throughout the day as well. After dinner is served we will have a parcel game to play where everyone here will have the opportunity to entertain us with either a song, dance, a poem or some act, determined by whatever parcel they choose, and then there will be dancing of course. Drinks are provided in the drinks tent. I hope you all have an enjoyable time, and thank you for being part of our celebration!" I said.

I was thrilled to hear the applause, and cheers, it was my very first speech, and I must admit that I was very nervous even though I was among friends. But it felt good, and I thanked them all. As I stepped down the first person to approach me was Reagan Chase. He had been listening to my speech, and then walked towards me.

"Really Jacqueline, that was good! You never cease to amaze me. One minute you are a typical country girl, the next an entrepreneur, is there no limit to your talent my love?" he asked. I smiled, as I looked up at him. He always had a way of complimenting me. *I loved him so.*

"Thank you Reagan, but I wouldn't go quite that far, though I did enjoy that immensely!" I replied. "You are here early Reagan, where is your Uncle?" I asked. "Yes, he is around here somewhere, most probably the stables. We came over early in case anyone wanted some help, but it looks as if you have it all under control! Just by your speech, I can tell you have everything available to entertain your guests, a big crowd too. I bet they will remember this Garden Party in many years to come!" he was saying as we got swamped by my closest friends Anne Giles, Rebecca Strickland, and Helena Ball, who had rushed to our sides.

Their excitement was infectious as they all jumped up and down, trying to speak all at once. "Settle down ladies, take it easy, there will be plenty of time for you to do what you want to do!" said Reagan, with a laugh.

"Hello Reagan, thank you kind sir for your advice!" said Anne as she giggled. "Thank you Anne, Hi Rebecca, Helena!" he replied. "Oh Jackie, this is going to be the best time ever, and a good speech too by the way!" said Anne. "Thank you Anne! Yes I am sure we will all have some great fun!" I replied. "Hi Reagan, Hello Jackie!" chimed in Rebecca, and Helena. "Hello, good morning Rebecca, Helena. I hope you have in those packs what you need to stay over, a room is made up next to mine for the three of you, so you can have the latest night ever if you wish to!" I said, as I laughed. "Sounds too good!" said Anne, the others agreed. "Reagan I will just show all the girls to their room to take their things up, shall I meet you back down here?" I asked.

"Yes, you go ahead Jacqueline!" he replied.

So in a way that only young girls could do, I whisked them away, and amidst all our giggles, and chatter as we joked together, we all proceeded towards the big house, toting their belongings.

Camp Drafting was quite a unique competition that thrived in the Outback, and a true Australian sport which tested the skill of the rider, and his horse as they worked selected cattle in a specific yard, and a course within the rules for points awarded.

As I returned with the girls, all activity was happening in the pavilion. I picked out Reagan's position, and gave him a wave, then we moved forward to meet up with him just as the announcement was blaring out an alert that Camp Drafting was first on today's agenda, and would commence in half an hour, and a final call announced for all riders entered in the first of the two day competition, to report to the yards.

"You are just in time ladies!" he said. "The events are starting soon!" "Aren't you entered in the camp drafting event Reagan?" asked Anne. "No Anne, I will watch the professionals at work, it is something I have never done before, so it will be interesting to watch!" he replied.

## JENNY MAC

Rows of seats had been arranged around the yards for the spectators, and with a rush of anticipation, the guests headed towards them for the best vantage points.

"Come on Jackie, shall we all go over now? We don't want to miss it!" said Rebecca, as Helena added. "Yes let's get a seat if we can!" "Let's go, and watch Mitch!" said Anne, full of enthusiasm. As we walked across the lawns I explained the rules, and concepts of the camp draft to Reagan. "The object is for the rider to maneuver his horse to cut out one beast from a mob of about eight cattle in the yard. He must turn the beast at least two times, proving to the judges that he has total control, then he calls for the open gates. He then drafts the beast around left, then right pegs in a figure of eight course in a larger yard. Once completed the rider guides the beast through a pegged gate, once gated, draft is complete, and points are awarded!"

Reagan's face took on an astonished look. "Wow Jacqueline, I didn't realize it would be so involved!" he said. "Yes Reagan it is a real test of horsemanship."

"It might also be a good time to tell you that Mitch has entered in everything, and we have a deal!" I said rather hesitantly. "What deal is that?" asked Reagan.

"He wants to donate all his prizemoney, if he wins any, to a charity!" I said. "Very generous, good for him!" said Reagan. "That is in return for dances with me!" I continued. I am sure Reagan's face paled, I did not think he was the jealous type, but he recovered quickly, and then spoilt it. "Then a deal is a deal, let's hope the band is playing a quickstep then." he said laughing.

The announcement for the first rider stopped my reply as the cattle were let out into the yard. I looked at Reagan, but he was too intent on the action to notice my concern as the rider cut his selected heifer out from the mob, and proceeded with his round. Great prestige was awarded to the winning horse, and rider of the camp draft event and the riders were very serious competitors.

Each ride for the two days could award them up to 100 points. Usually it was 26 points for the 'cut out' horse handling another 70 points and 4 points for the course. Points were awarded for horsemanship and for control of the beast, within a set time limit.

Disqualifications were for losing the beast more than twice on the course, losing control of the beast, or by running a beast onto the fence, and was signaled by the crack of the judge's stock whip.

Mitch rode in elegantly to a roar of cheers from the crowd, as he was introduced to the yard, and the girls beside me yelled out. "Go Mitch!" He turned his horse towards us. It bowed, and he tipped his hat to us, then proceeded his serious task of the cut out.

I took particular note of the bay mare he was riding, one of his own I noted. A good stock horse, agile, and alert, and very clever. Horse, and rider was groomed to perfection, the seriousness of the competition was set on Mitch's composed face until he coaxed her forward, and they became one, exploding into a flowing action.

## JENNY MAC

I could not help the feelings of huge pride that I was experiencing as I watched Mitch expertly cut out the heifer from the mob, and wheel it away, turning it three times, and in total control, as he faced the judges, and called for the gate. "That was neatly done!" said Reagan.

"He can ride this boy, I mean really ride, he looks like he's glued to that horse, and the horse is very good too, it is so quick to act on his demands. Let's hope he can maintain that form for his round, this is really good to watch." he said.

Reagan Chase never ceases to amaze me. 'He always gives credit where it is due.' 'I *guess that is why I love him so much.*' I thought. "I am pleased you are enjoying it Reagan." I said." "Quiet now Jacqueline, this is the difficult part, watch Mitch!" he said. Mitch was in his element, and loving it I noticed, as he maneuvered his mare to draft the heifer right, then left, in, and out the pegs of the eight figure course, then finally through the pegged gate. He stood up high in the stirrup irons, pumping his fist into the sky, and the crowd roared, and stood in ovation. "That was just spectacular Jacqueline, I cannot see anyone beating that round. If Mitch wins tomorrow, he will deserve his dance with you." Reagan said quite genuinely.

"So pleased you said that Reagan, but I would like to point out that Mitch will be riding Sailor in the mile race tomorrow as well!" I said, as I giggled. Reagan laughed. "He's a cunning rogue. I guess you, and I will have to do our dancing tonight then my lady!" he replied.

## APRIL RAIN

Stars amassed across the cloudless sky, the night air cool as darkness closed in, and the pit fires were being lit. Coloured lights altered the atmosphere as they twinkled throughout the pavilion, and gardens, and the music took us to a new place.

Reagan held out his hand, and then led me onto the dancefloor, and our bodies seemed charged as we came together, and he enfolded me into his arms, then I was lost in his embrace. I just felt so safe there, my heart pounded against his chest, and I thrilled to the scent of his body filling my head as I rested on his shoulder, as we swayed to the beat of the music. He moved his head to whisper into my ear. "I love you Jacqueline Coby!' he said softly. I looked into his eyes deeply. "I will always love you Reagan Chase!" I replied.

There was so much activity all around us, but we were oblivious to it all, as we were in another place where love enveloped our existence. Our minds were one, but our bodies wrapped together seemed to suffer a huge longing that shocked me deeply as I experienced these new unknown feelings that were surging through me from his touch.

We both started, and sprang apart when the voice boomed beside us. "Mind if we cut in!" Father said, as he tapped Reagan on the shoulder. "Yes for sure!" said Reagan, embarrassed. Mother saved the moment, and stepped forward as she said. "Let us dance Reagan!" then whisked him away. I looked up at my Father. "May I have this dance Jackie?" he asked. "The pleasure will be mine

Father!" I replied, as I held up my arms, and for a big man he guided me around the floor effortlessly. I was laughing as we swirled around and, he said.

"You know Jackie, you look so amazing tonight, you are a very beautiful girl, but just remember one thing, you are still young, try to hold on to that youth Jackie, it is most precious!" *'Was that a lecture I just had'* I thought, as I looked up to my Father's face which was already set in that way that he had.

*'Yes'* I thought. *'That was my lecture'*

I smiled up at him and giggled, as I said. "You do have a unique way of telling me things Father. But don't worry, I have Coby blood, and I think you, and Mother have both set the guidelines for me I think. You both just have to trust me!" "So it was that obvious Jackie was it?" Father asked. "Yes Father it was! But please know that I love Reagan Chase, and I will marry him one day!" I said, as I looked deep into his concerned eyes.

"Ok! Enough said now then Jackie. You are always so damn direct. I don't know where you get that from!" he said, as he laughed, and I laughed too, knowing exactly where my thoughts come from.

"I will trust your judgement Jackie, now let's have some fun!" he was saying, as he whirled me around.

"Thank you Father!" I said, as I looked over to where Mother, and Reagan were dancing, and talking, and I could imagine what was being said there.

"You dance beautifully Reagan!" Mel Coby said, as

they glided across the dancefloor. "You do too Missus Coby. I can see where Jacqueline gets it from. You, and Mister Coby have taught her just about everything I can think of, you must be so proud of her. You have a very beautiful, talented Daughter!" he said. "I am so pleased you mentioned Jackie, Reagan. We are so very proud of her, but she is still very young Reagan, she needs time to grow, and to reach her full potential. Sometimes in our youth we tend to forget all consequences which could change our futures!" Mel said. Reagan guessed what Mel Coby was trying to say to him. "Missus Coby, I love Jacqueline, and I would never do anything to hurt her, and I am hoping one day her future will be with me!" he said. "Thank you Reagan!" Mel said.

It was the final day of our Garden Party, not a cloud in the sky, and the sun in all its splendor, was a welcome sight as it broke through the trees instantly warming the cool, crisp air. There was so much activity everywhere, the pavilion was alive with the chatter, and much to the annoyance of the late night revelers who cupped their ears in despair, the loud speaker announcement blared out across the gardens. It was time for the mile race, and all riders, and their mounts were being called to the starting point.

I wanted to wish Mitch good luck so Reagan, and I walked across to the stables. Mitch was about to mount Sailor as we got there. Sailor was so well behaved, I couldn't help but admire Mitch for the way he handled him, and I guess a little of my heart cringed with regret as my thoughts were wishing it was me riding today.

"Hi Mitch!" I said, as I moved to Sailor, and took his beautiful head in my hands and kissed him on his velvet nose. Sailor snorted, and I laughed.

"Hi Jackie, Reagan!" Mitch replied. "Doesn't he look beautiful Jackie?" "He certainly does look wonderful Mitch, thank you, you have done a great job." Sailor was groomed to perfection, and his coat shone with a black brilliance. I looked at them both, and took particular notice of the colours that Mitch had chosen. Sailor had purple reins, and purple ribbons woven throughout his mane. The new saddle with my initials embossed sat neatly upon the purple saddle cloth, and Mitch was wearing a purple silk shirt, and black moleskins with a black, and purple cap, and black boots. I guess Mitch knew that purple was my favourite colour. I brushed away a tear, and said. "Good luck Mitch, do me proud!"

"I will Jackie, thanks. But luck is not going to come into it!" he said laughing. I laughed too. Reagan shook his hand. "Go well Mitch!" he said.

We went quickly to the starting point, and as we breasted the railings at the first paddock waiting for the contestants to gather, parade, and settle for the start, I couldn't help but notice the good job that Mitch, and his Father had done in setting out the racetrack.

Very appropriately the race track was shaped like a horseshoe, and every aspect of the mile race could be seen from our position, with the signed, and flagged finish line appearing after the final stretch.

Sailor was in his glory, he was prancing, and putting on a show for the crowd. He had done this many times with me on his back, but I couldn't help noticing that he didn't even seem to miss me. Mitch had him well in hand, and I could tell he was loving it too.

There were ten of them as they lined up. As the crack of a stock whip determined the start, they were away, and Sailor bounded forward in eagerness, but was soon checked by Mitch as he jostled for positions, guiding him over to the rails. Mitch sat Sailor like a real pro.

Horse, and rider seemed to be one, and Sailor, true to his naming, his hooves were sailing over the ground, as if he were flying. I laughed, thrilled with the sight of it.

"He is a magnificent animal, what a beautiful horse!" said Reagan, with the excitement of the race evident in his speech. "Look at Mitch! He is so switched on with horses, it is quite unbelievable, he has a talent that boy. I thought you always said that Sailor was too difficult to ride Jacqueline!" he asked. "Believe me when I tell you Reagan, that no one, but me, has ridden Sailor before, till Mitch. I think Sailor loves Mitch, Reagan!" I said, as I looked sadly into his eyes, and Reagan laughed loudly.

"Jacqueline Coby, I do believe you are jealous. I didn't think I would ever see the day that happened. Especially not of your horse loving someone else!" he taunted me, and I had to laugh too.

The excitement mounted towards the half way mark as a

few of the contenders made their moves, and the crowd went wild, cheering them all on, but it was all about Sailor at the top of the straight as he took the lead, and seemingly extended his flight even more, and drew away from the field to cross the finish line.

Then, as if it was his trademark. Mitch stood high in the stirrup irons, pumping his fist to the sky. He patted Sailor, and waved to the crowd, and as he passed us, he called. "That is one Jackie!" holding up one finger.

I laughed, I knew he was counting dances, and I called back. "Well ridden Mitch!" The whole crowd chanted! 'Mitch, Mitch, Mitch' Reagan, and I were breathless from cheering, and the excitement of it, and as the girls joined us we all chatted about the race as we walked over to the gardens for refreshments.

"Mitch was just so fabulous!" said Anne. "We have nearly lost our voices from all our cheering!" uttered Rebecca. "Wasn't Sailor great?" said Helena. "Yes Mitch, and Sailor have done us proud today!" I replied.

'We had so much fun that day. Things I have never forgotten.' Mitch won the second round of the Camp Drafting in style, making him the outright Camp Draft winner, and on his own horse, he won the short-course horse race. He was the big winner for events over both days, and was quick to remind me of our deal when he joined us that night in the pavilion, all showered, and changed. "I'll have you know Jackie! That makes three!" he said laughing. His outfit was loud, outlandish, but very Country. We all stared at him.

## APRIL RAIN

"I know that Mitch! And congratulations on all your wins, you never cease to amaze me, but what is with the outfit?" I asked. "Thanks Jackie! Well! I have good news first-hand that there will be a square-dance on tonight. Can you rustle up some Country Dancing Clothes?" he asked me, grinning with his widest grin.

I laughed. "Better come with me girls!" I said. "What about you Reagan. Do you have anything appropriate?" I asked. Reagan got up. "I will see what I have in the car Jacqueline, but they won't be as loud as Mitch's I'll bet!" he said laughing, as he walked off. "Don't worry about a shirt Reagan, I have a spare. A real bright one!" Mitch called. "Ok Mitch!" Reagan said, laughing.

Reagan almost reached the car park when he noticed someone lurking in the shadows, so he veered off the path to walk through the trees, and as he got closer he was surprised to see who it was. The intruder started in alarm, as Reagan spoke out from behind him. "What are you doing here Deakan?" Reagan asked. Deakan recovered his usual aloofness, and retorted rudely. "Ya mind yor own business Chase, I be just lookin, that's all, nothing ta do with ya, so git lost" "I think you are the one that should leave Deakan! This is a private party, invitation only! Do you have one?" he asked. "Ya no I don't Chase, damn Coby's wouldn't invite me!" he said.

"Then I would suggest you leave now, or would you like to speak to Mister Coby?" Reagan asked him. "Nah don't bother, am goin now, only be toffs here anyway!"

he said, pushing past Reagan to leave. *'He has got a huge problem that boy.'* thought Reagan, shaking his head as he watched him. Then walked to his Uncle's car.

When Reagan returned to the pavilion, amidst all the excitement from the girls who had returned wearing their special outfits, darkness was closing around them, and Jacqueline was busy organizing her four couples for the square-dance. "Reagan, I have partnered you with Anne, and my partner will be Mitch!" Jacqueline was saying, as she stood up to face him. Her exposed skin glowed, as thin straps held up the bodice of her green, and white polka dot dress which flared out with lots of petticoats from her waist to mid length. Green leather boots snaked up her calves to her knees, and a green cowgirl hat to match. "That leaves Rebecca, and Helena with Bob, and Sonny!" Jacqueline said.

"Beautiful!" said Reagan. "What is?" she asked. "You are!" he said. "Thank you kind Sir!" replied Jacqueline.

Dinner was served amidst the uproar of everyone chattering, presentations were awarded, and then to everyone's amazement some local talent showed as everyone competed fiercely in the parcel game. Then the band music changed as a fiddler started to play a real Country Rock Beat. A caller made an announcement for the Square-Dancing, and tables, and chairs were pushed aside to make room for extra teams. As I looked around, Mitch was standing before me. "Shall we show them all how it is done Jackie?" he asked, a huge grin on his face.

## APRIL RAIN

"I believe we will do just that Mitch!" I replied, with a giggle. "Come on team, get ready!" I said.

The moves set the pace, the caller in form as his voice boomed out loud, and the dancers were challenged to a real Country Hoedown. The pavilion bounced, the night was in full swing as everyone joined in.

It was late when they played the final song, and Mitch stood before me to claim his last dance with me. I took his outstretched hand and we laughed out loud together as we approached the dancefloor, but as he enclosed me in his arms some very strange feelings overcome me.

It felt so warm, so secure, in the circle of his arms. My smile paled. Then a seriousness overtook me, as I looked up into his eyes. What I saw there made me blush, and warm feelings rushed through me.

As the song finally ended we were just so oblivious to what was happening around us, we still stood looking at one another, just lost in the bond that we shared. Until so suddenly, a rush of well-wishers crowded around us for the finale, breaking the spell between us.

Mother, and Father joined us all, and people came up expressing their deep gratitude for their invitation to our Garden Party, and giving them accolades for its success.

Then everyone joined hands to start dancing around in a circle. It seemed that dancing was a huge connection for us Country people. I looked at Mitch as he laughed. I laughed too as he reached out for my hand, and then we both joined in the fun.

# JENNY MAC

*'The Hall' ... Shallow Siding ... The Year ...1962*

## Chapter 23

Ironically it had been at a dance in Shallow Siding that I had first met Jake Hardy during the more happier times in my life when we were very young. Jake was a fun-loving person who soon became an important part in our circle of friends. He was to become a very special, and dear friend to me personally, almost like the brother I never had, sharing some special years of my life.

Jake was just eighteen, and a total stranger to Shallow Siding when he had arrived looking for work, and was fortunate to get a position at 'The Siding,' and started work there. Initially to everyone, he was known as the new boy in town, however it was through my very best friend Anne Giles that I really got to know Jake Hardy.

Anne had first met Jake while working in her parent's bakery shop, and they had got to know one another as he became a regular, until Jake summed up the nerve to ask her to go out with him to a dance that was coming up on the events calendar in Shallow Siding.

Anne was just beside herself. I had never seen her so excited about anything before, and I could say that was an understatement. I knew at once, when she told me about Jake Hardy, and how she spoke of him, with her big brown eyes all lit up, that she had met her special someone. Particular emphasis, I recall, was required on selecting a specific colour for the material of her dress, and of course, I was requested to help her with the design so she could get it made up. We laughed together as we planned, and planned.

Anne wanted everything just right, and I was really looking forward to meeting this newcomer who had captured my best friend's heart.

I felt so happy for her, and in the following weeks leading up to the dance, many important decisions were made, as we giggled endlessly about them, and we were as close as two friends could ever be.

Eventually the big night for the dance had arrived, and everyone at the Homestead were making their final preparations to get ready. Mother had arranged for us to have some pre-supper delicacies, and drinks served in the sitting room before we left, and Emily was busy in the kitchen making the final preparations.

I walked down the steps with my high golden sandals tapping, as I stepped into the living room of our house.

My hair fell around me massed with curls entwined with green, and gold ribbons, and Mary was still fussing with my skirt. It was a green taffeta creation that fell full, to mid length from the waist, but underneath there were petticoats, lots of petticoats, and an edge of netting was exposed at the hem. The bodice was overlaid in a cream coloured lace but highlighted by the thin straps crossing over my shoulders, which was a new fashion out. It was a beautiful dress, and it made me feel very special.

I looked up to where Mother, Father, and Reagan were chatting while they waited for me. "All ready!" I said as I stepped out, and as they stood to greet me, I felt it was a special time in my life that I will always remember.

# APRIL RAIN

My heart swelled as I was overcome with love and pride as I looked at them. My parents, and the one I loved.

Finally, I had come to terms with my changing body, and I was growing up with new interests now, and a whole new outlook on my life. I was just absolutely, deliriously, and hopelessly in love with one Reagan Chase, and every moment that we spent together was a treasure to behold, our feet walking on the same path through the sands of time. I could never have imagined a love like ours ever happening during my lifetime, but I was living it, and loving every minute, and my life, my future, seemed mapped out before me with no question, and it was the happiest time of my life.

Deep feelings emerged within me, to surge through my body like some unknown power was possessing me, and finally, for the very first time in my life, I felt like a woman, and I was very pleased to be one too, as Reagan sauntered slowly towards me. *'He is just so beautiful.'* I thought. My heart thumped, just from the site of him, our eyes locked together, as he took my hands in his.

"Jacqueline you have a special beauty that is beyond all belief, you look radiant, and so lovely I could just eat you!" he whispered. "Best if you don't do that in front of Father!" I whispered. We laughed together then Reagan came back with his retort. "Exactly! Though the promise of a rain check is quite appealing I think, if you would agree?" he asked in a whisper, giving me a cheeky grin.

I couldn't help but giggle, and as I looked up to his face seeking his deep green eyes to give him my reply, a thought crossed my mind. 'What is it about Reagan Chase that I love?' I mused. 'He makes me come alive, and he excites me with his taunts, and jests. But more importantly, his desire makes me feel so young, and beautiful and my heart sings with feelings of importance from the love, and respect that he shows me.'

*He really is the perfect man.*' I thought.

"Quoting my Father's opinion now!" I whispered as I smiled. "That is a debatable issue, one to be discussed fully in the future!" I replied, with a giggle. "By the way Reagan, I think you look very handsome, and beautiful tonight too!" "Thank you for your kind words my lady." he said, with a bow. "I will think very carefully on what you have said!" he replied. We both laughed together as my parents moved up to join us, and my Mother smiled tenderly at me. "Jackie you look absolutely stunning!" said Mother. "Clayton, I think our little girl is all grown up now, and has now become a beautiful woman!"

My Father's face told it all, as usual, and the pride I saw there in his eyes just for me, was something special for a Daughter to see. As he spoke, once again I was reminded of how much love I had for my Father, and how I could never discredit him in any way.

"Jackie!" he said, as he walked towards me. "I can still remember the times I bounced you on my knee. They were special times, but none more special than looking at you now, and seeing how you've grown, not only into a beautiful woman, but a beautiful person Jackie! You have made your Mother, and me very proud parents!"

## APRIL RAIN

A tear slid down my cheek as I choked out my reply.

"Thank you Father, and Mother but it is me that is proud to be your Daughter!" Reagan didn't know where to look, he had not seen such a display of affection from any family before, it was a very special moment. "Look what you've done now Clayton!" said Mother.

"We are not being melancholy tonight, we are going dancing, so let us have some refreshments now, come on Jackie, and Reagan, let us all go through. "Well, I guess your Mother has spoken Jackie!" uttered Father.

"As quick as you like then!" he added, with a laugh.

Laughing as we went, we moved to the sitting room which was a special room in our house that was mainly used for formal occasions, to greet, and meet people for pre-dinner drinks, and cocktails. Designed for comfort, leather chairs were strategically arranged captivating the views of the landscape through the large bay windows, and double glass doors opening out to the balcony.

Just a hint of the sun remained, the sunset turning the sky into a huge array of colours of pinks, purples, and yellows. It was a magic time of day, but as we looked out over the property, huge banks of dark clouds were forming, the threat of a storm to come.

Coloured lights were twinkling in the semi-darkness, to adorn 'The Hall' in splendor, as we drove into Shallow Siding, and into the busy parking lot where the locals, and people from the surrounding properties were converging like flocks of sheep now for the all-important dance night, and a huge social event in town.

## JENNY MAC

Father parked our car, and we all got out. He popped the boot, and then proceeded to help Mother with her contributions for the night. She had brought along some cakes, and slices, and also two hot dishes for the supper, which would be held at halftime. That is what I loved about our community, everyone always helped out.

The welcome sign greeted us at the entrance to the front doors, and as we walked through we noticed that 'The Hall' was decorated with bright coloured lights, balloons, and streamers. Table-clothed tables, and chairs were set along both side walls, and rows of single chairs placed around the dancefloor were usually reserved for the young ladies who would wait to be asked to dance by the young men. The back area of 'The Hall' was split with bathroom facilities one side, and a separate kitchen area on the other side. We headed that way so Mother could put all her donations inside.

As we returned, and selected our table, music flooded the huge room of 'The Hall' as the band members tuned their equipment in the far corner, giving us an insight, as to what was to come. Many people were arriving now, and they selected their places as they entered 'The Hall' in their numbers. I anxiously watched the front doors through the mix of people as the very first of my friends started to arrive with their parents, but it was only one particular couple that I was seeking, and as I searched they finally emerged from behind a group of people, and privately, I was able to scrutinize them.

## APRIL RAIN

Jake Hardy provided an arm to guide Anne through the crowd, and she seemed to take it with huge pride, I noticed, as she looked into his eyes, and smiled. Jake was not at all what I imagined. He was not tall, more on the stocky side, but a fit body beginning to show muscle, a perfect complement to Anne's petite frame. His carrot-red hair swept back at the sides, and was cut short at the back, but his side-burns were long, and seemed to suit his handsome face.

Anne looked around 'The Hall' anxiously, then as she noticed our table, made a bee-line towards us, dragging Jake along with her. When they reached our table, Anne was really excited, and was quite jubilant as she spoke, and acknowledged us all, and made the introductions.

"Good evening Mister, and Missus Coby, Hi Jackie, and Reagan!" she gushed. "May I present my friend, Jake Hardy. Jake, this is Mister, and Missus Coby from Shallow Downs, their Daughter, and my very dearest friend Jacqueline Coby, and her boyfriend Reagan Chase from Ainsley Downs. "Hello Anne!" said Father, and he extended his hand to Jake. "Very nice to meet you Jake!"

"Thank you Sir!" replied Jake, as he returned the handshake. "Hi Anne, well met Jake, I am Reagan!" he said as their hands met. "Hi Reagan!" Jake said. Mother greeted Anne, then added. "Welcome to Shallow Siding Jake, lovely to meet you. Please join our table, and tell us more about yourself!" "Thank you Missus Coby!" said Jake. "Jackie, this is going to be the best night, ever!" said Anne. "You always say that Anne!" I giggled, as I faced Jake. I was captivated by the warmest, friendliest brown eyes I had ever seen. "Well finally! We are to meet, Jake Hardy! I am Jacqueline Coby. Strange though, I feel like I know you already!" I said. "Hello Jacqueline, funny you should say that, I had the same feeling!" Jake said, and he smiled. Mother arranged the seating, and offered Jake a place next to Father, and Anne a seat next to me. I could tell in the first instant, that Father had taken a liking to Jake, as the conversation seemed to flow between them, and Mother also joined in eagerly.

Anne looked at me with a question in her big brown eyes, and smiled. "That would be a 'Yes' from me Anne!" I whispered, and her smile broadened. "I might add, too, you look beautiful Anne!" "Oh Jackie, thank you so much, I feel so happy I could bust, but I am sorry I have been selfish, here you are looking more stunning than I have ever seen you, and I haven't even told you." she said. "Well you have now, and thank you! But I want to tell you, that your dress is amazing, the colour is just so cool." I replied. "Thanks to you Jackie! I feel real special in this dress. Jake just loves it, he said it's the loveliest dress he has ever seen, and, he has been calling me 'pumpkin.' of all things." Anne whispered, then giggled. "Pumpkin! But why pumpkin?" I asked in a whisper. "For the colours in my dress, I guess, but I rather like the pet name, it feels special." she said. As I looked at the dress, the colours seemed to change under the light. Rustic orange, turning to a paler orange, even yellow. It was amazing material, and I could see why Jake thought it resembled the colours of a pumpkin, and like Anne, I thought the pet name was rather cute, but it was the dress design which brought it all together. On top of the bodice, a small capped sleeve draped the right shoulder, but the other shoulder was completely bare, and highlighted Anne's lovely tan where the two thin straps crossed. A full skirt fell from the waist to mid length, and flared with the help of lots of petticoats.

Yes it was a beautiful dress, and I felt a smidgen of pride that I had a hand in its design.

Conversation got very intense as we talked amongst ourselves. Jake was prompted by Father to tell us about his upbringing in the city which they had been discussing, and then Jake's desire to travel, which had then brought him to Shallow Siding, and to the Outback Country. Jake had a very deep, and hearty laugh, which was infectious, and we all laughed as we listened to his stories about his travels, and what he had experienced along the way. He had such a way about him that made you feel so comfortable, and at ease, so everyone joined the conversation unaware of the events surrounding us.

The Hall had filled, the band had started up in full swing, and couples were filing out to the dancefloor, the dancing had begun. It was Mother who alerted us all as she said. "I trust all you young people are here to dance, I certainly am! Clayton?" Father stood, holding his hand out to her. She took it, and smiled as they came together, and he whisked her away. "They certainly do make a wonderful couple, but we can't be outdone pumpkin!" said Jake. "Shall we?" he asked Anne, as he rose. "We certainly will Jake!" said Anne as she joined him, and I smiled fondly at them.

Reagan took my hands in his, sensing my feelings I guess, and I looked into his eyes. "I hope they will be happy, just like we are Reagan. Anne is a very special person to me!" I said. "Yes I know that Jacqueline, but I really like this Jake Hardy, I think he will be good for Anne. Anyway, time will tell! Shall we dance also?" he asked. "You know Reagan, as always, I think you are right, it is only early days yet. I guess nature will take its course! And yes! I would love to dance with you Reagan Chase!" I said as I rose, and smiled at him.

He flashed his special smile, then took me into his arms so tenderly, and as our bodies came together, the thrill of it overwhelmed me.

It was a special night for everyone, and when we came back to our table for the break we were joined by all my friends, and their parents. 'Anne sensed' I thought. 'That it was a great opportunity to introduce Jake into our circle of friends,' and she lost no time in getting him to mingle, and meet everyone.

I noticed Mitch coming towards us. Anne, and Jake had joined Mother, and Father, and were in a deep conversation with Jeffery Stringer. "Hello Jackie! Hi Reagan!" said Mitch. "Hi Mitch, have a seat." said Reagan, and pulled out the chair. "Thanks Reagan." replied Mitch. "Wow! Just look at Jacqueline Coby! All grown up, and looking so beautiful tonight, must be because you are a year older tomorrow." Mitch said.

## APRIL RAIN

"Mitchell Stringer! Are you suggesting I am getting old?" I asked, and giggled as I looked into his deep blue eyes. "I'm not so sure if that was meant as a compliment, but thank you anyway Mitch. Happy Birthday for last week, but I guess I will be saying that again tomorrow, at our joint party! I hope you are coming early?" I asked. "We have a lot planned!"

"Whoa!" replied Mitch as he held up his hands. "Too many questions! Firstly, you do look beautiful tonight, and it was a compliment. You aren't old, or else I would be too." he laughed. "It seems, seeing we are having a joint Birthday Party tomorrow that your Mother, and my Father have been arranging, it looks like Father, and I will be staying over tonight at your place, as we have some jobs to complete for your Father early tomorrow."

"Really! What jobs Mitch, how come I don't know about it?" I asked. "Because Jackie, it is a special surprise from your parents, and I am not saying anymore!" he said. "But Mitch… "No buts Jackie. My lips are sealed, please save me a dance." he said as he got up.

Anne wasn't letting him get away though. "Wait Mitch!" she called. "I have someone I would like you to meet!" "Jake, please come, and meet my very best male friend, Mitchell Stringer. 'Mitch, to us all.' "Mitch, please come, and meet my friend Jake Hardy." Mitch, and Jake looked long, and hard at one another, then a huge grin spread across Mitch's face, and he laughed.

"Well Jake, if you're Anne's friend, you can be mine too. I guess you are the newcomer we have all been waiting to meet, welcome to Shallow Siding, pleased to meet you, but just look after our girl!" he said, as he extended his hand for a handshake.

'*I am about to meet a real cowboy!*' Jake thought, as he noted Mitch's swagger, a country accent, and tanned skin, and as he stepped forward to shake Mitch's strong hand he saw the muscles flex in his forearms. "I too am pleased to meet you Mitch, I have heard so much about you from Anne, that I feel I know you. She warned me you were protective, like a big brother. Well don't you worry I have this lady's best interest at heart!" Jake looked up at Mitch with his warm friendly eyes, then added. "Now if I have passed the test, can we sit, and chat for a while Mitch?" his face broke into a huge smile. Mitch could not resist but laugh, and patted him on the back. "I think we will do just that Jake Hardy!" he said.

I watched as they were talking. Mitch would throw his head back laughing, and Jake's deep hearty laugh would ring out, and I witnessed a special bond forming between them both. Jake Hardy seemed to get on with everyone, and I smiled at Anne. Her face was radiant, her big eyes lit up, but the smile she returned was a treat to see. I was so happy for her. I knew that Anne needed approval from all her friends. It was so important to her.

So much fun we had that night. Jake very politely asked me to dance, and I soon learnt that he was a very special person. Then as we danced, he said to me.

"Jacqueline Coby, you would not believe the stories Anne has told me about you, and quite frankly some of them, I found hard to believe, but having met you, I feel almost guilty for even thinking that. I am convinced you are everything, and more, than how she has described you. She loves you like a sister, and I hope we will have a similar relationship Jacqueline?" I laughed. "Jake you will have to remember that Anne is a little bias when it comes to me, and I guess I am the same about her!" Then I looked at him very seriously, and said. "I love her too Jake! I want the best for her, and if you end up by being that best then I will love you like a brother, but you treat her right Jake!" "Wow! Are you always that direct?" he asked. "Mostly! Or so they tell me!" I said, with a giggle, as his hearty laugh joined me. "I think I love you already Jacqueline Coby!" he said, just as the music ended.

Mitch stood waiting at our table with a big grin on his face. "Come on Jackie, the night is getting away, you've promised me a dance!" "Of course Mitch!" I said, as I looked for Reagan, but he was out on the dancefloor. "Thank you Jake!" I said. "It has been my pleasure Jacqueline!" replied Jake. "You are a hard girl to get a dance with Jackie!" Mitch said, as he put his arms around me. As he did, I shivered, and a warmth spread throughout my body, my eyes unable to meet his. "You ok Jackie?" he asked. "Of course Mitch!" I said, as my feelings went haywire. "I hope so, we have a big day tomorrow, one to always remember!" said Mitch. "Yes I know Mitch!" I said softly. Sadly the night finally ended, but with us, an eagerness for the coming day.

*Our joint Sixteenth Birthday.*

# JENNY MAC

*A joint Celebration, and Sixteenth Birthday Party:*
*1962*
*Jacqueline Coby, and Mitchell Stringer*

## Chapter 24

Mother had organized banners at the entrance to the big marque. Happy 16th Birthday Jackie, and Mitch it read. It was dark out as we all converged in the pavilion for our breakfast. Coloured lights twinkled, and candles lit up the tables. Massive clouds were banking up across the sky, cheating us of the usual sunrise, and distant thunder rolled across the heavens.

The first event on the agenda was to be a trail ride after we had eaten. Some people had stayed over from the night before, but others arrived early, and everyone who was invited was now present. Only I seemed to be missing a few important figures, so I asked Mother.

"Good Morning Mother!" I said, as I walked up to where she was busying herself in decorating a special table. "Oh! Good Morning Jackie, and best wishes for a Happy Birthday!" Mother replied, as she wrapped me in her arms, and kissed me. "Thank you Mother!" I said, as I kissed her back. "Everyone seems to be here Mother, but where is Father, and why aren't Mitch, and Mister Stringer here, and Reagan, and Anne are missing also, where are they?" I asked.

"Don't worry Jackie, they are all here, and were all up before first light this morning helping your Father. Jake Hardy, and Anne arrived early ready to help, and they are with them. Your Father arranged it when he invited Jake out for your party. So they should not be much longer!" she said. "I am so pleased that Jake was invited Mother. I really like him a lot!" I said. "Good! I would suggest that you greet your guests now, and if they give you presents Jackie, could you put them unopened on this table please, as I would like you, and Mitch to open presents later at morning tea, when you come back from riding!" Mother said. "If you wish Mother, but what are the others doing?" I asked. "Patience Jackie!" Mother replied.

There seemed a mystery in the air concerning my party, which I was obviously not included in, so I decided to let it go, and take Mother's advice, and join my friends and their families. This was the first time that Mother had arranged a joint party for Mitch, and myself, and simply because every year we usually all attended Mitch's Birthday party, and then mine the week later.

Mister Stringer was a sole parent, his wife had passed away some years back, and he was finding it difficult to entertain, so this year Mother had suggested to him a joint Birthday Party, and they made all the arrangements together.

Breakfast was a buffet style, and Ashton, and Emily Banks had everything ready to serve as I walked up to them. "Good morning Mister, and Missus Banks! This all looks amazing. Thank you both so much for going to such detail!" I said. "Good Morning Jackie, it has been a pleasure I can assure you, and a very Happy Birthday to you!" said Emily Banks, as she hugged me, and kissed my cheek. "Thank you Missus Banks!" I replied.

"Happy Birthday Jackie!" said Ashton Banks, as he kissed my cheek. "We both hope you have an enjoyable party. Everything is ready here, we are just waiting on your Father now!" "Thank you Mister Banks!" I replied.

My friends became impatient, and quick to seek my attention, so they were quite loud with excitement as they grouped around me to wish me a Happy Birthday, and loaded all their gifts upon me. "Happy Birthday Jackie!" called Rebecca, and Helena in unison. "But where is Mitch, Jackie?" queried Rebecca. "Anne is not here either!" said Helena. "Thank you girls for your Birthday wishes, and I believe everyone is here, but there is some secret going on about their whereabouts, obviously I am not meant to know!" I said.

"Really Jackie! How very mysterious, but I do love surprises, don't you?" said Rebecca. "Well, I guess so Rebecca, we will have to wait, and see, unfortunately!" I replied, as I looked out over the gardens. "Looks like they are coming now!" I said, as I noticed Father striding out across the lawn, with all the others in his wake.

Father hastened to my side. "A very Happy Birthday Jackie!" he said, as he picked me up, and swung me around, then set me down with a kiss on both cheeks, and wrapped both arms around me in a huge hug. I looked up at his handsome face. *'He has that look in his eyes!'* I thought, and I giggled. "Thank you Father! No doubt you have been up to something, but I guess you will tell me in due time!" I said, laughing now. Father laughed too. "Is my face an open book Jackie?" he asked.

"Only to me Father!" I replied.

"I can't seem to keep anything from you Jackie, and

you are so damn direct! I don't know where you get that from!" he said, and everyone around us laughed.

"Ok then Miss Birthday Girl! You will be kept in huge suspense now, so you will need to dig deep for some patience, which I know is not your strong point, as we plan on having 'ALL' the presents for you, and Mitch during morning tea, which is after your trail ride.

"But Father…"No buts Jackie! It is all planned" he said, and threw his head back laughing.

Jake Hardy stood at the back watching the interaction playing out between the Father, and Daughter, and he couldn't help but smile. 'Such a lovely family, but what a special bond between Father, and Daughter.' he was thinking. Then the big man's voice rang out to take control as Clayton Coby stood proud to address all his guests, and to bid them welcome, as only he could do.

'With such pride, and determination, he delivered a speech straight from the heart.'

Clayton Coby's face beamed when he completed his speech, and everyone clapped. "Now if you would all be upstanding, we will toast to the two Birthday people dearest to our hearts. So best wishes to my Daughter Jacqueline Coby, and also to Mitchell Stringer. A very Happy Sixteenth Birthday to you both!" Father said. "Hear! Hear! Everyone cheered, and broke into the Happy Birthday Song.

"A word please folks!" said Jeffery Stringer as he held his hand up at the close of the song. "First of all, Happy Birthday Jackie, and Happy Birthday Mitch. I can see now that this day is going to be a memorable one, I owe it all to Mel, and Clayton Coby! I would like to express a special thank you to you both for suggesting this joint Birthday Party, it is a great idea, and I'm sure all Jackie's and Mitch's friends, and family will have a great day!" Thank you all, he said.

"Thank you Jeffery you're most welcome, but we are all friends here so let us celebrate, and let's eat now everyone. I am famished!" Father replied. So everyone found their places, and proceeded to get their breakfast from the buffet table.

Brief glimpses of the sun were just visible through the trees as I sat amongst my friends, and family, there was still the threat of a storm to come though, as ominous dark clouds hung low, but no one seemed to mind, and they chattered endlessly. I felt happy, and fortunate to have such very good friends. Father rose to speak after breakfast, and said.

"Listen up all! Jackie if you would like to take your friends on the trail ride now! Roy has all the horses saddled ready to go at the stables, see Emily before you leave, and be back in three hours for morning tea, and the opening of the presents!" "Thank you so much Father, and Mother, and thank you Mister, and Missus Banks.

I guess that's our cue to leave people!" I said.

Jacqueline gathered all her friends around her, and then Emily Banks joined them. "Jackie, I have goodies for you, and your guests in these packs. All the other packs contain drinks, and water on frozen bricks, so they will last you for the ride!" she said. "Thank you Missus Banks!" I said. "If everyone is ready, we will go now!" I said. The boys all grabbed a pack each, and they left the pavilion chatting as they went, as Jacqueline led them on the short walk to the Inner Stables. There was thirteen of them, and all trying to talk at once. Jacqueline had a secret place to take them to this morning, and she was excited about sharing it with them.

Jake Hardy, and Anne Giles moved up alongside Jacqueline. "Oh, there you are Anne!" I said. "Hello Jackie, it's going to be the best Birthday Party!" replied Anne. "Thought you might say that Anne, but Yes! We will have a lot of fun today!" I replied. "Hello Jake, I am so pleased you could come out for our party, it will give us a chance to get to know one another a bit more!" I said. "Thank you Jacqueline, that means a lot to me. I am just starting to realize, that what Anne has told me is spot on, when she said The Coby Family usually do things in a certain way, and I can see now what she meant. I have enjoyed myself so much this morning, however Jacqueline, I do have a confession to make! I can't ride a horse!" said Jake, as he laughed that deep hearty laugh. "I laughed too, as I said. "Don't you worry Jake, we will look after you, and you will be a Country Boy, before you know it!" "Sure Jacqueline!" he said. I laughed, but turned my attention to Anne then. "So Anne, you are about to tell me what you were doing this morning, aren't you Anne?" I asked. "Oh no you don't Jackie! You can't trick me! It's a surprise, and I am not to say. No buts either!" said Anne. Anne started to giggle when I looked at her. "Thank you so much my dearest friend, now I will be in suspense all morning!" I replied.

"Have patience Jackie!" said Anne. "I think you have been with Father too long this morning, you are starting to sound like him Anne!" I said, and we both laughed.

We reached the stables, and all the horses were lined up ready to go. "What is so funny you two?" asked Mitch, as he joined us. "Oh! Jackie was trying to get information out of me about this morning Mitch!" said Anne. "But I refused to tell!" "Good for you Anne!" Mitch said, and laughed. "Good things come to those who wait Jackie!" "So they tell me Mitch, it is nice to have real friends though!" I replied. Reagan led a horse as he walked towards us. "What is happening here? Shouldn't we be leaving Jacqueline? Your Father expects us back on time!" he said. "Yes, you are right Reagan. I will get Sailor now, these very best friends of mine are not sharing any secrets!" I said. "Oh! I see! Jacqueline, and I'll not be saying either!" he said, and chuckled. "Thank you too, Reagan!" I said. As I headed to the holding yard, I turned to call to Mitch.

"Mitch, Jake said he couldn't ride. Would you select a quiet horse for him, maybe the grey mare, she is gentle!" I suggested. "Yes sure Jackie!" Mitch called. "Come on then Jake, and Anne, let's get you sorted. Don't worry Jake, I will ride with you today!" said Mitch. "Thanks Mitch. I don't want to hold you all up, but I am usually a quick learner at most things, but horse riding? I am not so sure!" replied Jake. "You will be fine Jake, trust me!" said Mitch, as they reached the saddled horses. "Oh I have faith in you Mitch. It's me I'm worried about!" Jake said laughing, as he looked at his horse. Mitch laughed too. "Let's mount up Jake!" he said.

Jacqueline led Sailor through the holding yard gate, and then closed it. She climbed up into the saddle, and Sailor started showing off as usual, prancing along as she rode him towards the others. Jake Hardy sat very tensely in the saddle, his face full of apprehension. 'Just a little fear,' thought Jacqueline, as she tried to suppress the smile which escaped her lips, but all of a sudden Jake's eyes flew wide when he looked at Sailor. "My goodness what a beautiful horse Jacqueline, he is just magnificent!" said Jake in awe. "Please meet Sailor, Jake! My very first love, and the fastest horse in the district. You can ask Mitch, he won a race on Sailor last year, and he has stories to tell about himself, and Sailor!" I replied, with a giggle.

"Thanks Jackie!" uttered Mitch. "It was my pleasure Mitch!" I said, giving him a cheeky look. "Well, I guess a few stories on the ride today will take my mind off the horse!" said Jake laughing.

"Ready everyone? It is time to move out now!" called Jacqueline, as she maneuvered Sailor towards the head of the line. "We can ride two abreast for about a mile or so, until we reach a sandy bank where there, we will cross the creek, then we will stop there!" I said. "Ok Jackie!" they all voiced their replies, and "Lead the way Jackie!"

## APRIL RAIN

The weather had changed again. It was still cloudy, but in patches intermittent sunshine, making it a pleasant morning for a ride.

They were making good time, but when Jacqueline looked back, she noticed Jake had dropped back a bit, so she reined in off the track to let the others pass. "George, just up ahead there is a track which veers off this one, take that down to the sand bank. We will stop there, and have a break. I am going to check on Jake!' I said. "Ok Jackie!" said George Worthington. Jacqueline started back, but to her surprise she noticed Mitch was teaching Jake how to ride the horse.

All of a sudden they were both trotting slowly along the path. "Oh very well done Jake!" I called, as I got closer. "Oh it's not me Jacqueline, it's this cowboy friend of yours, he knows everything about horses, he is just a genius, and such a good teacher!" said Jake. "Yes I have to agree with you Jake, Mitch does have a lot of skills, but still, you are the one riding, and doing well too, from what I can see! You might be pleased to hear we are almost at the sandbanks, and we will rest there." I said.

"Oh thank goodness Jacqueline. I might have trouble walking when I get off this horse, and my rear end has real problems too!" he said, with a chuckle.

Mitch, and I looked at one another, then broke out laughing. "Don't you worry Jake, the first time is always the worst!" said Mitch through his mirth, and I could tell he was enjoying himself. "Now you tell me Mitch! At least my car has a proper seat!" replied Jake.

## JENNY MAC

I looked at Mitch. His grin was spread wide across his handsome face. "Thank you Mitch, you are really a true friend." I said, as I looked into his deep blue eyes. "No thanks needed Jackie, we are having fun." he replied.

"Come on then let's catch up to the others." I said.

The Sandbanks were the shallows of Shallow Creek. The water narrowed at this section, and flowed over rocks, and then widened further upstream. We arrived amid the mayhem, and chatter, the girls busy laying the blankets under a big gum tree, and the boys, George Worthington, Bob Jones, and Arthur Bell were tethering the horses, and Matt Sole, Cliff Gibbons, and Sonny Peet were busy unpacking the packs to get drinks, and food.

"Thank you all, but don't get too comfortable we only have a half hour here. I was watching Jake. Mitch has him trotting now!" I called. They all cheered him as Jake climbed very gingerly to the ground on his wobbly legs.

As the gradual slopes meander through the hillside seeking a destiny, a natural phenomenon becomes visual from the huge formation of ochre coloured rocks, which bunched together glistening in the early sunlight, and water, as it tumbled from the above crest, and spilt into a small waterfall out over the rocks, and then into the creek. 'This is what I wanted my friends to see.'

It was only a short ride there to see it, and on this particular morning the view was a spectacle, a treat, and it did not disappoint. As our horses climbed up the last rise, and we came out on level ground again, what we saw before us was just too much to comprehend, and we all lined up on the crest awestruck with the wonder of it.

Anne was first to speak out. "Oh Jackie, thank you for bringing us up here, this place is magical, look at the colours! Are we staying for a while?" "That pleases me Anne. I hope you all like it, this place is special to me, and I just had to bring you all here today to share it with you on my Birthday, and Yes! We can stay for a while, so dismount people, enjoy!" I said. "Thanks Jackie!" they all called.

Activity was everywhere. Some tethering the horses, others were setting up a small camp area, and George had a new-fangled camera, and he was calling everyone to pose for shots to be taken. There was laughter as we jostled for positions, and several voices talking at once as photos were taken of us with the magnificent waterfall, and the view of the rock formations as our backdrop.

Reagan moved closer to me. "Jacqueline! You have been holding out, I have never been up here. It is really a remarkable place, but you have never mentioned it!" he said. "I am sorry Reagan, there are really many places I haven't taken you to yet on our property, everywhere is different, and a joy, but here is special!" I said.

Needless to say, our morning ride was a highlight for all of us, but it was pleasing to soon discover that the other generation were having a good time also, back home. After arriving back at the stables, Roy Anson took total control of the horses, so in need of a shower and some fresh clothes, we all walked to the homestead.

Everyone was waiting for us, and we all reached the

pavilion just as morning tea was being served, and a beautiful Birthday Cake, shaped like a horseshoe, graced the center table. Mitch, and I cut the cake together, to the cheers, and clapping, from our friends, and family, and we blew out the candles together.

We heard speeches from Father, Mother, and Mister Stringer, and then it was time for opening the presents. I was excited because I had a special present for Mitch that I designed myself, and had the saddler make it for me, and Axel Hall had done the artwork.

Father, and Mother were first in with our presents. Mother had brought me a lovely watch, and Father's present was a music box. It was so beautiful, and when I opened it, and wound it up, a lovely dancing lady in a pink dress, revolved around inside to the music. I could only imagine what time, and effort it took them to get those gifts here for me. "Thank you so much Mother and Father. I will cherish these gifts forever!" I said. "That is not all, Jackie!" he said, with a hint of mystery. "If you be patient, we have a little surprise for you later!" "What surprise Father?" I asked him. "Patience Jackie!" he said, then they were giving Mitch his present, so obviously the subject was closed. We spent ages opening presents, then I gave Mitch my gift. "Happy Birthday Mitch!" I said. He opened it, and I watched his face as his eyes lifted slowly from the gift to mine, his gaze mesmerizing me. "Oh Jackie, what can I say?" said Mitch.

On a plaque that was lovingly planed by the saddler, and finished with the creative artwork, and writing done

## APRIL RAIN

by Axel Hall, was mounted, four horse shoes painted in black, and the letters on the plaque read.
'The Mile Race 1961 Winners Mitch Stringer, and Sailor.'

I could see Mitch was overcome with emotion, so I tried to smooth the situation with a joke. "Presents are meant to be happy things Mitch. Lighten up, you look like you have seen a ghost!" I said, and I giggled.

'I will never forget Mitch's face as he spoke to me.'

For once Mitch didn't laugh at my joke, he was very serious. "Jackie! I can't thank you enough for this gift, it is so thoughtful!" Mitch replied, his voice almost a croak. "This is something that I will treasure, and keep forever, it means so much to me!" "Thank goodness for that! I thought that I had given you a melon Mitch! Now smile!" I said to him in jest. His huge grin that I loved, spread across his handsome face, and he took my hands in his, and kissed my cheek. We hugged, and that warm feeling overcome me again. "Happy Birthday Mitch!" I said "Happy Birthday Jackie!" he said.

Then as a twinkle appeared in his deep blue eyes he chuckled, and released me. "I too, have a special gift for you Jackie, but I want to savour that moment, besides I left it in my room, if you don't mind waiting till later, I will go, and get it!" he said. "Of course Mitch." I replied.

"Ok you two, we have to move on now if you are both ready." asked Father as he joined us. "Yeah for sure Mister Coby, let's go!" said Mitch eagerly. "Move on where, Father?" I asked. "Your Mother is going to speak now Jackie!" said Father, then he clapped his hands.

"Attention all, Mel would like to say a few words!" he called out. Mother moved to my side, and addressed our friends. "Thank you all so much for being here for this special day, and a very Happy Birthday to Jackie, and Mitch. Because you all know us so well, you will not find it unusual that we have a special surprise in store for Jackie for her Birthday today, and at this same time I would like to thank all the people involved for helping us to bring this about.

"Jackie!" said Mother, as she turned to me, and took my hands in hers. "Your Father, and I have something special for you today, something we hope you will enjoy for many, many years to come. It entails just a short walk from here, so Father will lead the way. Is everyone ready? We are about to leave!" Mother called out. Our guests clapped, and got to their feet, ready to go.

Bewildered, I looked around the pavilion thinking to myself. *'I am sure everyone here knows what is going on. All except me.'* So I turned to ask Mother, but knowingly she was quick to speak first. "Come along Jackie, let's go!" she said laughing as she coaxed me.

So we all trailed across the lawns, and then skirted the gardens. A big following of people all chatting together, it was rather exciting. My eyes went to the head of the procession as Father led the way, his massive physique towered over the others as he surged ahead.

*'He is a man on a mission'* I thought to myself, and couldn't help but feel the love I held for him surfacing, and surging through me.

## APRIL RAIN

We moved onto the path which led on to the tennis courts, but only walked a short way before veering right onto an old, hardly used, bush track, that I noticed had been cleared of all debris. The first thing noticeable to me, as I peered eagerly through the huge gum trees, was a small building of some sort, and as we got closer, I could see it was a grass thatched hut, and a shelter. "Whatever is that Mother, and why is it there? No one ever comes here!" I said. Mother laughed, and looked at me saying. "We will now Jackie!"

As we emerged from the tree line into the clearing, I came to a sudden halt. For an instant I was totally mesmerized, trying to comprehend it all. Huge boulders, strategically placed, hugged the sides of the cemented, kidney shaped swimming pool with wide rock steps that disappeared into its depths. A rock pool in every sense of the word, but enhanced, and adorned with colourful gardens. I was so ecstatic, a scream escaped my lips as I rushed over. "Happy Birthday Jackie!" said Mother, and Father in unison. "Oh Mother, Father, this is just great, thank you both so much, what a surprise! Can we swim now?" I asked. "I am pleased you like it Jackie, and the grass hut is a dressing shed. Inside there you will find swimming costumes for everyone, and even a dressing mirror!" said Mother.

"Be as quick as you like though Jackie, if you want to swim. I don't like the look of the clouds coming in!" uttered Father, as he looked skywards. "Will do Father!" I said, and I was off running to get everyone organized.

## JENNY MAC

There was a race to the dressing shed, but the ladies won, so we changed first. When I emerged, Reagan was outside waiting for me. "Jacqueline come, and see this!" he urged. We went out back where another small shed housed pumps, and the pool equipment. "Your Father is amazing getting all this here, it must have taken ages to arrange this, and keep it secret! You have loving parents Jacqueline!" he said. "Yes I know Reagan, I love them dearly too, but I cannot imagine what it all entailed to complete this pool?" I said. "So come in for a swim, let's enjoy it." I urged.

"Just one moment my lady, I haven't given you your present!" he said, as he pulled me close. "You did too, a beautiful bracelet with my birth stones in it…His soft lips cut off all my protests, as they found mine in a smoldering kiss, which left me breathless.

Jackie, Jackie! Anne called. "Where are you?" Reagan released me, and started to laugh, and with a cheeky grin on his face, his eyes smoldered as they sort mine.

"Hopefully Jacqueline! One day I will have you all to myself, so I'd better hold onto that thought I guess!" he muttered sadly. Then he kissed me again, deeply, and longingly, until I thought my heart would burst.

Regretfully our lips slowly parted, but he held me close to him, I felt my face flushed with the realization, that the same feelings hounded me also. As I looked at his beautiful face, I could see the strain there, so I spoke to him softly, and tried to ease his pain.

"I know just how you feel Reagan, because I feel the

same way, but just think for one moment. These are our young years. Years, never to be replaced, so please try to be patient Reagan, so I can try too!" "You are well aware that patience isn't my best attribute Reagan!" I said, then started to giggle, and that got him going too. "You can say that again Jacqueline, I guess you are right!" he said in mirth.

"Come on Reagan, let us join the party now!" I urged him, and pulled him along. As we turned the corner, I called out to Anne. "Over here Anne!" "Oh there you are. I couldn't find you two! Are you ready to have a swim now, the others have already gone in!" she said. So we all joined hands, and jumped into the pool.

As I came to the surface, the cold temperature made me gasp, and took my breath away as the water was freezing. I looked up at the darkening sky, a cold wind had sprung up too but no-one was complaining, they were busy enjoying themselves, so we joined them in their fun, and games, and we all spent ages in the pool.

Eventually it became too cold, and I told Reagan I was going in to change my clothes, and to get ready for lunch, so then I went to the hut, and the girls came with me.

Later when I emerged from the hut, I looked up, and noticed Mitch ambling along the path, so I headed towards him. "Where have you been Mitch?" I asked, as we met on the track. "I went to get your present Jackie. Happy Birthday!" he said as he handed me a small purple covered parcel, dressed in purple ribbons.

"Love the colours Mitch!" I gushed, as I pulled at the

purple paper. "I thought you might Jackie … His words stilled amid huge claps of thunder, which menaced the dark, ominous wind-swept clouds above us, lightning lit the heavens, and my parcel flew from my hands.

Spilled from its protective coat, the miniature black horse with white markings rearing up high on its timber stand, now lay in the dirt. As I retrieved it, I looked at Mitch, and tears sprang into my eyes. "He is just so beautiful Mitch, and looks just like Sailor!" "Should do Jackie, I carved him myself. A very special present for a special girl!" he said. "You're so talented Mitch, thank you, and no words can describe my gratitude for this thoughtful gift. He will be by my side, and in my heart forever!" I said. "Wish I was!" Mitch whispered sadly.

What materialized in his eyes as I looked up at him, was no surprise to me, and realization hit me for the first time in my life that I loved him too.

*'Probably have done all my life.'* I thought.

"But you ar … I whispered softly as a huge raindrop smacked him square in the face to slide down to his chin. We were startled, and laughed out loud together.

"April Rain!" he said, as he looked up to the heavens laughing, and he held his hand out to capture the falling raindrops. "Yes! I guess it is Mitch!" I mused.

"Hmm! That is a perfect name for my little horse!" I said decisively. "What's all the mumbling Jackie, let's make a run for it, we are getting wet." Mitch urged me.

"I said! The little horse's name will be."…

*"April Rain."*

# APRIL RAIN

*1964: Drought in The Outback :*
*Cattle Muster: Shallow Downs*

## Chapter 25
*The Year 1964...Was significant in more ways than one.*

It was mid November, and already the lack of rain was becoming evident in the paddocks which baked in the unforgiving sun, as it scorched the land. Temperatures soared, and ultimately, drought prematurely plagued The Outback Country, and still the threat of the summer heat was yet to come. Many properties were suffering, their paddocks drying up, feed, and water was scarce.

Shallow Creek had always provided ample water supply for the stock, and some pasture irrigation at Shallow Downs Poperty, but the paddocks were quickly becoming dry now, and in stress, and the numerous growing plantation of wattle trees, were seeking more water. Drastic measures needed to be taken, and Clayton Coby moved quickly to organize a cattle muster so that he could sell off some stock, and have them railed to the sale yards. The irrigation needed updating as well, and seeing Christmas was not far away, and all the family were coming home, he had planned ahead with June, his eldest daughter, and family, to go back with them to the city when they returned after Christmas, and stay for two months. He had heard a whisper of a new irrigation system that he wanted to see in operation, which could hopefully solve his problems for watering all the extra wattle trees, and for setting up more irrigation and plant lucerne seed in some of the paddocks for future fodder.

The property was a buzz of activity as it was just breaking day, but already the heat from the sun was oppressive, just a reminder of what was to come, and the muster would be a long exercise. All property hands had been notified, and all required to assemble at the outer stables, opposite the cattle yards for a briefing, and their final orders. Anyone who could ride was to be included.

Clayton Coby stood tall, as he addressed his workers from the back of the Jeep. "Good Morning all! A huge job we have men, and Jackie! So let's get down to the organization of it all. 'As quick as you like!' So listen up everyone!" he called.

"My aim is to cull the main herd, and segregate the weaners from the cattle to be sold, then do any branding needed, and the vet will do a check, so they will all have to be brought in for assessment, this will mean camping out, until we can get them together from all paddocks, and back to the yards. "Roy?" "Yes Boss!" Roy replied. "Select your own men, you will have total charge of the horses, and the wagons, make sure you take everything required, but work with Ashton to find out what he will need, maybe two wagons, one for a cooking galley, and one for swags, and other things." "Ok Boss!" said Roy.

"Ashton! Total charge of your galley, so pick what staff you will need to take with you, and get the stores you will require, probably for four or five days, but take extra!" Clayton said. "Will do Clayton!" said Ashton.

"Mick?" "Yes boss!" replied Mick. "Would you allocate what men you need for the main muster, and give them their orders. I want you to move my breeding stock to the two paddocks on the hillside near the creek where the grass is best. I want to retain one bull, and ten of my best heifers. I will tell you which ones before you leave. The others you can take to join the main muster, and bring them in." said Clayton. "Yes Boss!" said Mick.

"Jackie! If you can join the main muster, that would be good, and take Jacob with you. I want you both to move the weaners to the smallest paddock close to the creek!" he said. "Yes Father!" I said. "Good! When you are all ready, then move out. I have to organize trucks, and rail wagons. I will catch up at some point!" he said.

Mustering was very tough, long hot days of endless riding through fly infested terrain to maneuver cattle at their own comfortable pace. As night closed we made camp, but the thought of any relief, was in vain.

Our evening meal was eaten in haste, making way for our much greater need, and our only blessing, to seek out our swags which lay upon the bare earth, where only the drone of mosquitos flitting around, could interrupt our sleep, and our last thoughts.

*'Tomorrow was another day.'*

'Six days actually!' I thought, as I watched Father climb into the Jeep to follow the last truck of cattle to the yards at The Siding. It had taken all that time to muster, sort, and brand, and to have the animals checked. Our remaining cattle had already been moved out to better pastures, the ones for sale were trucked, ready to go.

"Thank you Jackie!" said Father, as he looked at me. "What a huge job you, and the men have done. Mother has always said that you should have been born a boy, though I must say, you are far too beautiful to be that, and I rather like that you are a woman Jackie. A strong woman Jackie, one who I am certain, can take over from me here!" "Thank you Father, my pleasure!" I replied. "I must admit I am used to that fact now, but this woman needs a hot bath!" I replied, with a giggle, and Father laughed. "We shall celebrate tonight Jackie. Invite the men in for a bar-be-que. I have to go!" he said. "A good idea, leave it to me, Father, I will see you at The Siding later!' I said. "Ok Jackie, no rush." he said, and drove off.

I watched as my Father left in a swirl of dust, and I reflected how my life, at this time, had changed yet again, and so dramatically. I had turned eighteen now, and, true to his word. Father, and I had signed the final papers that gave me part ownership of Shallow Downs.

Celebrating my Birthday came not only with all the responsibility of being a Property Owner, of which I had taken very seriously, by being hands on with all the organization of it, but with the gift of a new car as well.

Not any car, but a 4WD Jeep. Orange, and Black, and beautiful. Unlike Father's Jeep, which he had bought through the army supplies, my Jeep was a special edition with doors, cabin, and a proper roof. Specially ordered by Mother, and Father. As I recalled, when it had arrived by rail, and I saw it for the first time. 'I had a new love' and with it, came independence, and freedom.

I was exercising this freedom on this particular day as I packed the Jeep with my rugs, and belongings, and the hamper of goodies that I had so lovingly packed for a picnic, and as I climbed into the Jeep, my body shivered with excitement. I was going to meet Reagan.

Reagan was getting used to me picking him up now, he had a special name for my car, and as we sped along the road beside the creek, he asked. "Where is the 'Mean Machine' taking us today Jacqueline?" and he started to laugh. "You can laugh Reagan Chase, but I will have you know that we have something special in store for you today, this 'Mean Machine,' and I!" I replied, as I took a quick turn off the road, along a sandy track, and over a causeway, which crossed the creek, and headed bush. "And! I might add that my 'Mean Machine' can go where other transport fails!" I replied triumphantly, as we weaved through the bush, emerging out to a flat, but rocky area, where the river gums dominated, and a track led down to a wide, sandy bank, which surrounded a deep pool of clear water, where a waterfall cascaded down the rocks into it. "Well, this is more like it Jacqueline! This is beautiful Country, and alone with my beautiful girl, at last!" he said, as he smiled.

Jacqueline shut the Jeep down, and climbed out to grab their belongings. Reagan toted the rugs, and hamper, but grabbed her hand, and they walked hand in hand, down the track to the sandy bank, where they selected a place under the gum trees for the rugs, and their gear, then they both fell down laughing. "I just love hearing you laugh Jacqueline!" said Reagan, as he brushed a lock of hair from my face, to look deeply into my eyes. "I love you so very much Jacqueline Coby!" he choked out the words. His gentle touch, and his show of emotion, sent a shiver up my spine. "I love you too, Reagan Chase, I always have, and I always will!" I replied.

His hands framed my face, his mouth smelt so sweet, and was so soft, as he searched for my parting lips. Our kiss was long, and passionate, the heat rose inside me, threatening to choke me. I sensed Reagan's urgency as his desire built, and I was overcome with a deep love for him. Our lips slowly parted as I gently eased him away, trying to stall, not only my own feelings, which were racing madly inside me, but his as well. So on a lighter note. I said.

"Come on Reagan, let's go in for a swim!" I said as I giggled, discarding my clothes to reveal my swimmers. I raced down the sandy bank, taunting him as I ran. "Last one in is….I laughed, and he was up, charging after me, and tearing off clothes as he ran. I swam across the pool towards the waterfall, and was climbing the rocks as he grabbed me, and helped to pull me up onto the ledge.

We both stood there breathless, our fits of laughter echoing around us were stilled in a heartbeat as we were lost in each other's eyes. Reagan pulled me close, and as our wet bodies merged as one, we were heedless of the world around us, only conscious of our need, our love as our lips met, and water cascaded over our heads.

Marry me! Reagan rasped, his voice became hoarse, and whisper like, as he sank to his knees. His distraught face uplifted searching my eyes for a reaction.

"Jacqueline, will you be my wife? Today, tomorrow,

or very soon? Because the waiting is just killing me!" he repeated in anguish.

"Reagan Chase! Is that really a proposal?" I asked in wonder. "You can bet your life it is Jacqueline Coby, and …"Yes please Reagan!" I whispered to interrupt him.

"What did you just say?" he asked. "Yes!" I replied.

He stared at me in disbelief, until the realization hit him. "Yes, yes, and Yes!" he yelled.

Reagan was ecstatic, he grabbed me, and swung me around, then folded me in his arms, and kissed me deeply, until I could barely breathe. "You will be Missus Jacqueline Chase!" he said, smiling with total conviction. "I think that would be Missus Jacqueline Coby Chase!" I corrected him.

"Why is that Jacqueline?" he questioned me, with a puzzled look. "That is a promise I made to my Father, to always be a Coby!" I replied. "I see!" he said. "Does that matter Reagan?" I asked. "No it does not matter at all Jacqueline, on the contrary, I think we both owe him that gesture for different reasons, and to honour him in some way, he deserves that! "Thank you Reagan, that means so much to me!" I said. "And speaking of your Father Jacqueline, I have to ask his permission to marry you."

"Things must be done correctly, or I will never live it down. Should I ask him tonight? The sooner, the better!"

"Yes ask tonight!" I said. "I will never forget the first time I met you, and your family, especially your Father!" he laughed at the memory. I laughed too, as I recalled. "But what will I do if he says no Jacqueline?" he asked in desperation, and I giggled. "If that happens Reagan, 'There is always a way! Father always says.' I quoted.

That evening Reagan asked my Father's permission to marry me, and was welcomed into our family. Father looked pleased as he directed us into the sitting room to have a celebration drink, however I sensed reservation in my Mother's eyes. As she rose to check on the dinner, I excused myself to help her in the kitchen.

"What is it Mother?" I asked. "Goodness me Jackie, are you physic? But so direct too! Then I guess I will be also!" she replied. "What about Mitch?" she asked. "I love Mitch also Mother, you know that. But I can only choose one husband!" I replied. "Then, why the rush Jackie, why not wait to be sure!" Mother said. "I am sure Mother! I have chosen Reagan because I have loved him from day one, I know him. Mitch however, confuses me with his casual manner, but then surprises me with his thoughtfulness, and his talents." I said. "He is younger Jackie, still learning, and a bit shy to speak out, but is becoming a fine young man I must add!" she defended.

"I have noticed Mother, but I made my decision today to marry Reagan in April. Will you please support me, and be happy for us so we can make plans?" I asked.

"Yes of course Jackie, please forgive me. I just had to be sure!" "I know Mother, and thank you!" I replied.

Mother was her usual composed self when we joined the men. "Clayton we have a lot planning to do! Jackie, and Reagan plan to marry in April on Jackie's Birthday.

But we have a problem, as to when we will have the

## JENNY MAC

engagement party!" she said. "You will think of a way Mel!" said Father. "I have, I think! A family celebration at Christmas, the engagement party on the 3rd April, one week before the wedding when everyone will be here!"

"How does that appeal to everyone?" she asked. "Oh that just sounds wonderful Mother, thank you!" I said.

"That is perfect Missus Coby!" said Reagan.

"Yes Mel. That will suit nicely!" replied Father.

*Christmas... Shallow Downs... 1964*

## Chapter 26

Christmas was still weeks away, but already the festivities were happening within our homestead.

All of my sisters would be home this Christmas. June, Latisha, and their families were driving, and Lainey was travelling home on the train, so we were all making final preparations for their arrival. They had decided to come home earlier to spend more time with Father before he left with June in January, and he would return home by train. In his absence, I was to run Shallow Downs, with the help of Mick Jones, Father's overseer. Christmas was a special time that Mother, and I shared as we both had a passion for decorating, and when it came to Christmas decorations, it had become a ritual to adorn, not only the Christmas tree in all its glory in its privileged place, but the whole house too.

As we stood back to peruse our handiwork, Mother laughed with joy. "We have outdone ourselves this year Jackie, it is just perfect!" she said. I watched as the pure pleasure emanated from her smoky-blue eyes, and as I looked around, I noticed everything was glittering, and the Christmas spirit filled our home.

"It is beautiful Mother!" I replied, with satisfaction.

We still had two more days before our family guests arrived, so tonight we all planned to rest.

Father, and Reagan joined us with drinks, and snacks full of praise, and accolades for our combined efforts. "Wow Jacqueline, and Missus Coby, great job!" Reagan said. "You two will never cease to amaze me, well done Mel, and Jackie!" Father said, as he turned the wireless on. "Let's relax now, and hear some news." he said.

Amidst the crackling of all the background noise, a guest speaker's voice came through loud, and clear, and seemingly echoed around the room. Our gaiety ceased, as we were riveted to our seats, and thrust into silence, as we listened, gripping our chairs in despair.

*As a special announcement was made.*

Australia is at war in Vietnam. *'The voice blared out'* The Menzies Government of Australia will now be introducing The National Service Scheme in November 1964.

The First National Service Ballot will be drawn out 10th March 1965. A birthday ballot of all 20 year old men is to be introduced by way of selection for new recruits to be trained to fight, and serve in The Vietnam War, and requires men who turned 20 years to register their names with the Dept Of Labour and National Service.

*'We stared at each other as the voice went on.'*

If balloted in, the men will perform two years of continuous full-time service within The Regular Army Supplement, followed by three years part-time service in the Regular Army Reserve. National servicemen on full-time duty are liable for what is called 'special overseas service' which would include combat duties in Vietnam.

## APRIL RAIN

Jacqueline felt like her heart had stopped momentarily, and she just stared into space, and was only vaguely aware of her Father standing up beside her. Her stomach seemed to lurch, and sink to the floor as her eyes tried to focus on Reagan's sad, blank face. He sat so quietly, his face had become as pale as the wall behind him, his eyes dull, and had fixed into a stare. He opened his mouth to speak, and then closed it again, and resumed his silence.

Clayton Coby flicked a switch when the newsreader resumed. Silence followed the cut off voice.

"I am so sorry Jackie, and Reagan, but be patient, we don't have an outcome yet!" Father said, concerned.

*However.* The National Service Scheme was a threat to Jacqueline Coby's future plans, as the unknown hung heavily over her head. Reagan turned 20yrs on 20th Feb 1965, and would have to register.

*'The first chink in her armour began to appear'*

Jacqueline's mind was thrown into turmoil, thoughts consumed her as they raced wildly through her head. 'What will we do?' 'We have only just commited to one another!' 'What of our future together?' and 'What about our Wedding?' "It is just not fair' For the first time in Jacqueline's life, the unfamiliar feelings of insecurity, gripped her. 'Please don't take him away from me!' she pleaded to herself in desperation.

Mel Coby crossed the room to take her daughter into her arms. As she looked into Jackie's sad, green eyes, they immediately filled with tears that welled, and slid down her beautiful face, and Jackie began to sob. Heart wrenching sobs, which bought Reagan to her side, and tore Mel apart. Reagan grasped Jaqueline's hands in his.

"Jacqueline just know how much I love you, and somehow we will work this out!" Reagan's voice trailed off as it broke with such emotion. Mel Coby came to the rescue. "I am so sorry, Jackie, and Reagan! However we will deal with this together. You both will have to be very positive until you know the outcome, but you will have our support." Mel said, as she rocked Jackie.

Jackie's reply was barely a whisper. "Yes Mother, I will try." "Thank you Missus Coby." Reagan said.

Clayton could sense Jackie's dilemma. He looked at the forlorn features of Reagan Chase, and his heart ached for them both as he realized the deep love these two young people had for each other. "Jackie! Reagan! We both feel your pain, and you will have our support, but you have to face reality too. Life is hard, and we can't dictate our future, or what will come. All I know is, that you both have to be tough to face what lies ahead, but you will survive it somehow. If you need advice, ask us! Try to cheer up now Jackie, your family is coming, and they will want to meet Reagan!" Father said. "Yes Father, I know." I said. "Thank you Sir!" said Reagan.

Lainey was the first to arrive. Reagan insisted that he come with me to 'The Siding' to pick her up. We stood waiting on the small platform for the train to pull in, and noticed, the only head poking out of the train window, was Lainey's. As she saw me, she called out, and waved. "Jackie, Jackie! Over here!" I smiled, and waved back. I detected the first chuckle I'd heard from Reagan in quite a while. "My Sister!" I said.

"I guessed!" he said, and we laughed.

Reagan, and Lainey got on tremendously, but later when we talked privately, she said. "Wherever did you find him Jackie? He is such a dreamboat, and a real nice person too! Funny though, I always thought you would end up with Mitch Stringer!" 'There it was again, what was with my family' I thought, as I looked at her.

"Yes well, surprise! Surprise! I am going to be Missus Coby Chase!" I replied. "I can see that little sister, and Congratulations!" Lainey said, with a laugh. "Thank you Lainey!" I said, and we hugged.

My two sisters June, and Latisha arrived the next day with their families. We reminisced, and hugged a lot. It was so good to see them, and my nieces, and nephews dictated the mood, but once again, Reagan won over all their hearts. "He is so perfect Jackie, such a gentleman. I will pray for you both!" said June, when we talked later of all my fears. "Yes, you have a real man there." said Latisha. "Congratulations Jackie!"

Jacqueline approached Christmas in total confusion, though all around her, the family were all trying their utmost to create a joyful time, and so she tried earnestly to join in their festivities. However deep down inside, her fear was her constant companion, and for Jacqueline, and

Reagan it was a time of uncertainty, and fear of the unknown, as they anxiously suffered the long wait for an outcome of the birthday ballot, which could have a huge impact on their lives.

Mel, and Clayton Coby were deeply concerned for their daughter Jacqueline, and for Reagan, their future son-in-law. So once again in their usual style, The Coby's took the situation totally in hand by arranging a surprise for them both.

It was the week just prior to Christmas, and Shallow Downs, once again, was busy with activity, as Mel, and Clayton Coby hosted a Pre-Christmas Party, especially to invite all Jackie, and Reagan's friends to. Their smiles were just the reward that Mel, and Clayton sought, as their friends rallied around the couple to offer love, and support to them both, and the laughter rang out. "It was just the tonic they needed' Mel thought, as Jackie rushed to their side.

"Mother! Father! Thank you both so much, what a wonderful surprise!" I said, as I kissed them. "It's made us both realize, we have to stop moping, and enjoy this time we have together, especially at Christmas. "You are welcome Jackie, but you are so right, enjoy yourselves!" Mother said. "Yes Jackie, just have some fun now!" said Father softly, as he hugged me to his chest. I will always remember that special party with all my family, and with my very dearest friends.

*'It was to be our last.'*

## APRIL RAIN

Christmas morning was one I will always remember. I walked slowly down the stairs into our beautiful living room. It was all lit up now, and so welcoming, not only with decorations, and lights, but with smiling faces, and their laughter rang out.

I paused, as I looked up. They were all there, all the people in my life that I loved so dearly. They had come home to Shallow Downs for the Christmas Celebration.

'My family! My whole family!' I thought, as I watched them closely. And there watching me, was Reagan Chase who had become a very close addition to our family, and I guess. 'The love of my life.' He moved slowly towards me, then took my hands in his, and kissed my cheek.

I did not realize it at the time. But then how could I have known? 'That this would be the very last Christmas I would ever spend in my home with all my loved ones at The Homestead on our Property at Shallow Downs.'

*Ever again.*

# JENNY MAC

## Chapter 27

Shallow Downs seemed to be deserted now. 'Just the absence of Father, makes it feel that way' Jacqueline thought to herself as she walked over to the stables. 'But Mother too, that was a surprise.' When my other sisters left, she decided to travel back with Lainey on the train, to stay with her for a while. I arranged to meet the train on her return. 'I am really missing her too.' I thought.

'All the property workers are here, but it is my family who I miss. Father, Mother, and my Sisters.' I thought. Jacqueline had never been separated from her parents before, and it felt strange.

Sailor was in his stall when I walked inside. It was so good to see a familiar face so I hugged him, planting a kiss on his velvet nose. He snorted his approval, and my spirits lifted as I saddled him, tied my pack on, and slid my rifle into its sheath. I had pre-arranged to meet Mick Jones this morning at the small paddock by the creek to check on the weaners, and he was bringing some hay.

Axel Hall's bungalow seemed deserted as I passed at a slow trot. All was quiet anyway, but as I left the house paddock to reach the path beside the creek I urged Sailor into a canter. It was then that I heard yelling, and wild laughter. Warily, I reined in to dismount, and led Sailor down through the bushes. I paused to mount up again on the bank at the edge of the clearing, and what I saw was unbelievable.

Two young aboriginal men were soaking, and naked to their waists. They were laughing. One was wielding a knife, and Deakan Hall stood next to a fire, yelling, and urging them on to slaughter a small calf. "Stop!" I called.

"What is going on here? Who are you people? This is private property!" The one holding the knife stood up threateningly, and raced quickly towards me, but I was quicker, as I wheeled Sailor away. Grabbing my rifle, I loaded, and fired two shots into the air.

Mick Jones had just arrived at the small paddock, and was in the process of unloading the hay, when the two distinct shots rang out. A well-known distress signal out in the bush, so he lost no time in contemplation. "Hell Jacob! That is rifle shots, jump in!" Mick called, as he quickly jumped in to start the rover, and they went tearing back along the track.

Sailor was stretched to a full gallop along the track. Jacqueline was leaning forward, urging him on. She was headed towards the rendezvous with Mick Jones, but then looked up, and saw the rover coming.

Mick was quick to sight the Stallion galloping down the track towards them, and Jacqueline Coby riding him, as if possessed. She was down low on his neck, pushing him hard, the wind was whipping her long, golden hair out around her in her haste. He had watched Jackie racing Sailor before, but this was different. He felt panic inside, then noticed her reining in, to ease the stallion down. He braked in a swirl of dust, as they met on the roadside.

Jacqueline jumped down, as Mick rushed to her side. "I heard gunshots Jackie! Are you alright?" he asked.

# JENNY MAC

Jacqueline was very calm, and in total control. "I am fine Mick, I fired the shots. I came upon a situation that I couldn't handle on my own, thank you for coming!" she replied, and began telling Mick what had happened.

"Smart girl Jackie! I knew straight away something was amiss. Now, if I know your Father, I know exactly how he would handle this. I just need your confirmation Jackie. I plan to get rid of these trespassers, it may even have to be at gunpoint, if they are armed."

"As for Deakan Hall, we will have to speak to Axel unfortunately, but Deakan has no chances left, we have to ban him from Shallow Downs! Do you agree Jackie?" he asked. "Yes Mick, I do!" I said.

"Then this is what we will do!" said Mick, and we both listened. Mick Jones was thirty-six, a very fit man, solidly built. Hard work had honed his body to muscle, and his strength was well known. As arranged, when they returned, they left Sailor tied to the rover, well back off the track, and Mick went ahead alone, unarmed.

Jacqueline, and Jacob, armed with their rifles followed closely, but watched from the clearing as he ambled down the bank. She could see a calf lying in a pool of blood on the sand, the three men stood over it gloating, and laughing, as Mick walked up to them.

"What the hell do you think you are doing here? This is private property! You've killed a calf by god, and who lit that fire? Put it out now!" Mick said. One of the men stepped forward. "Well why don't ya make me Boss!" he said, and he flashed the knife. "Throw the knife down now boy, don't make me hurt you!" said Mick, and the other two laughed when he lunged at Mick. Deceiving the eye, Mick's hand shot out to grab the wrist holding the knife, and he squeezed until the bones snapped. The boy screamed in pain, and fell to the sand, dropping the knife from his useless fingers. Mick retrieved the knife, saying. "Now! Who else wants to cause more trouble?"

"Start walking, all of you! To Axel's place first!" said Mick. "You have outstayed your welcome here Deakan! You cause more trouble than you are worth! You leave here immediately. I want you gone from Shallow Downs permanently, and take the scumbags with you!"

Deakan scowled, his face livid with anger, his fists bunched as he moved in on Mick. "Don't you push your luck Deakan!" Mick said, grabbing him in a bear hug. "I be workin here ol man!" Deakan spat, and spittle flew into Micks face. "No more, you don't!" said Mick. "Ya not me boss, ya can't tell me what ta do!" he said.

"I can, and I will Deakan Hall, as Clayton Coby has given instructions regarding you to Jackie, and myself, now we have to exercise that. We have discussed it, and decided that this time, it is best that you leave, so move!" said Mick. Deakan Hall's temper flared, his eyes glaring wildly at Mick. His aggression was paramount, as he punched, and kicked him, trying to wrestle his way out of his grasp. Deakan Hall had grown to a tall, strong boy now, and it took Mick all his strength to contain him, and he almost dragged him to the rover.

"You drive Jacob, and Jackie keep your rife aimed at Deakan!" he said, as he tied up his hands to apprehend him. If he moves, shoot him in the foot!" Jacqueline was startled, but she looked at Mick's stressed face, and did what he asked. Axel Hall met them, as Mick dragged Deakan to his door to explain what he had done. "Sorry Axel, but he has to go, get his things!" said Mick. "How could ya Deak, ar ya mad?" asked Axel. "You be mad ol man!" Deakan yelled. He wrenched free to barge Axel, knocking him to the floor, then he went on a rampage through the bungalow, smashing things. Mick tackled him, and at gunpoint they got him to Axel's truck.

Jacqueline sat on Sailor's back watching, her rifle on her knees, as Mick followed Axel's pick-up out of the house paddock. Then, as planned, he would trail them to the front entrance, and to town, making sure they left Shallow Downs. Deakan Hall sat hunched up in the back of the pickup, but his face was murderous, his hands were tied. His two mates sat desolate beside him, still not believing the violence he was capable of, as they had witnessed the destruction.

Deakan yelled as the truck pulled out, his face turned ugly into a vicious scowl. "Think ya smart, don't ya Miss Jacqueline Coby, but I'll get ya. I'll get ya all, an I wont forget ether. Ya all will be sorry, yeah ya gonna pay Miss Jacqueline Coby!" he screamed.

Jacqueline was frantic, she felt threatened, and Deakan's taunts scared her, and bad thoughts plagued her, she needed an escape. It had been a rough few days, being a boss wasn't at all what she expected it to be she realized. 'Please come home Father, and Mother' she thought.

## APRIL RAIN

Reagan Chase provided the solace that she so needed though as they had arranged to spend the whole day out riding. It was just the type of therapy she had needed in her anguish. When they eventually met, she fell into his arms. "Whoa!" he said. "What is wrong here Jacqueline, why all the tears?" Jacqueline explained the events that occurred at the creek, and the taunts from Deakan Hall. As usual, Reagan had a unique way of explaining things.

"Put it all behind you Jacqueline, your Father would have done similar, only worse!" he chuckled. "Deakan Hall is bad news, he seeks trouble! It's a good thing that he is banned from Shallow Downs!" 'I guess so!" I said.

Time seemed to stand still that day, so they were both amazed as the sun started to sink from the sky.

"It is time to leave Jacqueline!" Reagan said, and they mounted up. Light was fading fast as they reached the halfway mark where they were to part, and to go their separate ways. "You take care Jacqueline!" he said, and kissed me. "I will Reagan!" I said. 'Though the day had been perfect as usual, Jacqueline still felt uneasy as she dismounted at the Inner Stables.'

'There was a dampness in the air as it crept in.'
'Dusk turning to darkness, an eeri feeling, as it closed around her.' Jacqueline sensed her return to the Property was later than usual, but led her stallion Sailor to his stable, and reached for the lamp. Close at hand the sound of a match striking, shattered the complete stillness of the night, and echoed loudly in her ear.
*'The flame rose up high into her face'... 'Startling her'...*

# JENNY MAC

*1965...Inner stables...Shallow Downs Homestead...*

## Chapter 28

Jacqueline felt her scalp crawl, all the hairs on her neck stood erect as a shiver shot down her spine, and she tried desperately to adjust her eyes quickly enough to the dim light, to see who was there.

Startled by the flame, she stared at it, to look beyond.

"Who is it?" her voice trembled, as the flame moved to light up his dark face, and only then, recognition become evident. She could smell his foul breath now. 'Vile, and reeking of alcohol.' His body exploded into action, as he kicked the stable door shut, and grabbed a handfull of her long hair in his fist, wrenching it back so hard, she felt as if it was being torn out by the roots. Her mouth gaped to scream out loud, but one rough hand clasped it tight, stifling her, and then her senses rocked, as his fist connected with her face, and she sagged down to the floor. In her semi-concious state, she heard his laughter.

From a dark place, she was aware of rough hands on her body. She tried to lash out, but her hands were tied behind her back, and she was gagged with a foul cloth. Her legs seemed to be pressed to the floor, and her fuzzy eyesight seemed only to focus from one eye now, as she strained hard to see. Then as he rose up before her, the weight lifted from her legs. He pulled something from his clothes, and brutally rolled her over, and she knew instantly, that it was a belt, as the lashes whipped her bare buttocks, again, again, and again. Her last wish as she passed out, was. 'Please let it be over soon!'

She was roused by the water splashing into her face, but as she looked down at her naked body, and her legs spread wide apart, and tied, she knew this nightmare was only just beginning as he started laughing. 'Then he spoke for the first time' "Well Miss Jacqueline, ya not so smart now are ya? An where's ya gun, ya not so brave without that now are ya?" he jeered. 'Hate consumed Jacqueline for the first time in her life.'

There was a faint light glowing from somewhere now, her one good eye adjusting to its glow, and outlining a shape which started to take form as he bent over her.

Calloused hands pulled at her naked breasts in haste, roughly twisting her nipples, squeezing them tight. Her screeches were in vain, just pathetic, stifled noises, as his hands demeaned her, to grope the soft bush between her thighs, and huge tears welled up in her eyes, and rolled down her beautiful face. She screamed a silent scream, as he repeatedly thrust his fingers deep inside her, tearing at her most intimate parts, scratching at her secret flesh, and she groaned with the pain of it.

Shame overwhelmed Jacqueline Coby. Her complete, and utter self respect depreciating in her tormented mind, her body racked with muffled sobs as the torture continued. He laughed at her antics, and she glared back with pure hate as he tore off his clothes. In the defused light he stood naked. Sweat dripped into her face, and she gagged at his rank odour, but more offensive was his manhood standing rigid before him, seeming to have a life of its own as it reared up in front of her vision.

Jacqueline's eyes widened with terror. She tossed her body trying to break the bonds, and tried her hardest to scream out, but all she could manage was a guttural sound deep in her throat, which was cut off severely, as he drove his knees roughly between her thighs, then he thrust himself deeply inside her to tear a path through her maidenhood. Shock ripped right through her body, and her soul, as the excruciating pain took over.

Disgust threatened to choke her as he continuously thrust into her, grunting like a wild animal, until he fell spent in a spasm on top of her. From the depths of her despair his words echoed."If ya tell Miss Jacqueline, yor dead! Ya parents too!" he was saying.

Mary Higgs was puzzled. Earlier she had looked out the kitchen window just as Jacqueline Coby was riding in at dusk, so Mary started preparations for their dinner. They had a habit of eating together while Missus Coby was away. Now it was very dark outside, and Miss Jacqueline still hadn't come up from the stables to The Homestead. Mary left the kitchen, and wandered through the living room, grabbing her jacket from the peg as she passed on her way to the verandah. The cool night air closed around her as she stepped outside. 'Tis damp,' she thought, as she peered out into the darkness to see the fog creeping in to mask the Homestead, outer buildings, and also the Inner Stables. 'Tis windy too,' she thought, as it whipped around, so she pulled her jacket close. There were no lights visible over at the stables, and suddenly an uneasiness overcome her.

Quickly Mary turned the outside light on, and went to get the battery powered lamp out of the store, at the end of the verandah. 'Miss Jacqueline may hav accident' she thought, as she rushed to the steps, and guided by the light, headed out towards the inner stables.

Silence was unbearably oppressive in the darkness, and visibility was getting poor. Mary shuddered.

'Tis scary,' she thought, as the dark shadows danced around upon the inner stables, as she flashed the beam through the trees, and the branches seemed to reach out at her in sympathy, as she passed in her haste towards the stable doors.

Mary felt scared, so she began running, to almost fall inside the building with relief when she threw the stable doors wide open. It was so dark so she composed herself initially to lift the lamp higher as she walked in, calling.

"Miss Jacqueline, ya be here?" She flashed the beam of the lamp back a little, and what she saw would stay with her forever.

Jacqueline Coby lay very still on the cold, cement floor amongst shreds of scattered straw, her knees drawn up tightly against her body into a ball. Mary paled in the darkness, her hand trembled as she held up the light to convince herself of what she was seeing, and the beam flashed on Miss Jacqueline Coby lying there.

Although her naked body was pale in the lamplight, she noticed huge welts exposed upon her skin. She had been beaten badly everywhere, and as Mary moved the beam she noticed her lower body streaked with blood.

# APRIL RAIN

Mary rushed to Jacqueline's side, and set the lamp down. She was in tears at the sight of her young mistress. "Miss Jacqueline! Oh please be ok, please wake up Miss Jacqueline!" she cried, and shook her shoulder gently.

Jacqueline screamed out in torment, as the feelings of hands upon her body triggered her sub-conscious state, and she reared up to lash out violently to knock Mary aside. "Please stop Miss Jacqueline. It be me Mary!" she said in anguish, but as she rose from the floor her eyes followed the beam of light which captured Jacqueline's face now, and she sat down again, in total shock.

It wasn't only the swollen, beaten face that completely closed one eye that shocked Mary to the core. It was the good eye, which glared wildly, and stared viciously with anger, like a mad person. 'What be happen here to my Miss Jacqueline' Mary stressed. When she held out her hand though, she detected some recognition emerging now to soften Jacqueline Coby's face, so she reached out to her, grasping her hand firmly, and pulled her closer. Shrugging off her jacket, Mary then encased Jacqueline's body with it, to hug her close, and rock her.

Somehow in her own distress, Mary managed to help Jacqueline to stumble along in a slow trek towards the homestead, and up to her room, where she bathed her injuries, and put her to bed.

"Miss Jacqueline, I go call doctor now, an I get Mister Mick ta com ta see ya!" said Mary.

Mary was immediately startled, and took a step back

from Jacqueline's wild outburst when she lifted up the covers to scream at her. "Don't dare call the Doctor out here Mary, do you hear! I do not want the Doctor to see me! No Doctor! Do you understand me?" "No, me not understand Miss Jacqueline, ya be hurt there, ya need a Doctor!" Mary replied, rather sheepishly.

"Please Mary, Jacqueline uttered in exhaustion as she lay back, her body racked in unbearable pain. She sunk deep under the covers, trying to blot out the world. Her mind was distorted as thoughts ran wild of her Mother's past words echoing in her ears, over, and over again.

"You know that you can produce life now Jackie." *'Produce life!'* "A precious gift for your husband, would be your virginity." *'Virginity!'*

"Pride, is a huge factor with your Father Jackie. He would frown on any discredit to his name, or to your name!" *'Pride!'* "As a Coby you're expected to do things the right way. Respect that!" *'Respect'*

Jacqueline threw the covers aside to rise slowly from the bed, her good eye glaring in anger.

"I will say this only once Mary, then we will never speak of it again. 'Tonight my life ended.' I was beaten, but violated in the worst possible way that if a man tried to touch me again, I would shudder with revulsion.

'My self-pride is gone! Shame is choking me! Eating away at my soul.' So it is my Coby pride that forbids me from shaming my loved ones Mary. I have to live with that or I will die trying. But I will not subject them to this embarrassment, or to see their pity. We tell no one about this Mary! Not Mother, Father, Reagan, my friends, or staff! So don't get Mick! Send Reagan, and my friends away! I am asking you to lie for me now Mary? Please promise me! I need your help!" I said, as I sobbed. "Trust me Miss Jacqueline, me be beside ya!" said Mary.

As the very first rays of sunshine burst through her windows at daybreak, Jacqueline Coby woke. Very gingerly, she rose from her bed, grabbed a mirror from her bedside table, then she trailed her coverlet behind her to the window seat, where she sat curled up to look out over their property.

'It's so beautiful out there, but in this room, and in my heart, it is cold, and ugly! Oh how I wish I could change it!' 'Reality is a bitter pill to swallow!' she was thinking, as she was jolted into realizing her predicament.

'Why has fate cruelly played yet another twist in my life, but for the worst?' she wondered.

Her mirror reflected someone's swollen but saddened face staring back at her, though it was not her own.

Vicious wild looking eyes that 'Frightened her' glared back at her through the swollen slits that were bruised to blackness. There were no facial cuts, though it was her body that screamed out in anguish, and the deep ache in her chest cleaved her apart, as her heart throbbed in the deepest agony with every beat.

'There would be no wedding' she thought. 'No future plans.' 'I have to face up to those facts now.'

# JENNY MAC

Despair overcome me, as I made the heartbreaking decision to forsake my true love, the love of my life, and set him free. 'I cannot face Reagan, my shame is too deep, and my revulsion far too strong, he doesn't deserve that.' I thought. 'This is something that, even he could not accept, but how could I expect him to, when my own disgust violates my whole being, and the shame eats at my pride. I could never face my closest friends about this, or even to let them see my injuries, but more heartbreakingly was my Mother, and Father. My heart would just tear apart if I saw hurt, or judgement in their eyes, and to discredit their name would be unspeakable. It was not The Coby way, where pride runs deep in our family. 'My life will never be the same again.' I thought.

Jacqueline's thoughts were suddenly interrupted by the raised voices outside on the verandah, so she moved closer to the shutters to listen. Mick Jones was there, and he called out, as he climbed up the stairs. "Are you there Jackie?" his voice boomed out, and as I peeked through the slats I saw Mary opening the front door. 'Poor Mary! I have really asked too much from her!' I thought, as I watched her speak out. "Mister Mick, good mornin! Ya be wantin Miss Jacqueline, me thinks?" "Hi Mary, yeah I arranged with Jackie to work together today, is she up yet?" he asked. "So sorry Mister Mick, Miss Jacqueline, she be still in bed, she have some flu me thinks, might be betta she stay there for few days!" said Mary.

"No worries!" said Mick, tell her to stay put, and get well!" "I will Mister Mick!" replied Mary.

## APRIL RAIN

Reagan was not so easy to deter though. Each day he phoned but I refused his calls, and once again Mary made excuses for me, until early one morning, he just turned up. From my room I could hear the arguments between him, and Mary, and my heart went out to him as I peeked out through the slats. "He is so beautiful' I thought. Tears just rolled down my face, and huge sobs came from deep down, as I ran to throw myself on the bed. Secretly, I wished to rush out to him, to fall into his embrace, so he could comfort me, and make it all right, but it could not be, not now! 'I was a used person now!' 'Not worthy of him!' 'But in my heart, I knew I would be appalled by him, and repelled by his touch, as complete revulsion, and horror resurfaced from the depths of my brain to take over from where it seethed inside, haunting me. Nothing would be the same again.'

Alerted by Reagan's voice, I went to the window as he left the stairs, and watched him walk away, and out of my life forever. At that instant I decided I would write to him to end our relationship.

If I recall, at that point in time I realized everything went from bad to worse! Many weeks had passed now, and I tried hard to immerse myself in work. My injuries had almost healed on the outside, but inside it was like a living hell, as nightmares plagued me, and the threats from Deakan Hall haunted me, to the point of fear.

Mother was coming home soon, and I fretted for her safety. However, deep inside another fear nagged at me. 'How could I face Mother, and the million questions she would have for me that I could not answer?'

# JENNY MAC

'I was completely changed now, and if anyone could detect that, it would be my Mother, or my very closest friends. I really fixed that with my friends, didn't I.' my thoughts raged in disgrace.

Jake Hardy had driven slowly up the driveway that particular day, and parked under the Jacaranda trees to face the homestead. Anne Giles rushed to climb out of the vehicle when she saw me leaving the stables. I was distraught, and trembling uncontrollably, hardly able to set one foot in front of the other. It was the first time I had gone to the stables since that night, and once inside, fear gripped me in a vice.

My breath choked in my throat, suffocating me, as I gasped for air. My face broke out in a cold sweat, and my whole body began to shake all over, and I ran, bursting out the double doors into the sunlight, where I gulped for air, and fought to gain control. Anne was so excited as usual, I noticed, when she called out to me.

"Jackie! Jackie! We have just arrived, came to visit, it's so good to see you!" As I got closer, she stopped dead, to stare at me. "What is it Jackie, what is wrong with you? Aren't you well?" 'I managed not to burst into tears, but I was so ashamed with what I had to say to them.'

"Go home Anne! Take her away Jake! I cannot talk to you both now, or ever again!" Jake was startled, and took a step backwards, but Anne reacted quite differently.

'My best friends face fell in a heap.'
*'That is how I remember her'*

## APRIL RAIN

Anne Giles was devastated, the tears sprang into her eyes as she looked back to watch her best friend go inside. Jake put his arm around her, and said softly.

"Come on Anne let's go now, you are getting upset."

"You don't understand Jake Hardy!" Anne sobbed.

"Something is terribly wrong with Jackie! Didn't you notice? I know Jacqueline Coby, like she is of my own blood. Believe me when I tell you, something is wrong here! That person there was not the Jacqueline Coby I have loved all my life, and have grown up with. I should go back to help her!" said Anne. Jake faced her, and said.

"Anne, I know Jacqueline too, and I am as concerned as you, but now is not the right time I don't think, we will come back another day!" "Promise me Jake?" she said. "I promise." he said. So they got into the car, and Anne sobbed her heart out as they drove away.

Jacqueline barely made it to her room. She pushed through the door, and rushed in to seek the solace she needed as she collapsed onto her bed, and into a fit of hysteria. Huge sobs racked her body, her heart pounded so severely in her chest, and it ached like it was being torn apart. 'I am rejecting all of the people I love.' I sobbed. 'One by one Mary has been sending them away, and now my best friends Anne, and Jake!' 'Is there no end to the pain?' I cried out.

*'Unfortunately it was just starting for me'*

Mary closed the door softly as she came in, and sat by my bed. Tenderly she folded me into her arms, and rocked me gently, trying to calm me, as my tears flowed down my face to dampen her tunic, and she whispered.

## JENNY MAC

"Miss Jacqueline, might be not tha right time, but me needs ta talk to ya, tis important! I thinks ya missed ya moon Miss Jacqueline, an if ya dont get that there soon be far too long now!" I stared bewildered, realizing what she meant, and panic hit me.

We left Shallow Downs two weeks later. The long wait was driving me crazy, and throwing my mind into chaos. I had to have a definite answer, and I could not see a local Doctor, so the only other answer was to travel the two hundred miles to Laidley.

Mary had arranged the Doctor's appointment for me. So we left together in my Jeep at first light.

Confirmation when it came that day, hit me just so hard that my senses reeled, my tormented mind was in turmoil, as the last hope of redemption was shattered, as I was faced with the enormity of my situation. Waves of shame, and desperation consumed me, as I realized this was just unforgivable, the ultimate shame, and disgrace upon us all. 'I was pregnant' and this was not the Coby way!' On the return trip I became overcome with huge sobs which shook my body, and tears flooded my vision, until I could not see. I pulled over to leap out of the Jeep, and submitted to the excruciating pain, and thoughts.

Torn apart, and tortured with huge guilt, Jacqueline struggled with the deep feelings of remorse which consumed her as she groped blindly with heartbreaking decisions that were now facing her but would ultimately define her fate, and change her life forever.

## APRIL RAIN

My eyes filled with tears, and I stared up at Mary's anguished face, as I told her with the utmost certainty what I had to do! "I am leaving home Mary! Leaving my Family behind, and also my life at Shallow Downs. My destiny is mapped out for me now!" "Then me be goin with ya Miss Jacqueline!" she replied, then she cried. I felt relieved, but answered. "Thank you Mary, when we get home I want you to pack all our clothes, and then I will get everything I need from the stores shed. I will meet Mother's train tomorrow, but I must leave before Father gets back! We will leave tomorrow night!"

Jacqueline was frantic, it was her last night at Shallow Downs. She looked around her room sadly, and her thoughts ran wild. 'My home! My beautiful home, and I am leaving it a self-made outcast, to be alienated from my Family, and my dearest friends. To never see their faces again will be so devastating, heartbreaking.' 'Then there is Reagan, my true love. To forsake him seems a huge price to pay for a life of pain! Oh, why did this have to happen to me?' she cried. She could hardly keep the hysteria at bay so she could concentrate on her tasks. Her priority now was to finish her packing, and to pen the two letters that nagged her subconscious.

Anxiety gripped her as she sat down on the window seat, with pen, and paper in hand. Cruel words began to appear upon the paper, her tears fell to smudge the page as she wrote to her love, Reagan. It was an unforgivable way to end a perfect relationship, and she thought of the life they could have had, but she would not sugar-coat it, her mind was made up. She could not bare to face all the embarrassment she would cause her loved ones. Her heart would break to give this letter to the mail driver tomorrow at 'The Siding.'

Jacqueline thought about her parents. 'What to say to them' she wondered. 'Nothing would really suffice.' She was at a loss, so she poured out her love for them on the alien pages which would be their only salvation.

She offered them no explanation for her leaving, only that she would never return. That she could not bear to shame them with the sordid details. 'Mother would be devastated, and just thinking about leaving her Father, who was her idol, brought tears to Jacqueline's eyes, but somehow she just knew deep in her heart that he would understand. They were both two of a kind, Father, and Daughter, their Coby pride ran deep.' 'Leaving Father is unthinkable, he had plans for me!' she thought sadly.

Jacqueline paused for a moment, then quickly added another sheet to her letter. This note was business-like as she penned it releasing her shares in the Property back to her Father, Clayton Coby, then she signed it. As Jacqueline dragged her eyes from the papers in despair to look around her room, the bedside lamp attracted her.

Beneath its glow upon the table, the timber carving of her miniature black horse with white markings, rearing up on its timber stand just seemed to beckon to her. She thought of Sailor, and of Mitch. 'Oh Mitch! I loved you too! If only you knew that?' she thought.

## APRIL RAIN

Retrieving the carving, she slipped it into her bag. 'I may not have Sailor anymore!' she said sadly as the tears sprung into her eyes. 'But I will have you April Rain!'

She added another note to the letter. 'Please Father. Give Sailor to Mitch! I know that he will love him like I do, and please give him my special racing saddle also!'

'Enough!' Jacqueline cried, as she grabbed the letters to sweep them into her bag, and throwing herself on the bed, she cried herself to sleep.

Next morning Jacqueline had arrived at 'The Siding' early, and waited for the train to arrive. Her head ached, her eyes were puffed from crying, but Mel Coby looked refreshed from her break as she stepped on to the small platform. Jacqueline's heart almost burst with love for her as she ran into her embrace.

As she predicted though, her Mother's intuition took over very quickly as she eased her backwards, and just stared at her. "Hello Jackie! Whatever is wrong darling, you do not look your best?" she asked. "Welcome home Mother! I have missed you so very much. I am just tired I guess!" I replied, as Mother's questions continued on.

I was finding it difficult to hide things from Mother all day, so it was late when Mary, and I packed the Jeep.

I drove over to re-fuel, and went to the stores shed to pack all the things I had put aside to take with me. Then I drove into Shallow Siding to pick up some things there, but mainly to bide my time until we were to leave.

## JENNY MAC

*As I look back to recall.*

\*\*\*\*\*

*My thoughts continuously plague me for not spending more time with Mother that day. Instead, I was avoiding her.*

*'It has been one of my deepest regrets in all my life.'*

\*\*\*\*\*

Reagan Chase thanked the mail truck driver, then he stared at the small envelope with the unmistakable flowing script. 'Why is she writing to me?' he wondered.

'I would have thought by now, she would have come to see me in person, but he knew that Jacqueline Coby was definitely avoiding him, and shutting him out. But he did not know why!' She was not answering his calls, and he was refused access to see her at The Property.

'Maybe Jacqueline is still just upset about The Army Ballot, and my possible call-up, which was still hanging heavily over our heads. They had both lived with fear of the outcome of that!' he thought.

But deep down the nagging feeling in his gut told him otherwise as he tore at the paper to open it, then started reading the heartbreaking words, which changed his life forever, and realized his instinct had been correct.

## APRIL RAIN

He felt angry, and devastated, but was at a loss for an explanation as he sensed something was terribly wrong here! 'I must go to her!' he thought, as he ran to jump in the Land Rover. He gunned the engine, and with his foot flat to the pedal, he sped out through the front gates in a swirl of dust to join with the main road.

His thoughts raced wildly, like the vehicle he drove, but when he topped the next rise he braked the rover abruptly as an unmistakable glow against the darkening sky filled his vision, and he came to a halt in a spray of gravel, and just stared out over the countryside to the direction of the property Shallow Downs. Fear gripped him in a vice as he urged the vehicle forward, and drove like a mad-man towards the threat they all feared most.

It was late when Reagan reached the portals of Shallow Downs. He stared in disbelief, then drove on towards the Homestead. His heart thumped wildly in his chest, his fear threatened to choke him. 'Where is Jacqueline?' he stressed, as he looked to her car park, but her Jeep wasn't there. But something else caught his attention, as someone came into view, someone he knew well.

*Then Reagan ran.*

# JENNY MAC

*1965 ... The Fire ... Shallow Downs*

APRIL RAIN

## Chapter 29

Shallow Downs was burning. Huge flames, fueled by the dry undergrowth of leaves, and twigs, was soon alight, and crackled then spit out sparks to ignite other areas, that soon became a raging fire as it burst through the massive forest of wattle trees, and raced on the wind, then down the escarpment. Very quickly the devastation became so much more ominous when it headed towards an obvious awaiting disaster as it threatened the Shallow Downs Homestead, which sat in its path.

People were everywhere. Mick Jones had rallied his men to try, and beat back the flames. Their faces were blackened with soot, their clothes singed, their bodies drenched in sweat as they beat the flames with heshion bags, and sprayed water from the hoses, and buckets, but nothing could stop the intensity of the flames.

Reagan Chase ran quickly amongst all the chaos to find Mick Jones. He yelled above the roar of the fire, and the men trying to combat it, to get Mick's attention. He beckoned him to follow, and keeping his sights firmly on the figure he had seen emerging from the smoke, and flames, he pointed him out. Mick acted at once, grabbed a length of rope, and ran closely behind Reagan.

Reagan looked back helplessly as he ran on, to watch in dread as The Shallow Downs Homestead seemed to disintegrate before his eyes when the great wall of fire engulfed it, consuming all its timbers. Deakan Hall saw them coming. Though his bare feet were all blistered, the flesh peeling off, and his body singed, he summoned up a last effort to get away, but he was also overcome with smoke, and his lungs heaved with the effort. 'He had lit the fires alright, but he hadn't counted on the wind, and his escape route had got cut off by fire so he ran through it.' 'Damn Coby's had ta pay!' he reveled in the thought, as he was tackled to the ground by Reagan Chase.

Mary was helping Mel Coby to prepare the evening meal, and she was being questioned by Missus Coby about Miss Jacqueline. Mary hung her head low, barely able to look up for she feared Missus Coby would know she was lying.

"I be goin ta set tha table now Missus Coby! Where ya want that there set?" she asked, in haste to escape. Mel Coby looked hard at her. She knew Mary very well. 'But something was not right here!' she thought. 'I will let it go, I have asked enough for now!' "Thank you Mary, set up the sunroom please. I missed that room while I was away!" replied Mel. "Ok Missus Coby!" said Mary.

Mel Coby was deep in thought, but she completely froze when she heard the agonizing scream from Mary piercing the stillness around her, and she rushed out to the sunroom to Mary's aid. She stopped dead at the doorway as a great wall of fire filled her vision, only just a few yards outside the sunroom of the house. Fear, and disbelief overwhelmed her, but she tried to console Mary who was hysterical, and crying.

"Come quickly Mary, we must get out!" Mel said with

urgency in her voice, as she pulled Mary up from the floor. Mary's limbs were weak, her hands shaking as she stared over at the fire. Mel's heart thumped wildly in her chest as fear overcome her, but she shook Mary hard to alert her. "Get out Mary, now!" she screamed. "Run! Get outside of the house! Do you understand me Mary?" she yelled. Mary looked vaguely at Mel. "Yes Missus Coby, me know now, me must get outside, ya must come too!' and Mary ran. Mel had no time to dwell on her beloved home or to salvage a thing, the fire was too close, so she raced through the living room, but in haste she tripped on a rug. Her head thumped the hardwood table solidly as she fell, and she slumped unconscious to the floor.

Jacqueline had purposely planned to return home late to Shallow Downs as the Jeep was packed for the trip now, and she wanted to keep it from prying eyes. From the front entrance of The Property, a gold, and red glow seemed to highlight the scenario in the failing daylight as huge flames leapt high in the air to surge through the Property. Jacqueline slammed on the brakes hard in total shock, and stopped to stare in unbelievable dread at the devastation as the fire consumed her home. "Oh no, no! Please God! Not our home too!" she screamed out loud, but no one was there. She jumped from the Jeep and ran.

Mary was groveling in the dirt just out of reach of the burning Homestead. She rocked from side to side, and she kept repeating some gibberish over, and over again, then she wailed out with the most mournful sound that pierced Jacqueline Coby's soul. Jacqueline rushed to her side, and then took her in her arms. She tried not to let the fear, and anguish appear in her voice as she tried to console her. "Try to calm down now Mary, then you will be ok!" she said. "Not be ok Miss Jacqueline! Cause me thinks tis all be me own fault!" wailed Mary. "What is all your fault Mary?" Jacqueline asked her. "Ya Mother! She told me ta go! I be left her Miss Jacqueline!" cried Mary.

As a first reaction, Jacqueline began to tremble at the mention of her Mother. "You left Mother where Mary?" Her voice rising, then she shook her hard. "Where is she Mary?" she asked. "Me be so sorry Miss Jacqueline, but Missus Coby she not come out there, she tell me go, but she not come out there, she be in tha house!" Mary cried.

Jacqueline Coby's shrill scream could be heard from everywhere as she madly tore herself away from Mary to race towards the crumbled ashes of her home. Reagan Chase heard her as he, and Mick were tying up Deakan Hall, and he sprinted after her as fast as he could.

When he reached Jacqueline, she was so hysterical, just like a person possessed, as she threw bits of burning timber aside, and crying uncontrollably as she scraped aside the hot ashes with her bare hands, trying to get through. He noted with his own eyes, the blisters appear on her soft skin, and her clothes were blackening.

Quickly he grabbed her arm hoping to coax her back, but it was flung aside just as quickly, and he was sure he saw revulsion upon her face as she turned. He recoiled in amazement. "Jacqueline, please come out of there! I am sorry about the Homestead!" he pleaded an apology.

Slowly she rose. Beneath all the charcoal smears, her skin was pale, and ghost-like, her eyes shut tight, puffed, and with dark circles underneath them but were rimmed red from crying. Her eyes slowly opened, and his shock was magnified. He stepped back as she seemed to look right through him with those dead, un-seeing eyes that frightened him. 'What happened to her?' he wondered, as the smell of smoke, and burned flesh lingered in the air. Then her voice rasped with emotion, and was almost haunted-like. "It's not only our Homestead I lost Reagan Chase! My Mother was trapped in there!" she wailed.

Reagan gaped at her response, he opened his mouth to speak to her, but then closed it again. Suddenly she walked away in a dream-like state. 'It was so useless attempting to talk to her, she was beyond all sensibility.'

He felt saddened with this revelation, devastated! 'No one even dreamed that anyone would still be inside the Homestead!' This shocked him to the core, and the tears welled up to fill his eyes. He wished that he could help Jacqueline, but she was not letting him in at all. 'What happened to our love? She hates me now! But why? This is not the Jacqueline Coby I know, and love! Something is wrong!' he thought. His last sighting of her was when she was reaching for Mary's hand, and they hugged.

Mick Jones distracted Reagan then as he appeared at his side. Mick had Deakan Hall all trussed up, but he was fighting him every inch of the way. "I need help Reagan!" Mick said, in a breathless voice, as he wrestled to contain

Deakan Hall. Reagan grabbed him as they both struggled to drag him along. "Let's get you all nice, and cozy in the local jailhouse Deakan, and there you will answer for all your crimes, and that is going to be quite a lot, if I have anything to do with it!" said Reagan bitterly. "Ya git ya hands off me Chase, ya aint takin me ta no jail, or ya will be next on me list, an ya too Mick Jones!" yelled Deakan. "Save it for the judge Deakan, where you're going, you won't have a need for any list!"

"You won't get any sympathy from me either, I will do everything in my power to see you put away!"

"Mick, and I will both be witnesses at your trial! We have caught you in the act of escaping from the fire at Shallow Downs, a place where you are banned from. We have your lighter fluid, and matches which we found on you. You are as guilty as hell!" Reagan said.

Deakan Hall was quite proud of the fact that he got even with the all the Coby's, and he didn't mind admitting the fact either. He wanted everyone to know they don't mess with Deakan Hall. "Ya be crazy Chase! Corse I lit tha fire, jus gettin me own back I was, twas payback time! Damn Cobys kicked me out o me home, now they hav ta pay, now they got nothing, jus like me!" he laughed. "He won't be laughing soon when they add murder to all his charges!" Reagan whispered to Mick.

"What murder Reagan?" Mick whispered back. "I just had to stop Jacqueline from going in the rubble to get in to her Mother. Mary got out, but Missus Coby didn't!" he whispered. *"My god she is still in there!"* said Mick.

## APRIL RAIN

They buried the charred remains of Mel Coby in the family graveyard which was situated in a separate paddock that overlooked Shallow Creek, where the big river gums grew in amongst the hills, and where all the Coby's before her, lay to rest. Clayton Coby stood alone beside the graveside under the river gums, and as he looked up, sick with his grief, they were all there. Their many friends, families from town, and the surrounding countryside came, also their loyal workers. His three daughters, and families were there too.

*'Everyone except Jackie!'* he thought, as a deep crease furrowed his brow. They all stood back quietly as they grieved, but mingled respectfully, giving him his space.

He had returned to Shallow Downs to its devastation. His home was completely gutted, half his Property, and stock, and his wattle plantation, all gone! His life! His being! All he worked hard for all his life, destroyed by a raging fire, and the fire within him raged. But above all else, from the depths of his soul, he felt the loss of his wife, his best friend, the worst tragedy that cut deeply.

As Clayton Coby looked down into the pit where his only true love in all his life was being interred, his heart almost ceased from the pain, and loss. 'It had all taken it's toll,' as his body sagged. His once massive shoulders, and physique seemed to shrink, as if the life was being sucked out of him. His sullen face had paled to stretch tight, and masklike to emphasize the lines which now etched deeply into his once handsome face.

When the Preacher spoke the final few words for the

passage of Mel's life. To Clayton it seemed so pitiful in relation to who she was, what she had been to him, their family, and to all her friends. 'She was just everybody's rock! She deserved so much more!' he thought sadly, as the tears slipped silently down his face.

After the service, and when everyone had paid their final respects to Mel Coby, they all then quietly approached Clayton Coby to offer commiserations, but the obvious absence of Jacqueline Coby was also at the forefront within everyone's minds, and this presented Clayton with many questions from them that he could not answer about his Daughter's disappearance.

Ashton Banks moved in to try, and alleviate Clayton's stress which was now plainly draining his face, so he discreetly directed the guests away to a place along the sandbanks of the creek, where he had previously set up an area for the many guests to celebrate Mel's wake.

Temporary tents were erected. Tables, chairs, a buffet table, cooking facilities, and a healthy supply of food, and drinks on ice. Ashton thought that would be more appropriate than sitting out in view of the devastation of the demolished Homestead.

Clayton watched in relief as they moved away, then Mick Jones moved up beside him. "Clayton there is no best time for this, so I am just going to tell you now of the controversy that Jackie, and I had with Deakan Hall, and why we decided to ban him from the property!" He handed Clayton an envelope. "I'm not sure, but this may be a clue to the mystery of Jackie's disappearance! It was in the mail box at the front of The Property!" Mick said.

Clayton Coby looked longingly at the flowing script upon the envelope, and his heart flipped over as the tears flooded his eyes. He slid down to sit with his back hard against a gum tree, and he replied to Mick.

"Leave me for a minute Mick. When you return, we will talk then!" "Sure Boss!" replied Mick with heart felt sorrow. Clayton at once was puzzled, the letter was 'To Mother, and Father.' *'This was written before the fire!'*
*'Why was Jackie leaving then?'*

His thoughts consumed him, and he almost tore the paper in half trying to get to its contents. He read it over, and over, trying to read between the lines even. He was persistent in trying to understand the specific message that his Daughter was leaving him. 'It had to be pride.' he realized. Jacqueline could not stay to face the shame that she undoubtedly knew would ruin them all, to then ultimately discredit Clayton, and Mel's name, as well as her own, and all their friends as well.

*'Whatever could be so bad to make her leave her home though? And what was the shame?'* he wondered.

Clayton beckoned to Mick. "We will talk now Mick!" he said, as Mick stood before him. "But! I want you to arrange for me to speak privately with Reagan Chase!" Clayton wanted to speak to Reagan in depth! "Then find young Mitch for me?" "Yes Boss!" said Mick, as he sat down beside him to tell his side of the saga.

# JENNY MAC

Mick laid it all out in bare details, but leaving no stone unturned as he related the events. Clayton could picture the vengeance festering in Deakan's sick mind. When he spoke to Reagan, he was quite satisfied that he was not involved in her disappearance however he was shocked that Jackie broke up with him, and of her recent peculiar behaviour. 'Something just doesn't add up!' 'This is not like my Daughter at all!' *'What had happened to her?'*

*'I should have been here!'* he thought.

Mitch found Clayton Coby alone, and so forlorn with his grief. "Mister Coby, I can't begin to say how sorry I am for all your loss!" he said sadly. "Thank you Mitch!" said Clayton. "Sir, where is Jackie? Shouldn't we all look for her?" he asked. "I don't know where she is Mitch! I only have the letter she left me, it said not to follow. I am instructed to give Sailor to you, he belongs to you now!" "Sailor? Goodness, isn't she coming back Mister Coby?" he asked in deep stress. "Sadly, no Mitch!" said Clayton.

They drove into Shallow Siding in silence, each one to their private thoughts as the countryside slipped by. Idle talk was irrelevant as the talking had been done, and their sole purpose united them.

It was early on Sunday morning, there was a calmness in the little town. It was so quiet, as if sleeping.

Not a soul graced the street either, so the sound from tyres crunching on the gravel seemed deafening amidst the stillness as they came skidding to a sudden halt as Mick Jones braked the Land-rover, and stopped outside the front of the little Jailhouse.

## APRIL RAIN

Clayton Coby was first to get out. Slowly he walked to where the Constable who was expecting them, waited at the front door. Ben Jarvis was young man of thirty, slight of build. Black hair fell into his blue eyes.

He was most efficient, and he spoke very politely. "Morning Mister Coby, I am so sorry for your loss, the sooner we do this business the better! "Thank you!" said Clayton. "Morning Mick, Reagan. Please come on inside everyone." "Hi Ben!" they said. Ben had the paperwork ready, and he began taking their statements. "Witnesses Mick, and Reagan, are you willing to testify in court?" Ben asked. "We sure are Ben! We will travel on the train with you if need be!" said Reagan. "Good! Clayton, the prisoner has confessed. I believe you have other charges to press against him!" "Yes I do!" answered Clayton.

When all the formalities were final, they shook hands, and filtered out but then a ruckus in a cell nearby alerted Clayton, and he turned back towards the cells.

Clayton looked sternly through the bars at Deakan Hall. "Well if it's not Clayton Coby com ta visit me, ya not be so smart now Coby, ar ya?" said Deakan, with a laugh. "You will pay for a long time for what you have done!" said Clayton, and turned to walk away. "Yeah, got ya all Coby! Got ya Miss Jacqueline too, that was tha best!" he laughed. Clayton turned, a fierce scowl creased his brow, his face livid, and inside him a fire raged.

'Suddenly, with great sorrow! He understood it all'

*'This was the missing link he needed'*
*'To explain why his Daughter had left.'*

# JENNY MAC

## Chapter 30

Jacqueline Coby was raised in Outback Country, but to leave it now was the hardest thing she had done in her protected life as her upbringing with loving parents, was the only world she knew. Her life had been completely shattered by disaster, and total devastation, and plucked away from her, to be left in tatters.

*'As her whole world, as she knew it'*
*'Was turned upside down.'*

Her heart was heavy, like the clouds above her. She stared blankly, her knuckles turning white as her hands gripped the steering wheel tightly, and she tried hard to focus as she drove along the dark road. Jacqueline had not uttered a word since they left Shallow Downs, but there was nothing to say, she was just shattered, so she submitted to the constant pain deep within herself, and sat rigid on the seat, her face pale, and mask-like.

Huge bolts of lightning startled her as they shook the heavens, to strike with a vengeance up ahead, breaking open the night sky to turn it into day with its brilliance, while the ominous thunder rolled, and clapped loudly above them like a huge whip being unleashed.

Jacqueline watched in horror as the deluge descended upon them. They had protection inside the cabin of the Jeep from the weather, but the windshield wipers were struggling to keep up pace with the downpour, and her visibility was poor. Jacqueline began to shake, and tears slid down her face when her mind began to wander, and the constant thoughts recurred to plague her again as she relived the past months. *'It was never-ending.'*

'If only the rain had come earlier!' she thought sadly. 'Father wouldn't have gone away, he would have been at home to protect us. Mother would still be alive, and I would be at home! *'Our home'* Lost because of me!' she screeched loudly. *'My life was ruined, taken from me in the worst way'* But Mother! *'It was all my fault we lost Mother!'* she called out loud.

Mary jumped in her seat with fright, and amidst the storm raging around them, Jacqueline's screams scared her, and her eyes flew wide as she strained to see Jacqueline's pale face, but as she listened to her ravings, even the darkness couldn't hide the fact that Jacqueline Coby was under huge stress, and out of control.

Softly Mary spoke out so as not to startle her, and laid a hand gently upon her arm. "Please be stop now Miss Jacqueline, ya be need ta rest. Stop the Jeep please Miss Jacqueline, ya need ta sleep!" she said.

Jacqueline seemed jolted back from that awful place, and once again she tried to function to face reality. "I am really sorry Mary, I didn't intend to frighten you, and I know that I must be acting strangely, but I cannot seem to help it. My grief is such now that I do not feel normal anymore! You are right, we will find a place to stop for the night!" she said. "You be not well Miss Jacqueline!"

"Ya hav had too much goin wrong there, an too much pain, an a lot more ta go through yet! We be fight ta get ya right agin, an me be help ya Miss Jacqueline!" replied Mary. "Thank you Mary!" Jacqueline said, as she noticed a gravel track which left the road, so she veered off to park in the protection of the bushes, and the towering gum trees.

Mary leaned over the back to reach the tucker box, and handed Jacqueline some cold cuts of beef, and broke some bread for her. "Now we hav ta eat somethin, then we sleep Miss Jacqueline!" she said. "Stop it, stop it now Mary! Stop calling me Miss Jacqueline! I am not worthy of that! I am 'Miss' to you no longer, just Jackie! You are my friend not my employee Mary! Do you understand?" Jacqueline asked her. "No me not understand at all Miss Jacqueline, ya hav been that ta me since ya was born. Me just can't call ya Jackie, tis not right!" said Mary. "You just did Mary, so get used to it!" Jacqueline replied.

In total contrast from the previous night, the morning brought with it total sunshine as it shone through the trees, and Jacqueline Coby stirred, as the heat from its presence filtered into the closed cabin. She woke up to a feeling of desolation as it overtook her, and her head pounded, but deep inside her chest, her heart seemed to tighten as it continued to ache in her sorrow, and there was an emptiness inside her.

She felt desperately alone, and lost, for the first time in her life as the pain consumed her. Her body ached, and her hands were blistered, and bleeding now from driving.

## JENNY MAC

Her clothes were blackened, and partly burnt, and her hair was a matted mess, but her red, puffy eyes had lost their light as she stared out at Mary sitting at an open campfire.

"Mornin Miss Jacqueline! Come out here ta tha fire!" called Mary. "Good morning Mary, but you have forgotten! That would be Jackie!" Jacqueline said, as she got out of the Jeep. "Yeah me forgit!" said Mary. "I did not know you were familiar with the ways of bush life Mary!" Jacqueline stated with surprise. "Me thinks me memory be comin a bit back, twas all I be used ta growin up. We be livin in tha bush, not be in house, jus a ol tin shack, then Mama, an Papa got killed here in thet car crash, twas when ya Mother found me, an took me in ta her home. She be jus like a Mamma ta me too, ya Mother was, and I miss her bad!" said Mary, as she sobbed.

Jacqueline rushed quickly to her side to fold her arms around her, and said. "Mary, I am so sorry! You loved my Mother too, didn't you? I really didn't think Mary! Please forgive me?" Jacqueline said, and she started to cry too. "Don't cry Miss Jacqueline. Me be ok, jus sad is all, but ya be lot worse, so much lost, me know ya pain. Hav wash now, ya will feel better!" she said.

While Jacqueline dried her eyes, she looked hard at this person who was always around for her when she was growing up. 'I am just getting to know more about her' she thought, as she realized that they had never had a conversation like this, and she felt guilty for not asking these things before. "Tell me what it is you are making?" asked Jacqueline, trying to change their mood. "Me be makin damper ta hav with treacle, an hav tha billy on for cuppa tea, ya need ta eat Miss Jacqueline, an ya will like!' Mary said, as a smile lit her face.

"Thank you Mary, damper sounds great, but please try to remember to call me Jackie!" Jacqueline said. "Me no forgit Miss Jacqueline, me cant do tha Jackie, tis too strange ta me." she replied. "Well how about Jacqueline then? Will you at least try Mary?" she asked.

"We don't know who we will meet from now on, so I cannot have a servant calling me Miss! Can you at least try to understand what I mean Mary?" asked Jacqueline.

"Me thinks so Miss Jacqueline, will try me best ta call ya Jacqueline!" she said.

"So where we be headin Jacqueline?" Mary asked, as she giggled. "Very good Mary! That is a good start!" "I have no idea where we are going Mary! I only know I had to leave, but to where? I don't know, and I feel too sick to concentrate on working that out yet. However, the compass in The Jeep reads we are heading north!" said Jacqueline.

"Me be from tha north, too far, way away north, twas when I be a kid, long time ago now!" said Mary.

Jacqueline raised her head, her puffed eyes searching Mary's face with interest. "Where in the north did you come from Mary?" she asked. "It be in The Territory, Jacqueline. Way to north at Tenna Creek, be me home."

"Hav lots a cousins there, an Aunties too, somewhere me thinks. We hav tha big family, but twas long ago, but maybe they still there!" said Mary.

My senses reacted at last to my situation, and I then became more realistic about the thoughts that had been brought to my attention. 'I have nowhere to go! I have to bear this child I carry, and I can't go to a hospital!'

I had begun to hate this child inside me. It was only living proof of my shame, and the humiliation. I just wanted to be rid of it. As my thoughts hounded me. 'I finally accepted in my own heart that this birth would have to be kept secret, no one must know.' I could not bring this disgrace upon my Father, and all our friends. I would have to go to somewhere distant, remote, where there would be no chance of anyone recognizing me.

*'I owe them that at least'*

"Mary! I have made my decision now!" I said, as I looked at her very seriously. Mary looked at Jacqueline, whose face was set in that way she had, as she became determined about something. Mary knew that look, and also that nothing would ever change Jacqueline's mind, either.

"So, what ya decided on now Jacqueline?" Mary asked.

We will keep going north, Mary! We will go to The Territory, and to your Tenna Creek! What do you think about that? Jacqueline asked. "Me will be ok bout that Jacqueline, but are ya sure? Tis a long, long way ta go!" replied Mary. "Do you want to come with me Mary?"

asked Jacqueline. "Of course me com with ya Jacqueline, me be with ya always, ya no that!" she answered.

"Good that's settled then!" Jacqueline replied, having the first positive feelings inside her since she had left her home, and her family at Shallow Downs.

"An we hav ta wash an change our clothes Jacqueline, yor ones be all burnt there, ya need ta throw em away, then we be eat!" said Mary.

"I guess we should Mary!" replied Jacqueline, looking down at her clothes. "You have plenty of water on there heating, so we could wash our hair too, I guess! Then we will leave for Tenna Creek, it will still be there when we get there!" she answered.

Mary sunk deeply into her thoughts. 'How me life be changin so much! No Mamma, or Papa ta raise me, only Missus Coby, but she be gone now! An only life I no be Shallow Downs, but it be gone now too! An now, I be goin back ta me home country, The Territory.'

'Me be changin lot since then. If me hav family there, would they no me now?' she wondered.

# JENNY MAC

# APRIL RAIN

## *Chapter 31*

We travelled slowly, but stopping along the way to make camp. Many weeks had passed by. I had to take particular care on the dirt, and graveled roads that were still in some places, but noticed in other sections, to my amazement, the roads were tarred. Eventually, late one afternoon we crossed the border into The Northern Territory to the brilliance of the red setting sun.

As I recall. In another circumstance, or another life even, if it wasn't for the fact that every single mile was taking me further away from my home, and from my Father, then the trip could have been enjoyable, but I was not seeing the beauty of it all. Bitterness, and regret consumed me. My heart was broken, my body in stress.

In light of the new day brought a change in scenery once again to the vastness of the elevated plains of the Tablelands where the black soil, and Mitchell grasses spread endlessly, seeming to roll on forever. Particular skill was required to negotiate the black muddy road.

This was huge cattle grazing area here, and a very large property. Only one big rambling Homestead stood out barely visible through the trees, as we drove along for miles past the paddocks on the way. 'This was cattle country at its very best, the cattle stations so much larger here than at home. Maybe they were the largest in Australia!' thought Jacqueline. Our destination was so close now, and our long trek was almost to an end. Until finally we entered the township, then I spoke to Mary.

"Well Mary we are here now, your old home at last!" I thought Mary's excitement would be evident, but instead she was apprehensive in her reply.

"Not be me home Jacqueline! Me home Tenna Creek. This be a town now, twas only minin huts here afore. Me no live in tha town Jacqueline, me home be bush!" Mary replied. Realization hit me then that Mary was a true aboriginal, and came from a clan, or a tribe.

Then we will go to your Tenna Creek. We will just get some supplies, and petrol, then we move on!" I said. "Yes be betta me thinks! Thank ya Jacqueline!" said Mary. "What type of mining did they do here Mary?" I asked. "They be look for tha yella gold, an they be find it too! Twas big minin place here long, long ago when I be a young girl, then lots a people com here ta look for tha yella gold, an lots o drovers be here ta move the cattle. It be rough place afore a town be startin ta build, an afore that, be just Aboriginal people! My people! I belong ta a tribe, but ar lots o other tribes be in this here area, an our ancestors be livin in this area for thousands o years afore us!" said Mary.

I was dumbfounded, there was so much history here, and Mary? 'Did I really know Mary? I am finding out more about her all the time!' I thought. "You have never spoken about your childhood Mary!" I said.

"Yeah me no, me be mostly forgit me thinks, tis comin back ta me now!" she replied. So we headed north again for about twelve miles, then Mary directed me onto an old bush track as she seemed to know her way now, which was strange after all these years. I was thankful for the 4WD as we weaved through the thick scrub.

Suddenly I became aware of a natural clearing as it appeared ahead, and when we reached it, we drove out onto the sandy bank of a creek bed, where the water, pushed along by the surging of a small waterfall which tumbled into it, ran pure, and clear. "Me be home, me thinks Jacqueline!" said Mary. I was past all believing by now, so I just replied. "That is good Mary, let's set up camp!" We found a good campsite, unpacked The Jeep, and set up our tent. "Will we find your relatives here Mary?" I asked. "Me not be sure Jacqueline!" she said.
*'We did not find them!' 'They found us!'*

As the sun slipped below the tree-line, and daylight faded, we built up our fire, and sat around it to drink our Billy tea. As the flames leapt higher I looked beyond. Something had attracted my attention so I focused hard. Shadows seemed to be moving now, and a shiver went up my spine as I started to realize what it was.

They moved slowly forward, and squatted just out of the light of our camp-fire. I noticed at least seven aboriginal men, maybe more, just sitting there staring, and my fear gripped me. Immediately I was poised for flight, and ready to get my rifle, when I saw the women were coming forward towards us very shyly, and to my astonishment, Mary had left my side, and was walking out to meet them. It was the elder of the clan of women who shuffled forward to speak first, as the other women of all ages stood back respectfully, with their little ones hanging onto their skirts, pretending to hide.

The Old Mother who came forward was very ancient, and the weather-beaten signs were evident as deep lines of age produced grooves upon her crinkled face, as she hobbled towards us on legs as thin as sticks.

Mary spoke to her in a tongue that was alien to my ears. My shock was obvious, and I stood gaping at her, as I had no idea what was happening. Then the Old Mother touched Mary's face, and she cried out in urgency to the younger women as Mary then kissed her hands. They embraced, and the others swarmed Mary for their turn. All talking in that same language which only they could understand.

All of a sudden, I was the center of attention as they all turned, and came towards me. "Jacqueline, this be me great mama Ngani, she be want ta meet ya!" said Mary, as she spoke my name in that strange tongue. The Old Mother touched my hair, and tried to say my name, but called me Jacini, as her steely old eyes bore straight into mine, and as she touched my tummy she clucked with a toothless grin.

"She be love all tha babies!" explained Mary, as she proceeded to introduce me around to them all. "I can see that Mary!" I replied, as I got lost in the thrall of many names, and hands that were totally obsessed with my hair, as they touched it, and of course, my tummy. They chattered in their own language, giggling as they all came in close to meet me.

## APRIL RAIN

We sat around the camp fire, and I don't think I have ever seen Mary more happier as she talked earnestly with her Old Grand Mother. 'They are friendly people.' I thought, as the others were jabbering away, and to me too, so Mary had to relate what they were saying. I noticed though that the men didn't join us, and I wondered about that. Then suddenly one called to Old Mother, who replied. Then, just as they had appeared, they disappeared into the darkness. Gone!

"What happened Mary?" I asked, concerned. "Is ok, nothin be happin Jacqueline. Great Mamma want me ta talk ta ya bout baby, she need ta talk with elders now, so they go, but be comin back!" said Mary. "What about the baby?" I asked. "Ya dont hav much time left Jacqueline, where ya be havin the baby?" Mary asked.

"Mary we haven't spoken in detail before, but I will have the baby here on this creek bed! No hospital, and no one is ever to know! I have only revulsion for this baby growing inside me, and to keep it would sicken me. It was not conceived from love, but from hate! I will never forget that. I will give this baby away, but who to give it to, is a problem!" I said.

"Tis what I hav be thinkin, jus had ta ask ya ta be sure Jacqueline, if tis what ya want then great mamma help ya with tha birth. She go talk now, an if elders agree, an if ya sure afta ya hav it, she be raise tha baby for ya!" offered Mary. Jacqueline was amazed, but she thought about it seriously. 'This baby will be part aboriginal, so I guess it would have a life here among its own, it seemed right.'

"Then I will agree Mary!" I replied.

# JENNY MAC

My time passed quickly, and the baby inside me kicked brutally, as if it was punishing me for my decision to abandon it. My body was becoming quite awkward, and so heavy, but in one way, the physical pain helped to take my mind off my deep mental pain, but in the night my nightmares lived on.

When the aboriginal clan had originally returned, the elders of the tribe called a special meeting, but this time all the men were introduced to us, then they all squatted in a circle to speak. Mary was interpreting during the discussion, and it was consented, and agreed on that Old Mother would take my baby at birth. Two of her granddaughters who had babies to suckle, would share in the feeding. It was by my request, not to see the child when I gave birth, it was to be taken from me. They really didn't understand why, but they agreed to my wishes.

Life in the bush was so peaceful, and quiet. I became accustomed to the aboriginal women now as they visited us so often to help Mary remember her heritage, and to source food in the bush, and I even learnt a few simple words of their language. Then the day arrived.

I was in thick scrub with Mary, and her cousin, and as I bent over to dig into the dirt with my stick, the first pain gripped me. Mary told her cousin to find great mamma. True to her word she came as quickly as her old thin legs could carry her, and my preparation began.

'Endless walking.' Then as I squatted over the birthing mat, my nails scraping the tree that I leaned on, and the excruciating pain tearing me apart, was how I gave birth, and the baby was whisked away. As arranged, I planned to leave Tenna Creek at once. Mary was coming too. We took the tent down, and packed. I bathed in the creek, and changed. Then we said our goodbyes, and left.

Once again, I had no idea as to where I was heading, and I searched my soul for a decision as we left Tenna Creek, but there was no way I could go home, my pride forbade me from doing that. I was a lost person, alienated from my home, and from my family. 'I had to go on.' But somehow! Even though I had no regrets for abandoning the baby, there was this distinct feeling as something tugged at my heart, that I had left a part of me behind, and doom overcome me, as I struggled with mixed feelings. I was destined to a life of punishment beyond all. I could not have foretold, or prevented the events that had dictated my future, and ruined my life.'

We were on an endless trek, camping, and driving on until late one afternoon I became aware of changes to the countryside as the earth turned red, and the huge rock formations becoming domineering high above in their magnificence, but bull-dust lined the road making it difficult to drive. We were in Kimberley Country now, the top end of Australia. We set up camp, only this time, amongst the rock formations reaching high above the flow of a natural spring. Mary was overjoyed to discover aboriginal paintings inside the caves close by, but my interest waned, and unable to appreciate the true beauty of our surroundings, so at first light we moved on.

## JENNY MAC

Something deep inside me was constantly pushing me forward, and always urging me to keep going, as my determination tried to overrule my twisted thoughts. I seemed to be always searching, forever searching, but never finding peace in my heart. Weeks became years. I wandered to seek out redemption that never came. Until quite by accident I had decided to take an inland road through the Flinders Ranges, and we happened to find a place that reminded me of home. I braked, to stop the Jeep so I could look deeply into Mary's patient face.

With the utmost certainty, I spoke out to her. "Mary, this may come as a complete shock, but I have reached a decision! I would like to stay here permanently, there is something about this place here that I like. Would you like to settle here Mary, and stay with me?" I asked.

"Well tis bout time Jacqueline Coby, me be think ya neva goin ta stop roamin round, so this be good news, tis good ta hear, an o course I be stayin with ya, I got no home too Jacqueline!" she said.

"Thank you Mary, we will look around to see what we can do. I would like to work somewhere so I can start to live a normal life. What do you think? Do you want to work Mary?" I asked. "Been waitin long time ta hear ya say that, an hav been wantin to settle an go ta work like we used ta Jacqueline, tis good idea!" she said.

"You do realize that I do not need to work, don't you Mary. Father has provided for me very generously! I just want to feel normal again, do you understand?" I asked. "Yes me thinks so. Maybe ya can go ta home Jacqueline, has bin too long!" she said. "I wish I could Mary, but I can never go home to face all their questions! I just can't discredit Father in that way. No, we stay here!" I said.

'So determined this one be, me thinks that be tha key ta git her through.' "Ok we be stay here!" Mary replied.

I really cannot recall what lured me inland to the bush which directed me into a certain area of the ranges, but I knew when we arrived at Waverley Downs that it felt right, and unknowingly to me at the time, it was to be my salvation. Waverley was not only a working cattle station, but a great hub for tourists who came to stay in bungalows for a bush holiday retreat where they rode horses, and reveled in the camel trail rides, fished, and swam in the river, and simply enjoyed the hospitality of the Restaurant, and Bar available.

Initially, it was very easy for Mary to get work there. She was hired immediately as full time housemaid for the bungalows, and even was offered shifts as a waitress in the Restaurant. However, because I wanted to work outdoors with the animals, I had to go on trial for three months, and we were given a bungalow to share for our lodgings. Mary was excited, and deep down, I was too.

I hadn't ridden a horse since my Sailor, but I picked a spirited stallion for my very first trial, and the Owner of Waverley looked at me to say. "You might want to pick another horse Jackie, this stallion likes to take control!" "I will be fine Mister McKenzie!" I said, as I walked up to the horse to caress his muzzle, and in one leap was on his back, and the Stallion soon learnt who was in control.

Within one month, after trials on horses, and with the camels, which I had never ridden, but I soon learned to master their ways. I worked beside the men to muster cattle, or branding, and anything else that needed doing.

Then my boss called me aside, and he said. "Jackie, if half of my men had your skills, I would be pleased. You are now on the payroll young lady!" "Thank you Mister McKenzie!" I said. I found that in company of my work mates I was mostly in control, but in my room at night was when the heartache, and pain continued.

My only remaining connection, or remaining link to my past life at Shallow Downs was 'April Rain.' My miniature black horse with the white markings that reared up proudly on its timber stand upon the bedside table. When I looked at him, the memories filled me with a sadness beyond belief, and the tears stung my eyes.

As years rolled on, needless to say. I spent my entire working life at Waverley Downs. The Cattle Station was good therapy for me. It was there I regained confidence, and my determination was returning too.

It was towards the later years of my time at Waverley, when a small parcel was delivered to me. My shock, at first glance, was not only to be receiving mail, but the recognition of the flowing handwriting which jogged my memory. I ran to my bungalow to rip open the seal in haste, and my lost years were revealed in the sadness which emanated from each page, and, between the lines.

## APRIL RAIN

I realized for the first time of the grief I had caused my loved ones by leaving, and not returning. Pain was evident in the words from my sister June, when she said Father had passed away ten years ago, and was buried beside Mother at Shallow Downs. He had always hoped that I would return, so he built a Homestead, re-planted wattle, and had built a timber mill. In his passing, all holdings would be left to me, trusts funds would still operate, but a Manager was to be employed to run the Property. He provided for us all to the end.

Heart wrenching sobs shook my body for the loss of my Father, my idol. I loved him so. Photos, and another letter scattered as the parcel fell to the floor. Shaking, I picked out the letter, and opened it. As I read it Reagan Chase poured his heart out. "Just to see your face again Jacqueline is all I want! I love you! Always have! I will be on the train to Shallow Siding on your Birthday. I am hoping that you will be there to meet me. There is a reunion to be held too. Now we have contact, please confirm, and please come!" Love always, Reagan.

"Mary I have received mail!" I called. "Me be sorry Jacqueline, but I wrote ya sista!" she said. "It is ok Mary, but now I have just made a decision! I think it is time to face the demons of my past, and go back home. Are you coming with me?" I asked. "Will ya be comin back?" she asked. "I guess so!" I said. "Why wouldn't I?" I asked. "I not sure, I be stay, ya let me no Jacqueline!" Mary said.

*'Now my life takes another twist.'*

*'But a chance for redemption'*

# JENNY MAC

*The Historic Railway Station...Shallow Siding...1996*

## CHAPTER 32

Jacqueline Coby jumped in her seat, as she was jolted from her reverie by all the commotion on the platform, which had startled her. People were jostling each other in their haste to depart The Station, and panic rose inside her as she tried to comprehend the situation.

'Whatever is going on, why is everyone leaving?' she thought. She jumped up off the bench seat, and grabbed desperately at a man's shirt sleeve as he passed, to ask him. Her hand was shrugged off just as quickly, and he hurried away mumbling away to himself. Jacqueline just stood rigid, her dilemma twofold now, her face stricken.

"Better get moving lady!" someone said, from behind her. "Do you have anyone to help you?" the voice asked. Jacqueline turned quickly, and faced a young man. "I'm sorry, but I do not understand! Where do I have to move to, and why would I need help. What is happening?" she asked. "We have been told to leave The Railway Station, and go to our homes Ma'am!" replied the young boy.

Jacqueline soon realized that she must have missed the announcement earlier, and maybe that was what had startled her so!' "I am sorry! I didn't hear that message, but could you tell me why we have to leave here? I am waiting for the train to arrive!" she replied. "The train won't be coming now lady!" answered the boy. "There has been big trouble on the train, an armed fugitive is at large. That is why we have to go to our homes!" "A fugitive! In Shallow Siding! Are you quite certain? What has happened then?" asked Jacqueline. The young man's reply was drowned out by the next announcement.

Jacqueline looked down the platform, and noticed the familiar face of Jake Hardy weaving a path through the multitude towards her, as he spoke seriously into the loud speaker. "Please do not panic folks, leave sensibly, and go to your homes, so we can do our job!" said Jake.

\* \* \*

Word had come in from one of the Outback Property Station hands, and Jake eagerly took the call in his office. He had tried several times to contact Old Riley, the train Conductor on the inbound train, but all his attempts had been futile, and there was no response. At least, now, someone had called in.

Earlier he had told Sam Hind to pass out messages, requesting a sighting of the train, and location, to all the hands who travelled home by way of the train route, one of them was on the line now.

"Yeah mate! I know the place!" replied Jake, as he spoke into the phone. "Are you sure Mark? No, there's no need to go back to the train! Leave it to me now. I can't thank you enough! That is a great help! I'll get back to you with an update!" said Jake, and hung up.

Sam Hind noticed the concerned look on Jake's face. "What is it Jake?" he asked. "Had a call from Mark Dunn, one of the hands from Curloo Station. He passed the train the other side of the river at Billberry Creek, so that's about four or five miles out of Shallow Siding. He said the train was stationary, with no lights on. All the passengers were disembarked, but they all seemed to be in a panic!" Jake said, just as the phone rang again, and he grabbed it up in haste.

"Jake Hardy! The Siding Station!" he muttered into the mouthpiece. Sam could hear the voice yelling on the other end of the phone, but he watched Jake's face as it paled, and then he swayed on his feet.

Somehow Jake managed to stay calm, and to make his reply. "Try to settle everyone, let them know that help is on the way, but please stay in a group, do not leave the train! If someone there has medical experience, get them to attend to Old Riley. I will send a medical team from the hospital. The voice on the phone became hysterical.

"Where is the culprit?" Jake asked. "Are you positive that was the direction he went?" asked Jake. "Thank you for all that information, now please give me your name, and phone number, so I can call you back! I have a lot of organizing to do, so tell the passengers to stay positive, and I will get back to you!" Jake scribbled the details on his note pad, and said. "I will hang up now, and thank you once again!"

Jake's face had reddened in his anguish, the signs of grief were well marked upon his face, as a cold sweat broke out across his forehead, and his shoulders shook. His body swayed, as he faced Sam Hind. Sam took only three steps forward to go to his aid, and steadied him.

"You better sit down Jake, I'll get you some water!" he said, as he pulled up a chair. Jake slumped down into it in disbelief, and in total despair. When Sam returned, Jake drank deeply from the glass. Sam waited patiently for him to speak. 'When he did, he could not believe it!'

There has been a murder committed on the inbound train Sam! Jake rasped. "But that is not the half of it! Old Riley is severely wounded, and he is not expected to pull through! And to make matters worse, the murderer has fled the scene, but he is armed! He was last seen heading in the direction of Shallow Siding! We have a huge problem here Sam!" he said.

"Hell Jake! Murder in Shallow Siding is unbelievable! My God! Rebecca is on that train! Who was murdered?" he asked, getting quite upset now. "I don't know Sam!" replied Jake. "I must go out there!" Sam said.

Sam's distress seemed to pull Jake from his dilemma, and he stood forcibly to face him. "No you will not be Sam! I forbid it! We will do things correctly. Ring Pete Stringer, only he can help us here. He is a well-known bushman, and tracker. I will ring the hospital, and get the Constable to take a medic out to the train. We also need to clear this Station, make the announcement first, but don't mention the murder, we don't need a riot here! Then get me Pete on the phone please!" said Jake.

As Jake picked up the phone once again, he could hear Sam outside making an announcement on the loud speaker, trying to calm people, and advising them for their own safety to leave the Railway Station as quickly as possible, and go to their homes.

## APRIL RAIN

Jake spoke to the Constable at the Police Station first, to advise him of the murder, and told him that he was trying to contact Pete Stringer to track the murderer. The Constable thought that would be best, so they would have a better idea of the fugitive's movements, but he also asked Jake to locate the local shooters just to have them on standby in case things got out of control. In the meantime he would go to the hospital to pick up a team of medics, and head out to the train. No doubt he would meet up with Pete there, and discuss tactics with him.

Jake hung up the phone. 'At least now we have a plan in place!' he thought. 'They had a Town to protect here, but he also knew when the going got tough, the Country folk stuck together!' 'He had more calls to make.'

Mitchell Stringer had just returned to The Homestead as the phone rang. He threw his hat on the chair, picked up the phone, and moved to the couch as he lifted up the handset to speak into it. "Mitch Stringer here! Outback Gardens!" he drawled. "Hello there Sam, how might you be?" Suddenly his blue eyes darkened in anger, his disbelief obvious, as he listened to Sam at the other end.

"Hells sake Sam, are you sure? This is Shallow Siding for god's sake! Who has been murdered?" he asked. He listened intently while Sam relayed all he knew, and that they needed Pete to help.

Pete was down at the yards last I saw him Sam! I will drive over there immediately to ask him to call Jake." "Jake is right, if anyone can help, it will be Pete! I'll head off now before he goes somewhere, bye Sam!" he said.

Jake took the all-important call with relief, and began to brief Pete Stringer. "I cannot thank you enough Pete, and good luck!" he said, then hung up the phone.

\* \* \*

Jacqueline detected the deep concern evident on Jake Hardy's face, as he got closer to her. "What is it Jake?" Jacqueline asked. Jake reached out his hand to her, and she took it firmly. Gently, he pulled her towards him, then he put his arm around her shoulders, as if to shield her, or offer protection, but then he spoke urgently to her.

"Come with me now Jacqueline!" he muttered, as he coaxed her to follow him along the platform. "It is not safe here Jacqueline, we will go into my office to talk in private. I have to wait anyway until all the people have left here, then I will lock up!" Jacqueline stopped dead in her tracks, and she retorted with irritation.

"Enough Jake!" she stated, as her deep green eyes darkened in annoyance. "Just tell me when someone is going to offer me some explanation as to what is actually happening here? Tell me this instant Jake!" she said.

Jake looked deeply into her beautiful green eyes as his thoughts roamed. 'Whatever happened that possessed you Jacqueline Coby, to abandon your home, your loved ones, still remains a mystery. Though, that fire is still burning inside of you!' he shook his head in admiration.

"You haven't changed a bit!" he said, as they reached the front doors, and ushered her inside. "Oh yes I have Jake Hardy! I came back specifically to bare my sole, to face the demons of my past! It has taken me a long time to get to this point, but at some time I plan to tell you, and Anne, of my sordid life. Then Jake Hardy, you may have a different opinion of me!" replied Jacqueline.

"I doubt that very much Jacqueline Coby!" replied Jake in earnest. "But right now, and to answer all of your questions! I have grave tidings to disclose!" he said.

Murder has been committed on the train Jacqueline, and also Old Riley is fighting for his life!" he said sadly. "Who's Murder? Are you serious Jake Hardy?" she asked. "Yes! I am very serious Jacqueline! But I don't know who was murdered yet, the only news is that the murderer was seen heading towards Shallow Siding!" he replied. "My goodness, this is devastating, and what has happened to Old Riley?" asked Jacqueline.

"This is not very pleasant Jacqueline! Apparently, he was gutted like a fish. No-one expects him to survive!" said Jake. Then put his arm around her as she burst into tears. "Oh no! How could this happen here?" she cried.

"Not much of a home coming for you Jacqueline I am afraid, and on your birthday too!" said Jake.

Jacqueline looked up at him. "You remembered!" she said in astonishment. "After all these years you never forgot me, and you still remembered my birthday Jake Hardy! What a friend you are!" she replied, and started crying again. "Only because we all love you Jacqueline. Anne, and I both know you well, always have. You were never, ever, forgotten to us Jacqueline!" he said.

# JENNY MAC

## Chapter 33

Reagan Chase was elated, and it showed. His jovial mood became infectious amongst the passengers on the train, and he was making a lot of new friends. Riley Summers was one of them, and they had taken to having meals together, and a drink in Reagan's cabin at night. Reagan's heart was bursting with new life, new purpose.

As the train rocked along, he peered out through the window at the never ending beauty of the Countryside, and as he reminisced, his thoughts turned to Jacqueline Coby. He could see her in his mind's eye, just standing there so beautiful, so strong, and full of life, and so very determined. 'Was she still like that now?' he wondered.

All his life he had suffered, and the heartbreak it had caused him for losing her was relentless. It haunted him, taking a huge toll on him over long endless years.

Shallow Siding wasn't an option for Reagan to return to initially so coming back now felt very strange. It was a long time ago, a lifetime really since he was shunned, to be cast off by his only true love, his soulmate, to have his engagement broken, and their wedding plans cancelled.

'Their love had been so pure but so deep that it hurt!' he thought. Then it was over, ending in a heartbeat, but without an explanation. 'What went wrong?' He was at a loss for a reason why, and then his only opportunity to reconcile was crushed by Jacqueline's sudden departure from her Father, and her home at Shallow Downs! Never to be seen, or heard of, again! 'Her behaviour then had been really strange though!' he recalled. 'Something had happened to her, he was sure of it!'

'Maybe it was the fear that they both shared, which emanated from the threat of his possible call up in The National Service Ballot on March 10th 1965?' After which became a reality, as within the month a notification letter advised he was balloted in, and was required to report for duty, to be trained to serve in The Vietnam War.

Reagan had spent many years of his life in Vietnam. He had fought for Australia, and had done his time over there, but his lost love was on his mind continuously, so contacting Clayton Coby was the very first thing that he done on returning to Australia, but to no avail. Clayton had not heard from her, and told Reagan that Jacqueline just disappeared, and he had no way of contacting her. Reagan's endless search had extended over many, heart-breaking years, but it had proved fruitless.

He had kept in contact with The Coby family though, in hope that someone would hear from Jacqueline one day. He started work for his Father in the city, at Chase Enterprises, as he could not face life out in the Country without Jacqueline, he was not interested in anyone else, and had never married. He just wanted his love back.

Then surprisingly when he was not expecting it, one phone call changed everything when June contacted him to say that she had received a letter from Mary, and knew now how to contact her sister. Reagan was quick to visit June in the city, taking with him a letter which he had penned painstakingly for Jacqueline. June promised him she would enclose it in a package she was sending.

Jacqueline Coby's reply astonished him so much that he could not believe it. After all their lost years they had made contact again. 'He told everyone!' 'His Father, his workmates at Chase Enterprises, and even all the wharf workers unloading crates from their trucks to the ships.'

*****

Now aboard the train to Shallow Siding celebrations were in order as well-wishers amongst the passengers, who listened to Reagan's tale, and his imminent reunion with his lost love, all wished him luck. He was ecstatic.

Reagan relished every mile as the train was getting closer to his destination, enjoying it immensely. Because finally at its end. 'His true love, the only person he had ever loved, would be waiting for him! Jacqueline Coby!'

*****

Revenge was his sole purpose for going to Shallow Siding. It seethed inside him like a living thing that had obsessed his twisted mind. Nothing would ever sate his appetite, until the job was complete. He lived for it, planned extensively for it, and thrived on the thoughts of the eventual outcome. His long-term jail sentence had seen to that. Every day, every year he had sat locked in a small cell, he became possessed with his obsession for revenge. This escalated his raving thoughts, and fueled by intense anger, and hate, it festered to eat away at him.

He had come prepared now, and was unrecognizable. Matted hair hung long at his back, and a wild curly bush of beard covered his face. His massive body was all out of proportion, and forged by continuous hard labour, it had become tempered with muscle, but honed, and lean.

His life-long scheme to get even with Reagan Chase was foremost on his mind on his release from prison, so he had cunningly pushed for a job at the wharf when he heard that Chase Enterprises sent their trucks there.

He then knew how to get to Reagan Chase, and was secretly planning his demise. But his original plans had somewhat altered when out of nowhere his excitement was heightened to another level, when fresh information reached him from the workers, and he was compelled to alter his plans. Reagan Chase shared a close relationship with the workers, and had been so excited he told them all of his plans for a reunion with his only love back in Shallow Siding with One Jacqueline Coby! She would be meeting him at the Railway Station on her birthday.

'This new information was vital to Deakan Hall, as he knew only too well the birthday date in question!' It was branded into his memory. 'I will be on that train too!' he thought. 'Yes! Revenge will be sweet when it is all done!'

He had kept a low profile on the train, but had taken particular interest in all the habitual movements of Reagan Chase who he would not have recognized if not for the passengers mentioning his name in conversation.

It was almost daybreak on the last day of the journey, and only eight more miles to Shallow Siding, then Chase would shower, and head for the diner. So he laid in wait above the buffers for him to return. It was a simple plan.

## APRIL RAIN

Pete Stringer was totally focused. His mindset stolid of the job he had to do, and he was transported to his own world. The world of the Hunter. He checked all his preparations with finesse, making sure that he had omitted nothing. Everything had been so meticulously organized, but only one certain thing annoyed him, and his thoughts kept reverting back to the same issue.

'Many a wild animal I have hunted in my life, many situations of danger I've overcome, but the outcome was always inevitable.' 'However! To hunt a human being is alien to my way of life. With wild animals I am ecstatic amidst the thrill of the chase, and the kill is an ultimate pleasure, but always keeping a Hunters respect for the animal. 'How can I hunt a man with the same passion?' 'To me that is impossible!' he thought.

Mitchell Stringer looked at his son closely now, and he noticed the tell-tale signs, as Pete's brow knotted, as it often did when he was puzzled. As if reading his mind, Mitchell spoke up. "You know Pete, we've never hunted man before! This is a completely different scenario to what we normally do!" 'He knows!' thought Pete in his amazement, as he looked up at his Father, and their eyes locked. "I have trained you only to hunt wild animals, not human beings, and this will require, not only great skill, but great compassion!" added Mitchell seriously.

Rather than an irritable response Pete Stringer looked at his Father, and he laughed. "You know me too well Father!" he said. "Yeah I guess I do!" replied Mitchell.

"Want to talk about it?" he asked. "Yeah, I would like that Father! To be honest I am somewhat confused!" said

Pete. Mitchell looked at his son. His only son, and when he spoke it was with true feeling. "The way I see it Pete, is this! I want you home safe, so please! Just don't take unnecessary risks! We don't know how the murderer is armed! If he has a rifle Pete, then that is dangerous!"

"You had better be prepared for that by taking all the precautions to protect yourself! Keep in mind though, as opposed to hunting wild animals, you have to act within the law, so I would suggest when you meet up with the Constable at the train, talk to him about that!"

"Just do what you always do best Pete. Hunting, and tracking! But be certain you find out your rights about apprehending the fugitive, and once again, unlike a wild animal! You don't have to shoot to kill Pete!" "Does that help at all, or make sense to you Pete?" Mitchell asked.

Pete looked at his Father with pride. 'He always tells it how it is!' thought Pete. 'He has been my rock, all my life!' "Yes! It makes real sense to me Father. It's what I've been trying to get my head around! So once again, thank you Father, you have helped me a lot!" said Pete.

"Just be careful Pete!" Mitchell said. "I will Father!" said Pete. They were so engrossed in their conversation, they hadn't noticed Royce, and Riana Chalmers walking towards them until Royce spoke. "Hi Mitch! Hi Pete!" Royce said, as he joined them. "What is happening Pete, are you going somewhere?" he asked. "Guess you could say that Royce! Good morning to you both" said Pete.

Mitchell Stringer steered the conversation to himself as he spoke. "I wish I could say, 'Good Morning!' Royce, and

Riana, but it is not! It is a very sad day for Shallow Siding! We have very disturbing tidings to tell you both. Murder has been committed on the inbound train, and another person is fighting for his life!" said Mitch sadly.

"My goodness, how horrible!" said Riana. "In Shallow Siding? I don't believe it!" said Royce. "You can believe it Royce. Pete was asked to track the murderer down, so I think it might be best for now, seeing you are the only guests remaining, you had better come to my house for your own safety!" said Mitch. "Thank you!" said Riana.

However, Royce instead, was looking at Pete. "Have you got any help Pete?" he asked. "Not this time Royce! I work quicker on my own!" said Pete. "I will go with you Pete! I can pull the pack horse, but I won't hold you up, and I will stay back out of your way. You might need some help Pete, or you could use my phone to call someone!" Royce said.

"Now, just a minute Royce! You are a guest here, do you think I would put you in the path of danger? I will be hunting an armed murderer, and mobile phones? I don't need! So no!" said Pete. "But….started Royce. "No buts either Royce!" answered Pete. Mitchell was deep in thought, then he said. "Now hold on Pete, you might want to think this through. You don't know what you will be expecting, and having another person with you could be an asset, and the mobile could be turned off, and only used to send messages when needed, maybe to the Constable with updates!" "Father, Royce is a guest!" said Pete. "And he will hold me up." "I won't Pete! I promise, please let me help you?" pleaded Royce.

Pete looked in exasperation to his Father. "Your call Pete, but it might not be a bad idea!" offered Mitchell. "What are your thoughts Riana? Would you like Royce to be facing danger?" asked Pete, hoping to finalize their dilemma. But much to his surprise, Riana said. "Royce loves a challenge Pete, and, if that is what he wants to do? Then so be it, and I am sure he will be of help to you!" Pete looked hard at Royce. "I have rules then! To go forward, I must go back to the source. 'The train,' to search for tracks. We will go over rough country to get there, and at some point cross the river. You ride behind! Your phone off! No talking! No noise! If you can handle that, grab a pack, and a horse, then we ride!" said Pete.

Royce Chalmers followed as best he could. Pete rode steadfastly setting a fierce pace, but Royce would never complain. 'How Pete knows his way through this thick bush is beyond me!' he thought.

Royce had no idea where they were, or where they were heading to for that matter. 'Well! I always wanted an adventure with a real life bushman, but this has got to take the cake! I hope I survive to tell the tale!' he was thinking, as he peered ahead to keep Pete in sight.

After about an hour of grueling riding, Royce noted the river in sight again, and Pete headed upstream, until he stopped to beckon him. "We cross here Royce! How are you holding up?" asked Pete. "I'm ok! But there is a bank there, and no way to get down!" replied Royce.

## APRIL RAIN

Pete laughed. "We will jump Royce! This is the best place to cross, just trust me!" Pete said, as he grabbed his rifle, and ammo to wrap them tight in a waterproof bag.

"Just watch what I do, but be sure to clear the stirrups when you jump from the horse into the water. Grab his mane, and swim beside. Steer him across, don't hamper him. You can swim?" Pete asked, laughing. "Swim? Yes Pete! But jumping off a bank on horseback is not exactly what I am used to. But, what the heck, let's do it!" Royce said. "Good man! We will rest on the other side!" said Pete. 'That is if I make the other side!' thought Royce.

Much later, due to an easier ride across open plains, and much drier from the sun, Royce was amazed as Pete led them exactly to where the train stood.

Pete spoke earnestly with the Constable, then lost no time locating the tracks of the murderer, and they set off.

Pete tracked him for two miles along Billberry Creek, then he turned off. "What's up Pete?" Royce asked, as he caught up with him. Pete replied in concern. "Whoever I am tracking, knows this Country like a local Royce! He is heading to the only crossing of the river!

\*\*\*\*\*

He crouched low watching them through the crevice of the rocks as they rode on. On a knoll earlier he detected them trailing him. They followed relentlessly, and now he looked hard at the imposing figure of the big man in front. 'He is good' he thought. 'All the efforts to screen my tracks have not deterred him, he comes on still.'

# JENNY MAC

'I can't shake him off. I just have to have that horse!'

Screened but protected by the huge boulders which formed an overhang of the pass he had selected to go through, he sat in wait. 'It has to be now.' he thought, as he watched the leader enter the pass, and ride through. He hesitated just long enough for the other man in the rear to appear beneath him, and as he sprang, he noticed the leader rein in, and dismount, to peer at the ground.

Totally unaware of any danger Royce unsuspectingly yelled in fright as the massive body hit him, knocking him off his horse to the ground. He watched helplessly, and in total disbelief, as his attacker then jumped on his mount, and in a flash, was galloping away.

Pete's skin seemed to crawl as all the tell-tale prickles inched up the back of his neck. He had dismounted to scrutinize the terrain, and the rocky ground where the trail had momentarily faded away, then realization hit him. "He doubled back, he is behind me, or somewhere close!' he thought, and the fear of being exposed gripped Pete. He turned to beckon to Royce just as he yelled out, as he was hit, and went sprawling in the dust under the monstrous body of a black man, their obvious runaway.

Pete reacted instantly to grab his rifle from its sheath for their protection, but noticed that the fugitive was not attacking Royce. He seemed more interested in the horse as he jumped upon its back, and goaded it into a gallop.

The murderer laughed loudly in his escape to call. 'Ya won't catch me now!' Then relished reminiscing about what had brought him here, and what he had yet to do.

## APRIL RAIN

Reagan Chase hauled heavily upon the doors to open them, then sidled through to step out, and make the crossing over the buffers. A fist of iron stunned him, and a massive body dropped from above wielding a knife in his hand. Riley Summers pressed close behind Reagan, and he screamed out in fright as he felt the sensation of a knife slashing across his torso. Old Riley looked down at his stomach in disbelief. He paled as sweat bathed his brow, then slid slowly down the wall to sag to the floor, as he tried desperately to push his innards back inside.

Reagan's head was yanked aside roughly to bare his throat by the iron-like arm that held him. Then their eyes made contact, and recognition showed in Reagan's face in his final moments as the knife slashed deeply across his throat, and his life's blood was pumping away.

Only one thing really mattered in Deakan Hall's life-long obsession, it had propelled him forward. He felt so rewarded to have accomplished a part of it. He relished murdering Reagan Chase in cold blood. To watch him without empathy as his life slipped slowly away, but he was not satisfied fully because the best was yet to come!'

*****

Now as he lay secluded amongst the bushes beside the car park something kept nagging him. Shallow Siding Railway Station looked deserted now. 'Where is everyone? Maybe me be too late!' he thought in panic.

Then instantly, he felt ultimate relief as he noticed two people turn the corner of The Station then stepped down into the carpark. He watched closely as the unmistakable woman, Jacqueline Coby, walked straight towards him.

JENNY MAC

# Chapter 34

Jake Hardy locked his office then he put an arm around Jacqueline Coby. "All set! Are you ready Jacqueline?" he asked her. "Yes I guess so Jake!" she replied. "Then let's get you home to Anne, where you will be safe!" said Jake, as he guided her out towards the front doors, and was about to lock them, when the phone rang.

"I had better go back for that call Jacqueline, it might be important! Come back inside!" Jake urged. Jacqueline followed him into the office, and sat in a bucket chair, as Jake went around the desk to lift up the handset. "Siding Station! Jake speaking!" he said quickly.

"Hello Constable! Yes we are all secured here, and the Station has been cleared, I am about to leave!" said Jake.

"Oh really? Pete did get word back of a sighting! That would put the fugitive only about a mile, or two away."

"Yes I have contacted the shooters, they will wait at your office!" said Jake. "What's that you say? Oh no! Not poor old Riley! "Can you please repeat that bit again?"

"Who did you say Constable?" Jake's voice altered.

"Can you be absolutely positive of that identification Constable?" Jake asked, his voice shaking uncontrollably now, as he looked directly at Jacqueline Coby.

Jacqueline was watching Jake closely when he spoke, then as their eyes connected, his face turned grey, and he stammered, and stuttered through the words that ended his call. "Whatever is wrong Jake, are you alright?" she asked. "You look like you've seen a ghost!" Jake looked at her, and tears smarted in his eyes when he spoke.

"Jacqueline, was Reagan Chase on the train, were you to meet him here?" "Yes Jake, he was coming to see me. I told you that I had made up my mind to put things right with everyone!" I said. "Oh Jacqueline forgive me! I hate being the one to tell you this information. I am so sorry! But the Constable has just confirmed that it was Reagan Chase who was murdered today!" he said sadly.

Suddenly the room was spinning. I tried to maintain my stance, but I felt faint, and a weakness overcome me as I swayed on my feet trying to regain my balance, and the screams that could only be mine, filled the room.

My body shook uncontrollably, as the tears filled my vision now, and I screamed out in my pain. "It is all my fault. It is always my fault." I stressed.

"But why? Why Reagan? He would still be alive if it wasn't for me! He was coming to meet me! Who would want to kill him anyway?" I screamed out at Jake.

Jake slowly pulled me towards him, and I grabbed at him thankfully as I sobbed into his chest. "I am so sorry Jacqueline, please stop now! It is not your fault at all, so stop blaming yourself! Do you hear? We don't know any details, please try to calm down!" said Jake.

I looked up as I sensed his stress, and witnessed the sadness, but the tenderness that filled Jake Hardy's eyes.

'Such a real friend he is!' I realized. 'Many years had separated us, but the connection was still there, he was still just like a big brother, and he was suffering too.' I noticed. "I am so very sorry Jake, please forgive me?" I blubbered. "Nothing to forgive Jacqueline, you have had a huge shock! Well, we both have. So try to stop crying now, so I can take you home. You will need your best friend now! Anne will help you!" he said.

We left the Siding Station platform, and crossed the carpark to where Jake helped me into his car. I screamed out in fright when Jake's head was smashed against the dashboard, and then he fell inert to the ground. Then shock gripped me as a huge hand struck out at my head.

Darkness was closing in on me! White lights starred, and crept in threatening to block out my vision as I tried desperately to stay conscious, as I stared at my attacker, and into the face of the person who had ruined my life.

'In my dazed state, I realized two things!'
*'I knew who killed Reagan Chase'*
*'And that I too! Would die this day!'*

\*\*\*\*\*

Pete Stringer had pursued the murderer, to track him to a point at the river where his stolen horse was left abandoned, and grazing on the river bank. He detected the well-identified footprints heading into town, so he grabbed his binoculars from his saddle bag, and climbed a tree at the edge of the escarpment.

He knew who he was looking for now, as he had got a real close look at the huge black man that he had been following, and he focused on the streets in town. They seemed to be deserted now, there was no one around, and all was very quiet. 'He could be anywhere by now!'

thought Pete, as he searched. 'I will just follow him in!' he thought, with conviction, as he prepared himself for the climb down. Suddenly though, movement caught his attention, and he looked harder into the lens. He picked up The Siding Railway Station. All was quiet there, but once again the movement attracted him coming from the carpark, as the unmistakable black man filled his vision.

Pete watched in horror as he crept up behind a car to viciously attack a man. Pete knew that car, and he knew it was Jake Hardy being attacked, as he tumbled to the ground in a heap. Then the fugitive attacked the woman inside the car, and Pete's blood began to boil.

He paused just long enough to get a direction, and he watched earnestly as the huge man raced around the car, jumped in the driver's seat, and then gunned the motor to speed from the carpark in a spray of gravel.

Pete quickly reacted calling to Royce as he slid down the tree. "What's up Pete?" asked Royce, as he brought the horses up. "I found him! He stole a car, and took the left fork of the river road. He has a lady captive, so I will have to follow fast now. Get your phone out now, and get some help! We have a man down in the carpark. This is dangerous now Royce, you best stay there!" said Pete.

"I'm ok, I will stay back Pete!" said Royce.

*****

Deakan Hall could not believe his luck. All his plans had worked so far, and now he had the means of escape. He hadn't thought about that, but now he had a car with a full tank of petrol. That would get him a long,

long way, away. He laughed. 'Nobody had even seen him, and no one knew where he was, so he could take his time now, to savour this last part of his obsession, the final act that he had waited so long to play out.'

He plotted in his mind how it would all unfold. 'He would have some fun with Jacqueline Coby at first, but most decidedly, he knew that she would die slowly!' He could see it in his mind, could taste it in his mouth, and his excitement grew. 'Yah! Revenge will be so sweet!' he thought, as he looked at her hunched up on the seat.

Jacqueline could barely function properly but her mind screamed at her to focus, and in her chest, she seethed with hate for Deakan Hall, as she watched him through one closed eye. She was now at a loss for a way out. He was far too powerful, hitting her about the head when she tried to retaliate, she was already feeling her injuries. She could not believe this was happening to her again, for a second time in her life.

Deakan knew of a place that would suit his purpose, and took the left fork along the river road in his haste. He drove wildly until he recognized a place, and veered off to drive down to the river, then braked. He flung the door wide, then grabbing Jacqueline Coby by the hair, pulled her from the car, kicking, and screaming. "Yeah, fight me ya bitch, will be all tha better!" he said, as he threw her to the sand, falling on top of her, to straddle her body. He ripped shreds off her clothes in haste, as he repeatedly slapped her face. Then amidst his frenzy, he was startled.

## JENNY MAC

Apart from Jacqueline's screams, there was complete silence in the river bed around them, but it was suddenly shattered, as a voice rang out, and the country accent seemed almost comical to Deakan when he spoke.

"Let the lady be Mister, or you are going to be very sorry!" said the unknown intruder.

\* \* \*

Pete Stringer dismounted in the thick scrub. "That's close enough Royce, keep the horses quite! I will go in alone, and do not come any closer until I call you!"

"Understand?" he stressed. "Yeah sure Pete! Will you be ok, or should I come in with you for back up?" Royce asked, as he quickly tied the horse's reins up to a tree. Pete's eyes seemed to darken in annoyance as he looked at Royce. "That is a no, Royce! Do you get that?" he asked, starting his usual ritual of checking, and loading of his rifle, then slung his shot belt over his shoulder.

"Wait here!" he said. "Ok Pete!" said Royce.

Guided by the screams, Pete worked his way through the bush towards the voices echoing deep in the river bank, and surfaced on the edge of the sand. There he lay his rifle down near a bush, and laid his shot belt beside it. He looked up as the big black man was attacking the lady who lay beneath him, and Pete called out.

Deakan Hall was riveted to the spot by the sound of the voice close at hand, and he turned quickly to face his intruder. He laughed, as he noticed the young Cowboy standing there. He was big, but he was unarmed. "What a fool!" he uttered. 'He can't stop me!'

Then he tossed Jacqueline roughly aside, and was up quickly, and running hard.

Jacqueline Coby raised her head, straining hard to see clearly through her hazy vision as a Cowboy emerged to stand by the edge of the clearing. "Mitch, Mitch?" she asked shakily. "Is that you?" she pleaded.

Royce crept up slowly through the thick scrub behind Pete. He followed secretly so that Pete could not see him, knowing that he would send him back. He could hear the commotion now. Then he heard Pete calling to the attacker. 'What's Pete doing?' he thought. 'Why is he warning him?' He started to run but as he finally broke through the tree line, he stopped dead. Unable to believe what he was witnessing.

Pete was standing his ground very calmly as he faced the charge of the huge black man who was running like a wounded bull straight towards him. Royce became just mesmerized, and it seemed to him that it was almost too late when Pete finally exploded into action when he dived onto the ground, and rolled to grab his rifle.

Before Royce could even blink an eye, the first shot was ringing out, and the massive black man screamed, as the bullet shattered his kneecap. Then just as quickly, his other kneecap collapsed, and then his right arm hung useless at his side as two other shots, fired in succession, made their mark, and the murderer fell before Pete onto the sand. Pete came to his feet lithely, and cat like, and smashed the rifle butt into the side of his head. "You shouldn't have hurt the lady Mister!" he muttered.

# JENNY MAC

Royce Chalmers gaped. 'How amazing this Country Bushman is!' he thought. 'But how ruthless is he in the face of danger!' 'I'm pleased I am on his side!' he was thinking, as he looked up, and Pete stood glaring at him.

"I thought I told you to stay back Royce?" he asked. "But seeing you are here! If you want to help, get some rope, and tie this monster up. He's going to be mighty angry when he wakes up!" drawled Pete.

"So he's still alive then?" asked Royce shakily.

"Of course he's alive, a bit battered up, but alive. If I wanted him dead, it would have happened with the first shot! I guess the authorities can do the rest!" "Oh Royce! By the way! Bring that god-dammed phone back, so you can call the Constable for me! I must get myself one of those damn things!" said Pete, with a laugh. "Yes Pete!" laughed Royce.

Pete walked slowly to where the lady lay, and knelt down beside her. She was knocked about, and a trickle of blood ran down her face. He started when her eyelids fluttered, and her beautiful deep green eyes squinted at him. "Mitch? It is you!" she whispered, then passed out.

\* \* \*

Shallow Siding was in mourning. The town folk were strangers to violence in their little town, but murder was unthinkable, and a deep feeling of insecurity had spread amongst the community. A special meeting was called to be held in The Community Town Hall.

Constable Evans stood to address the congregation to explain all the events, and to assure them of their safety.

## APRIL RAIN

"We owe our thanks to the tenacity, and bravery of Pete Stringer who tracked, then apprehended the murderer, who has been transferred to a larger town's jail." he said.

"Hear, hear!" they called. It was decided unanimously to postpone the Town's Reunion to a date to be decided, and the funerals were to be arranged for Riley Summers, and, for Reagan Chase, who had been murdered. It was a sad day indeed for the community of Shallow Siding.

But in the Hospital, Jacqueline Coby lay unconscious.

As the meeting closed, people dispersed out onto the street, and then Anne Hardy scanned the lawns until she located Mitchell Stringer. He seemed to be in a private conversation with Pete she noted, so she walked slowly.

"You make me feel so proud Pete, a great job, and you didn't hold back either I hear!" Mitchell said, laughing. Pete laughed. "No I couldn't Father. He was hurting that lady, I didn't take too kindly to that. But strange though! Before she passed out she called me Mitch! I am positive she thought I was you Father! Why is that?" Pete asked.

Mitch's eyes clouded as he looked at his son. 'What to say?' he wondered. "I will just have to tell you straight Pete! Please try to understand all this! Jacqueline Coby is her name. She was the love of my life, although I guessed she would never be mine. Besides your Mother, she is the only other woman I ever loved, and I love her still. Thank you for saving her son, she means so much to me!" "Father I ... Pete was cut off when Anne spoke. "Are you ready to go Mitch?" "Yes Anne!" he said.

# JENNY MAC

# APRIL RAIN

## Chapter 35

Mitch Stringer's mind raced, he could not overcome the apprehension, and mixed feelings that stirred inside him as he drove out to the hospital. 'All those lost years!' he thought. 'But what to say to her?' 'Will we still have a special bond?' he wondered. He took a quick look in the rear vision mirror at his son. Pete was looking out the window, and he seemed to be lost in deep thoughts, but Mitch knew Pete well, and Pete would stand by him, whatever happened! 'He was sure of that.' he decided.

Anne Hardy babbled on though, full of excitement as she sat on the seat beside him. "It will be like old times Mitch. Let us make it a home coming for Jackie, Mitch. I am so excited I can hardly wait to see her! Just wait until you meet Jacqueline Coby, Pete! Then you will love her too, as we all do!" she said with conviction. "I'm looking forward to that meeting Anne, everyone can't be wrong! But do I call her Jacqueline, or Jackie? Like you all do!" asked Pete. "Good point Pete! Call her Jacqueline, and if I know Jacqueline Coby, she will soon set you right."

"Only two people that I know of called her Jacqueline. One was Reagan Chase, and the other my husband Jake, who is a little old-fashioned, and very much set in his ways as we all know!" said Anne.

"Anne! You are getting way ahead of yourself here, we don't know if Jackie has regained consciousness yet!" said Mitch. "Let's just be positive Mitch! Besides, I spoke to her doctor yesterday, and all her tests were clear. So she will recover, and wake up. You will see!" said Anne.

When they finally arrived at Jacqueline's room, she was not only conscious, but conspicuously missing, and so too was Jake Hardy. They found them sitting under a trellis laden with Wisteria, within the hospital gardens. Jake sat in a wheelchair, and Jacqueline sat wrapped up in a blanket. She lifted her head to the sound of footsteps falling heavily upon the pavers, her eyes weren't healed, but they flashed deep green at their approach. She stood to stare as a warm feeling filled her. "Mitch?" she asked.

Just to see her again was like turning back time, and he stood riveted to the spot. His heart thumped, but the love that he still felt for her was so obvious to see in his deep blue eyes, as Mitchell Stringer just stood staring at Jacqueline. Everyone else had become silent, sensing the moment between them, and Mitch was aware of it.

He quickly became his usual jovial self, to say. "God damn it, Jacqueline Coby! I turn my back on you for five minutes, and then you disappear for thirty-one years!" he said, as his laughter rang out.

Jacqueline just looked at him in disbelief. Somewhere deep inside, his country voice struck a chord in her heart as memories of their past flashed before her. 'He has not changed one bit! He always was the typical cowboy!' she mused, as the first smile for days escaped her lips, then her giggle caused infectious laughter amongst them all.

"Yes it is me Mitch, but just a bit older Jackie!" he said laughing. "But this young man here, you may very well enjoy meeting. My son Pete, your rescuer!" "Pete, please meet my very best friend Jacqueline Coby!" Mitch said.

## APRIL RAIN

Pete looked at his Father's flushed face, and then at Jacqueline Coby. His observation led forth his own conclusion. 'This was a love that moved mountains!' he thought. He didn't know their history, but sensed their unbreakable bond. 'What were the odds of them finding each other again?' he wondered.

'Fate has had a hand here!' he thought.

'Jacqueline's injuries seemed quite obvious.' he noted. Both her eyes were almost closed, though he sensed a deep sincerity in them. Her hair had been shaved where the stitches closed a long cut in her scalp, but there was no complaint coming from her, or self-pity. He detected a strength in her that seemed almost unique, and a sense of pride like no other, but there was something else. As he looked into her beautiful face, he felt almost humble in her presence, as he felt her virtuousness.

Jacqueline knew that she was being scrutinized so she spoke first. "This is my utmost pleasure to finally meet you Pete, you are my hero! Many people have told me how you saved my life, and to what extent you went to."

"I really cannot thank you enough! I guess I owe you now, but rest assured Pete Stringer, I always pay my dues! So I guess I am at your beck, and call, if I can ever return the favour! Oddly though, I seemed to feel it was Mitch rescuing me! I have no idea why, but you are so much alike! Having said that, would you mind calling me Jackie like he does, I would like that!" she said.

"I too am pleased to meet you Jacqueline Coby! You don't owe me at all, but thank you! I am just pleased that

# JENNY MAC

I got to you in time, and yes, you were calling me Mitch, but you were a little out of it! I wasn't sure what to call you, but the others said that you would set me right, and I guess you have in more ways than one. I'd love to call you Jackie! I hope we can be friends too?" stated Pete.

Jacqueline's face saddened, then she said. "I can only wish Pete! But I have returned to Shallow Siding with a specific purpose in mind, to face the demons from my past, and explain to all those I have hurt, my reasons for leaving! Then! After I tell my story, you may not want to know me but I will understand that!" Jake Hardy's brow furrowed, making his face look ferocious as his stitches knotted up across his forehead. "Jacqueline don't upset yourself!" he said. "I am fine Jake! This is something I must do! Everyone please sit, and I will begin!" she said.

Jacqueline's voice caught as her heart felt tale unfolded. They all sat in silence as they witnessed the grief, and shame it caused her. They all shed tears as they felt her pain too, but with huge determination she continued.

Anne Hardy sobbed uncontrollably at the horror of it, each word tearing her apart. She had always known that something was not right with Jackie, she felt it deep in her heart. She pulled Mitch aside. "Mitch I must make it up to her!" she said. "I will care for her!"

"We all will! But please Anne, could I take her out to my place? I couldn't bear to lose her again!" Mitch said, his eyes pleading. "Jackie would have more to occupy herself in her recovery at my place anyway. I also have staff to tend to her every need!" he said in his defense.

# APRIL RAIN

Anne looked at her friend, and felt his struggle as his face saddened in deep concern. "Yes of course you can Mitch! I guess that would be best for Jackie after all!" she said. "Thanks Anne! I will ask Jackie her thoughts!" he said. But both Jackie, and Jake agreed to his idea.

Sunshine seemed to bless his day as Mitch collected Jackie's belongings from the hotel, but his heart fluttered with anxiety, as he drove in with Pete to collect her from the hospital, and then take her out to his home.

"Good morning Jackie! You look heaps better today!" he said, when he entered her room. "Hello Mitch, thank you. I do feel a little better, I guess. Good morning Pete!" she said. "Good morning Jackie!" replied Pete. "Jackie, if you are ready to go, we should get moving now?" Mitch said. "Yes I guess so Mitch!" she replied.

So they walked down the long hallway of the hospital towards the entrance. Then Mitch stopped specifically to point out a plaque to Jacqueline. She stared, as the name 'Clayton Coby' stood out proudly in bold letters on the plaque. She paused to read the script of his involvement with the foundation of the hospital, and the memories of her Father flashed in her head of a time so long ago.

As they drove into the Countryside, the beauty of it attracted Jacqueline's attention, remembering it all so vividly, and her thoughts drifted back in time.

But nothing could overshadow her sadness, and grief she felt for Reagan Chase. It was eating away at her, and she felt almost responsible for his death. 'He was just so beautiful.' she thought. 'And I loved him so, but would our love have lasted?' 'That I will never know now!'

'Somehow I feel that our love was never meant to be!'

"You ok Jackie?" asked Mitch. She stared at him as if he had read her mind. "I will be fine Mitch!" she replied.

"I am so sorry about Reagan!" he said. "I am sorry too Mitch, because of me he is gone!" she said. "You have no blame Jackie, it's not your fault." Mitch replied.

Jacqueline Coby had loved only two men during her lifetime. One, being Reagan Chase! A newcomer to the Outback Country, who had swept her off her feet at a very tender age, and the other! Was Mitchell Stringer, a real Country Cowboy who not only shared with her the same birth month of April but was the same age. They had grown up together, were best friends, and shared a very special bond.

She looked at Mitch beside her now. 'So handsome, so strong, and so very dependable, but I guess he always was!' she thought, as warm feelings seemed to multiply with his closeness. 'It is so strange to realize that after all these years he could still stir those feelings inside me as he did so long ago!' Jacqueline thought to herself.

Memories swamped her then so suddenly from out of nowhere her thoughts returned to her Mother, and the words that she had spoken to her a long time ago.

'What about Mitch Jackie?' she had said to me. 'Why the rush to marry? Why not wait until you are sure? He is younger Jackie, still learning. A bit shy to speak out, but he is becoming a fine young man I must add!'

## APRIL RAIN

'I guess my Mother was trying to tell me something.'
'She was usually right too' she thought.

Mitch had never pressured Jacqueline for a closer relationship, but she remembered though, there were many frustrating times when she wished he had.

He confused her, and never pursued her as she would have liked. Mitch seemed just content in being around her, and part of her life, but secretly she thought that he assumed it was only a matter of time until they would become a couple, as the chemistry between them was the one thing she could not explain.

They always were the very best of friends, had grown up together sharing many similarities, and a very special bond, but there was something else. Though the words were never uttered, she always knew they shared a deep love, and a total respect for each another, something she had always wanted to pursue further. 'I guess he was a little immature, or even shy, back then!' she thought.

'However Reagan Chase was much older, and he was very ardent in his pursuit, even from the very first time they met. Their love blossomed, and he had been a true gentleman in every way. Her decision to marry him did not come lightly, she could not fault him in any way. He was the perfect man.' she thought.

Then prematurely, she was forced to reject him. 'He was so beautiful!' she remembered tenderly.

*'They were two very different people!' she thought.*
*'I loved them both!'*

# JENNY MAC

# APRIL RAIN

## *Chapter 36*

The Outback Gardens was a huge enterprise, and it exceeded all Jacqueline's expectations when Mitch drove around the complex to show her the extent of it, and in some respect The Outback Bush Camp brought back memories of Waverley, the place she had lived out her life, and finally reached some normality amidst the thoughts in her head that plagued her, and the sorrow in her heart that would not cease. She thought deeply of her friend Mary, who she had left there, and she made a mental note to contact her soon.

Suddenly an idea struck her, and she turned to speak to Pete. "Pete, I imagine you have a dining area for your camp guests, but what if you had a Restaurant, and Bar? You would have all year round trade from the locals, and visitors, if you had that attraction as well!" she said.

Pete gaped. "Jackie you are a legend. That is a great idea! What do you think Father?" he asked. "Well Pete! I guess that may be the extension we were looking for."

"Seeing this place has taken off, we can probably look at that idea soon. Would create a lot of jobs for the locals too!" replied Mitch. "Yes you're right there!" said Pete.

"Good idea Jackie! Jackie?" called Mitch frantically, as he braked. "Jackie?" Jacqueline was staring at him, but not seeing him. Beads of perspiration wet her brow, and her face was as pale as a sheet. "My god Pete, I think she is going to faint. I'll hold her, you drive, and get her to the Homestead quickly!" said Mitch, in deep distress.

# JENNY MAC

From nowhere the blackness started creeping in, and I could hear voices, but the noises in my head were much louder. Visions became intertwined, clouding my mind of my attacker, the murders, then flashes in recollection of my past, as I drifted into oblivion.

Apparently it was much later in the day I discovered as I woke that I was in a specially selected room of the beautiful Homestead. Secretly I knew as I looked around the room tastefully decorated in the colour purple, and out through the double doors at the setting sun, that it was Mitch who had a hand in selecting this room for me.

I was so thankful, and realized immediately it was the peacefulness that would be my solace, but also a way to recuperate from all my hurt. It was then that I made the decision to hibernate until I was completely recovered. So I took it one day at a time, never leaving my room or my private balcony, to live through my personal drama.

'Until one special Morning.'

Jacqueline Coby woke with such a start. It wasn't only the sounds of chatter from the birds outside, but from her disturbing feelings. Somehow she felt very different, like a big weight had lifted from her. She felt strong once again, free of guilt, and determination surged inside her.

Covers were tossed aside negligently in her haste to reach the balcony doors where she flung them aside just in time to witness the huge golden orb peeking over the distant hills, flooding the earth with its brilliance, and warmth. 'So beautiful!' she thought.

'This is the first day of the rest of my life!' I thought.

## APRIL RAIN

'And I am not going to waste a minute!' I had a spring in my step as I raced inside to shower, and dress in my best riding clothes. As I walked into the dining room, Mitch almost dropped his cup as he looked up at me from his paper. "Jackie? What a surprise!" he gasped.

"How good it is to see you come down finally, and all dressed to go out riding I see! You look just wonderful today, welcome to my humble abode! Would you care to join me in some breakfast?" he asked.

"Good morning Mitch! Isn't it a beautiful day? I feel absolutely wonderful today, and yes! I would very much like to join you for breakfast, and yes Mitch! If you have a horse for me, I would love to go riding this morning!" I replied with a giggle. Mitch laughed, his deep blue eyes twinkled, as he replied. "Yes Jackie it is a beautiful day!"

"However Jacqueline Coby! Such good news calls for a celebration. It just so happens that I have been saving a special surprise for you! 'A gift! Just for this moment!' So after breakfast, we will go riding together!" he declared.

"Oh Mitch! That sounds so wonderful, but what is the surprise?" I asked. "If I told you that Jackie, it wouldn't be a surprise!" he replied. "But Mitch … I was about to protest, as his words stilled my speech. "No buts either Jackie!" he said, as he laughed. I laughed too, at the jest which was Father's favourite.

As we drove over to the stables, I could not help but feel that Mitch was enjoying the moment. 'He even looked rather smug.' I thought. "Everything should be ready!" he was saying. "I sent word over to the boys, so we shouldn't have to wait!" "Wait for what?" I asked.

"Jackie be patient!" he said, as he braked, and got out to open my door. "Are you there Sam?" he called. "Hi Mitch, all set for you here!" he said, as he materialized. "Thanks Sam, good man!" said Mitch.

"Hi Jacqueline!" Sam said. "Good Morning Sam, what is happening?" I asked. "I am not to say Jacqueline. That would be telling!" Sam replied, as he grinned.

"But... I was about to say. "Jackie have patience!" said Mitch, as he headed to the yards, then he took my hand. "You have to wear this blindfold Jackie, I will lead you!" he said. "Lead me, are you serious?" I asked. "Yes, come on now!" he laughed, as we proceeded slowly, then we came to a halt. "Okay, you can look now Jackie!" he said.

I tore the blindfold away, not knowing what I was to see, but stood staring in disbelief, as if someone had turned back time, and tears filled my eyes as I looked at the Black Stallion, with white markings standing there. "He is just so beautiful Mitch!" I said. "May I?" I asked.

"Yes go in Jackie!" said Mitch. I swung the gate wide, and proceeded towards the Stallion. He stamped a hoof in protest as I reached out to him, but when I placed my hand on his velvet muzzle to caress him, he snorted, and I laughed. "He looks just like Sailor, Mitch, and snorts like him too!" I said. Mitch laughed. "Should do Jackie! I've bred only black horses with Sailor's foals, and he is beautiful! Best one I've had yet!" replied Mitch proudly.

Jacqueline looked unbelievingly up at Mitch. His eyes told it all. 'For so many years he continued doing this!'

## APRIL RAIN

'He had never ever forgotten me!' she thought.

Without hesitation or thought she rushed quickly to wrap her arms around him, wanting to hug him madly, and to kiss his cheek ever so lightly, but instead she felt the softness as his lips brushed hers. She stepped back startled, but already her eyes were seeking his, and they stared at each other, just lost in the moment.

Jacqueline felt the firmness of his body as Mitch very gently pulled her closer, and his country aroma of all the things that she loved, of horses, of leather, and the bush air, filled her senses. She surrendered to his touch as she swayed closer to meld to his body, and experienced such a warmth flooding through her that made her feel safe.

His lips sort hers so very tantalizingly at first, then his tenderness mounted to such a passion that she shivered just from the shock of it. 'I often wondered what his kiss would be like!' I thought, and I felt shaken by it, as his urgency, and passion became the one thing I had waited a lifetime for. I became lost solely with the thrill of it, as I melted within the circle of his arms, and his warmth.

"Geez I love you Jackie, I always have!" he choked. "I should have told you thirty-one years ago, but I was too shy. I thought we had heaps of time!" he said. "I realize that now Mitch, but I have loved you also, ever since we were kids Mitch, but you are not shy now!" I said with a giggle. He laughed, as he said. "Welcome Home Jackie!"

"Thank you Mitch!" I replied, then sadly, as tears slid down my face. "But somehow I don't think I deserve ….

# JENNY MAC

Tenderly he folded his arms around her. "Please stop Jackie! You have already suffered enough. I know what you were about to say then, but please don't! It is time you moved on. It was not your fault Jackie! Do you understand?" He eased her backwards, so that he could look into her eyes. "It was not your fault!" he repeated.

Jacqueline buried her face deep into his chest as huge sobs racked her body. Mitch then slowly lifted her chin so she could face him. "Ok?" he asked. "Yes Mitch!" she replied. "It is in the past Jackie! Live for the future now!" he said, as he very tenderly, and lovingly kissed her lips.

She responded with a passion that she did not know still existed inside her. "That is much better!" he said, as he held her at arm's length. "Now let's regain that mood you had earlier, and enjoy your surprise!" he uttered.

Jacqueline looked so longingly at the beautiful horse. "What is the Stallion's name?" I asked. Mitch became serious as his eyes found mine, then smiled as he spoke.

"The Stallion is my gift for you Jackie! Your surprise! There can no other name for him but!"... 'APRIL RAIN!'...

'He remembered!' I thought, and I retrieved the little black horse with white markings from my pack. Mitch gaped in shock. "You still have the carving?" he asked in wonder. "I did tell you he would be with me always!" I said. "Stay with me Jackie! Will you please marry me?" Mitch asked, as he fell to his knees. As the tears filled my eyes I knelt beside him, and we hugged. "Of course I will marry you. I love you Mitch Stringer!" I said, as I added.

"Besides, we have Country in our souls Mitch!"

"Our love has stood the test of time!"

## APRIL RAIN

## *Epilogue*

*Jacqueline Coby was Home.*

I stood watching the magic of the setting sun.
Its descent produced such an array of colour that
seemed to say. 'Welcome Home!'
I shivered with the thrill of it.

Still I lingered, in thanks, and gratitude, for my life back.
Until the first hint of mist drifted in to cloak the trees.

'Sheer determination got me through my tortured life.'
'Only now I realize! All the pain, the grief I suffered,
and that others had suffered, and the sacrifices I made!'
'Was all to no avail.'

'All the people I tried to protect.'
'Would have in turn, protected me.'

'Pride was my huge self-indulgence, and it came with being a Coby. Though in hindsight, it was my fiercest enemy. It forbade me from facing my own shame, and from shaming others, by snatching me away from those I loved most, and those who loved me the most.'
*A Lesson to be learnt in the Book of Life*

# JENNY MAC

Printed in Great Britain
by Amazon